"Why do you care what he thinks?"

His eyes, a rich brown, crinkled in thought. He was only eighteen, but already small lines were etched at the corners of his eyes and between his brows. His life so far had not been an easy one. But the lines just gave his strong, handsome face a touch of character. I could already see the thoughtful, kind man he would be in twenty years. "Mostly to avoid more conflict for you. But there's this tiny little part of me that wonders what it would be like if we could just be . . . brothers. Or half-brothers, or anything other than enemies. I know it'll probably never happen."

"But you can't help hoping," I said. "I don't blame you."

"Why do *you* care what he thinks?" Lazar asked.

I hesitated. I couldn't tell him the truth: that I didn't want Caleb to think poorly of me. Caleb had broken up with me because of Lazar. If he saw us together now, he might think I'd cheated on him. I hadn't cheated, but still. He might never get over it; we'd never be friends. *Or anything else.*

MORE FROM NINA BERRY

Otherkin

Othermoon

Othersphere

NINA BERRY

KENSINGTON PUBLISHING CORP.
www.kensingtonbooks.com

KTEEN BOOKS are published by

Kensington Publishing Corp.
119 West 40th Street
New York, NY 10018

All Kensington titles, imprints, and distributed lines are available at special quantity discounts for bulk purchases for sales promotions, premiums, fund-raising, educational, or institutional use.

Special book excerpts or customized printings can also be created to fit specific needs. For details, write or phone the office of the Kensington special sales manager: Kensington Publishing Corp., 119 West 40th Street, New York, NY 10018, attn: Special Sales Department; phone 1-800-221-2647.

KENSINGTON and the KTeen logo are Reg. U.S. Pat. & TM Off.

ISBN-13: 978-0-7582-9238-4
ISBN-10: 0-7582-9238-4

First Trade Paperback Printing: January 2014

10 9 8 7 6 5 4 3 2 1

Printed in the United States of America

First Electronic Edition: January 2014

ISBN-13: 978-0-7582-9239-1
ISBN-10: 0-7582-9239-2

For Max

ACKNOWLEDGMENTS

I didn't realize how difficult it would be to say good-bye to these characters who have changed my life. My debt to all the people at Kensington Books for making these books a reality, and for making me a real-life, actual, no-kidding, honest-to-goodness writer can never be repaid. In particular, all gratitude goes to the insightful, supportive Alicia Condon, queen of editors. Additional fountains of thanks to publicist Vida Engstrand and to fellow KTeen authors Jennifer Estep, Brigid Kemmerer, Marni Bates, and Erica O'Rourke.

Thank goodness for the essential support, both emotional and editorial, of my gorgeously talented critique partner, Elisa Nader, and beautifully sharp fellow TV/YA writer Jen Klein.

A special hug of gratitude to my agent, Tamar Rydzinski, the first professional in the business to take a chance on me.

Friendship has been an important theme throughout these books, and I couldn't have written about it without my friends, who not only help me laugh my brains out, but provide endless inspiration and encouragement: John Mark Godocik, Brian Pope, Michael Musa, Valerie Ahern, Ruth Atkinson, Cathleen Alexander, Maria de la Torre, Peter Shultz, Pilar Alessandra, Pat Dodson, Cheri Waterhouse, Naomi Catalano, Paul and Dara Cuoco, Corey and Carrie Elliott, Pam and Scott Paterra, Frank Woodward, Jim Myers, Meriam Harvey, and Maritza Suarez.

Then there's the extraordinary group of buddies that got me through my own insane teen years and beyond: Diane Stengle, Roger Alt, Alden Zecha, Matt Chapman, Cathryn Kleigel, Kat Munchmeyer, Jennifer Frankl, Lisa Moore, and Chris Campbell.

A particular shout-out to Wendy Viellenave, whose friendship and support have never flagged, and whose game company and generous use of her frequent flier miles have made my life infinitely richer and more adventurous.

I'm deeply indebted to all those readers who said kind things about my books, whether at a signing or via Facebook, email, or Twitter. You keep me writing.

Lastly and especially, thanks to my parents, Paul "Doc" Berry and Jacqueline Berry, whose love and respect laid the foundation for all the good things I've been lucky enough to have in life.

We are born from the Milky Way
Of the great high heavens,
We are sent to this sacred earth
To protect its borders.
Mend what is torn,
Sew what is ripped,
Fix what is broken,
Weld what is cracked.
When the yellow sun of tomorrow's morning is rising
Prepare your horses to ride to battle!
—THE EPIC OF GESER KHAN, 12th century

CHAPTER 1

I balanced carefully on the first step of the ladder, the folded wallpaper in one hand, and used the other to steady myself as I moved up. My eyes became level with the toes of Lazar's worn brown boots, pointing at me from the other side of the ladder.

"Hey, look," I said. "You under-pronate more on your left foot than your right." And I grinned up at him.

From the top of the ladder, his tousled golden head haloed by the skylight above, Lazar smiled down at me. "I love it when you talk dirty."

My cheeks got hot, and I ducked my head down to stare at my own feet and took another slow step up the ladder. The knees of Lazar's jeans came into view, both blotched with a Rorschach of wallpaper paste.

Even after nearly four weeks of us, well, dating, I guess you could call it, it still surprised me when Lazar said anything risqué. He was normally such a gentleman, one with even less dating experience than I had. His strict father had never allowed him to go out with anyone, so I still couldn't quite believe it whenever he said or did something suggestive.

I moved up again on the ladder, the walls narrowing around me, and my eyes came level with Lazar's thighs. I concentrated on making sure I didn't drop the wallpaper as I put my foot on the next rung. *Hello, Lazar's belt buckle.*

"In that case," I said, staring at the simple brass clasp and brown leather above his fly, "you're going to wish you knew what I'm thinking now."

His hips shifted slightly. "But I can imagine."

I took a hasty step up. My stomach had the jitters. It scared me sometimes, that I could feel anything for someone other than my ex-boyfriend, Caleb, gone who-knows-where for six weeks now. Scarier still was that any feeling could push through the overwhelming grief that overwhelmed us all. Siku had been killed six weeks ago today.

Time to change the subject. "It's still hard to believe that wallpaper can block wi-fi signals from getting out and in-frared scans from getting in," I said. After we'd destroyed the particle accelerator built by Lazar's father, Ximon, Ximon and his remaining men had fled. At Lazar's urging, we'd plundered the abandoned facilities, taking whatever equipment we could that remained undamaged. This high-tech wallpaper had been one of our best finds, and once this skylight well was done, the whole school would be shielded.

Lazar's shirt rode up as he lifted his arms to check the primer on the wall beside the skylight, treating me to a glimpse of taut six-pack abs with twin vertical lines gliding alongside his hipbones.

I swayed slightly.

"You think I made it all up just to get you on this ladder with me?" Lazar placed a warm steady hand on my arm to help me to the next rung.

"I wouldn't put it past you." My head moved past the top of the ladder, eyes now at the level of his chest. When I glimpsed it this way, up close, in a simple blue T-shirt, I couldn't help thinking of Caleb. Although, Caleb's T-shirt would have been black. The half-brothers were so different in many ways, one blond, the other dark. Lazar was polite, reserved, more innocent and yet more wounded than the sophisticated, reckless Caleb, who had been all over the world and hadn't endured life with their abusive, manipulative father, Ximon.

But they did have the same shoulders and strong arms corded with lean muscle, and the same strong chin, high cheekbones, and thick, expressive eyebrows, even if their coloring was different.

And they had the same taste in girls. At least in one girl.

I rose another step, trying not to stare at the cords of muscle on either side of Lazar's long neck, or just above that, his lips, a bit fuller than Caleb's.

Stop comparing him to Caleb all the time. He's his own person.

"Can you blame me?" His eyes, caramel brown where Caleb's were black, sparkled with mischief. Then he bent down and kissed me.

He kissed more softly than Caleb, more gently. I leaned into him, the top of the ladder pressing against my chest, the wallpaper still in one hand.

He put his other hand on my ribs, next to my breast, and lifted me bodily up to stand on the next rung so that we were almost the same height. My lips opened beneath his.

There was something irresistible about Lazar's neck. I put my free palm over the vulnerable spot at the back where his hairline ended and slid my fingers up into his thick, silky hair.

He pulled me closer, his hand sliding up inside my T-shirt, fingers tracing the upper edges of my demi-bra. My nerves sparked, whole body flushed with heat. There was nothing but warm skin under my fingers, the taste of Lazar's sweet mouth, and his hand trailing fire.

The ladder rocked.

"Whoa!" We broke apart. I dropped the folded square of off-white wallpaper. It wafted down to land against a leg of the ladder.

Lazar put one steadying hand on the wall, and reality came rushing back in. When we did that, when he scooped me up and pressed me against him, I forgot about the hole in my heart left by Siku's death, and the achingly painful wound caused by Caleb was anaesthetized.

"My fault," he said, descending the ladder with light quick steps and stooping to pick up the paper.

"Mine, too." I mimicked him, flitting down the ladder and jumping down next to him, one hand on his shoulder.

He dropped the wallpaper and grabbed me, something dangerous in his eyes. I gasped, and he stopped my mouth with a kiss more urgent than any other we'd shared. His belt buckle scraped against my abdomen and he pressed my body against the length of his. I could feel every hard muscle on his frame. His hand supporting my lower back skated lower, lingered over my curves there, and then descended more to grip in and around my back inside thigh.

I writhed, held fast. A moan escaped me. He kept his hand there and lifted me up, off the ground, guiding my leg around his waist. The other leg wrapped around, too, my feet locking together behind his back as my hands pulled his T-shirt up so I could slide my hand over his smooth bare back.

My hip pocket buzzed. For a wild minute, I though Lazar was somehow making that happen. Then it buzzed again, and I realized. It was my phone.

"Ignore it," he said and bit my shoulder lightly. I shuddered.

The phone buzzed again, and through the heated red fog in my brain, I remembered one thing, one reason not to ignore my phone. A reason I couldn't reveal to Lazar.

"I'm sorry," I said, unwrapping my legs from around him and pulling away reluctantly. "I have to get it if it's my mom."

He lowered me, but his hand loitered a long moment, caressing, before I tugged myself away. His blond hair was pushed to one side from my hands, his eyes bright and hot.

The phone stopped buzzing. I looked down. It was the alert I'd been waiting for. Why did it have to happen now?

"I have to call her back," I said. A lie. "I'm so sorry."

His eyebrows angled in puzzlement. "For being such a good kisser?"

I laughed, more out of unrelieved tension and desire than anything else. "Well, my ability there is kind of criminal."

He laughed, running a hand through his hair, and nodded.

"Just sorry to, you know..." I looked down. "To not be moving things along faster. I want to, but..."

"Between us?" He put his hands on my arms, rubbing them lightly. "I know. I'm sorry for pushing."

"No, no, no." I leaned my forehead against his chest. He smelled like incense and amber, mixed with a little wallpaper paste. "I like it. Just please keep being patient with me."

"The past couple of months have been full of troubles," he said. "The psalms say at such a time to search your heart and be silent." He smiled, the dimple showing in his cheek. "I haven't allowed you much time for that."

I shook my head. "You've been great. Sorry, but I really need to..."

He exhaled, shaking his head in amused resignation, and waved me away. "Go. I got this." And he started back up the ladder with the wallpaper strip.

I backed up, checking my phone to confirm. It wasn't a call; it was an alert I'd set up. Amaris had just received a Skype call from an unidentified number. The first time anyone had called her since Caleb had left.

I hadn't been spying on Amaris. *Well, sort of.* I was keeping tabs on her calls because I knew that if Caleb got in touch with anyone, it would be his beloved half-sister.

Okay, so monitoring her phone calls is an invasive violation.

I felt bad about it. But compared to all the other terrible things I'd done recently, this barely registered.

I looked up at Lazar, now back at the top of the ladder, holding up the strip of wallpaper, aligning it just so. He trusted me, and I was about to violate that. I nearly put the phone away then. I wanted to shake the legs of the ladder and bring him back down to finish what we'd started.

I just need to know Caleb's okay. Then I'll be able to move forward.

"See you later," I said.

He grinned down at me. "Shirker."

"Workaholic." I smiled back, not quite as broadly, and left, straightening my T-shirt as I moved with practiced quiet out of the boys' dorm into the hallway. A sliver of light reflected off the whitewashed walls from the half-closed door of the main computer room. We had monitors and wi-fi throughout the school now, thanks to Lazar, but I sensed movement in the computer room. Sliding into the darkest corner of the hall, I stilled and waited.

Within a minute, Amaris darted out of the computer room, completely unaware of me, and dashed up the steps, doing her best to be quiet. She had her heavy winter coat in hand. She was sneaking out of school, and that could only be for one reason: to see Caleb.

It was wrong to secretly follow her. That fact alone should have stopped me, but it didn't.

She'll never know, I told myself as I padded up the stairs after her. If she did find out about it, Amaris would forgive me.

Caleb wouldn't. But Caleb still hadn't forgiven me for going behind his back to meet up with his hated half-brother, Lazar. Twice.

And because of me, Siku was dead. If I hadn't fallen for Ximon's trap . . . *Stop it! Don't think about that now, or you'll get clumsy and she'll hear you.*

Besides, I hadn't seen Caleb in six weeks, and no one else had heard from him since. It was making me more than a little crazy. Any chance to learn more had to be taken. Just a glimpse of him was all I needed, the knowledge that he was alive and well would sustain me through this, the worst time of my life.

I could hear Arnaldo's voice in the dining area, giving his two younger brothers a lesson in shifter history—the jaguar-shifter kings of ancient Central America—so I avoided that area and went straight to the front door of the school, grabbing my own coat off the hooks there. I slipped out in time to see Amaris zip up her coat and head for the garage.

I lurked behind some trees next to the hill the garage was concealed under until she backed the SUV out and turned it around. Then I walked in myself, ignoring Raynard's red pickup truck, and headed right for the ancient motorcycle.

The SUV was moving away pretty quickly now. The motorcycle's engine sputtered and nearly died before I remembered and put one foot to the ground, focusing on sending all my anxiety down into the earth. Technology had a tendency to stop working around me, particularly when I got emotional. Wearing the Shadow Blade around my waist all the time had helped with that a lot, and I was wearing it now. But I'd also gotten better at directing my feelings into something natural like soil or wood so that my anti-tech vibrations didn't destroy the metal I was touching. I'd also improved at using it to de-liberately sabotage technology, but this was not one of those times.

Tonight I was particularly tense. Amaris was sneaking out to see Caleb because he wanted to avoid me. I wasn't sure how it would feel to see him again, knowing he hated me. I couldn't let him see me, or he'd despise me all the more for invading his sister's private life.

I had a nice boyfriend now. True, he reminded me of my first boyfriend because they were half-brothers, but that shouldn't matter. I really should let Caleb go.

The red lights of the SUV got smaller as it disappeared down a hill, leaving only tire tracks in the snow.

And what if Lazar finds out?

I pushed that thought into an imaginary Dumpster and kicked the bike into first gear, carefully coordinating the throttle and clutch. Ice-covered tree branches brushed my face as I lifted my feet from the ground and puttered forward. I couldn't follow too closely, or else even Amaris, with her ordinary human ears, would hear the noisy old machine's engine.

I let the SUV's taillights disappear before I sped up, teeth clenched so I wouldn't bite my tongue as the threadbare tires of the bike clomped and bounced over the unpaved road. I got close enough to see Amaris turn right when she got to the main road, heading south.

Once on the graded asphalt, I could go a little faster. The wind buffeted my ears and forced me to squint into the cold. It was late February up in Nevada's Spring Mountains. Old piles of snow rimed with dirty ice lined the road. In the spare light of the stars, the frosty evergreens spread over the peaks like a chilly green-black cloak.

I'd followed Caleb like this not long ago, when he had sneaked away from the first location of the school to meet Amaris. That was before I'd known they were brother and sister. Perhaps it was fitting that I was making the same trek now behind Amaris to meet Caleb. Maybe this trip would also lead to a life-altering revelation.

Or maybe I was a crazy person with a propensity for stalking people.

Before long, Amaris turned the SUV downhill onto Kyle Canyon Road, and we swooped out of the mountains into the spare beauty of the desert at night. The landscape flattened out in a hurry, and the trees vanished in favor of low scrub and a lot of dirt and sand. It was very dark before moonrise, but my acute night vision made it easy to keep tabs on the lights from the SUV without using the motorcycle's headlight.

A glow up ahead resolved itself into lights around a building, and Amaris stepped on the brakes to slow down, about to turn into the complex. I remembered the place from the many times we'd driven past—a modest but attractive resort catering to hikers and snowboarders spending a weekend in the Spring Mountains, away from the hustle of Las Vegas, but still equipped with slots in the lobby and the bar.

The SUV pulled into the far end of a half-empty parking lot, away from the cluster of trucks and family vans closer to the main entrance to the resort. Warm light spilled from wide glass windows there, and music with a driving beat announced a party. Figures were bouncing around, dancing, and a woman in a long white dress twirled into view, held by a man in a black suit. *A wedding reception.* It must be Saturday night. Weeknights and weekends blended into one when you studied at Morfael's school for otherkin.

I drove onto the groomed dirt alongside the parking lot and came to a stop. The SUV's lights went dark, but Amaris did not emerge. She had to be waiting for Caleb, which meant I would wait, too. I killed the bike's engine and climbed off to walk it farther away from the arc of the resort's light so I could sit in deeper darkness.

My eyes went to the bright windows and the celebration ongoing behind them. The bride was petite, with a curly cap of dark hair, and the groom towered over her. They were laughing and stepping on each other's feet, until he leaned down and swept her up in his arms, to dance with her that way.

I heard calls of "Good-bye!" and an older woman emerged from the double doors at the front of the resort, buttoning up her coat. An early departer heading home.

A long black car rumbled into the parking lot, and Amaris's SUV flashed its lights twice. Alertness pulled me up straighter. The vehicle looked vintage, an old-time muscle car from the 70s, and exactly like something Caleb would steal for himself if he had to. Before we'd met, Caleb had made his way by taking whatever he needed whenever he needed it.

He'd probably gone back to those old habits in order to stay alive now.

I crouched and inched closer to Amaris's SUV as the muscle car approached it. The car's windows were darkened, but I zeroed in on the driver and peered closer. *Thank you, cat-shifter night vision.* I discerned a familiar brooding silhouette, the strong nose, the square jaw, the unruly black hair, and my heart rumbled with a guilty ache along with the car's engine. It was Caleb.

He stopped a space away from Amaris's SUV. Her door opened, and she stepped out, arms hugging herself against the bite of the wind.

I should go. I'd seen Caleb. That's why I was here. That and nothing else. I didn't need to overhear their conversation, to eavesdrop and possibly catch up on what Caleb had been doing. It wasn't my business anymore. The longer I stayed, the more likely it was that they'd spot me.

But with your hearing, you won't need to get much closer. It was so easy to justify not leaving. I crawled closer, down nearly on all fours now, moving right up to the edge of the parking lot asphalt. Caleb was a mere fifty feet away.

Just one real look at him. Then I'll go. Caleb was too much of a gentleman to let Amaris open her own car door. As I knew he would, he turned off his car engine and got out, his long black coat fluttering behind him like a cape as he swept around the back of his car and wrapped his arms around his sister.

For a crazy moment it was like his arms were around me. I remembered how he smelled, like the woods after a rain; how warm he was, how the beat of his heart sounded beneath my ear, how our bodies melted into each other and became one. . . .

Is it him or Lazar you're thinking of?

Something was beating very loudly, but it wasn't Caleb's heart. I shook myself from reverie and turned up toward the sound, at the star-pocked sky. Part of it was blacker than the other, and the black patch was moving, the thumping quickly getting louder.

Helicopter.

My blood raced, every muscle tensed for attack. I stood up to my full height to see it better, but it was painted black with no identifying marks.

It can't be the Tribunal. They'd attacked us with a helicopter before, one larger than this, and Arnaldo had single-handedly, well, single-talonedly, brought it down. In our most recent attack on their facility, we'd seen no signs that they had another. Copters were expensive, and Ximon had poured all his money into the particle accelerator, the huge underground device engineered to turn the otherkin into ordinary human beings.

But I had destroyed the accelerator, and Ximon was on the run with only a few followers left to shelter him. This machine had to belong to some humdrum rich person, arriving at the resort in style.

Caleb turned toward the sound, too. In the indirect light from the resort I saw Amaris's eyes widen in fear. Caleb said something to her, pushing her toward her SUV. She looked startled, and then turned to obey.

The air around me stirred crazily, whipped by the machine's rotors. The black insect form of the copter was lowering itself to the center of the parking lot, exactly where a wealthy person would get dropped off. Dust and snow lifted and swirled, obscuring my sight. I focused instead on my hearing, trying to discern any other noises that might be—

Wheels screeched. Metal hit metal with a horrible crunch. Amaris screamed. Caleb shouted. I lurched forward, pulled by their cries. Closer now, I picked shapes out of the whirling snow—a large pickup truck had slammed into Amaris's SUV, shoving it like a toy thirty feet away. Amaris had been knocked flat on her back, but was rolling over to get to her feet. Three or four figures in gray emerged from the truck.

The Tribunal. Their followers favored gray when they ventured out on a night mission. It had to be them. But how?

Another truck skidded to a halt behind Caleb's car. Two figures standing up in the bed threw a large net, enveloping Caleb. They yanked hard, bringing him down hard on his side, thrashing like a black shark pulled from the sea.

Fury surged through me, expanding my connection to Othersphere. I welcomed the darkness inside me as power surged outward from my heart, and I shifted. My jacket ripped like sheer cotton as my chest deepened, my shoulders rippled with muscle and striped fur. I shook my tufted ears and sent my hat flying, hind claws cutting the paving beneath them like cloth, haunches gathering.

I roared. The men hauling on the net around Caleb whirled. Their heads were covered with gray ski masks, but I saw the whites of their eyes and smelled their sudden nervous sweat. Beneath that I could hear the very blood pumping through their veins. I couldn't wait to taste it.

One of them, with good presence of mind, reached for a gun at his feet. I sprang, faster than his eye could follow, and landed on top of him, swiping at the other man beside him at the same time.

The man with the gun was slammed into the bed of the truck beneath my weight, his scream cut off as the skin of his neck gave way to my fangs. At the same time, my right paw caught the second man in the shoulder, claws slicing through tendon and bone as he twisted away, yelling.

I pulled my mouth from the limp first man, tongue hot with his blood, and bit the first place I could reach on the second man, which turned out to be his waist. His scream hit a new fevered pitch as I lifted him bodily that way, put my front paws up on the side of the truck's cab, and shook him like a terrier shakes a rat. He stopped squirming and when the truck's driver poked his head and the barrel of a rifle out his window at me, I tossed the body at him. The driver ducked, giving me time to leap from the truck, turn, and place my front paws on its side.

"Dez . . ." Behind me, Caleb's voice said my name in a tone that conveyed surprise and anger. I had never thought to hear him speak my name again. I wanted to turn to him, but I had to deal with the closest threat first.

I gave the truck a shove. It rocked, and I heard the man inside yell, saw his hands scrabbling for a hold. Getting a better angle, I pushed up and over again. The weight was almost too much. I called upon the power of the earth beneath my feet, upon the black hole to Othersphere inside me, and strength flooded through me like a river. With a sudden, startling ease, I pushed the huge pickup truck over onto its side, then continued to roll it until it was upside down.

Amaris screamed, "Help me!"

The sound shredded all my sense of power. Even though figures were emerging from the helicopter, I turned away from them to see Amaris being tossed into the back of the other truck like a sack of laundry by two men in gray. They'd bound her up like a mummy with some kind of thick brown twine.

"Amaris!" Caleb yelled.

Caleb was still ensnared by the net, a typical Tribunal weapon infused with silver, which weakened his ability to call upon shadow. He was painstakingly trying to pick his way out of it, even as the truck bearing his sister peeled out, taking her away.

Ximon wants his daughter back. The head of the Tribunal in this area, Ximon was the father of Amaris, Caleb, and their brother, Lazar. Lazar and Caleb were both callers of shadow, powerful conjurers able to change the shapes and abilities of objects and of otherkin. But Amaris was even more valuable. Amaris was a Healer.

"Dez, stop them!" Caleb shouted at me.

I wanted to spring after the truck. I was bigger and

stronger than an ordinary Siberian tiger, so I could probably catch the truck while it was this close.

But . . . I glanced over my shoulder, past the upside-down pickup. A silver-haired figure in white strode toward us through the spiraling snow. Ximon looked taller than I remembered, his handsome face so like his sons', but craggier, harsher.

Four men, two on either side, flanked him, and another truck was pulling up beside them. They would be here in seconds.

"Amaris! You must save Amaris!" Caleb was half out of the net, but he wouldn't be free by the time Ximon and his men got here.

I growled, shook my head, and jumped over to him. His black eyes were shot with gold, hot points of rage, focused on me. "Goddammit, Dez! Save Amaris! Please!"

The "please" cut into my heart. But I unsheathed my claws and sliced through the remaining metal strands on the net around him. The silver burned my paws. I ignored the pain, taking care not to cut Caleb instead of the net.

Weirdly, the truck with Amaris wasn't racing away. With one cupped ear I followed the sound as it circled away from us and up to where Ximon and the other truck stood, in front of the helicopter.

Caleb pushed free of the net. "I can take care of myself. Amaris can't—"

He broke off as I swiveled my ears forward and ran a few steps, using the up-turned truck for cover to see what Ximon was doing. I could hear the man inside the truck thrashing, trying to get free of his seatbelt and open his door to escape.

But he was of no consequence. Caleb moved up next to me, face bleeding from tiny cuts caused by the net, breath coming fast. There was a tear in the sleeve of his coat.

"Five of them, including Ximon, plus the four in the truck with Amaris and another truck." He shook his head. "How did they find us? And what the hell are you doing here?"

I turned one ear to him, but didn't move my gaze from the two men lifting Amaris out of the back of the truck. I growled, just low enough for Caleb to hear.

He squinted at them. "We've got to stop them from getting her on that helicopter."

I shook my head, a gesture which felt wrong in tiger form, but which was one of the few ways to communicate when I was in this shape. If they wanted to get her away from us fast, they would've driven away.

Caleb eyed me, thinking hard. "No, you're right. Why not drive away and have the helicopter pick her up down the road, far away from us?"

It hurt having him read my intentions so well. We'd always been in sync, finishing each other's thoughts, feeding upon each other's ideas. Why then, were we apart? It was partly Caleb's fault, for being a stubborn idiot with antique ideas about the Tribunal and the otherkin. But it was mostly my responsibility, for keeping him in the dark, for not trusting him when he needed me to trust him the most. For turning to his brother, Lazar, when I should have turned to Caleb.

"What if we circle around from opposite sides?" Caleb asked. "They'll never see you if you don't want them to. I could provide a distraction. . . ." He pulled a postcard out of his pocket, but shoved it aside to display some chewing gum. "These have some interesting shadows."

It was as good a plan as any. Caleb's ability to call forth strange and dangerous things from seemingly innocuous items was a game-changer. I chirped and nodded.

"Thank you for coming, Desdemona," Ximon said, his deep voice easily coming to us over the chop-chop of the helicopter's blades. Ximon's voice was his greatest weapon. "Or should I call you Sarangarel?"

I became very still. *Sarangarel.* That was what my biological mother had called me on two separate occasions. But Ximon hadn't been there. How could he know?

Ximon was still speaking. "And thank you, Caleb, for leading me to Amaris."

Caleb's sun-browned face went gray. "But how could he follow me? How did he know you'd be here, and how could he know that name for you?"

I had no idea how Ximon had tracked Caleb, but Ximon was an expert in predicting my decisions. He'd mistreated his son Lazar, knowing Lazar would turn to me for help, and counting on the fact that I would not be able to refuse him. Because of that I'd taken my friends into a terrible trap in the bowels of Ximon's particle accelerator. Only my unpredictable connection to Othersphere had saved us, barely. And it hadn't saved Siku. I still couldn't quite believe my friend was dead. His killer stood before me.

Without even realizing it, I was snarling.

"Put her there," Ximon said to his men, gesturing at a nondescript spot on the pavement. Two men in gray dragged Amaris there, still bound in thick brown rope, her mouth now stuffed with cloth.

Caleb was frowning at them over the wheels of the upside-down truck. "What is that they've got her tied with? It has a vibration I've never sensed before. Something's wrong."

My growl deepened. Something was indeed horribly awry. Ximon had Amaris and was about to do something to her. I couldn't believe he'd kill her. Her healing ability was too valuable, and in his own twisted way, he cared for her. But I gathered all my strength, ready to spring. Caleb noted this and got ready to throw the chewing gum.

Ximon said. "Now."

That one word pulled me, as if someone had lassoed my gut. Ximon dragged out the word, singing it, howling it.

I reeled, claws scrabbling at the metal side of the pickup truck. My vision blurred. I could barely see Caleb staring at me. His mouth was moving, but I couldn't hear him. A deep chord of what might have been music filled my head, something so harmonious, so beautiful, I could focus on nothing else.

Beside me stood a huge picture window, cut vertically out of the air between me and Ximon. It was as if someone had laid the world's biggest, thinnest flat screen between us, connected to us at the outer edges. It cut right through the body of the pickup truck. A breeze warmer than the winter Nevada air wafted out of it, bringing with it the scent of dew, soil, and leaf.

The view through that window was of an expanse of uncut white stone decorated with gnarled trees grown in the shapes of winged beasts, overlooking a limitless dark forest cut by a winding river. In the distance lay sharp sheer peaks, taller than any mountains should be. I breathed deep the sweet night air, and everything else receded into the distance. I was home.

A colossal moon rose, its light sending silver sparks down the river, glinting off waterfalls, polishing the white stone I stood on with a strange and potent glow that penetrated my every pore and filled me with its power. Fear, pain, uncertainty—all fled before the radiance of that moon.

It was not a moon from this world, but another. Its milky surface was shot through with dark veins, which seemed to pulse, as if inside it lay a vast heart filled with the blackest blood.

I knew that moon. The memory jolted me from my reverie. It was the moon I'd seen about a month ago, when my biological mother had briefly crossed over from Othersphere, the world that lay closest to our own, to beg me to return with her.

Something tugged at my arm and called my name. A voice that I loved, a voice that could not be denied, reached out to me. As if through deep water I saw Caleb, his black-clad form wavy and indistinct. All my troubles poured back, filling me up, drowning out the hypnotic energy of Othersphere.

I snapped back to the resort at the foot of the Spring Mountains in Nevada to see Ximon, his face strangely feral, shove Amaris through the window to Othersphere.

Amaris fell through it with a strange, buzzing snap, the rope wrapped around her body tugging at her oddly, as if guiding her through. She landed on the moonlit ground in the other world, eyes wide with terror, pale under the strange light, but alive.

"No!" Caleb leapt over the upturned pickup truck, shooting like an arrow for the doorway to Othersphere.

He slammed into it, as if into an invisible force field. He exploded backwards and skidded twenty feet, head bouncing against the parking lot with an audible thump, and he did not move. I tried to lunge toward him, but was held fast where I stood at the edge of the window. It tethered me somehow, and as long as it stood there, Ximon and I were both stuck.

How could a connection between Ximon and me create a portal to Othersphere? It made no sense, and the buzzy nearness of the otherworld was crowding out other thoughts, muddying my thinking. Maybe I could somehow get through the window to Amaris, even though it felt as if the window was an extension of me.

Ximon said again, "Now."

The window to Othersphere vanished, and Amaris with it.

The only evidence it had ever existed was that the pickup truck that had stood between me and Ximon now lay in two clean pieces, as if a giant knife had sliced down from heaven and slashed it in half.

Ximon slumped. Something wrenched inside me, like a knot coming undone. Weariness washed over me. I teetered back and sat down, still in my tiger form. Through the space between the two halves of the pickup truck, I saw Ximon begin to topple. Two of his men rushed up to catch him.

Two others moved toward Caleb's immobile body at a run.

That was all it took. I shook my head, whiskers bristling,

mustered the last shreds of my strength, and leapt over the truck to land on one of them. He folded under me like a doll. I didn't bother biting or slashing him, but instead used his body as a springboard to dive at the second man just as he lifted Caleb by the feet.

The two of us rolled, his cry cut off as the breath was knocked from him. I gripped his shoulders with front paws bigger than baseball mitts and brought my back legs up to rake him with those claws, tearing him open from the belly down.

He made a terrible gurgling sound, which pleased me. In tiger form I was the ultimate apex predator, ruthless to the bone, appeased only once a threat was annihilated.

I spun toward Ximon to put an end to him.

Two more men had emerged from the third truck, and were helping the others carry Ximon toward the helicopter. With a yowl that resounded off the pavement, I bore down upon them, ears back, teeth bared.

A fifth man in gray shuffled in front of me, holding something that struggled. A split second before I slammed him, I realized he had one arm wrapped around the elderly wedding guest's neck, his other hand holding a gun to her head.

There wasn't time to stop. I veered to the right, front paws braced as I skidded. My back end, still going faster than my front, circled around, and I came to a stop, facing the helicopter again.

Over the thudding of the rotor blades, I could hear the woman crying. Her white hair was whipping around her, a bruise forming on her cheek.

"Shut up!" barked the man holding her.

A low *grr* rumbled out of me. My tail lashed. I wanted to wade in, regardless of the consequences to the old woman, and destroy them all. But enough of my human side remained to keep me from doing that. Instead, I paced over to Caleb's prone form, standing over him as they loaded Ximon into the helicopter.

At the last moment, the man holding the woman released her and leapt into the copter. She collapsed as the helicopter's landing skids lifted from the ground.

Wrath narrowed my world down to the space between me and the helicopter. I tore through it in two enormous leaps, and with my last ounce of strength, I vaulted upward. My outstretched front paws caught hold of the machine's left skid, and I held on to it with all my might.

My extra weight tilted the copter drastically. Beneath my dangling back paws, the snowy parking lot swayed. For a dizzying moment I thought we would all crash. It might kill me, but it would be worth it to take Ximon down.

The pilot fought the controls, compensating. We dipped hard, and my back feet hit the ground. But we bounced upward again.

Through the open side of the aircraft I saw the Tribunal men staring down at me, their ski masks pulled up, faces drawn in surprise and terror. I hauled myself upward, biting down on the skid so that I could reach one paw up to grip the fuselage. The man closest to me drew back.

Ximon, awake but clumsy with fatigue, was the only one not frozen with dread. He gave me a crooked smile and shook his head. "Not tonight, my dear." He pointed his finger at me and hummed a dissonant note. "We send you back, back into shadow. . . ."

Stronger than the wind from the rotor blades, I felt the force of his objuration, pushing my tiger form back into shadow, pulling my human form forth. In a second, I would once again be a teenage girl, naked, hanging from the side of a helicopter. I tried to roar, to cut off the vibrations from his voice, but my strength was nearly gone. I snarled one last time at him, then let go of the skid. Still safely in tiger form, I dropped to land on all fours, about thirty feet below.

The old woman was sitting up, confused, but not drastically hurt. Over by the resort I heard someone shout, "Call 911!" And in a lower, astonished tone: "Is that a *tiger*?"

They didn't matter. I'd already generated several reports of escaped tigers in Vegas and Burbank. I dashed over to Caleb, sniffing his neck. Relief rushed over me as I caught the scent of his living blood and heard the air move in and out of his lungs. He would recover.

But Amaris was gone, sent to Othersphere for reasons only Ximon knew. As the helicopter shot up and out to vanish into the desert night, I sent one last despairing roar upward toward the uncaring stars.

CHAPTER 2

Getting out of there took awhile. I had to work quickly, sniffing out Caleb's satchel in his car so I could put on his clothes and become human again. By then the wedding guests had called an ambulance and the EMTs were working on Caleb and patching up the old woman who kept insisting that the "puma" they'd all seen was actually a tiger. And it hadn't come out of the helicopter, but actually had run out of the desert, swerved to avoid her, and then tried to bring the helicopter down.

"You just need a bit of a rest," the EMT told her in soothing tones.

I felt bad. No one would ever believe her, and I couldn't tell them she was right. I said I hadn't seen any kind of big cat, but that my boyfriend and I had been meeting up here just when what looked like some kind of drug drop was happening between the black helicopter and the men in the trucks.

Caleb came to while they were testing his vitals and re-fused to go to the hospital, even though they said he had a concussion. They dressed his scrapes and made him sign some kind of waiver, which he did illegibly. He then allowed me to help him into the SUV, one arm flung impersonally over my shoulders. But as soon as he was safely in the pas-senger seat, he drew away from me and did not touch or look at me again. The already cold winter air got positively frigid.

Amaris had left the keys in the ignition, so I loaded the motorcycle in the back as best I could, moved what belong-ings of Caleb's I could find from his car to the SUV, and drove back to Kyle Canyon Road, heading for Morfael's school.

A heavy silence lay over us in the car. I didn't say anything. I couldn't, although more than anything I wanted to talk about what had just happened. It made no sense to me, and we had to figure it out fast to get Amaris back. I had no idea how that was possible, but if she could be shoved across the veil to Othersphere, then she could be shoved back. I just hope she survived until we got to her.

"I guess it's a good thing you're a stalker with terrible boundaries," Caleb said at last. He was half sitting, half lying in his seat, the frosty window supporting his bruised head. "Or they would have gotten me, too."

"I'm sorry." The steering wheel creaked under my clenched hands, and I realized I was gripping it too tightly. "I wanted to make sure Amaris was safe, that's all. I wasn't going to stay."

"You weren't going to eavesdrop?" His flexible voice dripped skepticism. "You weren't going to use that ridiculous hearing of yours to listen in on our private conversation, maybe find out where I've been, where I'm staying. . . ."

"Not everything is about you, Caleb," I said, skirting the issue. "It's not safe for any of us to go out alone." I let a mo-ment of silence linger. "Obviously. But that's not what mat-ters. Amaris is—"

"I know." He lifted one bandaged hand to run his fingers through his unruly black hair. "I don't understand it."

He still hadn't looked at me. Not that it mattered. I was dating someone else now, right? I kept my own eyes on the road, and my thoughts on the problem at hand. "Ximon hates Othersphere. Why would he send his daughter there? And how? How did he do it? He connected himself to me and used my power to open up—what—a portal?"

"Pretty much," Caleb said. "There was a weird vibration around him and that rope they put around Amaris."

"It looked like the rope almost pulled her into Othersphere," I said.

"Somehow it helped," Caleb said. "It had a vibration that was friendly to both this world and Othersphere."

"That must be why you bounced off. I tried to go through the portal, but whatever Ximon did kept me here till the window closed."

"You were born in Othersphere." For the first time Caleb turned his head slightly to look at me. His dark eyes were cold, assessing. "And he seemed to have planned on you being there. Maybe he needed someone or something from Othersphere to get that window open."

"I'm sick of him predicting my every move," I said, putting my hand on the hilt of the Shadow Blade. Cool calm spread through me, as it always did when I touched the Blade. It didn't keep me from feeling emotion, but it helped me see through my feelings more clearly. "It keeps getting people . . . hurt." I almost said, "killed," thinking of Siku. The ache of missing him, which never left, grew even stronger.

Caleb was looking out the windshield again, his face remote. "You can't take credit for everything," he said. "It's not all about you, Dez."

My throat tightened and tears nearly spilled out of my eyes in spite of the Blade. His voice was so detached. Did I make everything about me? Or was Caleb maybe saying, in his new, unfriendly way, that I wasn't to blame for Siku's death?

I swallowed down my tears. No way was I going to let Caleb see me cry. It was bad enough he knew I'd followed his sister just to find him, no matter how much I denied it. I couldn't break down in front of him. Not anymore.

"Morfael's a traveler between worlds," I said, referring to our teacher at the shifter school. "Let's hope he can shed some light on this."

As we pulled into the garage, London pelted up to us, her half-blond, half-black hair flying. "Amaris?" she asked, peering through the SUV's windows as Caleb got slowly and painfully out, and I unpacked the motorcycle. "We all just figured you and Amaris were gone, Dez. You're back, but where is she?"

I looked over at Caleb, to catch his eye because we both knew that London and Amaris were crazy about each other, even if they themselves hadn't quite figured it out. But Caleb was looking at the ground, his face a mask, stepping carefully so as not to shake his injured head.

"Caleb?" London frowned. The two piercings in her nose glinted in the dim garage light. "Are you back now? Where's Amaris?"

"Ximon took her," Caleb said through gritted teeth. He was in more pain that he'd let on in the car.

London sucked in a gasp of horror. "What? Is she okay?"

"She was the last time we saw her," I said. "It's complicated. We need to get inside and tell everyone. Can you help Caleb? He's got a concussion."

"What? Sure." London, lean as she was, could lift more weight than most boys her age. Some of her wolf-shifter strength remained with her even when she was in human form. She grabbed Caleb's arm, steadying him. "What the hell happened?"

"Inside," Caleb said, his breath short. "I need to sit down."

I went ahead, carrying Caleb's satchel, walking sloppily in

his too-long black pants, too-broad black T-shirt, with his giant black sneakers flopping around my ankles.

Would it kill the guy to wear a color every now and then? Some part of me knew I was making up reasons to be annoyed with him. But it gave me a perverse comfort. *What kind of pretentious jerk wears only black?*

London helped settle Caleb on the couch while I ran around the school, yelling for folks to meet us in the living room. I found Lazar putting away the wallpaper and paste in the boys' dorm room. He took one look at my face and strode up to me, taking my shoulders. "What's wrong?"

I shook my head and pulled away. He was about to find out where I'd been. He wasn't going to like it. "Amaris. Ximon took her. I'm getting everyone together to tell them what happened. Come to the living room."

How different it was from the first day I'd set foot in Morfael's school. It was hard to believe that just a few months ago I had no idea there were thousands of shifters living secretly in the world with a school that took in a troubled teen from each of the five tribes to help them make it safely to adulthood.

One of those teens was now dead—the laconic, kind, handsome bear-shifter Siku had been killed by the Tribunal six weeks ago, just a day after he and our friend November had declared their love for each other.

When Lazar and I walked into the room together, November cast London an expression of mock-alarm, raising her eyebrows, and shooting her eyes over to Caleb.

London gave her back a slight headshake.

Great. So our weird, tense little triangle hadn't gone unnoticed. At least in a regular high school, my dating life would've been less obvious. When Lazar sat down, I deliberately chose a different couch. Best to stay focused on Amaris's disappearance and let my stupid love life not even be an issue.

November was on the couch holding a giant bag of potato chips. She looked like the same petite, pointy-faced girl with pixie hair, except for the black circles under her eyes. But Siku's death had changed the rat-shifter at an atomic level. She remained a casual smart-ass on the outside, but inwardly she was consumed with a bottomless rage, most often aimed at me.

"So Dez secretly followed Amaris." November popped a chip in her mouth and crunched down on it loudly. "Keeping secrets and trying to control everyone as usual, I see."

"It's a good thing she did," said Arnaldo, "or Caleb would be gone, too,"

I shot Arnaldo a grateful look. He was the eagle-shifter of the group, and he'd matured a lot in the last month. I'd turned his alcoholic father in to Child and Family Services for abusing his sons, and Arnaldo had stepped in to take care of his two younger brothers while his father finished an out-patient treatment program. The situation was promising so far. Mr. Perez was staying sober, sticking to his regimen, and determined to find a job so he could take care of his boys again. Meanwhile, Arnaldo had brought Cordero and Luis to stay at the school until he graduated in a couple of months. They were both asleep down in the boys' dorm room at the moment, but during the day they added a lot of crazy energy to classes.

"I saw her leaving and followed because I didn't think it was safe for her to go anywhere alone," I said.

I cast a glance over at Lazar. He hadn't said a word since he walked in the room and saw Caleb there. He sat in a chair, elbows on his knees, eyes on his clasped hands, face unreadable.

"My father thinks Othersphere is where evil originates," he said, his normally deep, expressive voice flat. "Sending Amaris there makes no sense, unless he's developed some crazy new dogma."

Caleb shot a black glare at his brother. "As if his belief that the otherkin are demons in human form is sane?"

Lazar met Caleb's look stoically. "I'm otherkin, too," he

said. "I'm a caller of shadow now, not an objurer. Morfael's been training me himself these last few weeks. I don't have to prove anything to you."

"You have everything to prove." Caleb's voice was a growl.

"I've been here, every day," Lazar said in a hard tone. "I didn't run away."

"You ran the day that mattered," Caleb said with venom. "The day you killed my mother. You shot her and ran away."

"That's enough," Morfael said in a voice that brooked no argument. Our spindly teacher was clad in black that made him look like a statue made of bone and onyx.

The brothers shut their mouths in twin grim lines. It was confusing having them both in the same room. So similar, so familiar. Unlike Caleb, though, Lazar had grown up under Ximon's twisted care, which had effectively brainwashed him into killing a number of people. One of those people had been Caleb's mother. I understood why Caleb hadn't forgiven Lazar, but then he didn't know Lazar's deepest secret.

I did, and it had forged a bond between us, one I couldn't explain to Caleb without betraying Lazar. That, among other things, had pushed Caleb to break up with me and leave the school. Lazar hadn't even tried to hide how happy the breakup made him. He'd made sure to find me alone and talk to me, hugging me tight when I cried about losing Siku, listening whenever I needed to talk. Although I'd never talked about the other reason I was crying. I never talked about Caleb.

"How did Ximon do it?" I asked into the quiet. "He didn't use any kind of device to open up that window to Othersphere, not one that I could see. He just sang out, 'Now,' and it popped open."

"We can wonder how and why Ximon did it all we want," London said. "The real question is—how do we get Amaris back?"

Morfael was staring at me, motionless, with his glittering, colorless eyes.

"We have to go to Othersphere and get her," Caleb said.

"How you gonna do that?" November was licking salt off her fingers. "I know Dez was born there, but it's not like she can just go back any time she wants."

"Morfael can," I said.

The others stirred, turning to stare at our teacher. They didn't know what I did. Morfael didn't stop me as I said, "Morfael's a shadow walker."

"What the hell?" November was surprised enough to stop eating for a moment.

Lazar leaned forward. "What does that mean, exactly?" And I remembered that growing up inside the Tribunal meant he didn't have the same background knowledge the shifter kids had.

"Shadow walkers are legendary beings," Arnaldo said, his eyes on Morfael. "Well, I guess they actually exist. But the legend says they belong to none of the many worlds, but can move easily between them."

"The legends are basically correct," Morfael said. "There are an infinite number of worlds which exist alongside each other, and the shadow walkers are the only beings who move unhindered between them."

"So you've been to Othersphere," London said. "You can guide us to find Amaris there."

As was his habit, Morfael took his time answering. "I have been there," he said at last. "It is the world that lies closest to your own, which is why when you shift, your shadow forms come from there, and why callers of shadow like Caleb and Lazar can draw objects forth from that world. Because it is so close, it is possible for creatures other than shadow walkers to move between that world and this. But only with great effort."

"What's it like?" Arnaldo asked. "Is the sky blue? Can we breathe the atmosphere?"

London looked alarmed. "We'd better, or Amaris is dead already!"

"That world is very similar to this," Morfael said. His voice was dry, not soothing, but London breathed easier. "With a blue sky and atmosphere you can breathe. It is a world where nature runs rampant and no race has learned to work metal. It is a world without silver, too, which is why Dez is so allergic to that metal, and indeed to all worked metal and technology. Because she is from Othersphere, her vibration interferes with that which is truly alien to her world."

"Which is why I can't wear a watch and don't carry my phone around much," I said. "But what . . ." I hesitated, fearful of the answer I might get to this question. Still, I was dying to know. "Are the people I come from there? The Amba?"

Morfael's glittering eyes assessed me, as if deciding how much to say. "The Amba are currently the ruling class in Othersphere," he said. "Not only are they able to change shape into that world's version of a tiger, but they have an innate connection to everything in that world—the air, the earth, the plants, which allows them to control some of the weather and terrain. They can ask certain plants to grow into useful or pleasing shapes, or request the earth to crack open and create a new valley. Their tiger forms are bigger, stronger than the tigers that dwell here. Many animals there are larger versions of the ones you find here."

"So that's why my wolf form is larger than a real wolf," London said. "It comes from Othersphere, so it's bigger."

Morfael nodded. "And even your wolf form here is smaller than the form you would have if you traveled to Othersphere. When shadow travels through the veil, as your wolf form does, its size and power are diminished."

"Oh, wow, so in Othersphere I could be an eagle as big as—what?" Arnaldo asked.

"It depends on the individual," Morfael said. "But your

eagle form there would perhaps be one hundred percent larger than it is here."

Arnaldo raised his straight eyebrows, and his jaw dropped.

"A hundred percent larger!" November exclaimed. "You mean in my rat form, there I could be as big as . . . a German shepherd?"

Morfael considered her calmly. "Very probably, yes."

"Shit, let's go now!" She slapped her open hand down on the table. When Morfael glared at the swear word, she smiled, showing all her little teeth. "Sorry. But can you imagine the look on people's faces if I pranced along the streets of Berkeley looking like *that*?"

"Could you take us there now?" London asked Morfael. "The sooner we get Amaris out of Othersphere, the better."

He looked around at all of our expectant faces, and finally said, "I cannot go there with you, no."

We gaped at him. "But . . . but why not?" I asked.

"In order to bring you through the veil when you were an infant and shield you from shadow until you were sixteen, I had to sever my tie to Othersphere forever and transfer your own connection to that world into the Shadow Blade. If I go back, I will die there."

I stared at him. He'd never told me exactly what the Shadow Blade was before. It had started off in my life as my back brace. But when I no longer needed the brace, Caleb had pulled forth its shadow form—a knife which cut through anything that had never been alive. "You transferred *what* into the Shadow Blade?"

Morfael took a deep breath, as if exercising some patience. It was as if he expected me to just know things I had no way of knowing. "I severed your connection to Othersphere when I brought you here in order to let you grow up as a normal humdrum human, and to hide you from those in Othersphere who wished you harm. I had to put those vibrations somewhere. So I formed them into the Blade and attached it to you via shadow." He looked around at all of us staring at him blankly, trying to work it out. "It's all quite simple."

"So this—" I pulled the Blade out of its scabbard and felt its reassurance rush through me like a sweet ocean breeze. "This is what connects me to Othersphere now."

"Without it, you would be like any other shifter," he said. "And before you ask me why I didn't just destroy it and make you like the rest of the otherkin—such a thing is not my decision to make."

I sheathed the Blade, nodding. Morfael wasn't much on sharing information, but he also let me make my own decisions. And as someone who had been adopted, I'd always longed to know more about my birth parents, about the world I came from. A little over a month ago I'd learned I was born in Othersphere. The last thing I wanted was to sever that connection now. I wanted to understand it better, and if possible to go there. I'd glimpsed my birth mother three times now. Perhaps if I got to know her, and her world better, I'd know myself better, too.

"So you're saying ties to Othersphere can be severed," Caleb said.

Lazar was also looking very interested in the answer. They were callers of shadow, though Lazar had been raised by the Tribunal to refer to himself as an objurer. The skills were the same—to conjure forth a person or object's "shadow"— whatever they were connected to in Othersphere. Only a few people had that connection—the shifters, each with their preferred animal form. Objects had a more random shadow form; I'd seen Caleb pull a whole range of white marble mountains out of a small red desert rock once. The effort had made him pass out. Since then, he'd learned a lot about how to control and conserve his power. Callers could also push shadow forms back to Othersphere, as Ximon had started to do when I was hanging by my tiger claws from his helicopter. It made for uneasy relations between most callers and shifters.

"So you cut yourself off from Othersphere's vibration?"
Lazar asked Morfael.

Morfael gave him a small nod. "Shadow walkers attune
themselves to the worlds they visit. The vibration becomes a
part of them. To shield Dez while I was here, I had to sever
my own connection to that world forever. If I walked
through the veil between this world and Othersphere, I
would cease to exist."

"You wouldn't be much use to us that way," I said, smiling
at him.

"What about that rope Ximon wrapped around Amaris?"
Caleb asked. "It seemed to vibrate on both our world and
Othersphere's frequency."

"It is twine made of the stuff between worlds." Morfael's
voice was dry, making his extraordinary words sound normal. "It, like me, can move between worlds, and no doubt
eased Amaris's transition into Othersphere."

"Otherwise, she would have bounced off the window between the worlds, like I did," Caleb said. "I figured it was
something like that."

"But you could open a window and we could go through,"
London said to Morfael. "Sounds like Dez doesn't need any
help to get there, but the rest of us need something like that
rope Ximon wrapped around Amaris."

"I could open a window to Othersphere under the right
conditions," Morfael answered. "With twine between the
worlds, the rest of you could travel through. After that, finding her would be up to you." He tapped his staff once on the
ground for emphasis.

"But then what?" Caleb held both hands with the palms
up. "How do we know where to find her? Ximon could be
hiding her anywhere."

"This is Amaris we're talking about," I said. "We can't
just leave her there."

"Of course not," Lazar said. "Which means we have to
find Ximon and make him tell us where she is."

"And see if he's got more of that rope stuff we can use," Caleb chimed in. For once he and Lazar seemed to be on the same page.

And having any kind of plan always made me feel better. "So we have to track down Ximon," I said.

Next to me, Lazar moved uneasily. He interlaced his fingers and gripped till the knuckles were white. "I might be able to help with that."

I pulled away from him a little to look him in the eye. "You know where Ximon is?"

Lazar looked down at his hands. "I can't say for sure. But I know all the safe houses we have in the area. . . ."

"*What?*" Caleb rose to his feet, concussion forgotten as his fists clenched. "You've known where the Tribunal has their safe houses all this time, and it only just now occurred to you to tell us?"

Lazar flinched a little, but looked Caleb right in the eye. "Ximon knows I know about these places," he said. "It's unlikely he'll spend time at any of them. But it could be somewhere to start."

"You should've told us you knew this stuff the first day you came to live with us," November said, tossing the empty bag of chips on the coffee table with a flick of her hand. "And you know it."

"There could be otherkin living right nearby, in danger from the objurers in those safe houses!" Caleb took two steps toward Lazar. "I always said you couldn't be trusted."

Lazar got to his feet, his body taut. "If I'd told you before, you would've told your shifter council, and they would have slaughtered all the objurers, and their families, living in those places."

"Families who would happily slaughter our families, given the chance!" London stalked over to stand next to Caleb.

"There are children living there!" Lazar's voice reverberated with something that filled me with shame. London flinched and looked a little abashed. "Shifters aren't the only ones with kids. And I wasn't about to have more innocent blood on my hands—or on yours."

London was almost hanging her head. November and Arnaldo looked embarrassed, and I felt mortified, though I wasn't sure what I'd done.

Only Caleb did not look guilty. His mouth twisted into a knowing smirk, his black eyes cold as space. "Your vocal tricks don't work on me, *brother*." His own voice dripped contempt, cutting through the emotions I was feeling like a cauterizing knife.

Lazar clapped a hand over his mouth. His voice, like any caller's, was a potent weapon to manipulate both shadow and emotion. "Oh, God help me," he said through his fingers. "I didn't mean to manipulate anyone. I just wanted you to feel the same way I do about the kids. . . ."

"Bull*shit*!" Caleb lunged in a blur of black, grabbed his brother by the lapels and threw him backwards onto the couch. "You're a liar and a killer!"

Lazar fell back onto the cushions, rolled over to get right back on his feet. Caleb moved to follow up, to grab him again.

I got in the way. "Stop it!"

Caleb backed off a step, still coiled and ready to strike. "For all you know, he's been lying to you the whole time, using his voice to control all of you!"

"All of us?" Arnaldo had gotten up and was standing a few feet away. "Even Morfael?"

London snorted in agreement with Arnaldo. "So, what—we've become idiots in your absence?"

Caleb exhaled in exasperation and turned to pace away from me, away from all of us.

"You haven't been around much lately, Caleb honey," November said coolly. "No calls, no e-mails, no texts, except to your sis, I guess. It's like you broke up with all of us when you broke up with Dez. No matter what we've been through." Her voice broke a little as she finished.

Caleb's shoulders slumped. He turned to her. "I'm sorry, 'Ember. I really am. I've thought about you a lot. But when Siku died, I just . . . I couldn't be here."

"You ran away because a girl didn't do what you wanted her to," November said, no mercy in her voice. "And you didn't like the competition. It was all about you: your hurt feelings, your breakup. Well, what about us? Not just me, but the group, everyone—*us?*" She dusted the crumbs off her hands, and got to her feet, radiating tragic fury. "I know you were on your own a lot before you got to Morfael's school, but when you came here you made us all think you cared. We faced things together we never could have survived alone. We were more than friends; we were a team." Her eyes reddened, but she didn't flinch, didn't look away. "But I guess nothing lasts forever."

Caleb swallowed, and for once had no reply. For the first time I realized that our breakup had affected everyone around us. I wasn't much better than Caleb, too caught up in my own pain to see it in others.

"Fighting isn't going to bring Amaris back," London said into the quiet.

"I'll tell you where the safe houses are," Lazar said. "But I doubt Ximon's in any of them."

"Then we go to the nearest one and force whoever's there to tell us where he is." London's voice was matter of fact.

A droning buzz slashed through her final words. I jumped before realizing it was the alert that someone was calling us via Skype. Lazar had set it up so we would hear it in all the common rooms. The living room had a monitor now, too. Raynard, the school handyman and Morfael's boyfriend, had helped him install it three weeks before. My mother had called me that way recently.

"Who the hell . . . ?" Arnaldo asked, as the buzzer whined again. "Anyone expecting a call from their parents?"

We were all shaking our heads. Arnaldo walked over to the living room monitor, perched on a side table.

"It could be my mom," I said. "I hope everything's okay...."

"Hello?" Arnaldo had picked up the call. A muffled male voice spoke, but the speakers were turned away from the rest of us. Arnaldo shook his head, looking up at us. "He says it's Ximon."

"What?"

"No way!"

Everyone stirred, exchanging looks. Arnaldo leaned in closer to the speakers as the voice kept talking. Arnaldo listened, and then pressed a button to mute the voice, his dark eyes wide with disbelief. "He wants to talk to you, Dez."

CHAPTER 3

I didn't want to talk to Ximon alone. "Can we put him on the big monitor?" I asked Arnaldo. "So we all can see him."

"Sure, yeah." Arnaldo effectively put the call on hold.

Lazar was already up, turning on the fifty-five-inch monitor he'd recently installed on the big blank wall in the living room. We weren't allowed to watch TV or recreational movies, but it served well when Morfael screened a documentary for a class, or when all five of the shifter council called, usually to castigate me.

Arnaldo pressed two keys, and Ximon appeared, larger than life, on the big monitor. He blinked. The room he sat in was very dark. A light from somewhere higher up, as if at the top of a staircase, caught only the glittering corner of his left eye and the sagging flesh of his cheek. His shoulders, cast in silhouette, were slumped. It was hard to see him clearly, but he didn't look like the strong, wild, confident man I'd just seen whisk Amaris off to Othersphere.

"Ximon," I said, taking my seat again next to Lazar on the couch. "To what do I owe this honor?"

"I need your help," came the familiar voice, strong as always, but carrying a new tremor. It sounded like fear, or weakness, or age.

"That's not a very funny joke," I said.

He moved closer to the monitor. I caught sight of his upper lip. It was trembling. "Desdemona, I beg you—hear me out."

I stared at the half-dark monitor. What the hell was Ximon up to? "Why?"

"Because I am under attack," he said. "And I won't survive without you."

My friends were all staring at him with identical blank looks of incredulity. "What a shame," I said. "I'd wish you good luck, but you'd know I was lying."

"The attack on me is the reason my daughter was taken away tonight." His powerful voice was thick, as if with emotion, perhaps with tears. But Ximon was a powerful caller of shadow, a master with his voice, who could control someone with a single word.

"You're not making any sense," I said. "You are the one who took her away tonight."

He breathed heavily. His body shuddered, as if in pain. "Allow me to explain and there's a chance we can get her back."

" 'We' can get her back?" My voice shot high with disbelief. "What game are you playing?"

"It's no game." He cast a glance over his shoulder. For a moment we could clearly see his profile, still classically handsome, but adorned now with drooping jowls, his lips thin with anxiety. "I don't have much time. He could come back any second."

"He—who?" I frowned over at my friends. November was rolling her eyes.

"You won't believe me, I know," he said. "But you will believe that I thought for a long time before placing this call.

The fact that I have reached out to you indicates the level of my desperation. My . . . my God has abandoned me."

"About time," London whispered.

His overacting was getting on my nerves. "How did you get this number?" I asked.

"What does that matter now?" A touch of impatience crept into his voice, and he sounded much more like the Ximon I knew. "I tracked all of Lazar's calls to you last month. I knew you would be foolish enough to keep the same number."

"Point for Ximon," Arnaldo muttered.

I made a throat-cutting motion to Arnaldo, who put the call on hold. The screen froze. "He's using his voice to trick us into thinking he's stressed out, right?" I asked, looking at Caleb and Lazar.

Lazar shook his head, but it was Caleb who spoke. "He's not using any vocal tricks that I can detect. But he's so good at it, I might not be able to tell."

"He sounded genuine when he spoke of God," Lazar said. "I still can't quite believe he said it, though. He has always claimed to be specially chosen."

I nodded at Arnaldo, who took the phone off mute. Ximon's image jerked back to life. If anything, he looked smaller, more hunched. "Why would God abandon you?" I asked. "Has he finally figured out you're insane?"

"Insane." It came out of the monitor's speaker as a low groan. "Insanity would be a blessing compared to this. First I started blacking out. I had strange dreams, even when I was awake. My lieutenants claimed I gave them orders that I didn't remember giving."

"He should stop hitting the bottle so hard," Arnaldo said, but kept his voice low.

"I understand that you can't believe me yet," Ximon said, glancing over his shoulder again. "Only let me finish. I don't know how long I have."

"He's acting like a prisoner sneaking a message out," Caleb said under his breath.

"Have you seen a psychiatrist?" I asked, knowing that would anger him. Ximon was the ultimate arrogant jerk who thought he was the strongest, the sanest, the one who knew all the secrets.

"They would not believe me," he said. "For they do not believe in Othersphere, or demons. Or in possession."

I caught Morfael's eye. He raised his nearly invisible eyebrows, urging me to ask the next question. I couldn't quite believe I was saying the words as they came out of my mouth. "Are you saying that you're being possessed, Ximon?"

Ximon exhaled heavily, as if in relief. "Thanks be to God you understand. Yes."

Muffled explosions of skepticism erupted from around the room.

"What or who would take up residence in you?" I asked, unable to keep the derision from my voice. "And why?"

"It is a demon from Othersphere. No, hear me out!" he insisted as I let loose a ridiculing hiss. "I know you don't believe that evil resides in the other world, because you yourselves are connected to it, and you, Dez, were born there, but you must believe this: Something from Othersphere has taken hold of me. I can't refuse when he calls. I need your help. I need an exorcism."

I almost said, "Oh, brother," but controlled myself. "One moment," I said, and Arnaldo put him on hold again. "What is really going on here?"

The others did not look as contemptuous as I felt. "There was something odd about him tonight during the attack," Caleb said. "His vibration was different."

November was hunched over, tense. "Whatever he's up to, we should go along with it so we can find him and kill him."

"I'm the last person to believe him, but it's possible he's not lying," Caleb said. "You've seen things from Othersphere take hold of me, back when I wasn't as well trained in calling things forth from shadow. Of course, Ximon is better trained than I am, so it's a very remote chance that anything could get to him."

"He was weakened by the lightning strike," Lazar said, referring to a battle back at Morfael's first school, when Caleb had called forth a bolt of lightning and struck his father with it, nearly killing him. It was weird to hear him say things that supported Caleb, but something about facing their father at the same time had muted their other conflict. For now. "And I'm sure his defeat at the particle accelerator was devastating. But still, it sounds like a very convenient excuse."

"Exactly," I said.

"We need to know more." Caleb strode over to the computer and resumed the call. "Who is it that's possessing you, Ximon? And what does it want?"

"My son." Ximon's voice was creased with weariness. The light caught his wide forehead below the white hair. The skin was creased with lines. "I don't know its name, but I have been locked in a battle for control of my will with it for weeks now. I've been forced to warn my lieutenants not to take any strange orders from me, to check my demeanor, to double-check with me on every order before carrying it out. And still this monster took me over long enough to plan and execute the kidnapping of your sister. He has sent her to Hell. . . ." The strong voice cracked a little. "To force me to yield my will to him forever."

I leaned in and spoke very clearly, to make sure he caught my every word. "I was there when you shoved Amaris into Othersphere, Ximon. That was you, not some creature from another world. I've seen things come through from Othersphere, and none of them looked human."

"You're from Othersphere, yet you look human," Ximon said.

I shivered, and caught Caleb throwing me a glance. He almost appeared concerned, and then he turned back to the monitor. Ximon was saying, "And it . . . he told me that he learned not to announce himself after you saw him possess Caleb, back at my old compound in the desert."

Caleb inhaled sharply. Our eyes met again, and for the first time in forever, he didn't look away. I knew that he, too, was remembering the night when he had called upon his powers for too long, and in his weariness had been unable to prevent a powerful presence from Othersphere from taking over his body. Caleb had altered under its influence, gotten sharper, taller, leaner, as if he'd been made of hard black stone. I'd understood then why Ximon thought Othersphere was inhabited by demons, for that creature had emanated a malevolence and power I'd never felt before. I'd known I could not defeat it physically. Instead, I'd called upon Caleb's love for me. That was what had given him the strength to force it back to where it came from.

Maybe Ximon wasn't lying. How else could he know about that night? Then I remembered: Ximon had been there, too. He and Lazar had been nearby in a small plane, taxiing for takeoff, and could have easily seen what had happened to Caleb.

"He got a taste of our world that night," Ximon was saying. "And now he wants it for his own."

"Why the hell would anyone want to rule this stupid world?" London said, mumbling and low.

November was nodding. "Total quagmire. Good luck with that, crazy Othersphere demon."

"But why kidnap Amaris?" Caleb said to his father. "How does that help him with his plans? Is it her healing ability?"

"No." Ximon paused. I could hear his uneven breathing. "His plan was to possess me long enough to capture either Amaris, or you, and then to hold one or both of you captive in Othersphere as hostage for my good behavior."

"Extortion," said November. "Maybe not such a crazy demon."

"Why—because you care so much for us?" Caleb's voice dripped sarcasm. "This demon of yours isn't very bright."

Ximon didn't answer right away. When he spoke, his voice was bleak. The light shining on his left eye showed that the white was shot with red. "Regardless of what you think, I love all my children. You may not agree with how I act upon that feeling, but in your heart you know that's why I have strived to save you, to keep you from falling victim to evil. This demon is proof of what I have always thought—that Othersphere is just another name for the abyss of Hell. And I may have given the devil himself a ticket out."

Caleb shook his head. The bruises from his concussion stood out like smears of blue-black paint against his skin.

Next to me, Lazar spoke, his voice clipped. "He believes what he's saying. That's how twisted he is."

"To be honest," I said to the shadowy form on the monitor, "I don't give a damn how much you do or don't love anyone, Ximon. Why come to us? Don't you have other Bishops or Cardinals, or whatever you call yourselves, to help you? Personally, I'd recommend a dose of antipsychotic meds."

Ximon raised a bottle of water to his lips and drank, swallowing hard twice. Then he said, "I think . . . I think the demon fears you, Desdemona. Perhaps because you're from Othersphere, too, but I can't be sure. That's why I called you."

Goose pimples pricked all over my arms. The soft, undramatic tone in his voice only underscored the strangeness of his words. I still didn't believe him, but the tone of his voice made me uneasy. "I've never understood how you knew more about me than I did, Ximon," I said. "How do you know I was born in Othersphere?"

"The signs are written all over you to one trained as I've been," he said. "The Tribunal has records going back two thousand years, and in all that time, no shifter ever echoed the frequency of the demon world so strongly as you. We did a series of tests on you when you were first captured. They made it clear you could only be a creature from Hell. And not just any creature, but one of the higher devils, the rulers of that world. They are the beings who have been manifested through weak or tired objurers in the past, revealing themselves briefly, only to be exorcised. They call themselves the Amba. And you're one of them, the only one I've ever known to come bodily through the veil whole. Probably thanks to that vile teacher of yours, Morfael. "

The Tribunal had been around long enough, and was obsessed enough with record keeping for all of that to be true. And they had captured me not long ago, the very first time I shifted.

"But now you've sent Amaris bodily through the veil, whole," I said into the phone. "How?"

"It was not I who did it!" Ximon's voice rose, and the cords on the side of his neck stood out. "The demon made me go to the oak tree, the one whose shadow is a perpetual storm, and there he pulled some strange rope here from Othersphere. He said that whomever it touched would be able to go through the doorway he created. He just needed you to be there as well. Somehow with you there, the doorway was possible."

"And how would he know I'd be there?" Damn, Ximon was good. He'd come up with a very elaborate series of lies to justify himself, but they didn't explain everything. Caleb opened his mouth to say something, but I shook my head at him, still speaking to the man on the monitor. "You're the expert at manipulating me, Ximon. You're the one who predicted I'd help Lazar escape from you. You knew that would lead me to your trap at the accelerator. Tonight was a trap exactly like that. One made by you, not some alien."

"I haven't been able to keep him out of my mind." Ximon's voice was hushed with humiliation. He bowed his head. "Although I pray for strength."

His shame sounded very real, but again, all we had to go on was his voice, which he used like an instrument—or a weapon. It was yet another reminder, as if I needed one, that he could not be trusted.

Caleb put the call on hold. "That's how it was when I was taken over by—whatever it was," he said. "It knew everything I knew."

True, that creature had spoken of Caleb's regret at not being able to return to me. It had also promised to swallow our moon and drink its blood. Now that I'd seen the veiny surface of the moon in Othersphere, it all made some weird kind of sense. But that didn't prove Ximon was telling the truth.

"All that proves is that he knows a lot about these things from Othersphere. You heard him. He's got two thousand years of Tribunal research to call upon. He's counting on my desire to help people to lure us all into some other trap. I'm not falling for it this time."

Caleb looked uneasy. "He'd never humiliate himself to you like this unless something was actually wrong—something to do with Othersphere. You're from Othersphere, and Morfael's actually been there. You two are the logical people to come to."

"With all their research, the Tribunal's got to know nearly as much," I said.

"But he can't go to them," London said. "The moment the other Bishops and whatever get a whiff of any otherworldly demons around him, they'll kill him."

"No!" I said. "He's so clever. Don't you see? That's what he wants you to believe. Remember how I fell for everything he told Lazar? He knew that would win me over. He knew it would draw me to the particle accelerator and get us all there so he could infect us with that virus that would've cut us off from Othersphere. At least that didn't happen, but . . ."

"Siku died," November said. London put a hand on her shoulder, but she yanked it away. "Dez is right—Ximon's a liar and a murderer. I vote that we let him think we believe him, arrange to meet him, and kill him."

"After we get the information we need to bring Amaris back," London said.

Arnaldo narrowed his eyes, calculating. "If he's lying about this demon, then he's got to have more of that twine, or a map, or some way to open up the veil and locate Amaris."

"We get that from him . . ." I said.

"And we get her back," Lazar finished.

"It's a plan," I said. Everyone had spoken except for one. "Caleb?" I asked. He was in this now, with the rest of us. "What do you think?"

"I want Amaris back," Caleb said. "But there's more going on here than just a trap."

"Caleb's vote doesn't count," November said. "Sorry, handsome, but you gave that up when you ditched us."

Caleb opened his mouth to retort, and then shut it again in a hard line.

"Or if it does count," Arnaldo said, his voice reasonable, "he's outvoted. This time we lay the trap for Ximon."

"Good," I said. I'd wanted Caleb to agree with us, but when he didn't, I felt a weird, shameful satisfaction when my friends put him in his place. And it just felt good to be doing something, anything, to get Amaris back. "I propose that we let him think we buy his story and make him agree to meet us. He'll think we're there to exorcise this demon, but instead we capture him, go through all his records and his stuff for clues, and force him to tell us the real story."

Everyone but Caleb nodded slowly. "Tell him we need a phone number where we can call him back with details," Arnaldo said. "We might be able to use that to track him."

"Cool," I said. "I'm going to play it like we're still skeptical but open to a meeting, so it doesn't look like we did a complete one-eighty." Arnaldo pressed the hold button again. "Okay, Ximon. We've discussed what you've told us. I'm not completely convinced, but my friends think you might be telling the truth, and we've got to take the chance on you to get Amaris back."

Ximon exhaled a breath so big, it sounded like he'd been

holding it for days. "I . . . thank you. I promise you won't regret this."

"I already regret it," I said. "Give us a number where we can reach you. We'll find a spot to meet up with you that works for us."

"I'm not far from Livermore," he said, and gave us a phone number.

I got up, moving toward the computer to disconnect the call. Caleb grabbed my hand to stop me. "One more question, Ximon." His touch sent an electrical jolt through me. I pulled my hand away. But Caleb was focused on his father. "What does this demon want from you so badly that he's willing to shove Amaris into Othersphere to force you to give it to him? We destroyed your particle accelerator. What else have you got?"

"I don't know the details yet," Ximon said. "But he's very interested in the files on a project I abandoned a few years ago in order to concentrate on the accelerator. I felt it was too dangerous, too likely to rip the veil between worlds completely." He took a deep breath. "It involved construction of the world's most powerful laser."

CHAPTER 4

While Morfael vanished and the rest of us made popcorn, Arnaldo pulled up a Google map of Livermore, California, on one screen of his laptop, and a program he and Lazar had created to track incoming Skype calls on the other. I kept wishing I could get a moment alone with Lazar, to talk about the fact that his brother, and my ex-boyfriend, was now back at the school. But it had been hard enough to get time alone on an ordinary day, let alone a day Ximon rang us up on Skype.

Lazar had never heard about his father's supposed plans to build a powerful laser. "Either he's lying, or it was something he worked on when I was too young to hear about it," he said.

"It's probably a lie," I said. "But he could be throwing little bits of truth into his overall lie to keep it real."

"Who cares?" London was impatient. "Exactly where and how should we meet up with him?"

We talked about it till all the popcorn was gone and November brought out the ice cream. We couldn't do it too near the school, or we'd risk giving away its location. I voted for a spot near Ximon's old particle accelerator, where the veil was thin and my ability to destroy technology was enhanced. The Tribunal relied on guns and other machinery, so if I could help disable those tools, it would help keep us safe.

"I think I found him," Arnaldo said, the blue light from his laptop screen washing out his bronze face.

Chairs scraped back, and we gathered around Arnaldo's screen. "Thanks to Lazar sharing what he learned from the Tribunal, we can track calls to our computer to a precise location. Check it out."

London's half-blond hair brushed my cheek as we both leaned in to look at Arnaldo's monitor. It was weird to see the brothers so close together, with just November between them, doing the same. We saw an overhead satellite shot of a suburban neighborhood, complete with tree-covered medians and an even grid of streets with the occasional graceful curve thrown in to keep it from being completely boring.

"Fourteen ninety-one Cherry Drive." Arnaldo pointed to a small red dot on the grid. "Here's the street view." He clicked the mouse, and the screen switched to a shot of a wide driveway next to a narrow, evenly cut green lawn fronting an ordinary two-story suburban house, painted tan, curtains obscuring the few visible windows in the upper story.

Arnaldo cued the street view around to show a neatly paved road, and on the other side, some narrow parkland with gravel paths and neatly spaced trees. Through their trunks you could see another street just like this one on the other side of the park, peppered with identical houses.

"That's not one of the safe house addresses I know," Lazar said. "What city is it in?"

"Livermore, California." Arnaldo zoomed out to show us a wider view, which included the 580 freeway and the word "Livermore" to the left.

"So he's not just 'near' Livermore," Caleb said. "He's right in the middle of it."

"Rich folks live mostly in Livermore," November said. Her family owned a chain of pawnshops throughout the Bay Area. "Haven't spent much time there because it's boring. They've got an old Spanish mission, like everyone else. It used to be farmland, now lots of tech types working and living there."

"What's this brown patch?" London circled an area to the east of the Cherry Drive address.

"Lawrence Livermore National Laboratory," Lazar said, before Arnaldo could reply. "It's a hub of research and development for the U.S. Department of Energy, various universities, and lots of tech companies. They do experiments on everything from cyber security to plutonium research."

"Nuclear fun again." November shook her head. "How do you know all this?"

"Because Livermore Labs was labeled Code Yellow by the Tribunal's Threat Assessment team." Lazar took in our blank gazes. "That means it shows a detectable level of damage to the membrane between universes—to the veil. Code White means there's no damage detected, then yellow, then orange, then red."

"What did they label the area near the particle accelerator?" I asked. "Red?"

He nodded. "Red, and technically off limits, to keep out anyone who wasn't authorized. It's the only red area in the Western U.S., thanks to all the nuclear detonations, although Los Alamos almost qualifies. That's orange, along with the nuclear energy facilities at Diablo Canyon and San Onofre and, of course, the oak tree in Dez's old neighborhood."

"The Lightning Tree?" I'd climbed the tree nearly every day as a child, only to learn later that I was probably drawn to it because it had a powerful shadow in Othersphere.

"Is that what you call it?" Lazar asked, and then looked a little shamefaced. "It's been code orange ever since the

Threat Assessment team first found it, before I was born. So of course we planted cameras around it to keep watch. Father noticed your connection to it. . . ."

"And that's how you originally found me, shot me up with tranquilizers, and captured me." I shot Caleb a look and found him looking back. He'd been the one to figure that out. As he pulled his gaze away again, I felt how much had changed since then.

Lazar cleared his throat. "It's the only code orange area that seems to have occurred naturally in this part of the world. There's a very old yew in Wales and a cyprus in Iran that are also code orange, I think. But most code oranges are because of damage human beings did to the veil one way or another. Meteor strikes, except for Tunguska, tend to be code yellow."

"Tunguska must be code red," I said.

"The reddest."

"So why is Ximon now living next to a site filled with fancy technology that's damaging the veil?" Caleb asked.

November licked a dab of ice cream off her own nose and clanked her spoon down into her empty bowl. "Let's go and ask him."

We called Ximon and told him we'd meet him at midnight the next night on the western side of the San Antonio Reservoir, about twelve miles from Livermore, to make our own assessment of him and confirm his story. He agreed without argument.

But that wasn't what we did. After much discussion, we agreed to get a few hours of sleep and left before dawn to make the eight-hour drive to his house on Cherry Drive.

Lazar and I got only a few moments alone in the computer room just before we left. He pulled me in and surprised me with a passionate kiss. It was reassuring to feel his lean body against mine, to run his thick blond hair through my fingers.

"Hey," I said against his mouth.

He didn't let me pull away, wrapping his strong arms around me and kissing the tip of my nose "Hey. You okay?"

"Yeah." I thought about just breezing past the whole Caleb thing, but that would only keep things awkward. "But it's weird with Caleb here, isn't it?"

"Just a bit." He put his forehead against mine so that our noses touched. "He doesn't know about us yet, does he?"

"Well, I didn't tell him," I said. Lazar smelled so good, so comforting, like clean laundry just out of the dryer. "I know I've been tiptoeing around you when he's here, and that's weird, too, and I'm sorry."

He laughed softly. "Don't be sorry. I'm doing it, too."

I pulled away a little to look him in the eye, keeping his arms comfortably around my waist. "Why do you care what he thinks?"

His eyes, a rich brown, crinkled in thought. He was only eighteen, but already small lines were etched at the corners of his eyes and between his brows. His life so far had not been an easy one. But the lines just gave his strong, handsome face a touch of character. I could already see the thoughtful, kind man he would be in twenty years. "Mostly to avoid more conflict for you. But there's this tiny little part of me that wonders what it would be like if we could just be . . . brothers. Or half-brothers, or anything other than enemies. I know it'll probably never happen."

"But you can't help hoping," I said. "I don't blame you."

"Why do *you* care what he thinks?" Lazar asked.

I hesitated. I couldn't tell him the truth: that I didn't want Caleb to think poorly of me. Caleb had broken up with me because of Lazar. If he saw us together now, he might think I'd cheated on him. I hadn't cheated, but still. He might never get over it; we'd never be friends. *Or anything else.* "I'm so sick of conflict and pain and anger. I think I just want peace."

He searched my face as if somehow it held an answer to an unspoken question. "I wonder if we'll ever get that."

Then the door to the boys' dorm opened and we sprang

apart, acting nonchalant as Arnaldo and Caleb passed by the open door to the computer room. We joined them as they headed up the stairs, careful to keep an arm's length between us.

The ride was quiet. Lazar drove, with me in the shotgun seat, and Caleb and Arnaldo behind us. November and London got stuck in the back with our equipment and two large bags filled with chips, pretzels, cookies, and soda.

Not long ago, it would have been Caleb driving with me at his side, and Siku next to November. The bear-shifter's absence was like a black hole in the group, sucking away any desire to talk. Where there once had been anticipation of danger pulling us together, there was now a cloud of vague conflict and tension pushing us apart. Maybe this raid on Ximon would dissipate that cloud.

As long as it succeeds.

I pushed doubt away. Caleb was the only one really mad at me, and that was for personal reasons. November blamed me a bit for Siku's death, but she'd agreed with me that Ximon was lying about being possessed, and she'd eagerly pushed us to go on this raid. Because Ximon's man had shot Siku, November wanted Ximon dead or captured more than any of us.

And at least a few things hadn't changed. London, Arnaldo, and Lazar had all readily agreed to my plan. If it worked, the biggest threat to the otherkin would be neutralized.

Lazar drove seated in a much more upright, alert position than Caleb had, often casting me a sideways smile and asking me unnecessary questions to fight off the soul-squashing silence. I couldn't help smiling back and keeping the conversation going, grateful to him, ignoring the black cloud of disapproval emanating from Caleb.

For the last six weeks Lazar had been in our classes at Morfael's school, honing his ability to recognize and draw out the shadows of objects, something his father had told him was the devil's work. Objurers were only supposed to suppress shadow when they found it, never call it forth. Lazar had struggled at first against his early training, but after a couple of weeks, he got kind of giddy at all the shadow he saw, and at his ability to manipulate it. He'd sneaked up on me and tried to make me shift into being a tiger one day. I'd been forced to yell a contradictory note to stop him from succeeding.

He became a bulwark against my despair at the loss of Siku. I'd actually been able to laugh. And Lazar's face had lost its debased, guilt-stricken cast. He made jokes, usually very clean ones, and volunteered to babysit Arnaldo's young brothers when we, the older shifters, were sent out on assignments too advanced for them, and irrelevant to a caller like Lazar.

Cordero and Luis enjoyed learning how to repair the refrigerator or build an elaborate fort out of bales of hay and tree branches. We'd come back from class one day to find that the boys had constructed their own Monopoly set using cardboard and colored pens. A bemused Lazar had never seen one before, and they were teaching him all about real estate, the hard way. I had a strong vision in my head of how Lazar would be with his own sons—bemused, loving, so careful to be the opposite of his own father.

And he flirted with me, always opening the door for me, helping me when it was my turn to clean the kitchen or take out the garbage. Every time he did it, my spirit would lift, my pulse would speed up. November made sarcastic comments about it in the girls' dorm room at night, but I didn't know how to respond. I missed Caleb so much I ached. Lazar's attention sometimes made me forget that ache. Maybe I wouldn't go through my whole life alone. Maybe I wasn't a complete failure at being a girl, and a girlfriend.

Then during our first week after Siku's death, during an exercise where Morfael made us wade upstream through an ankle-deep creek, feeling for places where the veil was thin, I'd slipped on a mossy rock. I would have fallen and gotten completely soaked, except that Lazar was instantly at my side to grab my elbow with a firm, steady hand, the other hand on my waist.

It was the first time anyone had touched me since the night Siku died. I'd had good crying sessions with Mom via video conference, but at school we were all just wandering around in our own isolated haze, going through the motions. Now here was a warm, living person holding me, keeping me from falling, supporting me.

I nearly collapsed right into him. I'd nearly asked him to pick me up and carry me away to somewhere safe, somewhere that grief didn't drip from every word, where no one mourned or blamed.

Instead, I fumbled to gain my footing and slipped again, falling hard against his chest. The contours of his body were strangely familiar under my hands, but he smelled different from Caleb, more like soap and amber than thunderstorm. I'd wanted to wrap my arms around him and bury my face in his neck, to pretend, for a moment, to find comfort there.

His heartbeat had sped up; his hands tightened around my body. His pupils dilated, and he smiled. Our faces had been close, our lips inches apart, and the ache inside me had changed from a great dragging weight into a light, soaring, burning thing.

We hadn't kissed. It was too soon for that. He'd set me carefully on my feet, laughing. We navigated that river side by side, steadying each other. And as we walked back to the school, he took my hand.

We strolled like that until we reached the school. We even let go at the same time, just before we walked inside. I'd spent the rest of the day quietly smiling to myself. It had progressed slowly from there, with him always patient, deferring to my reticence, but hinting at better things to come.

Until yesterday. I blushed just thinking about it, wondering what would happen next.

What would Caleb do if he found out?

The thought dragged at me. The others in the school had eventually figured it out. But no one had said much. We were all preoccupied with loss. Grief had drawn a boundary of silence between us. Except for me and Lazar.

Lazar still hadn't given any outward sign we were together, but Caleb was no fool. He might already suspect. I tried to keep my responses to Lazar's chatter as innocuous as possible as we drove. If Caleb left because of me being with Lazar, then it would really be my fault that the group of friends, the team, had disintegrated.

And I couldn't imagine never seeing Caleb again.

We reached Livermore late in the afternoon, stopped off for some fast food, and coasted slowly down Cherry Drive after dusk.

It reminded me a bit of the neighborhood where I'd grown up in Burbank. The trees here were smaller, the houses newer, and thus even more cookie-cutter than I was used to. So 1491 only differed from 1493 and 1495 because it had been painted a lighter beige and had a familiar white pickup truck parked in the driveway.

"That's one of the trucks we saw last night," I said.

"Then we're going in," London said, shooting Arnaldo a look.

"Reconnaissance is ready," Arnaldo said, pulling his sweatshirt over his head.

"Yeah, yeah, me, too." November rolled up the bag of candy she'd been dipping into for the last hour and stashed it.

We parked around a bend in the road, waited till an SUV filled with kids in soccer uniforms drove by, and let Arnaldo and November slip out. Arnaldo's eagle form was too large for him to shift completely inside the car, so Lazar slid the moonroof back. Arnaldo stood up on his seat, bare chest poking out of the roof, and, with a tremble of air, shifted.

I could just see a gnarled yellow talon holding the edge of

the open moonroof. Then his fierce head, covered in snow-white feathers, poked down, and he fixed us with one shining golden eye.

"Okay, okay," November said. She kept talking, but after a brief pause, the words became squeaks. What had been a girl in the back seat in a fatigue jacket and skinny jeans became a pile of clothing and crumbs. A lump under the jacket moved, chittering, and November's little pink nose peeked out, her gray-and-white whiskers bristling. London opened the door for her, and November leapt onto the strip of grass next to the sidewalk.

Arnaldo lifted his head and with a flap of his huge brown wings, rose from the roof of the SUV, shoving it away with his powerful feet.

"He's awfully big for the suburbs," London said, craning her neck to watch the eagle fly toward number 1491 Cherry Drive.

"But federally protected," I said. "The worst thing that happens is someone sights him and they think, 'Cool! The bald eagle is really coming back.' "

"Unless Ximon has infrared cameras on his roof," Caleb said, his voice bland.

"Unlikely," Lazar said, even more neutral. "They aren't cheap or easy to install discreetly, and it's not like he had time to take any with him when he ran off."

"And if they set off an alarm, they set off an alarm," I said.

London stepped out of the car. "Time for us to go."

We followed her out of the SUV and split up. Caleb and London strolled back around the corner toward the front of 1491, while Lazar and I headed in the opposite direction to go around the back. There was no alley behind the houses here. They sat back to back with another row of houses just like them, separated by a tall wooden fence. So we would have to move a little faster and do more climbing than our friends.

Lazar took my hand. Nervous, I glanced over my shoulder

before we rounded the corner to see the long dark line of Caleb walking next to the loping, lanky form of London, the blond top half of her head faintly green under the street-lights. Caleb turned at the last moment to look back our way. I yanked my hand out of Lazar's; then we turned the corner.

Lazar was staring at me. "I need my hand," I mouthed to him. But his face was blank. Did he realize I'd pulled away because of Caleb?

"Testing," I said, a finger to the receiver in my ear. Lazar had fashioned headsets for us a few weeks back, and we'd practiced using them in a few classes. Now that I could chan-nel excess energy into the ground, I could keep it from short-ing out. Probably. Caleb had refused to wear one, as if the fact that it came from Lazar and the Tribunal tainted it.

"I hear you." London's voice was tinny in my ear. "We'll wait for your signal."

"Thanks." I turned to Lazar. "Let's get ahead of them. Count down."

We picked up the pace to a slow jog. "One," Lazar said under his breath as we passed the first house on the street parallel to Cherry. Fourteen ninety-one was the fifth house from the corner, and with the lots all the same size, we knew we could enter its backyard with confidence, as long as we counted the houses on this parallel street properly.

We counted down silently. "Five." We slowed down in front of the fifth house. The lights were off upstairs, but the opaque glass near the front door was glowing. Dinnertime in house five.

The coast looked clear. We walked normally onto the lawn toward the fence protecting the backyard, and then stooped low as we moved in front of the opaque glass by the front door. The dark, weathered wooden planks of the fence only came up to my cheekbones, so I stood on my toes and glanced over it. A black four-legged form lying nearby looked up from the bone it was gnawing and barked.

"Oh, crap," I said to Lazar, who was right behind me. A

thump from the other side of the fence announced that the dog was on its hind legs, paws up on the fence.

"Then we go through that yard." Even taller than I was, Lazar looked over the fence easily and pointed at the sixth house next door.

"Frances! Quiet!" a man shouted from the fifth house.

The dog, a lion-maned creature with jet black eyes, fur, and tongue, kept barking. Frances was no fool.

"Let's be quick." I moved over a few feet to the fence guarding the sixth house's backyard. There were no lights on in this house, not even a porch light. My pupils were adjusting as I reached up and put a foot against the fence to leap over.

"Here." Lazar bent down and put both his hands under my foot, like someone helping a jockey into a saddle.

"Okay." Caleb rarely helped me that way, knowing I could handle myself, but a little extra push couldn't hurt. I put my sneakered foot on Lazar's hands and pushed off.

Lazar used his hands like a springboard and I vaulted clear over the fence in almost a standing position.

His help threw off my balance a little, though. I had to roll when I landed. I got to my feet just as I saw, right in front of me, the black water of an unlit swimming pool, unreflective beneath the overcast night sky. I teetered on the edge, and then pulled back, silently thanking my cat-shifter reflexes.

Frances was still barking, aiming her displeasure first at me, then at Lazar.

"Maybe you should go out and see what she's barking at, honey," a woman inside Frances's house said.

Behind me, Lazar had his own hands on the top of the fence, about to hoist himself over.

"Oh, hey," I said, keeping my voice low. "Look out for the . . ."

Lazar, unable to hear me over the sharp woofs, pushed himself up and over the fence in one smooth move. Frances sprang toward the top of her own fence, snapping at him, her teeth the only white thing about her.

Startled by her leap, Lazar jerked away, mid-jump, in time to avoid a bite. But he caught his knee on the top of the fence and tumbled to the hard cement. He twisted as he fell, curling to cushion the blow, and rolled, as I had. Right toward the swimming pool.

I grabbed for him, getting hold of the sleeve of his brown jacket. But his momentum was too great. He rolled faster than I had and teetered on the edge of the pool as I scrabbled to catch his wrist. Instead, the whole jacket slid off in my hand. Lazar splashed into the pool with a startled cry, abruptly cut off by a gurgle.

I watched the ripples in the water, ready to jump in if he didn't come up for some reason. But he bobbed to the surface, spluttering quietly, and then stood up in the shallow water, dark golden hair in whorls on his forehead, his T-shirt clinging to his shoulders and abs.

I held up his last piece of dry clothing. "It was you or the jacket."

A stray ray of starlight caught a glint in his eye; then he burst into laughter.

I convulsed, too, hand over my mouth to keep the sound low, not that anyone would have heard us over the renewed frenzy of barking.

Lazar's white teeth flashed. He held a finger to his lips. "Ssh! Frances might hear you!"

I giggled as he hoisted himself, dripping, out of the pool.

"What the hell is happening over there?"

I jumped, hand to my heart. Lazar let loose another laugh as I realized it was London talking through the receiver in our ears.

"Can you hear us from all the way over there?" I asked, making sure my voice was low. Lazar and I rounded the edge of the dark pool, moving toward the back corner of the fence, where we could jump kitty-corner into the yard of 1491. No lights had come on in any of the houses around us. In the fifth house, the back door squeaked open and Frances's owner shushed her, announcing to his wife there was no one in the backyard.

"No," said London. "I heard you gurgling or something through the receiver. I thought someone was choking you."

Lazar and I exchanged a grin. "We're fine."

We stopped at the back fence as Lazar did a quick check of the gun in his shoulder holster, and the other tools—lock pick, flashlight, silver and brass knuckles—at his belt. "Everything okay?"

"Yeah, all Tribunal guns can fire if they get wet. Thanks." He took the jacket from me and shrugged it on so the gun was covered. Then he held out his cupped hands. "Another boost?"

"Thanks." I put my foot in his hand, eyeing the landscape behind us—Frances's owner had taken her inside—and then scanned ahead. "No swimming pool," I told him.

He breathed a laugh. "Hallelujah."

We made it over that fence without a problem. "We're in position," I said quietly into my headset.

"No movement," London said.

"Waiting for lights to go out." Going first because I had the best night vision, I led Lazar across the dying grass of the back lawn, scanning the big curtained windows for any sign of Ximon. Rats could get in just about anywhere, so we'd sent November in first to chew through the phone lines and disable any kind of alarm system she found. When the lights went out, we'd know she'd succeeded.

Lazar and I flattened ourselves against the outer wall of the house, close to the back door. I looked up, but didn't see Arnaldo. He was probably perched on the roof, keeping his sharp eyes peeled for anything suspicious.

Something rustled in the grass. Lazar drew his pistol out in one smooth move, but I'd heard a familiar chitter and said, "Wait!"

It was November, her fur damp from sprinkler-wet grass. She stood up on her hind legs, her brown, pod-shaped body almost a foot tall and prattled at me in a rush of squeaks and hisses.

I squatted down. "You know I can't understand anything you're saying." I kept my voice low.

She exhaled in frustration, then made a sort of firework motion with one paw, then sliced another claw across her throat in a cutting motion. "Lights, cut?" I asked. "No, the lights are still on. Oh!" As she danced with aggravation, I realized what she was trying to convey. "You can't cut off the lights?"

She nodded furiously.

"What about the phones?"

She shook her head.

"So you probably have no idea if there's a burglar alarm."

She nodded, and then shook her head, and I realized my question had no easy yes or no answer. Her whiskers curled and she squealed, shaking her paws at me. I reached over to pet her reassuringly on the top of her head. Disgusted, she gave me a warning bite that didn't break the skin.

"They've rat-proofed the house," I said into my headset, glancing up at Lazar. "Which means we definitely have the right place. But we can't cut off phone or lights."

"I vote we go in anyway," London said.

I heard a distant male voice through the microphone. Caleb. "This is a bad idea."

I ignored him and turned to November. "I agree, London." I turned to November. "Can you climb up and tell Arnaldo we're going in?"

The rat put her pink paws on her round hips and shook her head at me.

"I know. He doesn't speak rat either. Just mime something, like kicking a door in."

With a chirp that sounded a lot like an angry "Fine!" November scurried to the wall and zoomed up its vertical surface.

"Just pick the lock, Caleb," London said tersely over the headset.

"Let us know when you're ready," I said to her and reached for the scabbard hidden under my coat to pull out the Shadow Blade. As always, it felt cool and calming in my hand. Its blade was so black it seemed to absorb the light around it, and the wavering edge wasn't sharp, but evanesced into smoke. "Be ready to move in fast."

"Yeah, they'll probably hear us coming." Lazar reached into a pocket and started screwing a silencer onto his pistol. "And to keep this from creaking..." He reached into a pocket, pulled out a tiny bottle and sprayed the hinges of the screen door.

"Clever." I kept forgetting how Lazar had broken into my own house very successfully, more than once. He knew more about this sort of operation than I did.

"Caleb's got the lock," London said into my ear.

I nodded to Lazar. He swung the screen door open noiselessly and pointed his silenced gun at the sky.

I slid the Shadow Blade between the wooden door and the lintel, and cut down. As soon as it hit the metal bolt, the blade sharpened, biting through it with what almost felt like relish.

I put my hand on the doorknob. "London, count down. On three."

"One..." London said. "Two. Three."

I shoved the door open and rolled in. Judging by the sounds coming from the opposite side of the house, London was doing the same. I was in an open dining area, empty of furniture. The kitchen looked like an army of teenage boys had been there. Dishes half-filled with unidentifiable food lay piled in the sink, chairs were knocked over or pushed away from the small table there. Bottles, cans, and plastic bags lay strewn on the dirty floor.

Lazar pegged the screen door open while I sheathed the blade and stood still, listening. Lazar paused at the sight of the filthy kitchen, brows coming together in puzzlement. It certainly wasn't typical of the very anal-retentive Ximon and his Tribunal.

Footsteps moved cautiously near the front of the house. Caleb and London. "Nobody in the kitchen," I said to London.

The ceiling creaked. I pointed up at it for Lazar.

"Nobody in the living room," London whispered through my earpiece, although I also heard her voice through the walls. My hearing was ridiculously sharp.

Lazar opened the door out of the dining area and found the stairs up and another door. London and Caleb stood silhouetted at the other end of the hall.

Lazar started up the stairs, gun ready, and then turned and mouthed, "Check the basement," at me, pointing at the door in the hallway.

I nodded, but I was worried. London stalked over, icy blue eyes anxious. Caleb moved up behind her, keeping an eye over his shoulder.

Or is he trying not to look at me?

Me, me, me. He'd said not everything was about me. I needed to focus on what was important.

"This is weird," London said in a voice only we could hear. "No guards in the kitchen or the living room?"

"I know," I said in a similar tone. "One set of footsteps upstairs? No traps?"

"Then get ready for something big in the basement," Caleb said, using his whisper that wasn't really a whisper.

I nodded, but it still made no sense. Just last night we'd seen Ximon attacking in full force, with multiple trucks, men, and a helicopter. Where were they all now? Was this some new trap?

A swish of wind and the heavy flapping of wings, and Arnaldo swooped into the dining room through the open door, carrying something large, wiggling, and brown in one claw. He curved to land on the filthy kitchen table, and set his burden down there.

November shook herself and chittered at him furiously, lifting one dainty paw out of what looked like a bowl of congealed oatmeal to wipe it on the bird's brown chest feathers. Arnaldo pecked at her paw, and she jerked it back.

"Arnaldo." The eagle's piercing gaze turned to me as I said his name. "If you could help Lazar upstairs . . . I heard one person up there at least."

He nodded and pushed off the table. With one sweep of his wings, he was across the room, curving through the doorway, turning sideways to get through and up the stairs.

I walked over and laid my hand out like a platform to November. She hesitated, looking down at my fingers. "I know it's not like it was," I said. "But I'd be honored if you'd catch a ride on my shoulder for now. We're heading into the basement to see what's down there."

She wiggled her whiskers at me, considering. Her favorite place to be when she was in rat form had been on Siku's broad grizzly bear back, or sometimes on top of his narrow head. She hadn't hopped on anyone for a ride since he'd died.

She cheeped softly once and clambered onto my hand. Her little claws tickled through my sleeve as she scrambled from there up my arm to sit on my shoulder.

"Ready?" Caleb said in his non-whisper. "It's not locked."

"This is so bizarre," said London. "But let's go."

Caleb swung the door open. Wooden stairs led down to a cement floor lit by a faint glow coming from the left. Not waiting for me, Caleb started down as quietly as he could, though the stairs creaked under his weight. London was about to follow when his head swiveled to the left and he stopped dead.

"Hello, son."

Ximon's voice echoed through the basement.

Caleb didn't reply. His dark eyes were darting all over the portion of the room I couldn't see. London stood frozen in front of me.

"What are you doing?" Caleb sounded a little unnerved.

"I could ask you the same question," Ximon said. "I don't recall inviting you for a visit."

"Why are you in there?" Caleb's voice held an edge.

Ximon sighed. It sounded weary. "Trying to keep you, and myself, and the world safe until our meeting tonight."

I sidled past London a few steps, ducking my head to look. November's claws cut through the stuff of my coat to dig tensely into my skin.

The basement opened up to the left, bare cement floor and walls illuminated by a single bare bulb dangling from a cord in the ceiling. There were shelves on the back wall covered with rope and boxes, but none of that mattered. Ximon was standing in the middle of a large silver cage, shiny as a new quarter, and big enough for a man to pace three steps in any direction.

That he was in a cage was shocking enough. But Ximon also looked like a different man from the one who had kidnapped Amaris. He'd always been tall, vigorous, and handsome. Even after the lightning strike that sickened him, he'd radiated power and will. But the man before me looked like a shrunken Ximon in old age makeup. The hints of encroaching age and weariness I'd taken for acting on the Skype call yesterday were obvious in the light of the bare bulb hanging from the center of the ceiling. His once-tan skin hung pale and loose, his collarbone protruding under his white turtleneck, which was smeared with dust. His white pants were belted tight to keep them up. His powerful hands were skeletal, patterned with large purple veins.

His head of thick hair, usually combed back in a perfect

white wave, was patchy and mussed. His formerly rosy face looked gray, haggard, and his large eyes held a strange, desperate gleam.

"Where's Amaris, and how do we get her back?" Caleb demanded.

Ximon's lips, thinned with age and exhaustion, pressed together into a white line. "I wish I knew."

"You might as well tell us," I said. "We'll get it out of you, one way or another."

"Ah, Desdemona. Of course." Ximon gave me a bitter smile. "I'm sorry I didn't anticipate this visit and plan something for you. But I am not myself lately."

The door to the cage was shut. "Is it locked?" I descended the stairs to the cold floor and took in the whole room again. Ximon was really down here alone, in a cage.

"Yes," he said. "The objurer you probably found upstairs has the key."

Thumps from the second story shook the walls. An eagle shrieked, and I heard Lazar grunt once in my earpiece. Something fell, hard, to the floor. "Got him," Lazar said.

"Search him," London said, jumping in before I could speak. "Look for a key, and anything else that might be tied to where Amaris is."

"Copy," he said.

Ximon was looking at me with what might almost have been fondness, if that was possible. "I see my son Lazar has introduced you to the use of certain technologies. You've learned how to keep them from shorting out at your touch."

"What's he doing in there?" London asked.

"Ximon?" I turned the question over to him. Inside the enclosure I saw a sleeping pallet, a bucket, some tins of food, utensils, and a large jug of water. I wanted to check the cage out more closely, but the silver exuded a painful hum that kept me back. I was far more sensitive to that metal than other shifters, because I was from Othersphere.

"I'm hoping that the silver will help to keep me from be-

coming . . . not myself," he said. "And if the demon does return, maybe the silver will keep him confined."

November hissed, ran down the length of my body, and
put her paws on the mesh between the bars in the door of the
silver cage, wincing as the metal burned her flesh. She
tugged, but the door didn't open. With a chirp that sounded
like, "Yep," she jerked her little hands away and scampered
over to the shelves, climbing up to examine their contents.

Ximon barely seemed to notice her, switching his feverish
gaze from me to Caleb. "I told all but one of my men to
leave, so that they wouldn't be used anymore by the demon.
When the time came to go meet you at the reservoir, he was
to release me, and I would have driven there, hoping I made
it without further transformation."

"So you really believe you're possessed by something from
Othersphere." Caleb walked to within ten feet of the cage.

"I would rather not believe it," Ximon said. "But the evidence is overwhelming."

"Not yet, it isn't," I said. "London, would you mind keeping an eye out on the ground floor? If you hear anything even
slightly like hordes of objurers about to swarm us, yell."

"Okay, but let me know if he says anything about
Amaris." London trotted back up the stairs.

"Found a key," Lazar said in my earpiece. "Some books
on Othersphere, too. Bringing them down."

"Great."

Caleb turned to me, thinking that I was talking to him. His
eyes darted to my earpiece as he realized I was responding to
someone else. Then he asked, "What should we do with
him?"

"He's coming with us," I said.

"Ah." His black eyes were scathing. "So you're just deciding that, without consulting anyone else? He's my father."

"We have to find out what he knows about Amaris," London's voice cut in. She must have heard Caleb speak over my
headset.

I looked at Caleb square on. "You lost your vote when you abandoned us, remember?"

November trilled what sounded like a short laugh.

Ximon said, "Having second thoughts on the Amba's methods, my son?"

Caleb's face was glacier cold as he gazed at Ximon. "If it were up to me, you'd be dead. Then it wouldn't matter whether or not you're lying."

Ximon didn't appear fazed. "Your father is weaker than he thought, Caleb. Be careful you don't also dreadfully misjudge yourself."

Lazar came running down the steps, leaving wet footprints from his fall in the pool. He slowed down as he took in the scene. "I've got the key; left the books upstairs with London. Arnaldo's gone back outside to keep watch," he said mechanically, his eyes on his father. He paced closer to the cage. "He looks ill."

"God failed to cure me," Ximon said.

Lazar nodded, his brown eyes accusatory. "And why do you think that is, Father?"

Ximon's eyes reddened, his lips twitched. "I'm sorry about your sister, my sons. I'm so sorry." As he said it, his face caved in with sorrow. Tears erupted from his eyes.

Lazar and Caleb's faces each bore the same astounded expression. Simultaneously, they pulled their eyes away from their father's distress. Caleb's hands were shoved deep into his coat pockets. Lazar's grip on his gun tightened, the knuckles going white. Staring at the once-arrogant man, now stifling sobs at his own failure, I had my first moment of doubt.

Maybe he's not faking it.

November squealed at an ear-piercing frequency. Over on the top shelf she was hopping up and down on top of a pile of thick brown rope. It looked familiar.

Caleb straightened. "Is that what I think it is?"

"What?" Lazar moved closer, as if relieved to have something to do other than deal with his father. Ximon was hunched over now, head buried in his hands.

"It's just like the rope they put around Amaris before they pushed her through the veil," I said, moving toward November. The rope looked exactly like the thick twine the Tribunal had wrapped around Amaris.

Caleb hummed, eyes narrowed at the rope, checking to see if it had a shadow.

"It is strange," Caleb said, ignoring his father. "There's something about it. . . ."

"Tell us, Father." Lazar stayed where he was to keep the stairs covered, but craned his neck to look at the rope. "Is that what you used to force your daughter into Othersphere?"

Ximon lifted his head, hurriedly wiping his eyes. "Yes." He squinted at the rope as if it pained him. "But it belongs to the demon. It might be better not to touch it."

"So you didn't order your men to use it on Amaris?" Caleb asked sharply.

Ximon shook his head. "The memory is like something from a bad dream. He . . . the creature ordered my men to wrap it around her once we got hold of her. He orchestrated the whole thing, using what I knew about you."

November poked experimentally at the rope with one pink claw, and when she didn't disappear or get an electrical shock, she took a coil and tossed it down to Caleb.

He caught it, pulling more down, humming under his breath. His black eyes sparked with gold. "It has a shadow, yes, but there's more than that. . . ."

"It casts a shadow into all the many worlds." Ximon was standing a little straighter, and his voice was more resonant. He was looking stronger suddenly.

"In every world?" Unable to resist, Lazar walked over beside Caleb and grabbed some of the rope.

"That's what I'm seeing," Caleb said. "Shadows upon shadows."

Lazar hummed. He was newer at this than Caleb, but his brown eyes took on the same golden sheen. He blinked, taken aback at what he saw, invisible to me. "Thousands of them. Millions . . ."

Curious, I moved nearer. The rope was a rough brown, like the dark bark of a tree stripped and wound into a cord. The closer I looked, the more variations in color I saw within it, the more alive it seemed. "What does that mean—it has many shadows?" I asked.

Caleb stopped humming. "With this you could travel to any of the many worlds out there, not just Othersphere."

"Why does he have more than one rope, then?" I turned to Ximon. "What were your plans for this length of rope?"

Ximon didn't answer me. He had hunched over and lurched closer to the silver bars of his cage. His temples glistened with perspiration. I didn't like how close I stood to the cage myself now. The pulse from it was irritating my skin. "Ximon?" I said.

"It's a lot softer than it looks," Lazar was saying of the rope. "Here." He held up a length of it toward me.

I reached for it automatically. Ximon reeled back away from the silver bars, sweat trickling down his face.

The rope in my hand did feel soft, like fur, but firmer. I closed my hand around it. It stirred.

"Oh!" I dropped the rope, but somehow it had wrapped around my wrist.

"What?" Caleb said.

"You all right?" Lazar asked at the same time.

I opened my mouth to say yes, to tell them that some kind of warmth was coming from the rope, a reassuring heat, as it were a purring cat.

But Ximon sucked in a long breath, stood taller, and said, "Ahhh. That's better."

His voice rumbled now like a V-8, so different from his earlier weary tones. His cheeks had turned pink. His shoulders looked broader. And his eyes. His eyes were molten gold, fixed on me.

In his right hand he was holding a shiny black staff, longer than he was tall, its glassy surface carved with animal figures that seemed to writhe. It was just like Morfael's staff, only our teacher's was made of wood. He tapped the staff on the cage floor and seemed to get bigger, taller, darker, like something that wasn't even remotely human.

"Get back!" Caleb shouted, yanking the rope away from me. "Everyone, out!"

"Little cub." It came out of Ximon as a growl.

Every hair on my arms stood on end. I'd been called that once before.

He smiled. His shiny black teeth were sharp. "Perhaps it's better I didn't eat you after all."

CHAPTER 5

Many things happened at once.

Ximon grew even taller, leaner. His skin blackened and shone. His fingernails lengthened into claws, grasping his staff. His eyes were worlds of gold shot with green and black.

Caleb shoved me back, putting himself between me and Ximon.

Lazar pointed his hand at Ximon, speaking with a tone of command, "I objure you. Back to Othersphere. Back . . ."

Ximon laughed, a deep, rumbling chortle that was not his own. He curled his black, clawed hands at the floor, as if pulling it toward him with an invisible rope.

The ground heaved. The walls swayed and shook, as if a giant hand was using the room as a rattle. The shelves and beams shuddered and cracked around us as loudly as a train hurtling past when you stand right next to the tracks.

Lazar and Caleb stumbled and fell. November hurtled off her shelf, catching the edge with her two right paws at the last moment to stop her fall. Paint cans, tools, and old rags rained down around her as the screws pinning the shelves to the walls jiggled outward. I kept my feet and staggered toward her.

The cage clanked and hopped around Ximon, or rather, the thing that Ximon had become. The silver bars rattled out of alignment. Nails popped from their holes. The cage roof swayed, coming away from one of the corner poles. The Ximon-thing had no trouble keeping its feet.

He tugged upward with his hands again, as if pulling on the reins of the earth below him. The ground shrugged upward.

I fell. Above me, the ceiling cracked.

The cage's roof came completely off most of its supporting posts. One side of it crashed down with a head-splitting clang, right on top of the creature beneath it.

The shelf November was hanging on flew off the wall and smashed into the shelves below. I lunged, trying to catch her. But she disappeared in a cloud of dust and debris.

The quaking subsided to a shudder. Lazar and Caleb stirred.

"November!" Coughing, I got to my hands and knees and pulled aside a broken shelf. "Where are you?"

No answering squeak. *Oh, no.* I didn't let myself think any further than that. Caleb, close by, stumbled over and helped me lift another shelf. Lazar got to his feet to lend a hand.

I glanced over my shoulder at the pile of debris that had fallen on the Ximon-thing. Was it dead?

Was November dead?

A high-pitched call and a swoop of wings announced Arnaldo's arrival. He landed on the cracked banister next to the stairs, half of which had crumbled into a pile of wood.

"November!"

I thought I saw a bit of her pink tail under broken shelving and brackets. "Here!" I said, motioning to the others. "Carefully . . ."

We cleared away the debris on top of that shelf. Then Caleb grabbed an end, Lazar another, and they gently lifted it together.

November lay there, unmoving, blood spotting her brown fur, a deep gash on her head, nearly severing one of her pale pink ears. My stomach dropped.

Then I realized she couldn't be dead. I'd seen what happened when a shifter in animal form was killed. After he died in his bear form, Siku had shifted back to human for the last time.

I laid two fingers over November's heart. The beat was rapid but strong. "I can't tell if anything's broken."

Arnaldo touched her dusty nose with his beak.

Footsteps upstairs, and London called out from the doorway, "What the hell is going on?"

"November's unconscious," I said through numb lips. *What have I done?*

"What?!" She started to clatter down the steps.

"The quake," Lazar said. "She fell."

"It wasn't a normal quake," Caleb said. "That thing that's possessing Ximon did this."

The ground stopped moving. It was quiet.

"So," said London. She had stopped at the bottom of the stairs, staring at me. "Dez was wrong."

I bowed my head and gently stroked November's whiskers back from her nose. Blood dripped from her mouth.

I had been horribly wrong. About Ximon faking his possession. About coming here. About everything. I was responsible for this.

"Where's that thing now?" London was asking.

"The cage fell on it," Lazar said. He was pulling bandages out of his backpack.

"We need to get November out of here and healed, fast," Caleb was saying.

London craned her neck at the fallen silver cage. "Do you

think it will go away if Ximon is dead? And if he is dead, how do we track down Amaris?"

"November," I said. It came out raspy. My throat was closed up, dry. "Wake up."

Lazar knelt down next to me. His voice was gentle. "Careful how you move her."

"She needs to shift in order to heal." I looked up at both Caleb and Lazar. "Can you guys make her do that?"

The two brothers shot each other a glance before looking back down at November.

"We can try," said Caleb.

"We'll try," said Lazar at the same time.

A metallic scraping came from the silver cage. We all swiveled to face it. The collapsed roof of thick metal, which must have weighed over a thousand pounds, shifted an inch. Then it heaved upwards in a shower of rubble.

"Shit!" London screamed.

"I don't think I can objure it," Lazar said.

"We can fight it," Caleb said. "Or we can run."

Everyone was staring at me, waiting.

I had always been the team leader before, the plan-maker, the bossy one. November, *oh, God, November,* often teased me, called me General Stripes.

I stared down at her bloody little body. My mind was a horrible blank.

The cage jangled again musically as the roof was shoved another inch to one side. More of its silver posts clanked to the floor.

I looked up at all of them, unable to form a coherent thought. "I . . . I don't know. I can't . . ." My mind was ashes. Ashes and death.

"We run," Caleb said, stepping into the pause. "It's too strong for us. We have to risk moving November. Here." He grabbed a flat piece of shelving slightly longer than November's rat body and thrust it at me. "Put her on this, and we go."

My hands were trembling. Tears spilled from my eyes. I was crouched over November's mangled form, and I couldn't move. Some small part of my brain made a note: *So this is what it's like when you fall apart.*

"Dez?" Lazar put one hand on my shoulder. "What's going on?" He peered into my face, and his mouth straightened into a grim line. Abruptly, he took the plank of wood from Caleb, set it down, and used both hands to carefully pick November up and move her to the flat surface. "London, I'm going to hand her up to you," he said. I stayed where I was, trying to control my shivering.

"What's wrong with Dez?" London's voice seemed to come from far away.

Caleb's black coat pooled around him as he knelt next to me. He was frowning with worry and haste, and I looked down in shame. For the first time in my life, I didn't want to look into Caleb's eyes.

"She'll be okay," Caleb said. His voice was unexpectedly kind. "Dez. You're okay. You're strong. You have to be strong to help us all get out of here."

His voice placed something small and warm inside me. The worst of my trembling subsided.

With swift, soldierlike proficiency, Lazar had removed his belt and secured November to the board with it. "She's set," he said.

Metal grated on cement. The cage shifted, as if it were alive.

"Go!" Caleb said to Arnaldo.

The eagle took one last penetrating look at me, and then took off, vanishing through the door upstairs, past London's silhouette.

Lazar took the strapped-down form of November and handed it up to London, who took her with great care. "Hurry up, you guys," she said, and trotted off with our friend.

The shiny black tip of the creature's staff poked out of the wreckage and pushed at the silver slab of the roof. An angular hand reached up through the crack to move it farther. Smoke rose from the black skin where it touched the silver, filling the air with a smell akin to burning rock and flesh.

Lazar unholstered his gun, aimed at the creature's hand, and fired. The bullet thunked into something, and the hand flinched back. Lazar was a deadeye.

"Come on, Dez," Caleb said in my ear. "Time to go." He took me by the shoulders and helped me to my feet.

Lazar switched the gun's magazine with another.

"Silver bullets?" Caleb asked.

Lazar nodded, looking slightly ashamed. "I kept some."

"Good," Caleb said. "Kill it if you can."

The cage roof tilted again, but this time, we couldn't see what was behind it. The creature had gotten smart, using the silver as a shield, lifting as it went.

"Not sure bullets will do the trick, but I'll hold it off as long as I can." Lazar moved to the right of the cage, trying to get an angle where he could see what was going on.

"Don't wait too long." Caleb steered me toward the broken wooden stairs. "Come on, Dez. This way."

"The rope!" Caleb looked back. The length of the multishadow twine was lying coiled on the floor where he'd dropped it. "I should get it. Can you make it to the stairs and wait for me there?"

I nodded, hoping I was telling the truth. This failure of mine, this weakness, was humiliating.

"Okay, go now. Wait for me. I'll be right there."

He was speaking gently, simply, as if to a child. I should have been offended, but instead I felt grateful. The tears had stopped, but every cell in my body was trembling. I wanted to collapse, to lie down and just let go of the awfulness of being such a failure. But the seed of strength Caleb's voice had planted in me wouldn't let that happen.

Just get over to the stairs. That's all you have to think about right now.

I shuffled over and put one foot on the stairway. The lower steps appeared intact. The middle of the staircase was basically gone. I'd have to climb, but I didn't think my rubbery limbs could make it.

Lazar fired twice, bullets clanging. The silver roof was raised nearly on its side, like a wall now between us and the creature.

Caleb grabbed the rope just as the ground quivered and hoisted itself unnaturally again. I tottered, but my cat-shifter balance kept me on my feet. Caleb went to his knees.

Lazar fell, sprawling, but keeping hold of his gun. The entire silver roof was lifted off the floor and flung at him.

"Look out!" I yelled. My voice was thready.

But Lazar was already rolling. Caleb lunged for him, trying to grab his arm. Not fast enough. The corner of the roof hit the floor with a thud I felt in the soles of my feet, and then the rest of the ten-foot-long slab dropped on Lazar.

"There now." The harsh voice of the Ximon creature filled the room. "That's much better."

It seemed to have grown taller with the silver fallen away. Most of Ximon's body was gone, replaced with shiny black angles of arm and leg, still wearing the shredded remains of Ximon's white turtleneck and pants hanging on it like a skeleton.

It reminded me of someone. It took a moment for my clouded brain to piece the resemblance together. He looked like a dark version of our teacher, Morfael, particularly with that staff in his hand. But Morfael looked more like he was made of polished bone and ivory, with opalescent eyes and thin, nearly colorless hair. This thing seemed to have no hair, just a fearsome, triangular head, but its eyes, though golden, were a similar slitted shape. The body, also skeletal, looked like onyx or obsidian instead of bone.

Caleb had crawled to the silver slab and was trying to lift it. Lazar lay half under, unmoving. I could see his head, bleeding from several spots and smeared with dust. His eyelids fluttered, and a tiny portion of my despair lifted.

"So." The gold eyes of the creature slid to me. "Should I call you Desdemona? Or Sarangarel?"

I swallowed, gripping the remains of the stairway banister for support. "Either one." My voice was fragile. There was probably something cool and smart-ass I should say back, but my brain was flailing around like a newborn kitten. I put my hand on the hilt of the Shadow Blade hanging at my waist, and some of the tremors inside me subsided. But still I was weak. Weak and wrong.

The only thing I had to hang on to was the tiny shard of strength Caleb had given me. He couldn't hate me completely if he'd given me that.

The creature tilted its head, as if puzzled, though the stony face was hard to read.

Lazar had lifted a dirt-streaked hand to help Caleb move the block from on top of him. The veins in Caleb's temples bulged as he pushed. Lazar bit his lower lip in pain, but made no sound. It slid a few more inches off his body.

"What's your name?" I forced myself to ask the creature. Might as well keep the thing distracted. I was useless otherwise.

"Don't you know? Did my brother not tell you?" It drew thin lips back to show pointed black teeth. A smile. "He's not one to share."

"Morfael," I said. That explained the similarities in their appearance, and the fact that they both carried staffs. Morfael's seemed to be connected to his abilities as a shadow walker, which meant this thing was probably a shadow walker, too. "You're his brother?"

"Half-brother," said the thing. "We are . . . like them." He pointed at Caleb and Lazar. "We share a mother instead of a father. I am Orgoli. I'll kill my half-brother soon. I'll tell him you said good-bye."

Lazar twisted and was free. Other than scrapes and bruises, he looked relatively unhurt. But both his hands were empty. His gun still lay under the silver slab.

To keep Orgoli's attention, I stepped off the bottom stair and tottered toward him. Caleb and Lazar got cautiously to their feet. "So you're a shadow walker like Morfael," I said. "Why haven't you walked into our world before?"

"I have responsibilities in my own world," he said. "But I have been here before. You remember."

I did remember. This had to be the same creature that had inhabited Caleb's body, just as Ximon had claimed. That transformation hadn't been as complete as this one. And something still didn't quite make sense. "But Morfael travels between worlds without having to use other people. Why don't you do what he does?"

Caleb and Lazar were backing up with exquisite slowness. It was agonizing, but my keeping Orgoli occupied was helping. That helped me stand straighter, to keep my voice going, to keep from running away.

"Only half of me is shadow walker," he said. "Unlike Morfael, I have a place I belong, a place of my own. That is where I live, and where I would have stayed if your world was not so bent on destroying mine."

Okay, so that made no sense. I was pretty sure very few people from our world even knew about Othersphere. Except maybe Ximon, and he hadn't tried to destroy it, just to cut us off from it completely.

"How are we destroying you?" I asked.

"*We?*" The thing leaned in a little closer as a chill ran up my spine. "You, my child, are one of *us*."

"I grew up here." The words rattled out in a defensive rush. "My parents were born here. This is my world."

The creature shook his head. "You would think differently if you journeyed back to where you belong."

Caleb and Ximon were very close to the stairs now. I

couldn't let myself be distracted by the crazy mix of feelings Orgoli's words churned up in me. I did want to go to Othersphere, to learn about my family there, but this wasn't the time to talk about that. I babbled something, anything, at him. . . . "So if you're half shadow walker, then the banishment tone Morfael used to push my biological mother back to Other—to your world, might not work on you."

"Might." Orgoli smiled. A hungry smile. "I like these words of uncertainty in your language. Probably. Possibly. Perhaps." Orgoli turned and looked at the two half-brothers, not surprised to find they were climbing the broken stairs. "Which one should I eat first?"

"Leave them alone," I said, squeezing my hands into weak fists. "Or perhaps I'll eat you."

"Little cub," Orgoli said. "You have grown."

"Then help me understand." I took another step toward the creature, getting between it and the stairs. Maybe he'd eat me first and give the others time to run. "You know Morfael. That means you might know my biological mother, the one who gave birth to me."

"Know her?" Its smile widened. "That is one way to say it."

My heart omitted a beat. Behind me I could hear Caleb and Lazar hoisting themselves up. The creature cast them an unhurried glance.

"Dez!" Caleb spoke from the basement doorway, silhouetted next to Lazar, his hand out toward me. "Dez, come."

His voice spoke of power, of strength, of the knowledge that I was the predator here. I was the one who ruled, not this thing. . . .

Inside me, the dark void linked to Othersphere roiled at his voice's encouragement. As a caller of shadow, he was pushing me to shift into my tiger form, the form that was strongest, fastest, most confident, most able to leap from here to the doorway.

The most likely to survive.

But I still just wanted to curl up in a ball and hide. I clung to the idea that Caleb cared enough to try to get me to change. That was the only thing keeping me on my feet.

"How do you know my biological mother?" I forced the question from my mouth.

Orgoli said, "Still you don't understand."

"Okay," I heard Lazar say. "Together." His voice joined with Caleb's:

"We call upon you, Desdemona. We call upon you. . . ."

Their voices joined, blended so perfectly that they sounded like one. The call to shift redoubled in power, pushing my weakness into a corner, becoming irresistible. The longing to unsheathe my claws, to hunt, pierced my lethargy. Shadow coursed through my veins, up my nerves, pushing back my human form. I leaned into the voices of my friends. . . .

"Oh, little cub," Orgoli said. "I permit you to come forth. For you are my daughter."

I roared, and with a lash of my tail, I leapt for his throat.

CHAPTER 6

My claws scraped against what felt like glass at his shoulders and chest. Desperate to damage him, I wrapped my legs around his tall, narrow body and bent my teeth for his neck. Orgoli had blood, somewhere in there. I could smell it. He had a heart, beating faintly, somewhere inside that strange body. I could hear it.

Then with a sweep of his arm, he flung me like a rag. I flew backwards.

I crashed into the staircase, destroying what was left of it. But the wood giving way beneath me cushioned me enough to keep my bones from breaking.

I struggled to my feet, refusing to think about what Orgoli had just said, knowing only that I had to delay him long enough for my friends to get away. Then I could collapse. Then he could eat me or whatever. It was hard to care.

From the corner of my eye, I saw Caleb take something

from his coat pocket and move out of sight. Lazar pulled something shiny from his boot.

I snarled up at them, thinking *Go!* And launched myself at Orgoli again.

He caught me in mid-air. His bony arms grew longer as he did it, holding all eight hundred pounds of me up in the air, the way a human would a kitten, too far away for my flailing paws to reach him.

"I could have eaten you when you were newly born," Orgoli said. I could find no emotion in the deep furrows of his flinty face. "As I did my other children. But I was occupied with a rebellion, and your mother used that to hide you from me. My own half-brother helped her take you through the veil. He blocked me from coming through with his tricks and traps. For years I sought a way to find you and to stop your world's destructive influence on mine. But my brother is clever. He hid you well. Your link to shadow had disappeared. So I sought a link in someone else. I kept my eye on many promising young ones, including your boy there. The one named Caleb. I almost had him, too, that night. I would have. But you were too cunning." He shook me, the way a child shakes a doll. I tried to bite his hand, but my teeth slid off his skin. "Now I don't know whether to embrace you or to gulp you down."

A gunshot snapped behind me, and a silver bullet struck Orgoli right between the eyes. It fractured the surface of his face the way a pebble cracks a windshield. The monster winced and bent molten eyes on Lazar.

A fine shower of dust tickled my ears and whiskers. The crack in the roof above Orgoli widened.

"Get ready, Dez!" Lazar shouted, and fired a series of shots past me, right into Orgoli, thwacking into his neck, chest, and jaw. More fissures snaked along the glassy skin, like the gap in the ceiling above us.

Orgoli shook himself. His grip on me weakened. I scrabbled to get some kind of purchase on his obsidian skin.

A chunk of ceiling split off and plummeted down behind Orgoli. Larger pieces of plaster rained upon his head, falling into his eyes. I was also getting hit, but because I was farther from the ceiling crack, the pieces were smaller, leaving only bruises.

A larger piece fell in front of him, sending up an explosion of plaster. Orgoli let go of me with one hand, using his black staff to shield his face.

That was all I needed. I used my rear paws to push off of the remaining hand that held me and wiggled free at the same time, bounding for the doorway. One of my hind feet slipped on Orgoli's slick surface, throwing off my aim, and I landed half in the door. My back legs and tail dangled over the empty space where the staircase had been.

Orgoli reached for me. I hoisted myself up, and he grabbed my tail in a terrible grip.

The entire basement ceiling caved in.

Orgoli lost his hold on me as he disappeared beneath an avalanche of cement and heavy wooden beams. I scrambled to my feet in the hallway as Caleb ran past, the floor behind him where the kitchen had been now nothing but a ruinous hole.

"Run!"

Lazar and I took off after him. Walls around us were creaking, tilting. Above us the weight of the second story swayed.

I bolted out the front door after Caleb, Lazar a few feet behind. The SUV was waiting at the curb, London in the driver's seat.

Brakes screeched a block away, and someone down the sidewalk shouted, "Tiger!?"

Arnaldo, hastily dressed in human form, opened the SUV's

side door and we piled in, not pausing to get out of each other's way. Caleb ended up at the bottom of the pile on the floor, with me still in tiger form taking up half the car and Lazar half on top.

London peeled out, and I got out from under Lazar in time to see 1491 Cherry Drive crumble in on itself like a failed soufflé.

I pushed my way to the very back of the SUV, staring out the window. As we rounded the corner, one edge of the roof of 1491 Cherry Drive was flung back, and something blacker than the darkness slithered out.

After I shifted back to human and changed into my spare set of clothes in the back of the car, I stayed there, arms wrapped around my folded too-long legs, head on my knees, staring out the back window at the receding streetlights.

He could be lying.

But he wasn't.

And if what I'd seen was any indication, he was still alive. Did that mean Ximon was also still alive? I could hear them discussing it in the front of the car. There was no way to be sure.

I'd encountered my biological mother three times now. I didn't know her name. She'd used my real mother's body to come through the veil at the base of the Lightning Tree, and then again at school. She was mostly human looking, but otherworldly—tall, beautiful, all striped red-and-black hair and terrifying yellow-green eyes. I'd seen her once more after that, the same night Siku died.

That night I'd also seen the moon in Othersphere, huge and pulsing, just as it had looked through the window that Ximon, or rather Orgoli . . . had opened when he kidnapped Amaris. My biological mother had called me Sarangarel; she said she needed me to come back to Othersphere with her. She'd hinted that Morfael had betrayed her by keeping me here so long. It seemed that their deal had been for him to keep me safe on this side of the veil until she wanted me back. But Morfael had cut me off from shadow entirely and arranged for Mom to adopt me, without consulting my biological parents.

I was beginning to understand why.

I'd always known that my mother had chosen me. Her profound, abiding love was never in doubt. But it hadn't stopped me from wondering who was responsible for creating me. Mom was short, practical, Wiccan, and willing to believe her eyes, which had come in handy when I shifted in front of her the first time. But still I wanted to know where I got my towering height, my untamed red hair. I'd grown up feeling out of place, a lumbering brightly-colored freak. Later, I found a joy in my tiger form, and then in my human form, I hadn't imagined before. But it had only confirmed that I was an aberration. Everyone seemed to think there were no other tiger-shifters left on earth. I was the last.

And now it seemed I wasn't a tiger-shifter after all. Or at least not completely. If that thing, Orgoli, was half shadow walker, and he really was my biological father, then I was well, what, exactly? I'd assumed my biological mother was a tiger-shifter. She had the look of one. And since shifters in this world only ever mated with other shifters of the same tribe, I'd also assumed my biological father was a tiger-shifter.

You were wrong.

Again.

So wrong that November had been horribly injured. So wrong that Caleb and Lazar had been forced to risk their own lives to save mine. If it hadn't been for me, for my arrogance in assuming I knew that Ximon was lying, none of that would have happened.

It was the same arrogance the tiger felt when she hunted. The same certainty of the predator, to whom all others were either prey or threats to be eliminated.

A length of familiar brown rope flew over the back of the

seat in front of me and dangled, as if I were a cat, and this a string for me to play with.

Caleb stuck his head over the edge of the seat to look down on me. He wiggled the twine.

"You remembered it," I said, trying to sound appreciative, but it came out flat and dull.

"London nabbed the books on Othersphere that Lazar found on the second floor. He also grabbed a laptop from up there. Arnaldo's trying to crack the password now."

"That's great." My second attempt at enthusiasm was as dreadful as the first. "How's November?"

"Didn't you hear us?" Caleb tilted his dark head at me over the shiny tan Naugahyde. "Lazar and I were able to get her to shift, so she's fully healed. She's wrapped up in my coat, sleeping."

"Oh, thank God." I rested my forehead on my knees, saying *thank you, thank you* to whatever was out there over and over in my brain. "Sorry," I muttered. "I didn't hear you."

"Lots to think about." Caleb pulled the rope back on his side of the seatback. "It's probably better if you don't touch this, for now," he said. "I think that when you touched it back there, you keyed in some kind of power surge from Othersphere. The rope's like a conduit for vibrations from other worlds."

"You think my touching it helped Orgoli to come through?" I'd thought my emotions couldn't sink any lower. "It did feel like it was alive in my hand. Did it feel that way to you?"

"Not really," he said. "To me it felt like it was . . . I don't know, searching for a signal. Like when your phone's looking for bars. Morfael will know more."

"Morfael." I stared out the back window. Red taillights whooshed by on the right. Off in the distance white headlights followed, and then turned away. I felt like I was on a spaceship, out amongst the cold asteroids and stars, far away from home. "I guess I should talk to Morfael."

"So you think that thing was telling the truth." He rested his chin on the seatback, looking down at me. His eyes were completely black again. No trace of gold.

"No way to know, really," I said. "He looked kind of like Morfael. He had a staff like Morfael's. Why would it . . . he lie?"

"To throw you off, to send you on a wild goose chase, to stop you from finding out who your real biological father is."

Father. I'd grown up without a father. My mother had gotten married to a nice man when I was eleven, but he'd wisely made himself more friend than dad. When I'd played games in my head about who my biological parents were, the father figure had been the hardest to see. I had no model. In my mind's eye he was a tall, red-headed man with bright green eyes and a big laugh. When he smiled, there had been no pointy black teeth, no claws, no desire to eat me.

"Male tigers will sometimes eat tiger cubs in the wild," I said. It sounded like a non sequitur, but Caleb seemed to follow my line of thought. "But I think they're usually some other male tiger's cubs. Genetic rivals."

"In Greek myth, Saturn ate his own children." Caleb kept his voice light. "Because they were threats to his power. Suleiman the Magnificent of Turkey had a number of his sons killed out of fear they would overthrow him."

"How did this become my life?" I asked. I didn't expect an answer.

"I thought the same thing when my mother died," he said. "I bet November felt that way last month."

I looked up at him again, into the eyes I'd loved so much, the eyes that had once shined with love for me. Now all I could see in his face was pity and a sense of obligation.

"Who am I?" It came out as a whisper.

A line appeared between his straight black eyebrows. "Whoever you decide to be," he said. "Just like the rest of us." Then he turned back around. We didn't speak again.

We drove straight back to school, taking turns at the wheel so everyone could get a little rest. November slept straight through, breathing evenly. When it was my turn to drive, I kept listening for that breath. Every inhale and exhale was a reassurance.

We arrived back at Morfael's very early in the morning. Caleb went to help Lazar carry November out, but I got there first.

Caleb put a hand on mine, as if about to say that he'd do it. Then he removed his hand quickly, as if scalded. I opened my mouth, to apologize, to say something, but he was looking down, dark lashes brushing his cheeks, and I turned away to help London instead.

As London walked away with Caleb, I heard her ask, "What does this mean about finding Amaris?"

Caleb gestured toward Arnaldo, who was hurrying into the school, carrying the laptop and books we'd taken from Cherry Drive. "Maybe he'll find something to help us zero in on her in the files we got from Ximon's stash. We've got to do *something*!"

Lazar and I followed more slowly behind and carried November in to the girls' dorm. We laid her down carefully on her bed. I helped him get her under the covers.

"Are you okay?" Lazar asked, keeping his voice low.

I finished tucking in November's blanket. "Not really,"

"I've never seen you look like that before," he said. His expression, unlike Caleb's, was easy to read. He was concerned. He cared. It should have warmed me. Instead, it felt like a weight on my heart.

"I've been kidding myself up till now." I moved away from November's bed so we wouldn't disturb her.

Lazar paced with me to the doorway. "You're the last person to live in a delusion."

I stirred, suddenly restless. I didn't want to hear that, though I know he meant well. "I'm not perfect, Lazar," I said.

His dimples showed in a private smile. "That's a matter of opinion."

I rubbed my upper arms with my hands. It was snug here under the ground, but I still felt a chill. "If you think I am, you need to think again. I'll just disappoint you."

"Never," he said. He put his hands over mine and rubbed my arms slowly. I felt their heat, and it moved up my shoulders and neck, flushing my cheeks. "You're the best person I know, Dez," he said. "Only dictators and crazy people never feel self-doubt."

"Can I be one of them instead?" I asked.

He laughed, and I leaned into him, resting my cheek on his shoulder, the bridge of my nose against his neck. He'd changed into dry clothes in the car, but I caught the faint scent of chlorine from his smooth skin.

His strong arms enfolded me against his long, muscular body, a cocoon of warmth and safety, a place where I didn't have to prove anything. Where I could rest. The long-held tension in my body relaxed. I felt light and liquid.

"It's going to be okay," he said softly. One of his hands brushed the hair back from my face.

"Thank you," I said. "Not just for tonight, but for these past weeks."

I felt his lips press against my forehead. He'd done that before, the first time on the night Siku died, after Caleb had left and I'd told my biological mother to leave me alone. I'd been so lonely, so scared. Lazar had been there for me.

"Stalwart and true," I said, my voice muffled against his shirt.

He drew back a little. "What?"

"That's you. Stalwart and true." I conjured a huge effort and smiled. "And prone to falling into pools."

His laughter rumbled through his chest. He bent his head down and kissed me.

His lips were warm and soft but slightly hesitant, a bit of reconnaissance to see if the terrain was favorable. One of his hands moved to the back of my neck. He slid his fingers up into my hair, cupping my head. The other hand supported my back, those fingers digging into my side with desire. He was trying not to push me, trying to be respectful of what I'd been through tonight. But he wanted more than just one kiss. I could tell.

An image of Caleb, chin resting on the back of the seat in front of me, flashed into my mind. Then I saw him and Lazar, brothers, using their voices as one to help me to shift, to save me.

Lazar pulled back, trying to sense my reaction. So I mentally told Caleb to go jump off a cliff and leaned in to give Lazar a kiss in return. He smiled, and then my lips opened under his mouth, and all his hesitation vanished. He pulled me in closer, a small groan of desire escaping him. His hipbones pressed against mine, and he half lifted me and pressed me back against the doorjamb, grinding into me. The friction between us blotted out the rest of the world.

It felt so good to be wanted. To forget everything but this. I wanted to pull him down onto one of the beds right there, in spite of November sleeping a few feet away. I wanted to be giddy, to forget everything and just wrap myself around him until my worries, until I, disappeared.

What if Caleb sees us?

The thought intruded and I couldn't get rid of it. Would he be shocked? Would he lose all respect for me?

And what about Lazar? He and Caleb had worked in unison back on Cherry Drive, in spite of all their enmity. Would my being with Lazar destroy any chance for the brothers to become friends?

Sensing my distraction, Lazar pulled his lips from mine and said, his voice thick as honey, "You okay?"

I glanced over his shoulder, down the hall. "What if someone sees us?"

He took a step back. My feet hit the ground with a thump. His brown eyes were suddenly wary. The places on my body he'd been touching felt cold without him.

"You mean what if Caleb sees us."

I opened my mouth to deny it, but no words came out. Lazar deserved better than a lie.

"I don't know," I finally said. Not the whole truth, but close enough.

He stood there, staring at me. His thick blond hair was ruffled where I'd run my hands through it. His lips were still reddened from kissing. I straightened my T-shirt hem and the collar of my coat.

Someone was coming down the stairs nearby. I could tell it was London from the sound of her light, loping footfalls.

"I'm an idiot," Lazar said under his breath, and walked out, down the hall to the boys' dorm room.

London hit the bottom of the stairs, her shoulders slumped with fatigue, and saw me standing alone, half in the doorway. "Arnaldo's pretty close to hacking into Ximon's laptop, but he's so damned tired, he's going in circles now. I told him to go to bed or he'll be useless."

"Good," I said.

Sensing something, London gave me a puzzled frown. The door to the boys' dorm room shut hard, and she shot a look down the hall. "What's wrong?"

"How about everything?" I said.

She regarded me, her eyes reflecting back the light from the room behind me like blue mirrors. Her mouth turned down. "November almost died," she said. "What do you have to complain about?"

"Almost died because of me, you mean," I said.

She nodded. "Well, yeah. Caleb tried to tell us, didn't he? He said Ximon was probably actually possessed, but you said he was lying."

She was angry, tired and angry and sick of me messing things up. I didn't know how to defend myself. Or why I should bother. She was right. "Why did you all believe me instead of him?"

She shook her head slowly, pursing her lips as her stare got colder. "I don't know. But I don't think we'll make that mistake again."

I pushed past her and ran up the stairs. I ran past Arnaldo, yawning as he shut down the laptop on the dining room table. I pounded through the school's gym and out onto the outdoor patio cut into the side of the hill.

The night was still and cold. Dawn had yet to smear the eastern sky with color, but a waxing half-moon glowed over the dark arrows of the treetops. Snow draped blue-white over the dry winter grass, dotted with the hoofprints of elk.

I inhaled deeply, trying to calm myself. The air smelled of pine needles and ice. I walked down the hillside, watching my feet sink a couple of inches into the snow with every step, feeling the Styrofoam-ish crunch of it beneath my sneakers.

Before long I was deep in the woods. I looked back and saw the line of my footprints disappearing into the dark. What if I just kept walking? I had come out like this one night and felt the presence of Othersphere very close. I'd heard a strange music in everything around me, and been greeted by a hare, owl, and bobcat. It had been wonderful. What if I walked straight into Othersphere now and never came back? Maybe everyone would be better off.

Something moved in the darkness. I wasn't alone. I stopped walking and listened. The snow stirred over to my right. Something was breathing. Not an animal. I put my hand on the Shadow Blade, still strapped to my waist, and got ready. If Ximon or Orgoli or some other threat was here, I would do whatever I had to—

Thunk.

Snow spattered off a tree trunk about twenty yards in front of me. I blinked. That looked like a . . .

Thunk.

More snow slamming against the exact same spot. A ball of white flew through the air and clunked against the tree trunk, higher this time.

I took my hand off the Blade and strode toward the tall form in black I now saw through the bare branches, stooping to gather snow in his gloved hands, packing it into a ball and raising it to throw—

Thunk.

"A little low that time," I said.

Caleb whirled, another snowball in his hand, raised and ready to hurl.

"Besides, what did that tree ever do to you?"

He lowered his arm. "It's there, isn't it?"

I scooped up some snow in my bare hands and cupped it back and forth to form a ball. "Fair enough."

I turned and threw my snowball. It smashed into the exact spot Caleb's first throw had hit. Cat-shifter strength and co-ordination for the win.

"What are you doing out here?" he asked, tossing his snowball a foot in the air and then catching it.

"Shopping," I said.

He breathed a short laugh and flung his snowball. It hit dead center in the tree trunk.

"What are you doing?" I asked. "Other than killing trees."

"Better than killing something else," he said, and dug up more snow.

I bent and grabbed more snow. "Killing's overrated."

He looked up at me. "Maybe."

"Killing is easy." I threw my snowball, but it went wide, missing the tree trunk completely. "Forgiveness is hard."

He stood there, packing his snowball, his expression derisive. "Not everyone deserves to be forgiven."

My fingers were freezing. "You don't forgive them because they deserve it," I said. "You forgive them because you deserve to live free of anger."

He tossed the snowball in the air. "Do I deserve that? I don't know. I let my mother go out alone to be shot and killed, when I should've known better. I let Siku and November fight way too many objurers all on their own. I let Siku die."

I rubbed my hands together. "You're right. Forgiveness is crap. Take the easy way out and run away."

His hands stopped moving. "You think it was *easy* for me to leave you? You think it didn't rip me to goddamn shreds to turn around and go away after Siku died? To leave November? To say good-bye to my sister and the school, and . . ."

"Yet somehow you managed." I was starting to shiver from the cold. "Somehow you deserted everyone who loved you because your ego had been bruised, because I'm just so awful, such a liar. . . ."

"I had to leave—or I would have killed him!" Caleb turned and heaved the snowball with all his might at the tree. It caught a branch, snapping it off with a crack.

"Who? Lazar?"

He said nothing. He stared off at the broken branch, his breath steaming around him.

"Is that your answer to everything? To kill?" I circled around to face him. "You wanted to kill everyone in the Tribunal for a while, and you sure as hell want Ximon dead, and now Lazar? Killing won't bring your mother back."

"She'll rest easier in her grave." He lifted his head, dark eyes glittering with fury.

"You mean you'll rest easier," I said. "You think your

dreams will be happier once you kill the boy who killed your mother. You don't give a shit about anything else."

"But you care." He took two steps toward me, pulled by anger. "You cared more about him than you did about me, about our relationship. You lied to me *for him*!"

"I had my reasons!" My voice was as loud as his now. "I told you I had reasons for trusting Lazar, but that wasn't enough."

He leaned in, black eyes narrowed. "You were asking me to trust the boy who shot my mother. On your word alone."

"That should've been enough for you!" Anger was warming me up. Could I go for more than five minutes without being blamed for everything? I took my hands out of my pockets and pointed at him. "Your hatred for him was greater than your trust in me. Your hatred is the most important thing in your life."

Caleb shook his head, also fuming. "You knew my reasons for distrusting him—my very good reasons. But you wouldn't tell me your reasons to trust him. He's a manipulator, Dez. A murderer. Whatever he told you, how could you be so sure he wasn't lying to you?"

"He wouldn't lie, not about this," I said. I could still remember how Lazar had reluctantly, tonelessly told me how his father had tortured and abused him. How when, one night when Lazar's cancer-ridden mother couldn't stand the pain any more, twelve-year-old Lazar had tried to drive her to a hospital. Only to have the car fall into one of his father's traps. Only to have Ximon beat Lazar till his bones broke, then put a gun in Lazar's hand, point it at Lazar's dying mother, and force Lazar to pull the trigger.

Thinking about it still gave me chills. After that, Lazar became a killing machine at his father's bidding. He hadn't thought it mattered anymore. He'd already lost his soul. Seeing his sister escape from their father had given him hope. I couldn't deny it to him.

"You still don't know," Caleb said. He took two more

steps toward me, lowering his voice, as if someone out here in the woods at four a.m. might overhear us. "He could be playing a very long con with us, luring everyone here into trusting him, waiting until the Tribunal is rearmed and ready to pounce . . ."

"Oh, my God." I lifted my hands helplessly. "You are paranoid."

"The Tribunal really is out to get us, Dez," he said. "You led a sheltered life until recently. That's why you fell for Ximon's long con to lure us to his particle accelerator."

"I know!" Tears threatened to spill from my eyes when I remembered the consequences of falling for that trick. "Don't you think I remember? But Lazar didn't know about that trap. Ximon tricked him right along with the rest of us."

Caleb got right in my face. "How can you be so sure?"

I flashed on the look on Lazar's face when he gazed at me. How his hands felt when he touched me. The longing in his kisses. "I just am, okay?"

Caleb's black gaze was traveling over my face. He leaned in and hummed, low and menacing. "What have you been doing? His vibration—it's all over you."

I flinched back, my cheeks coloring.

Gold sparked fire in his eyes. "You can trust him because he's in love with you, isn't that it? Because he's in your thrall, and you're . . . you're in love with him."

He turned, long coat flying like black wings behind him as he strode away.

I ran a few steps after him. "What do you care? You broke up with me, remember?"

He whirled, furious. "So you could screw my brother less than two months later?"

"Even if I was with Lazar." Rage poured off me in waves. "Even if I was having sex with him three times a day, what are you going to do about it?"

"You were *just* kissing him, weren't you?" His eyes were on my lips. His face was flushed.

"Yes, I was," I said. "And I liked it. I loved it! So to hell with . . ."

He grabbed me with hot, hard hands and pulled me closer. He dipped his head, his lips nearing mine. An electric thrill rushed through me. I breathed his airy thunderstorm scent, felt the heat coming off his body, and waited for one eternal second for him to press me against him.

He shoved me away and was gone. A distant dark figure against the moonlit snow.

CHAPTER 7

I woke to someone shaking me, hard. I groaned and blinked, never one to wake quickly, and found myself in bed in the girls' dorm room. Lazar was standing over me, his golden hair ruffled from sleep. It looked like he'd just thrown on a sweatshirt and half buttoned his jeans.

"Dez, it's your mom. She's on the computer, calling for you. She's all right, but she said it's urgent."

I rolled up, rubbing my eyes. "Okay. Coming."

He backed out and shut the door behind him. I looked down. I was wearing nothing but a T-shirt and underwear. In the adjoining bed, London was sitting up, and in another, November was holding a pillow over her head, her small hands the only thing visible in the tumble of pillows and blankets.

"You and your mom are pains in the ass," November said, her voice muffled by pillow.

"Glad you're feeling like yourself again," I said, pulling on the jeans I'd left in a pile on the floor and shoving my feet into sneakers.

"That makes one of us," said London, lying back down again.

I hustled down the hallway to the computer room. Lazar was sitting in the glow of the biggest monitor. He looked up. "Here she is, Ms. Grey." He got up and held the seat out for me stiffly, his face unreadable.

I sat down and scooted the chair in for myself. Lazar left, clicking the door quietly shut behind him.

On the monitor, my mother looked about as awake as I was. Her short brown hair was standing up on one side of her head, her hazel eyes underlined with fatigue. She'd pulled her laptop up onto the bed, so I was looking up at her sitting up against her headboard, surrounded by pillows. "Hi, honey," she said. Her voice was a little hoarse, as it usually was in the morning. "How are you?"

I shrugged. "Kind of a rough night, Mom. I'll tell you later. What's going on?"

"I had a dream," she said. "One of *those* dreams, you know. Where something is pulled through this black hole in my heart, and I become someone else?"

I inhaled sharply and nodded. She'd had dreams like that before, and shortly after that she'd been possessed by a person, I guess I could call her a person, from Othersphere. A person who happened to be my biological mother. Her link with Mom was still a bit of a mystery to me. Morfael said they were like one being in their love for me. I had a hard time seeing how a woman in another world who hadn't seen me since I was an infant could love me as much as the woman who raised me. I'd told Mom about her—how she'd named me that strange word, Sarangarel, and how she'd told me to leave this world and come to her in Othersphere. Mom hadn't said much, but I'd been quick to reassure her that no one else could ever be a mother to me.

"It was the same woman," Mom said. "And she said—I

remember the words exactly—'Her friend's in danger here. Sarangarel must come over now, or all will be lost.' "

I dropped my head into my hands. Amaris was in danger. When all I wanted to do was crawl somewhere far from otherkin and danger and boys and myself so I could sleep for a thousand years.

"What friend is she talking about, honey?" The frown line between Mom's eyebrows was etched deep.

"Amaris," I said, and gave her a quick overview of everything that had happened in the last two days. Everything except the part about pissing off Lazar, and then maybe, possibly, nearly getting kissed by an angry Caleb. I was infuriating everyone lately. When I got to the part where Orgoli said I was his daughter, I stuttered and stumbled a little over the words. It was weird to tell Mom. We hadn't talked much about my birth parents, even after my nameless biological mother had showed up. Mom made no comment till I finished.

"You can't trust this woman," Mom said. "She wants you to come to her, and this sounds like some kind of trap."

"Maybe," I said, weary through and through. "But we can't just leave Amaris in another world in the hands of who knows what. Even if it's the cleverest trap in the world, Caleb and Lazar would move the moon to get her back."

"They could go without you," Mom said. "You're dating one brother and used to date the other. If you go with them, you'll just come between the brothers even more, ruining any chance they might have for a relationship in the future."

"No, I know," I said. "I've thought about that a lot. But because I was born there, I might be able to do things other people can't."

"Until this thing that claims to be your birth father decides it's time to eat you. Or something worse!"

"He's busy right now on this side of the veil. It might be a good time for us to cross over."

Mom was quiet a minute. "Do you think he was telling the truth?"

She didn't have to say "the truth about being your birth father." That was the main thing on her mind. And on mine.

"Morfael will know," I said.

"Why doesn't that man tell you these things in advance?" Mom punched the pillows behind her, fluffing them up with sharp, angry jabs. "Why do you always have to find things out the hard way? Morfael should go to Othersphere, not you. You're the student, the child. He should be protecting you."

"He saved me by bringing me to this world," I said. Mom's bitterness set me on edge. Normally, she had nothing but nice things to say about Morfael. "He made sure you were the one that found me, Mom. And to keep me here, he had to give up being able to go back there."

"Yes, yes, I know." Her pillow punching was escalating. "But all this mystery and risk gets very tiresome. I must be crazy to trust you to a creature that travels between worlds, a shadow walker. I mean, really! I know I'm a flaky nature-worshipper and all, but I'm starting to think I've graduated from flaky to neglectful."

"You've trusted me and my judgment, Mom," I said. "And you should, because I was raised by you."

"Raised by a flake!" She tapped her finger against her own chest.

I heard my stepfather's soft voice say, "Caroline..." He must be right off camera.

Mom looked up, shaking her head at him. "No, Richard! It's about time I put a stop to all these life-threatening shenanigans my daughter gets herself into. It's my own fault for not being stricter. I'm too hippy dippy to be a mother, really."

"You're a great mom..." I started to say.

"About to get greater," she said. "Desdemona, I need you to come home, to our apartment. I'm pulling you out of that school. Today."

"What?" Surprise pulled me to the edge of my seat.

"No more baby-eating birth fathers for you, I'm not sorry to say. Pack your bags and get Raynard to drive you to Vegas this afternoon. I'll get your room ready."

"No," I said softly.

Mom frowned through the monitor. "What did you say?"

I was a good daughter. I never defied my mother. And she in turn had always trusted me. My gut was twisted into a sickening knot, but I couldn't let her take me out of things now.

"I said no."

Mom blinked rapidly. I hadn't said no much to her since I was a toddler. Her face got very stern. "Desdemona Grey. You will come home today, or I'll come up there and get you."

"I still wouldn't come." I didn't say, *There's no way you can make me.* It sounded juvenile, and she knew it as well as I did.

"What have you become?" Mom's eyes were red with anger and unshed tears. "Defiant, risk taking. Do you have some sort of death wish? I said, come home!"

"I need to know, Mom," I said. "You're my mother, and that will never change. But I need to know the people who gave birth to me, even if they're awful. To see where I came from, even if it's hell. I'm sorry if that threatens you or scares you. I'm sorry!" For the millionth time in the last couple days, tears were spilling down my cheeks.

"I am your parent!" she said. "My first job is to protect you. I order you to come home now!"

"I'm sorry," I said again. "But that isn't your choice anymore."

I stared at her terrified, angry face. I almost told her then that I was coming home. Instead, I cut off the connection. The monitor went blank.

I was sitting on the patio, a light snowfall flickering down from the overcast morning sky when Morfael walked outside. He looked down at me, snowflakes dotting his bony white cheeks and forehead. They didn't seem inclined to melt on his skin.

"How is your mother?" he asked.

"She ordered me to come home," I said shortly. I wasn't feeling very friendly to anyone right now, particularly Morfael. "She says I shouldn't be taking so many risks. I told her I'm staying anyway, and she's pretty mad. Orgoli is my birth father, isn't he?"

"Yes," said Morfael, his gaze flickering over my face. "He is my half-brother."

"Which makes you my uncle." It came out flat. I felt flat, too. All these revelations should have made me emotional or excited. Instead, I felt nothing. "All this time, we've been relatives."

And you didn't tell me.

I didn't say it, but it hung in the air between us.

He regarded me for a long moment. "If I'd told you that the first night you came to this school? Would that have been better?"

I remembered that first night, how terrifying Morfael had seemed, how strange the other shifter kids and their ways. I'd had enough to digest learning how to be a tiger-shifter. "I guess being told I was a creature from another world rescued by her shadow-walker uncle from her stone-skinned demonic father would have been a bit much to take in," I said. "Would you have told me?"

He shrugged his narrow shoulders. "Who knows what would have been? Whether you knew or did not know of our blood kinship, I would have looked after you and cared for you the same."

I bowed my head, shame battling with anger. Morfael had saved my life and my friends many times now. He didn't talk much, but he was there when it counted. I told my anger to be quiet, but it didn't want to go away.

"So you and Orgoli share a mother," I said. "She must have been a shadow walker."

"As was my father," Morfael said. "Orgoli's father was

one of the Amba, or what you might call the tiger spirits of Othersphere."

"Are they alive? My grandparents?"

Morfael gave one shake of his head. "Orgoli killed them some time ago."

I digested that for a moment. So it wasn't just his children he liked to murder. "What exactly is an Amba?"

"They are similar to the tiger-shifters that used to exist in this world," Morfael said, "but less human."

"More tiger."

He gave one short nod. "Your mother is Amba."

"What's her name?" How strange. To ask for your own mother's name.

"Khutulun." He pronounced the early consonants soft, the vowels like a song.

"Khutulun," I repeated, less musically. It was just a bunch of sounds, and they didn't make me feel anything.

Morfael considered me. "You are mostly as she, but one-quarter shadow walker. That made it easier for me to move you through the veil and easier for you to live here."

"Orgoli said that he . . ." I swallowed. It was very weird to think this, let alone to say it. "He ate his other children, and he would have eaten me. Is that normal over there?"

"No." Morfael's opalescent eyes were clear and cold. "It has been recorded that an Amba king will sometimes eat the infant children of his rivals, especially if he wishes to mate with their mother. That is why many mothers keep their children hidden until they're older. But I have also seen them adopt the children of others and care for them as their own. Orgoli is twisted. As he gained more power, slaying other Amba to gain territory, he began to see even his own children as threats. They and their mothers paid the price."

I nodded and didn't speak for a moment. I wished Mom was there, or Caleb, or Lazar. Someone I could really talk to. But I'd managed things so badly that all three were now off limits, one way or another.

"That's why you brought me here," I said. "To save me from him. Why didn't you send me back when Khu . . . when my biological mother asked you to?"

"She thought she had found a safe place for you in her world," he said. "I disagreed. As you can see, Orgoli has found you even here. But you are better prepared now than you would have been fifteen years ago."

"Why didn't you raise me yourself?" I looked up at him, so alien in looks, but familiar to me now. *He's my uncle. I'm his niece.* It didn't feel real.

"I considered it." He leaned on his wooden staff, inscribed with animal forms that seemed to writhe under his hand. He looked tired. "But Orgoli would have found you more easily through me. You were safest with someone who had no connection to otherkin or Othersphere. Someone kind and understanding."

"Someone who wants to pull me out of your school."

He nodded. "There are times when it's useful to listen to fear. And times when it isn't."

I put my hands on my hips. "That is so not helpful. What does it even mean?"

His mouth curved upwards in his version of a smile. I wondered if I ever smiled like that. I didn't think I looked like him, or Orgoli. I hoped not. "It means that when you feel fear, you must exercise your judgment. Good judgment will tell you whether the fear is wise."

"Well, whether it's good judgment or not, we have to go to Othersphere to get Amaris back."

Morfael bowed his head at me, in acknowledgment or surrender, I couldn't tell. He was still smiling when he said, "I will help you pierce the veil. We must go to the Lightning Tree."

At breakfast, the others were twitchy and tense. Nobody was looking anybody in the eye. Raynard brought out a pile of scrambled eggs, and no one would pass it around. They just leaned over and around each other to scoop out their portion as if everyone else was an obstacle to get around.

Caleb's concern for Amaris was enough to keep him there, but he sat like a black cloud at the very end of the table with his own pile of home fries, bacon, and half a grapefruit. Lazar sat at the opposite end, ripping the rind off a clementine with long, hard, angry pulls, as if it needed to pay for some wrong it had done. The rest of us scattered between these light and dark bookends, with at least one empty seat between us.

Only Arnaldo seemed mostly oblivious to the strain, eating with his laptop open in front of him, wiping his hands on a napkin tucked into the neck of his T-shirt before typing a flurry of commands. His two younger brothers, Luis and Cordero, sat next to him, tossing bits of egg at each other or saying "Quit it!" in low tones, but otherwise keeping their heads down. They'd had to deal with far worse tension in their own home, but I felt bad that they were here for this.

I cleared my throat and told everyone the message my mother had dreamed.

Caleb dropped his spoon onto his plate with a clatter. "When do we go?"

"Today," said London. Her hands gripped the edge of the table hard. "Now."

"What about this Orgoli creature?" Lazar asked. "Do we have to worry about encountering him while we're there?"

"He's definitely still alive," I said. "I saw him crawling out from under the house as we drove away."

"Let's hope he'll stay busy in this world," London said.

"Do you . . ." I wasn't quite sure how to put it. "Do you think Ximon's still in there, somewhere?"

"Maybe," Caleb said. He looked at Morfael, who was at the head of the table, calmly crunching into an apple

"There is no way to be sure," Morfael said. "It depends on Ximon's strength of mind. His willingness to remain."

"He doesn't matter," Lazar said. "Amaris is what matters. I hope she's okay."

"Of course, she's okay!" Caleb snapped.

Lazar turned on him, getting red, then shut his mouth abruptly and said nothing. The brothers were both on edge, each dealing with their sister's absence in his own way.

Morfael swallowed another bite of apple. "I can help three or four of you through the veil if we drive down to the Lightning Tree."

"That's interesting." Arnaldo lifted his head up from staring at his monitor. "I've been going through the files on Ximon's computer, and it looks like whenever he was lucid, or free of influence from Othersphere, he was trying to figure out where "the creature,' as he called it, came from, and how. The veil is thinnest near his particle accelerator, but his calculations placed the creature's entrance in Burbank instead."

"That must be where this Orgoli thing first came through the veil," London said. "At the Lightning Tree."

"How do we find Amaris once we go through?" Lazar asked. "Othersphere has to be as big a world as this one, but does it correspond, point to point, with our geography?"

"What the hell are you talking about?" November asked. "Speak like a normal person."

Lazar's mouth pursed in amusement. He never seemed to mind November's rudeness. "I mean, if I went through the veil right here"—he tapped the table in front of him—"could I walk ten feet that way"—he pointed toward the kitchen— "and come out of the veil next to our fridge? Or would I pop back into this world a hundred yards, or a hundred miles away?"

"The distances are approximately the same." Morfael said. "But doorways can be manipulated."

"And what the hell does *that* mean?" November asked, her mouth full of egg.

Morfael let silence hang for a moment. He didn't like her

swearing at him. But she didn't back down the way she usually did and just stared at him, chewing. Finally, he said, "When you create a portal, like the one Orgoli pushed Amaris through, the creator can decide to use it to move things over distance as well as between worlds."

"Aha," said Arnaldo. "So that stone balcony she landed on in Othersphere doesn't necessarily correspond to where that lodge is on Kyle Canyon Road."

"Which means she could be anywhere!" Caleb said. "Even if she's still where he dropped her, and there's no guarantee of that."

"Orgoli's dwelling is not far from the eternal storm which shadows the Lightning Tree," Morfael said.

London was listening closely. "So his headquarters or whatever won't be far if we go through the veil at the Lightning Tree."

"How do we know which way to go once we're through?" Caleb asked. "Can you draw us a map?"

"You or Lazar should be able to find Amaris if she is anywhere within a few hundred miles," Arnaldo said. "From what I found in Ximon's research on Dez after they captured her, creatures from Othersphere give off a very unique signature vibration when they're here in our world. I bet you the reverse is also true."

"So Amaris should give off a signal that's easy to distinguish when she's in Othersphere," London said. "Got it."

"So if Dez is from Othersphere, does everybody over there look like her?" London asked.

"There's a great variety of creatures in that world, just as there is in this," Morfael said. "And Dez's appearance here in this world may be different from how she appears when she is there."

"Really?" I looked at him, startled.

He simply nodded.

"So that's a 'no,'" November said. "If shadow walkers

move between all the worlds, then where do they come from? Where are they born?"

"We are born wherever our mothers wish us to be born," Morfael said. "In any of the infinite worlds that exist."

I was one-quarter shadow walker. Did that mean I could visit more worlds than just Othersphere? I didn't want to bring that up in front of the others yet, so instead I asked Morfael, "How many worlds have you been to?"

Morfael regarded me, deadpan. "A lot."

Everyone laughed at the colloquial phrase coming out of him. He was usually so formal.

"So that means Caleb, Lazar, and I need to go," London said. "Cool. Let's pack up."

"And Dez," Lazar said quickly.

I felt a stab of gratitude to him. He was right, from a strategy standpoint. I should go. But I also really wanted to go, to find out whatever I could—about myself, about my biological parents. There was only one real fear that haunted me about going there.

What if I don't want to come back?

"Why take Dez?" November arched a thin eyebrow at me. "She wasn't much use the last time out."

I gave her a helpless look. Her words cut deep.

"Neither were you," Lazar shot back.

November leaned across the table at him. "That's because I was too busy nearly dying."

"Dez is from Othersphere," Caleb said. His voice was more neutral than Lazar's. "Her connection to that world will probably be useful while we're there."

"If it helps us get Amaris back, she's coming," London said. Then she turned to me, looking uncertain. "You're not going to freeze up again, are you?"

"No," I said, not trusting myself to say much. "I hope not."

"How reassuring." November popped a sausage into her mouth.

"I'll stay here and do some research on that powerful laser Ximon said Orgoli was interested in," Arnaldo said. "I found some encrypted files on his laptop labeled 'laser' that I haven't been able to open yet."

Arnaldo had obligations in this world—taking care of his brothers—which he couldn't easily leave. Me, I had no obligations, really. Nothing to tie me here at all.

Lazar said, "November, maybe you can help him, or see if you can track Orgoli's movements here somehow...."

"Nope." November brushed biscuit crumbs off the front of her shirt. "I'm leaving soon to hang out with Siku's family before the shifter council meeting."

The table got quiet. Everyone was staring at November.

"What shifter council meeting?" London asked.

"They didn't tell you?" November showed all her teeth in a malicious grin. "Now isn't that funny. The North American Council called a big meeting of all available shifters for tomorrow night. They're going to discuss how they can work together to wipe Ximon and the Tribunal off the face of the earth."

CHAPTER 8

Everyone started talking at once. Luis and Cordero raised their fists and gleefully shouted, "Down with the Tribunal!" as Arnaldo shushed them. Caleb was on his feet, asking November how she'd heard, and Lazar was doing much the same from his end of the table. London called her a bitch, which only widened November's smile.

Arnaldo turned to London. "Did you know?"

London's nose ring was quivering with anger. "No! I stopped talking to my parents weeks ago. They're the only way I get information like that." She turned to November again. "I'm a shifter, too, you verminous sneak! So's Arnaldo! We deserve to know about an all-shifter council meeting, same as anyone."

"Same as me," I said.

November dabbed her mouth delicately with the corner of her napkin. "You're not a shifter, Dez. So thanks for your help with the Tribunal and all, but we can take it from here."

Blood drained from my face. My chest felt hollow. "What? I'm . . . what?"

"That doesn't matter, and you know it," London said, leaning into November. "If it wasn't for Dez, all the shifter tribes would still be fighting each other. It's only because of her, and the rest of us, that they're even considering banding together against the Tribunal."

"I'm a shifter!" I said, so loudly that everyone else stopped talking and looked at me. "I shift into an animal, just like the rest of you!"

"But you're not like the rest of us," November said. Her brown eyes were slits. Behind them lurked a dark and terrible rage. "You're some creature from another world who's good at looking and sounding like a shifter. Who thinks she's smarter and stronger and knows what's best for everyone. Only you don't. Because when you're around, shit hits the fan. When you're in charge, people die. Siku died. Because of you!"

"That's not fair," Arnaldo said.

I took a step back, reeling. "No. Let her talk. Obviously, she's been thinking like this since it happened."

"Let me talk?" November let out a scornful laugh. "Try to stop me."

"Don't be an idiot, 'Ember," Caleb's voice was icy. "Siku was his own man. He knew the risks, same as the rest of us."

"Siku wouldn't have blamed Dez," London said. "He would blame the guy who shot him! And Ximon."

"Oh, I blame them." November stood up. "I very much blame them. But I also blame the person who led us right into Ximon's trap. Siku took care of the guy who shot him before he died. That leaves Ximon and Dez."

"What the hell does that mean?" Lazar never swore, so even a mild word like "hell" coming out of him was a shock. He normally had a high tolerance for November's shenanigans, too. But clearly she'd crossed a line. "If you're looking to get revenge on Dez, reconsider. Now."

"Look who grew a pair in five minutes." November

smirked. "Don't worry, Loverboy. I don't have to do anything to get revenge on Dez. You're doing it for me by heading off into Othersphere with her and her ex-Loverboy. What a joke! You'll all be so busy fighting or trying to ignore each other, the monsters over there will have you for lunch."

"November, why are you being like this?" Arnaldo said. "We're a team. You're acting like . . ."

"Like I've got half a brain for once." November pushed her chair back and walked to the hallway where the stairs led down to the dorm rooms. "I gave you guys a chance yesterday. Even after Siku died, I followed Dez like a good little soldier right into Ximon's house. And guess what? I nearly died. No more chances, Dez. No more death for me. My bags are packed. My brother will be here in half an hour to pick me up. See ya."

Her footfalls ran lightly down the stairs.

The four-hour drive to Burbank was grimly quiet. Lazar drove faster than he ever had before, while Morfael sat, all long legs and arms, in the shotgun seat. Caleb and London sat behind them, while I curled up in the way back, afraid to be up front. Afraid to let any of them see me.

"You're not like the rest of us," November had said. The phrase repeated in a sickening loop in my head.

As we packed up the SUV, London had told me not to take it personally. She said November was crazy with grief, or maybe just plain crazy.

Lazar had stopped me when we were alone in the hallway for a second and formally asked how I was doing. I wanted him to wrap his big strong arms around me. To tell me everything was going to be all right. That I was all right.

But he kept a discernible distance between us, and glanced away quickly when our eyes met. He, too, told me that November was acting out of pain. Then he left me alone.

It was nice of them to try to cheer me up. But I didn't believe it. November was mourning for Siku, yes. But I *had* fallen for Ximon's trap at the particle accelerator. If it wasn't for me, the group never would have gone there and Siku wouldn't have died. And yesterday November had nearly died as well, because I'd been an idiot and hadn't believed Ximon's story about being possessed.

It was hard to remember a time when I'd ever been right. A time when I'd ever felt anything but disgust and horror at myself.

Morfael gave us instructions dryly in the car: He could hold a window open to Othersphere for us for four hours only. We'd have to come back with Amaris by then or wait another twenty-four hours, when he'd try to open the window again. We left our phones in the car; they'd be useless in Othersphere without towers or satellites to keep time or transmit messages. Caleb and Lazar were wearing watches synchronized to be sure we got back in time. London chose not to wear one, since she'd probably shift as she went through the window. And I could never wear one—they stopped working within a few minutes thanks to my anti-tech-fu.

Normally, the sight of the Lightning Tree would have soothed me. I'd climbed the enormous old oak many times as a kid and visited it nearly every day after I got the back brace. I hadn't known then that the tree had a powerful shadow connected to an eternal storm in Othersphere. But I'd been drawn to it nonetheless.

Now, in the gray winter light it looked strangely ominous, skeletal. The mostly bare branches cast gnarled, snakelike shadows on the grass before us.

Huge dark clouds had gathered over the Burbank hills. Rain began to pelt down, and the few remaining kids on skateboards scattered off home. Morfael, Caleb, Lazar, London, and I were the only ones in the park. We piled out of the SUV, throwing on our backpacks, moving with urgency, as if any moment we delayed might be the one in which we lost Amaris.

Morfael followed at a slightly slower pace as we jogged forward, dead leaves crunching under our shoes. The three callers—Lazar, Caleb, and Morfael—hummed instinctively as we neared the tree, gold glinting in their irises.

I couldn't see the eternal storm in the tree's shadow. But I felt its nearness, a familiar, almost comfortable buzz under my skin. I sped up. The closer I got to the tree, the better I felt.

When I got close, I pushed off the ground to climb up, landing in a comfortable spot where the branches first split, wide as a bumpy lap. I ran my hand over the rough bark, and for a moment I could've sworn the branches swayed closer to me, as if in greeting.

Plants had always liked me. With my green thumb I could make just about anything grow, even in bad soil or the wrong climate. Something to do with my connection to Othersphere, where nature ran rampant and technology did not exist.

I leaned forward against a large branch, wrapping my arms around it, pressing my cheek to the coarse surface, like a starving person who had finally had a meal. Through my skin a nearly undetectable pulse beat. It was the beginning of the music of Othersphere.

"The tree's vibration changed when Dez climbed onto it," Lazar said, gazing up at the bare tangle of branches.

"The storm always subsides a bit when she's near," Caleb said.

"It knows her well," Morfael said.

"It does?" I hadn't known that.

"Line up before the tree," Morfael said in a voice that cut through the rain and the wind. Thunder crackled in the distance. I dropped down off the tree as the others arranged themselves.

London removed her shoes and socks and handed me her coat, getting ready to shift. "I wish November was here," she said. "Like the old days."

"Me, too." I stuffed her coat into my backpack, guilt stabbing at me again. My earlier reluctance had vanished once I'd touched the Lightning Tree. I couldn't wait to get into Othersphere, to take action, maybe to forget for a little while just how wrong I had been about everything.

"I'm going to miss Arnaldo and his eyes in the sky." Caleb looked up at the branches of the tree.

"We'll need to stay sharp," Lazar said. "Watch where every footstep lands. You never know what you might be walking into."

"Will I be forced to shift when I pass through, too?" I asked Morfael, raising my voice over the rain, which was now pounding down.

Morfael's moonstone eyes still glowed with gold. "You will stay in a similar form. But you will find more variation is possible in all your forms."

I frowned. "Similar form?"

"Yes," Morfael said. "You may not recognize yourself. As a shadow walker, your form will be closest to that which the world demands. But as an Amba, you'll feel the greatest attraction to your tiger form. Use it wisely."

"Shadow walker?" Lazar stared at me, unsettled.

Caleb was nodding. "That makes total sense."

London couldn't have cared less. "Let's go!"

Lazar had taken the brown rope from Cherry Drive out of London's backpack. He wrapped the rope around his right arm, holding it in his right hand and held it out to London. She measured out a span of it. Then the air warped around her, and where she had been stood a huge, silver-gray wolf with electric blue eyes. Her pants puddled under her back paws. Her shirt ripped, hanging on her front legs. She took it in her teeth and yanked it free. Then she took the rope in her mouth and offered it to Caleb, who wrapped it around his left hand. I stood next to Lazar, my hand on the haft of the Shadow Blade, completing the semicircle around the knotty trunk of the Lightning Tree.

Morfael stood behind us. "Don't forget, you must return within four hours, or you will not be able to reenter this world."

Caleb checked his wristwatch. "Four hours. Does time move at the same rate over there?"

Morfael half smiled. "Close enough. If you're left in Othersphere, wait twenty-four hours. Then return to this spot, and I'll try to open the portal again."

"We'll try not to miss the four-hour mark," I said. Surviving there that long would probably be challenge enough.

"Unless we haven't found Amaris by then," Lazar said.

"We'll find her," Caleb said. "No matter how long it takes."

London gave a short bark of agreement.

"Enter as soon as the portal appears. Waste no time," said Morfael. "Take care of each other."

I looked down the line at Caleb, London, and Lazar, united by the rope, and swore to myself I would not let them down. Not this time.

They were doing much the same, exchanging glances, taking a deep breath. Lazar turned to me, his brown eyes alight with tension and excitement. He smiled, and held out his left hand.

I took it gratefully, pushing worries about Caleb from my mind. Lazar's hand was warm, thrumming with a tremor I hadn't felt before, and I wondered if it came from the rope in his other hand.

Then Morfael unleashed a deep note from the back of his throat that nearly knocked me over. The force behind it was palpable. It didn't waver, growing louder, and I half expected an ocean liner to come steaming up behind us. In my peripheral vision, I saw him point his staff at the tree.

The note changed. A question was being asked. Before me, the tree seemed to waver, like an old film jumping in a projector, and I glimpsed a vast bank of black and gray clouds, churning with rain and lightning.

Then the tree was back. But it was taller, darker. Its branches extended like crooked fingers, reaching for me.

Morfael's note changed again, running up the scale, and then down to an impossible deepness, something beyond my hearing, but lodged in my bones.

The air in front of us split, the crack widening, growing taller. Blackness roiled on the other side of the fissure, a cloud bank vaster and darker than anything our world had seen. Rain that was not from this world joined the rain falling from our sky. New wind whipped my hair.

I was smiling.

The window extended, and the cloud bank in Othersphere now blotted out the one above. It also hung low, nearly obscuring the sodden, vivid green, knee-high grass at our feet, lashed by the gusts like my hair.

The portal was as wide across as the four of us now, and taller than Caleb. Lazar was braced, jaw set, determined, pushing down his fear. London's ears were up, her tail high. Her eyes glowed.

Caleb was grinning like a kid. He shielded his eyes with his free hand against the rain and our eyes met.

"Ready?" he asked.

London yipped.

Lazar nodded.

"Let's go!"

As one we stepped across the line that separated our world from the other.

CHAPTER 9

The air hummed. Rain waltzed around me as lightning flared thirty feet away. The air cracked, punctuated by a blast of pungent ozone. I was drenched in a deep, pulsing melody, which played behind and below the crushed grass at my feet and the warm bluster of wind. The great black bank of fog wove around me like a lullaby.

Welcome.

"Dez?" Lazar squeezed my hand.

I blinked through the torrent. Lazar looked overwhelmed, and worried. Next to him, glowing like a pearl through the whorls of fog, London in her wolf form was bigger than before, her fur coat thicker, her eyes prisms of aquamarine fire. She had dropped the brown rope and Caleb, his coat darker than the vapor around us, was coiling it up, staring at me, smiling slightly.

"I . . ." My voice was different. I felt it moving through the air, connecting and bouncing off of the mist, the grass, and my friends. "Can you feel it?"

"Feel what?" Lazar had to half yell over the howl of the wind.

"Everything. It's working together." I struggled to find the right words as Lazar's puzzlement and concern deepened the line between his eyebrows. "Like an orchestra, or a choir. This place. It's like a hymn."

Lazar looked down at London, as if hoping someone else would explain it to him. London cocked her head at me. Caleb's smile widened; then he looked at the swirling storm around us and shook his head in wonder.

They can't hear us.

It was not my voice, yet as it spoke in my head, my thoughts coincided with it exactly. I looked around at the swirling fog, the pounding rain, the jabs of lightning briefly illuminating the darkness. As I did so, the downpour abated. The gale became a breeze. Fingers of fog withdrew around us.

It was the storm, itself, speaking to me. Singing inside me.

I have missed us.

I was home.

"Are you okay?" Lazar moved closer, uneasy, wiping rain from his face. "You're different."

He was looking up at me. Back in our world, I was tall, taller than most men, but both Lazar and Caleb topped me by a couple of inches. Not any longer. Not here.

I extended my hand. The long freckled fingers were mine, but more slender, with pointed nails like talons. The arms were mine, too, but thinner, paler, more graceful, like the arms of an alien ballerina. My jacket sleeves ended two inches above my wrists.

My pants were also too short, but they hung around my narrow hips. My sneakers felt loose, the socks sagging around my ankles. And the Shadow Blade was gone. That made a weird kind of sense. If it embodied my connection to Othersphere, then I wouldn't need it when I was here. That connection was everywhere inside me now.

"My hair..." I grabbed a wet lock of my own hair, plastered down the front of my chest by the rain. It was vibrant orange, brighter than the color back home, and striped with black. My new skin pricked with bumps as a chill ran over me. "I look like her, don't I?"

I saw confirmation in Caleb's eyes. London yipped. Lazar reached up to touch my cheek, and then suddenly pulled his hand away, as if afraid. "Morfael said your form would stay similar, but it's... different."

Caleb took a step in, pulling London with him, so that we could speak more easily over the wind. "Did the rain let up because of you?" he asked me.

"I think so," I said. "I'm connected to the storm. To everything. It's amazing."

London sniffed at me suspiciously; then as if she'd confirmed it was really me, she barked and bumped her nose against my leg. Impatience bounced out of her.

"We better get going," I said, placing my hand on her silver-white head, now higher than my waist.

Caleb was humming. Gold flooded his eyes, and he stopped abruptly, eyebrows arching upward.

"What?" Lazar asked sharply.

Caleb's eyes were still glowing like golden lamps. "It only takes a second here, the barest murmur of sound is magnified incredibly. Try it. Try to find Amaris."

Lazar intoned a hum of his own, turning in a circle. The volume was low, but I felt the vibration scan over me like a wave. He stopped, swaying slightly. "Wow, you weren't kidding."

"That way?" Caleb pointed in the direction Lazar was now facing.

His brother nodded in agreement. "Yes. She's that way."

"That way?" I pointed.

As I gestured, clouds parted. Lightning withdrew. A hundred yards away, sunshine fell in a golden descant through the haze.

London yipped and trotted off through the path the storm had made. Lazar, Caleb, and I followed more slowly, walking side by side.

"Handy having you here," Lazar said.

"Good to be of some use," I said. It was a little weird to see the world from this new height. Moving felt easier, more fluid, and my newly translucent skin was reaching out to the molecules around it, feeling every change in the air, breathing in the rain and the half-gray light.

"We should be able to find the portal the same way." Caleb looked over his shoulder.

Behind us, a window cut from the fog revealed the unkempt lawn and rainy gray light of Burbank in a thunderstorm. It looked like a painting—pale and foreign. Within that frame, a mighty tone breeched the softness of the veil. It came from a figure thin as grass, white as marble draped in black.

Morfael.

The storm knew him, too. I lifted my hand. He raised his own, and a farewell danced between us.

A few steps on we came out of the storm, shaking the rain from our faces, to find ourselves at the edge of a meadow. Behind lay the endless bank of roiling clouds. Ahead was a forest of slender, white-trunked trees with crimson and green leaves that shimmered in the rich yellow light. The sun hovered just above the horizon to our right. I wondered if that was west. Perhaps the sun set in a different direction every night here, or perhaps the days were thirty hours long.

A warm breeze, laden with moisture, came at our backs and rustled the leaves. Each of them whispered in a distinct way, as if all conversing at once. I caught a name, chanted in a language I should not have understood, borne on the fluted air.

"The Red Wood," I said.

My friends angled questions my way. They were all looking a little damp and shell-shocked.

I shrugged. "That's what it calls itself."

"Okay then." Caleb hummed briefly, and then pointed
into the wood. "That way."

London bounded off. The grass was shorter here, but
hardy. Around the ivory tree trunks it clustered into thickets
teethed with long emerald thorns. We followed the enormous
wolf through a blue evening mist that smelled faintly like . . .

"Fur," Caleb said. "Why does this place smell like the fake
fur on a stuffed animal you just won at a carnival?"

"I was thinking carpet," Lazar said. "When you're a kid and
your sister gets mad at you and rubs your face in the carpet."

"Trixie," I said. "The wonderful old cat we had when I
was little. She smelled so sweet and powdery. I used to bury
my face in her neck and huff her like a drug."

London barked, her eyes bright, tail wagging, and I knew
she was remembering something, too, something the scent of
the Red Wood had brought back.

"Speaking of cats, it's a bit odd that we haven't seen any
animal life in this forest." I looked around. All the trees were
the same—at least three stories tall with smooth milky bark
and branches thick with leaves of scarlet and jade. Back in
our world, it might've been called the Christmas Wood. The
only other living things seemed to be the spiky grass, which
crowded the bases of the trees like sentinels. "Any scent of
any creatures, London?"

The wolf lifted her nose to breathe deep, and then shook
her head once, in awkward simulation of the human gesture.

"The air here reminds me of Amaris. She was stronger
than she looked," Lazar said, a smile spreading over his face.
"And she could be sneaky. If I did something that made her
mad, she'd wait till I was doing my homework on the floor,
creep up behind me, grab the hair on the back of my head
and rub my nose in the rug." He laughed. "Good lord, it
burned!"

Caleb let out a small laugh. "She could be surprising, couldn't she? Once, when you and Ximon were away, we sneaked off to a carnival in Barstow, back when I was living on the Tribunal compound," Caleb said.

"You did?" Lazar slid his smile over toward Caleb in surprise. "That was sneaky of both of you."

"That's when we..." Caleb hesitated, then continued. "We started to plan how we were going to get away from there. After Ximon told her she'd have to marry that man."

"That horrible old man." The smile dropped from Lazar's face. "I knew it was wrong, but I couldn't believe our father would..." He broke off, staring down at the sodden leaves of red on the grass beneath his boots like a bloody green carpet. "Anyway. I'm glad you were there."

Caleb turned his head to glance at his brother and shoved his hands into his pockets. "Me, too. I won a purple turtle for her at the carnival ring toss that night, and she named it Penelope the Purple Turtle and rubbed it against my face...." His voice trailed away. His black eyes were staring off into the blue-gray mist, remembering.

My throat ached a little. Caleb had lost his mother not long before that, his only family up till then. How much it must have meant then to find his long-lost siblings, for one of them, at least, to show that she loved him.

London whined and shoved her wet nose between Caleb's arm and his body, forcing him to take his hand out of his pocket. He ran his fingers through the soft silver fur behind her ears. "You're remembering something about her, too, aren't you, London?" he asked, stopping to meet the wolf's aquamarine eyes.

London pointed her black nose at the sky and let loose a high piercing howl. I'd heard her do it before, but here, as the sunlight faded and the blue mist rose around us, the melancholy moan brought tears to my eyes.

It stopped Lazar in his tracks. He and Caleb, so sensitive to vibration, stared at her, mesmerized. The keening descended down a bleak scale. At the final heart-ripping note, Lazar moved over to her.

London lowered her head, doleful eyes like lamps in the deepening twilight. Lazar reached out and scratched the ruff of fur at her neck.

"We'll find her," he said.

"Guys, we really should keep going," I said. The three of them were standing next to a particularly large tree, sharing a nice moment, yes. But the moment was dragging on. The forest had gotten very quiet, except for our voices.

"We should make her bake more for us when we get her back to the school," Lazar was saying. "She's okay at making dinner, but there's this Bundt cake she does..."

"Guys?" I walked over to them, my footsteps dampened by the soaked leaves. On each fallen red leaf I noted a lovely black outline, a swoop that looked like a closed eye, the eyelashes brushing a red cheek.

"I remember the shortbread cookies most," Caleb said with a grin at Lazar. "She'd roll them in powdered sugar."

I patted London's head. All this talk of baking must be playing with my head because the air around us now smelled like fresh bread. "We all love Amaris, I know. So let's not stop looking for her."

"Oh, wow, the shortbread! With the pecans?" Lazar shook his head in wonder. "I ate, like, three hundred of those at one sitting once. I nearly exploded."

The huge white tree next to us was even larger than I'd thought. Or...was it getting bigger? I blinked. The spiny grass around it stretched farther than I remembered, encircling us.

"Something's wrong," I said. "The wood..."

"But you would've died happy," Caleb said to Lazar, as if I hadn't spoken. His voice was so happy, carefree. He was smiling and leaning into Lazar as if he'd never hated him, never wanted him dead. "Who's got the next birthday? We'll beg her to make a cake for us."

"There is something wrong here." I put a hand on Caleb's shoulder to make him pay attention.

He blinked at me. "You like cake, silly."

"No, the trees, the grass . . ." I turned and grabbed the front of Lazar's jacket. He lifted his eyebrows in mild surprise.

Tendrils of grass had reached delicately over his shoulders, tickling his chin. He brushed them away casually. I looked down. The barbed plants had intertwined over our feet. I could barely see my own shoes.

A shiny thorn, as long as my finger, reached for Caleb's neck. He jerked away, but couldn't go far, hedged in by the white tree on one side and a growing cage of spiny grass.

"What the hell?" He looked around, as if seeing the encroaching plants for the first time.

"It's moving. It's all around us!" Lazar yelled, tugging against the binding green ropes now wound around his arms and legs. A thorn drew a long bloody scratch down his neck. "How do we get out of it?"

"A chainsaw?" I proposed, ridiculously. The light around us dimmed as tentacles of green reached over our heads, blotting out the sky. The four of us were clustered close now, hugged together by insidious arms of undergrowth. I tried not to struggle, but barbs were drawing red lines on my exposed arms and wrists, puncturing my clothes.

It was hard to even see the others now, though they were inches away. The plants were entwined around us from every angle, a living screen. If we didn't do something soon, we'd all die of blood loss, trapped here. Unless being ensnared was just the beginning.

London made a pained yipping noise. The thorn-covered grass was making her paws bleed. The blue mist puddled there, as if drawn by the blood.

"I've got a silver knife in my boot," Lazar said. The plants bowed slightly as he tried to bend over to his shoe. "I can't reach it."

"Check the shadows!" Caleb said, and then began to hum.

Lazar joined him. I winced back as a thorn as big as an antler stabbed at my eye. My adrenaline surged. I broke out in a sweat. "Hurry up!" Being constrained like this was deeply disturbing. If I didn't get out soon, I might start flailing and tugging, which would only draw more blood. I forced myself to take deep breaths and craned my neck to avoid being blinded.

The vines squeezed me tighter on one side. I shuffled my feet to stay upright, fearful of falling into a thorny bed. Through the teeming mass of olive and jade stalks I saw the white tree trunk get closer. "It's drawing us to the tree!" I shouted.

"Barbed wire, darn it." Lazar's mild swear word spoke volumes. "In our world this thorny stuff is barbed wire. The tree is a post."

"No point in drawing forth that shadow," I said. "Ow! Damn it!" The thorns pressed in, drawing more blood, getting close to tendons, muscles, and bone. I could shift into my tiger form to heal the cuts, and that form was stronger. But it was also bigger. If I got even a little bit larger, the thorns would be driven in deeper. The one poised in front of my face was long enough to kill me instantly if it went through my eye or my neck. Why hadn't it stabbed me yet?

It doesn't want us dead. Not yet.

The smooth white tree trunk in front of me trembled. An ominous crack gashed the surface.

"What the f—" Caleb was cut off as our captor jerked us closer.

The fissure in the bark split, revealing a gnarled maw dripping with cherry red sap. The vines were pulling us inexorably toward it. I struggled to believe it even as it happened.

Lazar leaned back, trying to stop our movement. "Just when I thought this place couldn't get any weirder."

"I always wondered what it was like to be digested alive," Caleb muttered.

"Maybe we can cut our way out once we're in there." I tried to sound hopeful, but it came out desperate.

Lazar was humming again. He broke off. "There's a hut! With tools! On the other side of the veil in our world, just ten yards to my right! I think I see an axe."

"Ten yards too far," I said, wincing as more thorns stabbed into me, forcing me to limp six inches closer to the slavering cavity ahead. Caleb's arm was half inside it already.

"No, Dez!" Caleb twisted around despite the thorns, exhaling with the pain of it. I could see his black eyes flecked with gold through the twisting greenery. A streak of sluggish blood ran down his cheek. The mist was thickening around it. "You might be able to get out of this," he said. "If you shift into a cat."

"Of course!" Hope surged through me. As a tiger I was too big, but as a cat, I just might be small enough to slip out. I'd only made that shift twice before, but there was no time like the present to try again. "London, you should do it, too," I said. "Turn into that little fennec fox like you did before."

London yowled mournfully, not sounding very positive.

"We can help her!" Lazar said. "Right, Caleb?"

"Yes, yes, good idea!" Caleb gritted his teeth, straining away from the yawning wooden jaws beside him.

"We'll do it at the same time, London, okay? So they don't have time to react and grab us again." London barked sharply. "Great. On three."

"Ready, Lazar?" Caleb asked.

In response, Lazar let loose a baying note I'd never heard before. It pierced and wavered like a deeper version of the wolf's howl London had wailed earlier.

Caleb sent out a note to join his, forming a chord, and then pitched it higher, thinner, as if it was coming from an animal much smaller than a wolf.

Lazar mimicked him. I watched carefully as much as I could through the writhing plants. Lazar's gold-and-brown irises were locked onto Caleb's black-and-gold ones. The brothers were interweaving their tones into an eerie song with a story I could feel under my skin. It was the story of a wolf who asked the moon a favor. And to save her life, the moon granted her wish—to become a fox.

Do their voices tell stories back in our world, too? I was sensing things in Othersphere I'd never known existed before.

The song seemed to be reaching a crescendo. I focused myself on how it felt to be small, how I'd once fit on a bookshelf in my cat form, how Caleb had run his hand over my head and made me purr with happiness. I found that place inside myself easily. Othersphere made it feel completely natural. I could be the world's smallest cat in a heartbeat.

"Okay, London," I said. "One, two, three."

Like a diver slicing through the surface of the water, I dove into my cat form. It rushed over me and down I went, under the grasping tendrils of the vines, slipping past the cruel prickles and barbs dripping with my own blood.

My paws were tiny now, narrower than the blades of the grass, speckled in swirls of orange, white, and black fur. Above me, the feelers that had held me were flailing, searching. Two feet away, a tiny fennec fox gathered itself, pale fur easily visible amidst the seething greenery. It swiveled ears as wide as coffee cups at me and yipped.

I meowed and angled my sinuous body around a particularly large thorn, poking my head past a grasping tentacle, and slithered through the fluctuating gaps in the living net that had held my human-ish form.

The fox followed, ears now tucked tight to her head, black nose narrow enough to find the cracks between the blades, tiny paws dancing past floundering emerald antennae.

Our escape was a kind of song, too. I felt the rhythm of it, a flurry of tiny notes in counterpoint to the menacing fugue all around.

Then I slinked between the last lattice of shrubbery and was free. London popped out beside me and shook her enormous ears. We skittered farther away from the seething hedgerow now looming so high, and she woofed. We couldn't see the boys, but they could hear us.

"Are you free?" Lazar's voice cut through the vegetation.

I let out a hard meow, trying to make it sound like "yes" as London barked, louder this time.

"Okay, Caleb, ready?"

"We're going to call forth whatever we can from the hut," Caleb said. "Get anything you find quick as you can because—arrh!"

His voice broke off in a growl of anger and pain. I trilled a question, pacing, trying to see his black coat, something, but even the white trunk of the huge tree was invisible to us now.

"Like I said." Caleb's voice was more strained, but determined. *Thank the Moon.* "Be quick. Go, Lazar!"

Lazar intoned another note, different from the wolf and fox howls, happier, more workmanlike. Caleb's voice joined his, describing in notes a tin hut, padlock rusted and useless, abandoned and unused on someone's land, with tools hanging from rusty nails inside.

I felt more than heard the pop of something coming through shadow. The fox's ears swiveled in that same direction, and we took off. The hut was there, exactly as the boys' notes had described it, leaning to one side, door hanging open. I ran right in, London beside me, and shifted instantly to human. On the wall, a large, slightly rusty axe was hanging from a hook. A saw with broken teeth hung next to it.

I grabbed the axe as London ran yipping around my feet. Perhaps she wasn't able to shift. "Stay back!" I shouted, and raising the axe, I rushed right at the teeming foliage now nearly two stories high at the base of the white tree.

I brought the axe down with all my might. The blade didn't look very sharp, but it bit into the stalks of undergrowth with a satisfying *thunk*. The grass tore beneath it, oozing cherry red, and then turned black. More dramatically, the entire bank of greenery recoiled, fanning out as if afraid of the axe head.

Be afraid.

I swung the axe down again, ripping away stems and thorns. The stalks nearby reacted more like a crowd of people than a plant, heaving away from me, desperate to escape.

I heard growling and the padding of feet behind me, and I knew London had shifted back into wolf form and was coming, dragging something. I chopped downward again as a silver streak, big as a pony, lifted a large, flat, rectangular object in her mouth and flung it at the rippling hedgerow.

The object clanged, vibrating, into the main body of the plant. It was the entire broken front door of the hut, made of corrugated, rusted tin.

The plants beneath the door wilted and blackened before our eyes. Lazar, his right leg now mostly free, was pulling his way out. Caleb's black shape was still deeply embedded in squirming green, half in the quivering hole in the tree, half out.

"It's the metal that's killing it!" I shouted. "Do it again, London!"

The wolf darted into the fray to grab the edge of the door as I chopped at coiling tendrils all around her. She dragged the door back and with a mighty twist of her neck, launched it again at the center of the plant. Wherever the metal touched, the grass withered and died, and this time, most of it was around Caleb.

The entire tree reared back from the metal, shaking the ground beneath us. Caleb shouted with alarm as the great open maw trembled and began to close around his left arm. Branches swung down at the tin door, banging into it, trying to shove it away. Lazar shook bracken off his face and ran to grab it.

One branch stopped in mid-swing right in front of me. A clump of ruddy leaves at the end of one twig turned my way. Each one sported a single bright unmistakable eye with a sparkling garnet iris, prismed with veins like a leaf.

I gaped. The dozen or so leaf-eyes scanned me, unblinking. I turned my gaze higher, all the way up the ten-story tree. Every one of its red leaves carried an eye. Half were focused on the tin door Lazar and London were grabbing. The rest were trained on me.

The nearest branch slapped at my face. I ducked, feeling the sting as the lower leaves smacked into my forehead. Another, larger appendage thrust itself at the door, knocking it twenty feet back, then lunged for London and Lazar. Lazar rolled away, and London tore at a clump of leaves with her teeth, ripping them off the bough.

There was no audible scream, but the eyes on the red leaves around me squinted. The entire tree shuddered, and the ground trembled. I concentrated on keeping my feet, cutting away at the last few binding strands holding Caleb. He grimaced, kicked his legs free, and stumbled away, trailing vines and blood. The mist clustered around the droplets on the ground and the abrasions on his face. He waved his hands at it, but it was like batting at insects the size of water droplets.

"Let's get out of here!" Lazar said, tugging on my sleeve. "This way!"

Sleeve? I kept hold of the axe and tried to figure out how I had come to be clothed in a soft gown made of what looked like fuzzy white flowers. We all turned and ran after Lazar.

"What the hell are you wearing?" Caleb asked, jogging alongside me as we wove between more white-trunked trees, careful to avoid any thick clumps of spiky grass. London was outpacing all of us on her four long legs, looking back frequently so Lazar could point her the right way.

"No idea," I said, speaking between breaths. "It was on me when I shifted. Oh!" The axe I'd been holding was now a dried tree branch. I kept hold of it. If we needed an axe, Caleb and Lazar might be able to call it forth again.

"Maybe clothes come with shifting on your home planet," Caleb said. "So to speak."

"I guess." We broke to go around a tree, giving it a wide berth. I caught a scent of orange blossom. "We need to get out of here fast," I said. "Now the whole place smells like my block back in Burbank in summer."

Lazar had let us catch up to him and overheard me. "It's like my mother's perfume."

Caleb's face was grim. "My mother grew orange blossom in our garden in France."

He'd told me about that garden during one of our long phone calls last year. He and his mother had managed to spend five whole years in the same place in the south of France when he was a boy, before Tribunal scouts had forced them to move on. He'd liked southern California because it had the same climate, the same smells as those happier days.

"The forest, or maybe the mist is manipulating us," I said. "It smelled like bread when you talked about Amaris baking things. It's like it finds the scent of our memories."

"And it fosters good will." Lazar shot a look at Caleb and said no more. He was right, though. For a few minutes he and Caleb had been laughing together like . . . well, like brothers. And they'd cooperated seamlessly to get London to shift and to make the hut and its tools appear out of shadow.

Caleb nodded, giving him a considering look. "It probably wanted us to get physically closer to each other, so it could grab us all at once."

"Is it the trees?" Lazar asked. We'd slowed down to a brisk walk. London circled around behind us to end up beside Lazar.

"Maybe the mist." Caleb looked at the sun dipping below the horizon. The gray-blue haze seemed to thicken between the trees. "You saw how it was drawn to our blood."

"A cooperative relationship between the trees, the grass, and the mist," Lazar said speculatively. "The mist gives off an aroma or pheromone that makes you get lost in happy memories so that the grass can trap you. The scratches from the grass feed the mist."

Caleb was nodding. Figuring out the problem had drawn him into talking to Lazar in a civil tone again. It wasn't friendly or brotherly, but at least it wasn't hostile. "Then the grass hands the live bodies off to the trees for an evening snack."

"And the memory we all shared, that pulled us together, was our love for Amaris." Lazar leaned over and looked at me. "You noticed something was wrong before we did. Do you think that's because you're from here?"

I shrugged. "Wouldn't the trees mostly prey on creatures from here? No wonder we didn't see any animals. The trees eat them all."

London whined uneasily.

"Maybe . . ." Caleb started, hesitated, and then continued. "Maybe you weren't as affected because you have shadow-walker blood." He slanted his eyes toward me. "That's right, isn't it? If Orgoli is your father, and he's half-brother to Morfael . . ."

"Orgoli is half shadow walker, half Amba," I said. "And Morfael confirmed that Orgoli is my father." I told them everything that Morfael had said about my biological parents.

"Having a crazed, child-eating tyrant for a father doesn't mean I'll become like him, right?" I asked, only half joking.

"I'm not qualified to comment," Lazar said, and didn't elaborate. I knew he was thinking about his own tyrannical father and history of bloodshed.

Caleb pursed his lips but said nothing.

"On the other hand," Lazar went on, brightening, "Amaris grew up with the same evil dad and she turned out pretty great."

"Guess there's hope for all of us," I said. "Hey, look!"

I pointed ahead. The trees thinned out, the grass looked less spiky, and a distant winged creature flapped off into the dusk. It looked like a large black bird, but at such a distance it was hard to tell. And I wasn't going to take anything for granted in this place again.

We came to the edge of the Red Wood with relief, and then paused to take in the slow-moving pools of water and hummocks of what looked like dry land covered in slender, papyrus-like plants. Farther on, trees began to appear again, and the land climbed higher to verdant hills in the distance. Clouds on the sunset horizon were turning a violent pink streaked with purple. The sky then lightened to a bright azure, which reflected in the nearly still waters around us like a neon watercolor.

"That way," Lazar said, nodding toward the hills.

"Nothing like a nice evening's walk through the swamp," said Caleb, and took a cautious step onto what looked like dry land. We followed in single file, keeping to the high ground, which forced us to wind our way around ponds of brackish water.

London gave a low whimper and looked up. I followed her gaze to see the faint outline of the winged creature. "I hope that's a bird."

Lazar followed my gaze. "It's getting closer."

The airborne outline was indeed getting bigger, much bigger, and plunging right at us. I shoved at Caleb's back. He was ahead of me, picking out the driest spots to walk. "Run!"

"We can't outrun a flying thing," he said, even as he jumped quickly from one hillock of land to another. "And the last thing we need is to walk into living quicksand or something."

"Too late. Here it comes!" Lazar shouted.

We all turned, braced, to see a sharp-winged form swooping toward us. The wingspan, over thirty yards wide, blotted out the sky. The pointed beak was longer than my arm, with a prominent bony ridge jutting upward over the shining red eyes. The rubbery gray skin turned rust-colored at the tail and on all four feet. It was no bird; it had no feathers. The forbidding beak was aimed right at us. It lunged.

I flung my arm up to protect my head and ducked. A wind from its body whooshed around us as the creature swooped directly overhead, skinny front legs tucked neatly against its body, back legs moving to jut forward, claws extended. Then it slammed into the large pond beside us. The claws latched on to something and the giant wings swatted at the air again. The whole creature, big as a private plane, launched itself toward the sky again, holding something about five-feet long and wriggling in its talons. I caught sight of a humanlike head and flailing arms covered with fish scales. A horrific scream rent the air as the flying creature threw its captive high into the sky. Then the voice was cut off as the beak unhinged to an unnaturally wide angle. The flying thing caught its prey, gulped once, and flew away.

"Holy crap," I said. My knees were shaking. I put a hand on London's furry back to steady myself.

Caleb lifted one hand to shield his eyes, watching the creature get smaller against the brilliant, darkening blue of the sky. "I think we just saw a pterodactyl eat a merman."

"Tero—what?" Lazar stared at him. "How can you know what that was?"

"Well, it actually looked more like *Quetzalcoatlus,* given the size," Caleb said. "That's the biggest flying creature ever known to exist in our world."

Lazar shook his head. "You mean, like a dinosaur? Ximon wouldn't allow us to learn about them."

"Ximon should come visit," I said. "He might rethink a few things."

Caleb was still staring after the creature. "It went extinct millions of years ago. What's it doing here?"

"Parallel evolution maybe," I said. "In this world it got to live."

"Maybe." Caleb recommenced picking his way through the swamp. London hopped ahead of him, using her nose to sniff out where the ground was firmest, and our pace picked up.

We came across a strange section of the swamp where the water dried up and the plants disappeared. The ground was nothing but grayish dirt and a few rocks, uneven and dusty. It spread hundreds of yards to the left and right, and about two hundred yards across. It was easier to traverse than the swampland, but it made me uneasy. The air smelled foul. The undercurrent of song that always thrummed beneath my skin here died away.

"Someone forgot the fertilizer," Lazar said, kicking a rock. "Oh, wow, hey."

He knelt down and I walked over to see him brush gray dirt off of something brownish-white and hard. As the dust fell away, I saw it was the brow of a small skull, with two deep eye sockets staring up at us. It could have been human except it was too small, even for a child.

"Maybe it's a graveyard," Caleb said, gazing down at the skull over my shoulder.

London whimpered.

Lazar brushed the dirt back over the bones and replaced the rock he'd kicked at. "In that case, let's get through it as fast as we can."

Soon enough the swamp re-emerged around us. We saw a lot of movement in the cloudy water around us and were sometimes startled by sudden scampering in the weeds, but it wasn't until the land started to get dryer that we saw other large creatures.

The sky had darkened to cobalt by then, but the horizon to our left was aglow somehow, which gave us just enough light to stumble onward without falling into treacherous mud or a bottomless sinkhole. We were tired, muddy, and covered with dried bloody scratches, so we stopped for a drink of water and a handful of trail mix while London scouted ahead. Caleb's scratches were the deepest, still oozing, and I insisted he break out the antibiotic ointment and some gauze.

I helped him place a bandage on the deep puncture at the back of his neck, pulling down the collar of his coat and shirt to reveal the bloody skin along his upper spine. He didn't wince as I applied the antibiotic, but I saw the muscles along his neck tense up, felt the shudder.

"Almost cut your spine," I said. With the blood wiped clean, I could smell Caleb's unique, airy scent again, like the forest back home after it had been washed by rain. The heat and scent drifting up from the back of his neck was different here. Not warmer, but somehow more potent, filtering through the air, reminding my fingers and lips how it was to be pressed up against his skin, to feel it slide beneath my own.

Caleb's head turned slightly, showing his strong profile. He breathed deeply, and for a moment I thought he was going to turn completely around to face me, bury his face in my neck, as if he too were remembering what it was to be close.

"Guess he was lucky," Lazar said. Pulled out of reverie, I turned my head and saw him standing by uneasily, fists clenched. "Lucky that thing didn't kill him." He jerked his gaze away from us and walked off, water bottle dangling forgotten in one hand.

Had he felt or seen what I was thinking somehow? I didn't see how it was possible, but then our last time alone together hadn't ended well.

"Here." I handed the leftover gauze to Caleb.

He took it from me slowly, eyes darting back and forth between me and his brother. But he said nothing.

I grabbed my own water bottle, took a swig and went over to Lazar. "You okay?"

"Nothing I can't clean up myself," he said.

"That's not what I meant," I said, and put a hand on his arm.

The lean muscles in his bicep tightened under my touch; then he pulled away. "He's the lucky one," Lazar said, his voice low so that only I could hear. "He didn't have to grow up with Ximon as a role model. He had a mother who didn't cater to a madman. And he met you first."

"Technically, you met me first," I said. "Remember? You shot me through my bedroom window with two tranquilizer darts."

He let out a reluctant laugh. "Lucky me." He glanced up at me, eyes widening as he took in, once again, my altered appearance.

"Are you still mad at me?" I asked.

"Not mad," he said. "Not really. It's funny. When I first came to stay at the school, I was hoping Caleb and I could mend things between us. Then he left, and I started hoping instead that you and I..." He trailed off, staring at the weird, white light in one corner of the sky. "Now he's back. I don't know what to hope for."

"I just hope the three of us don't hate each other forever."

"I could never hate you," he said. His gaze, a warm, soft brown, traveled over my face. Then he laughed a little, and shook his head. "I can't wait to get back to our world, if only because there you'll look like the Dez I lo—" He broke off. "I care for."

My heart sped up to a sprint, and my face got hot.

He almost said he loved you.

But he hadn't been able to get the words out. I was almost... glad he hadn't. Because I didn't know what I'd say back.

"It's still me even though I look a little different." I leaned over to look at my own reflection in the still water of the swamp. There was just enough light for me to see how strangely elongated I had become—so tall, unnaturally thin, with inhumanly huge green eyes that slanted up at the tips, and a swooping pointed nose that wouldn't have looked out of place on Tinker Bell. My red hair, striped with black, floated around me like a storm. The look was new, and weird if I thought about it, but it felt right here. "Just like it's still me when I'm a tiger."

"The Dez I know is there," he said, still gazing at me. "But something else is, too. Something I don't recognize."

A low growl from London pulled our attention to where she was standing on slightly higher ground. Caleb was shrugging into his battered coat, pacing fast to join her. I ran up the hill behind him, then stopped and crouched down as I caught sight of a group of what might have been elephants moving beneath the low trees on the edge of the swamp.

"Mammoths?" I asked Caleb, my voice low. Over a dozen of the creatures were grazing less than a hundred yards away. "Oh, wait, no trunks."

"Exactly," he said. Although as big as elephants from our world, these creatures had dusty brown and yellow fur, and shorter snouts. They walked with a strange, rolling gate on the outsides of their feet with hugely muscled bodies wider at the hips than the shoulders.

Then one reared back on its hind legs, using its broad tail for support, and raked the leaves off a tree with black, knife-like claws, shoving them into its mouth. Several smaller ones, probably babies, tussled with each, rolling under the belly of an adult, who just kept eating.

"If those aren't Megatheriums," Caleb said, "I'll buy Ximon a cherry pie."

"More dinosaurs?" Lazar asked, creeping up to join us. London sat next to him as he put a hand on her shoulder. "They look like huge hamsters."

"Giant ground sloths," Caleb said. "Mammals. I think they lived on our earth until about ten thousand years ago. I saw a skeleton in the Natural History Museum in London a couple of years ago."

"Herbivores, thank God," I said. "They've got skeletons like that in the Tar Pits Museum in L.A., too."

"It's like whatever went extinct in our world kept on living in this one," Caleb said.

"Humans are pretty good at wiping out other species," I said. "And each other."

"Yeah, but dinosaurs and mammals that lived millions of years apart in our world living here next to each other? Still doesn't make sense." He glanced at his watch. "We don't have much longer before we have to turn around if we're going to get back to Morfael."

"Better get going, then." Lazar turned and looked up the hill spread out before us in the twilight. The short grass gave way to shrubbery and trees as it climbed higher. Lazar hummed, and then smiled. "She's not far now. That way."

We hiked rapidly up the hill, fortified by the snacks and the knowledge that Amaris was close. London, as usual, was in front, sniffing the ground and loping tirelessly. Even as the sky to our right darkened from indigo to black, the left side took on an ethereal glow, picking out the silver tips of London's thick fur and burnishing Lazar's blond hair to gold.

We entered another forest thick with trees, not white-trunked or red-leafed, but with thick, tangled roots forming house-sized clusters above ground. Multiple bronze trunks sprouted above to flower into thick umbrellas of green-leafed branches.

We gave them as wide a berth as we could, trying to keep to the patches of pearly light that filtered through the canopy. I heard movement in the gnarled limbs above us, and the scraping of feet or paws amongst the roots. But even my excellent night vision couldn't penetrate the tangle of limbs.

In the distance, one tree glowed as if someone had strung white lights all over it, but the lights moved, and strange rhythmic music stopped and started at odd intervals, echoing toward us through the wood.

Then London gave a soft woof, staring upwards. I slowed, searching the branches above. Small winged creatures flapped just above the trees, so many I couldn't count. "Bats?" I said softly.

London whined low and fixed her attention a little lower. Then I saw it—a two-legged, human-shaped figure standing on a very high branch near the top of one of the trees. It appeared to be looking down at us, but it was too dark to make out anything other than a silhouette. Another humanoid figure, smaller, more feminine in shape moved up behind it and stood there.

Caleb and Lazar had stopped to look, too. Lazar reached into his jacket to his gun holster.

Then with a breath of wind, the humanoid forms were gone. It was almost too fast to follow, but in their place, for a moment, were two bat-winged forms, which swooped off to join the swarm above.

"Where'd they go?" Lazar asked.

"They shifted," I said.

"What?" He looked taken aback.

"It was almost too fast to see, but she's right," Caleb said. "They shifted into bats."

We stood for a moment, trying to work it out. "Bat shifters went extinct in our world around the mid-fourteen-hundreds," I said. "We studied Vlad Tepes last semester in school. After his reign of terror in Transylvania, the Tribunal wiped them all out."

"Another species that went extinct in ours?" Caleb shook his head. "I don't get it."

London barked, loping away, and then looking back anxiously. She was right. We needed to keep going. The three of us trotted after her.

Finally, we came upon a chalk-colored wall of mountainside, rising at nearly ninety degrees to our right, so high we could not see the top. We seemed to be standing at the bottom of a cliff, which thrust out of the forest like an ivory building block. We skirted along it as Lazar and Caleb led the way.

"Is Amaris inside the mountain somehow?" Caleb asked at one point.

"That's what I was wondering," Lazar replied. "It feels like she's there." And he pointed at an angle toward the towering cliff wall.

"There's got to be a way in," I said. "A tunnel, a door, something."

Caleb glanced at his watch. "Half an hour. Then we have to turn around."

"Or be stuck here for at least twenty-four more hours," I said.

"If we don't find her, I'll stay," Lazar said. "I'll find her and keep her safe till you get back."

London yipped and shook her ears in protest, as if to say she would stay, too.

"No," I said, "If one of us stays, we all stay." And we picked up the pace.

Lazar was in front of Caleb, humming quietly, when he spotted something up ahead. I could just see him through the trees, outlined against the whiteness of the cliff face. "Some kind of cave entrance up ahe—"

A black four-legged form leaped down on him from the tall jumbled roots of a nearby tree. Lazar flung up his arm in time to block the slashing white teeth aimed for his throat, but fell under the shaggy, dog-shaped body. Caleb jumped toward them to help, but a brown-gray creature, bigger than the first, darted out from behind another tree and snapped at his leg.

"Ambush!" he called, and leapt straight up, catching a low-hanging branch of the looming "broccoli" tree, as we'd started calling them, pulling his legs up in time to avoid the creature's fangs. I swung my backpack off my back, prepared to use it as a weapon.

But London lunged under Caleb and slammed into the brown-furred creature. It flew backwards with a yelp of pain. I spotted something white moving between the netlike web of roots next to the cliff face.

"On your right!" I shouted just as the narrow, white-furred head shot out to snap at London's front legs.

Quick as a cobra, London clamped her jaws down on the back of that creature's neck, and dragged it out from between the roots. It whimpered, paws scrabbling, but couldn't resist her. It looked like a large white wolf, but with slightly shorter, sturdier legs, and a longer, narrower head.

London was twice as large. She issued a powerful, menacing growl as she pinned the white wolf to the ground, her eyes like lasers on the black wolf still wrestling with Lazar.

The black wolf saw her there, holding its pack mate hostage, and pushed away from Lazar. His arm was oozing blood from a couple of punctures, but he looked otherwise okay.

The brown wolf got to its feet and bared its fangs at London. She snarled back, still gripping the back of the white wolf's neck. It had tucked its tail between its legs and curled up under her, whining pitifully.

The black wolf paced back and forth in front of London with Lazar's blood on its muzzle, as if trying to decide what to do. Lazar got painfully to his feet. Caleb lowered himself from the tree limb and the three of us ranged ourselves behind our own silver wolf, ready. Lazar's wounds would have to wait.

The black wolf barked three times at London, still pacing.

London growled, shook the ruff of the white wolf in her jaws a little, and scraped her left front paw twice on the ground.

The black and brown wolves put their heads together, turning away from us slightly, glancing back at London.

"I swear, they're conferring," I said in an undertone to Caleb and Lazar.

Caleb nodded, not taking his eyes off of the wolves. "I think these are dire wolves, a prehistoric version of wolves that died out thousands of years ago in our world."

"Looks like they can still speak the same language as London though," Lazar said, using one hand to put pressure on the teeth marks on his arm. "So that's good."

Indeed, the black and brown wolves had tucked their tails between their legs and rolled over on their backs in front of London. She let them cower there for a moment, jaws still clamped on their friend. Then she released the white wolf, who crawled away and rolled over, too, showing its belly.

London dipped her head and walked over to sniff the

black wolf. He cautiously got to his feet, tail wagging low, and bent his head submissively. The others did the same, and soon all three were carefully sniffing London, ears down, as she towered over them. She cocked her head at us. I swear she looked triumphant.

Caleb quickly slipped some antibiotic ointment out of his backpack, along with some gauze and handed them to me. There were four deep punctures in Lazar's left forearm, but he didn't wince as I bound them up.

"Amaris is in there." He tilted his head toward the screen of roots along the mountainside the white wolf had emerged from. Beyond them it was empty and black. A cave entrance.

"I think we just befriended the guardians of the entrance," Caleb said. "London, can they lead us to Amaris?"

London growled and barked twice at her new followers, who cocked their heads and listened intently. The black dire wolf, who seemed to be second in charge, yapped and jerked its nose toward the roots covering the cave entrance.

London barked again. The dire wolf lowered his head, as if in obeisance, and then paced over to the roots, looking back over his shoulder to see if we were following. In front of him, the roots wavered and moved, like tentacles, making an opening wide enough to get through.

Beyond that even my eyes could see nothing but dark.

"London, can you ask him if Orgoli's here or nearby?"

London perked her ears and up and let out a series of yips and woofs. The black dire wolf shook its ears and barked. London turned to me and shook her head in that strange human "no." She accompanied it with an odd lift of her shoulders that had to be her version of a shrug. "So—probably not. As far as he knows," I said, speculating.

London nodded once.

Lazar pulled the sleeve of his jacket over his new bandage. "Let's go."

The black dire wolf ducked between the roots into the cave entrance. It reminded me of my first day at Morfael's school, when he'd tested me and Caleb by sending us into an underground cave.

I looked at Caleb. He was grinning at me, hefting his flashlight. "Just like old times," he said.

And we followed the black dire wolf into darkness.

CHAPTER 10

The cave was narrow and less than four feet high. It sloped sharply down at first, so we ran awkwardly through the mountain stooped over like apes, following the blue-white beam of Caleb's flashlight, which he kept trained on the black dire wolf in front. The cave seemed to be entirely natural, perhaps carved at one point by an underground stream, now dry and fairly smooth. Like everything else in Othersphere, it hadn't been worked or touched by a metal tool of any kind. We were moving fast, breathing heavily, and conscious of how little time we had. Behind me, Lazar tripped over the uneven floor, and would have knocked me over, but he threw a hand out, using the curved wall to stop his fall.

My back was aching, and my knees cramped by the time I sensed air above me rather than rock. We didn't stop as Caleb scanned his beam of light around. The walls on either side rose to a ceiling that rapidly ascended into the dark, too high for the light to reveal anything. The light startled a flock of creatures that looked like trout crossed with humming-birds, with long narrow bodies flashing iridescent purples and blues, wide staring eyes, and filmy wings that flapped too fast to follow.

I tripped over a protruding rock and pitched forward. Behind me, Lazar caught hold of my waist and saved me from a fall. Then he pulled his hands away, quickly.

"You keep doing that," I said softly, and reached back to take his hand as we continued trotting forward.

He squeezed my fingers. "What?"

"You keep saving me from falling," I said, my voice low. "Thank you."

"Don't fall behind," Caleb said, swinging the light around.

I pulled away sharply from Lazar. His hand fell away. Had Caleb seen us together? I couldn't tell. He kept jogging through the darkness, shining the light ahead once more.

"Wouldn't want to leave you here without a light," Caleb said. His voice was flat but strangely ominous. Or was that just my guilty imagination?

We passed a number of side tunnels, some at floor level, some high up in the side wall, most too small for us to pass through. The cave widened, and water dripped steadily in the distance as we wound between stalagmites pointing up like crooked fingers. A light glowed to our left, and then we were walking through a natural arch and out onto a flat stone terrace into the brilliant white radiance of a nearly full moon, just rising above the skyline. It was not our moon, with its familiar gray seas and splotches. This was the strange, corpulent moon of Othersphere, veined with black lines that beat like a living thing.

Its light fell like silk on my skin, pulsing subliminally through my body. It reflected brilliantly off the blanched stone at our feet, casting multiple shadows on the mountainside behind us. A faint breeze stirred my hair, which waved in a flutter of notes perfectly in sync with the anthem of the night.

The natural porch was about thirty feet at its widest; then

it plunged sharply down at least a thousand feet to reveal a vast forested valley cut by an old, winding river, silver and black under that moon. The swamp and the Red Wood must be on the other side of the mountain.

To complete the feeling we were on a kind of balcony, shrubs grew into a sort of fence along the edge, and a gardener had coaxed them into fantastical shapes—a winged horselike creature rearing up to take flight, a familiar tree with leaves bearing baleful eyes, a ringed planet with a ferocious face.

It was all too familiar. Ahead of me, Caleb flicked off his flashlight and raced to the edge to stare out over the basin below, every tree etched with black shadow by the moon.

"This is where Amaris was pushed into Othersphere," he said. "This is it!"

"Here?" Lazar walked out onto the flat stone surface. Now that we were standing on it I could see that it was like marble, milky white, smooth, but patterned with darker hues just under the surface.

"We saw this view through the portal Orgoli created when he kidnapped her," I said. "She fell through right here." I walked closer to the edge to take in the verdant land before us. To our right, I could see more of the mountain we had been inside. Its peak, darker than the white cliff sides, jagged down lower here to form the silhouette of a huge, sleeping cat, its black stone tail wrapped around its feet as if for warmth, ears jutting up atop its rounded head, still alert even in slumber.

This is the dwelling of the Amba.

I knew it with a sudden certainty. We were in the heart of Orgoli's kingdom, in his home. Now that I knew it, a part of me wanted to run, to flee back the way we'd come and never look back.

But the other part of me wanted to climb that mountainside, to hunt along its narrow trails, to find my den deep inside its caverns.

Caleb hummed, scanning, and we all saw the other doorway in the cliff wall at the same time. This one looked as if
something very large had tried to go through it recently, something too big but strong enough to break off large chunks of
white stone around the circumference. The shards lay around
the entrance still, white as broken teeth.

London barked once, and the black dire wolf trotted
through that door, not looking back. We broke into a run
after it, London first, Caleb's flashlight beam bobbing as he
moved.

The cave here was more like a hallway, wider, and covered
with strange hard plant roots that descended from above at
intervals to cross-hatch openings in the rock.

I saw movement in one of those holes, and something like
red eyes and white teeth before I ran on.

"She's here, she's here!" Caleb was shouting, pointing
ahead to a large patch of the black roots which ran vertically
like the bars of a prison cell across a cavity as tall as I was.
"Amaris!"

"Caleb?"

My heart leapt. It was her voice. Thin, dirty fingers poked
between the roots, reaching. "Caleb, is that really you?"

"It's all of us!" Lazar shouted as we clattered to a stop in
front of her cell.

"Lazar!" The fingers tried to shove themselves farther between the bars.

"And me and London," I said, reaching to touch her. We
all laid our hands, and London her nose, on Amaris's fingers.
London woofed softly. "Are you okay?"

"Oh, thank God." Amaris's hands clutched at ours. Between the black bars of the roots, her brown eyes blinked
rapidly in the sudden beam from the flashlight. Her face was
smudged with dirt, her buttery yellow hair frizzy and wild.
Her brown eyes blinked up again at me through the roots.
"Is that Dez?"

"It's me," I said. "Othersphere turns me into a cartoon character."

"Are you injured?" Lazar asked, reaching into his backpack. "Did they feed you?" He pulled out a water bottle and some energy bars.

"I'm okay," Amaris said. "Someone left me a gourd with water in it and some things that were kind of like nuts, which I never need to eat again."

London was licking Amaris's fingers, whining softly. Amaris laid her forehead against the roots and stroked the wolf's muzzle. "Oh, my darling," she said. "It's so good to see you. You're so much bigger!"

London stared at the girl behind the bars with eyes like blue planets, her tail wagging. She barked, and it was joyous.

Caleb was feeling all over the thick black roots covering the entrance to Amaris's cell. "Now how the hell do we get her out of here?"

Lazar wrapped his hands around one of the roots and tried to move it. His biceps bunched under his jacket and his face got red with effort till he let go with a grunt. "We might need to call forth that axe again," he said.

London growled something low to the dire wolf. He barked, then lowered his head and groveled over to me, tail wagging submissively, and cautiously nosed my hand.

London cocked her head, and he whined expressively at her. Her ears lifted, as if she understood, and then she, too, ran her nose over first my left and then my right hand.

"Me?" I asked. "My hands?"

London nodded.

"Good thing we brought an Amba along," Lazar said.

I put my hands cautiously on the roots. They felt as hard as iron, but I gripped them and tried to pull them apart, like some superhero. As I did so, they turned rubbery and soft. I spread them open easily, pushing them aside to form a person-sized hole. Amaris slid through, free.

She fell into Lazar's waiting arms as London barked joyously. Caleb hovered nearby, a hand on her back, until she loosed one arm and grabbed him by the neck to pull him into a three-way hug. For a long, wonderful moment, the three siblings embraced.

"Psst, hey!" A voice came echoing down the hall.

I turned. Did people in Othersphere say "hey"?

The others didn't react. My ears were more sensitive. Or maybe I was hearing things.

"Hey, English-speaking people down the hall there!" The voice was real, and speaking English with a distinct clipped accent that I felt like I should recognize. "Are you from our world? Are you really there?"

I took a couple of steps toward the voice. But how could it be? It made no sense in this place.

"Did you guys hear that?" I asked.

The siblings broke apart. Amaris threw her arms around London and buried her face in the silver fur.

"Hear what?" Lazar asked. He was still smiling, so relieved.

"Someone down the hall is speaking English." I pointed that way, as if the gesture somehow made it more believable. "They asked if we're from 'our world.' "

"Probably a trap." Lazar hastily shoved the water bottle and energy bars back into his backpack. "We've been too noisy."

"And stayed too long," said Caleb. "We have to get back."

I looked at the dire wolves, ranged behind London. They were alert, but relaxed. Surely they would be more wary if the voice was a trap for us. "What if Amaris isn't the only one Orgoli kidnapped from our world?"

"Please!" It was a man's voice. "If you're there. Please don't leave us here!"

Everyone turned to look down the hall. They'd heard it

this time. London snapped something to her wolves, and the black one issued a low whine.

"Other people from our world?" I asked London.

She gave me a single nod.

"Help us, please!" called the voice.

I gave the others a wild glance and ran down the hall, passing other natural caverns. Some were barred with black roots, others were open, and I realized: We were in a prison.

"Dez!" Lazar hissed after me. "We don't have time!"

"We're like you!" The man's voice echoed against the stone walls. "We're from Earth. Please let us out!"

Light bobbed behind me, and the thud of Caleb's boots. He was coming, too. My anxiety loosened a little, knowing he was with me.

I slowed down as I came to a corner and peered down the hall. With the barest light from Caleb's flashlight, I saw two huge openings facing each other across the hallway about fifty feet down. Each was covered with a net of black roots. The stench of old sweat and urine assaulted my nose.

"You, girl!" The man's voice rose with a heartrending combination of terror and hope. "Help us!"

Caleb reached my side and the flashlight beam flooded down the hallway.

Through the chinks in the roots the light reflected back from dozens of eyes, outlined dozens of hands clutching, gesturing, and reaching for us.

A female voice shrieked in terror as another babbled in a tongue I didn't understand.

"It's one of the Amba!" the same man said in English. I zeroed in on him. He was in the cell to the right, closest to us. A man about six foot four with matted dark hair, brown skin, and flashing dark eyes that took me in with horror, then blinked in surprise at Caleb. And I realized—I didn't look human anymore.

Caleb must have realized it, too. "We're from your world," he said, and took a step down the hall.

The man's eyes widened. Tears sprang forth to course down his cheeks. He turned to address the dozens of others we could only partly see and shouted something to them I didn't understand. In the cell opposite, a woman—she was also tall, but redheaded and pale, did the same to the crowd in her cell, but in a very different tongue.

A full-throated roar of delight split the air. I could see fists pumping the air, people jumping and hugging. There must be dozens of them, at least fifty in each huge cell.

"That's Russian," Caleb said to me over his shoulder. "They're speaking Russian in that cell." He pointed to the left. "Sounds like Hindi or no, Bengali over there." He pointed to the right.

With that, I knew who they were. Pale, Russian-speaking group on the left. Darker skinned people, one with a clipped Indian accent on the right. Russians and Indians, one of each able to also speak English, all tall, imprisoned here for who knows how long.

"Tiger-shifters," I said.

Caleb leaned in, eyes widening. "What?"

There wasn't time to explain it to him, but it all made a weird kind of sense now. We'd seen other once-extinct creatures from Earth here in Othersphere—dinosaurs, giant sloths, dire wolves, and bat-shifters. Now we'd found probably a more recent addition. Tiger-shifters were supposedly gone from our world, wiped out by the Tribunal. Instead, they'd been brought here.

What they were doing in prison cells was anyone's guess.

Somewhere farther down the hall, past the cells, under the cheers and back-slappings, I heard the growl of a big cat. And quiet, deadly paws coming at a run.

"The Amba are coming!" I yelled to Caleb, and pointed down the hall.

His eyebrows came together in a puzzled frown and he turned. The beam of his light skimmed past a huge, striped, four-legged form as it slid around a corner a hundred feet down the hall and shot toward us like an arrow. Behind it there were more.

"Run!" I screamed.

The tiger-shifters in the cells shrieked en masse a half-second later.

Caleb zoomed past me, taking the light with him. "Come on, Dez!" he shouted. "There's no time."

As the light faded away, I saw the hands reaching through the bars, taut, outstretched in terrible desperation. Voices called to me to let them out, to set them free.

Forty feet farther on four tigers, bigger than horses, flew toward me, fangs bared, ears back.

I shifted.

It took no more than a single pulse of my heart here in Othersphere. One moment I was an elongated version of my girl self, the next I was tiger-incarnate.

I had never felt such might, had never controlled my every muscle, every whisker with such ease. Coiled within me was all the potency of the earth beneath my feet, of the air within my lungs, of the great living moon outside. I was a nation, a symphony. And nothing in this world or the next would stop me.

In a single bound I was at the entrance to the cells. The people inside drew back, squawking with fear. The Amba were pouring down the hallway like water unleashed from a dam, two seconds away.

I touched the roots guarding the cell on the right with one paw, and on the left with my tail, snarling a command. They parted for me. I had time to see the astonished faces in the prison cells, time to find the flashing dark eyes of the man who had first called out to me. I nodded to him.

He smiled, and the air around him parted like a curtain. He was a tiger now, too, a Bengal tiger smaller than I or the Amba ahead, but unafraid and ready to fight.

The other tiger-shifters saw and followed suit in both cells. They spilled free like a striped, roaring river. It was an army of tiger-shifters.

The first Amba leaped, fangs bared, right for my throat. I swerved and whomped him in the head with one paw. His neck cracked under my blow, and he fell with a hard thump to the floor.

The next Amba grabbed me with one clawed paw and aimed her canines at my neck. I got my back legs up between us and raked her down the abdomen. She howled, and I sank my teeth into her warm fur. She struggled and kicked, stronger than anyone I'd ever fought before, but I wrestled her onto her back and bore down until the air left her lungs. She lay utterly still.

I looked up, blood dripping from my muzzle, and roared. Arrayed around me like a brood of kittens were the shifters in tiger form, snarling.

The remaining Amba backpedaled, trying to slow their charge, but the one in front couldn't help barreling into the sea of tiger-shifters. They set upon him like hounds on a fox. He reared up, yowling, and flung them off, but others leapt to replace them, and still more were frothing and snapping around the other Amba.

"Dez! We have to go!"

I looked over my shoulder to see Lazar holding Caleb's flashlight, standing where the hallway turned. He'd gone a little pale, and his eyes were as big as the moon as he stared at the mob of tigers.

I chuffed at him, licking blood from my whiskers. It tasted sharper, stronger than the blood in our world. It fed a longing inside me I hadn't known was there. I wanted more.

"The window closes in less than two hours!" he shouted over the snarls and roars.

The window. I'd forgotten about Morfael, Ximon, and the concerns of that world. The caterwauling and wrestling going on down the hallway pulled at my attention.

"Dez . . ." Lazar's voice cut through everything. He was blatantly using all his skill as a caller to grab me. I slid my eyes over to him. He put his hands out, palms up. "We won't make it without you."

The tiger-shifters were swarming the Amba, but the Amba were fighting back fiercely, flinging the shifters aside or shoving them back into the cells. This fight could go either way.

A wolf's howl pierced the sounds of cats' fighting. London was calling me, too. I looked around and found the Bengal tiger I knew, the one who had been the Indian man. He slid down a wall after being thrown aside by one of the Amba and shook his head. All around me shifters were swiftly changing to their human form to heal, and then back into tiger form to fight, as if they'd been preparing for this moment for a long time.

"Dez!" Lazar's voice spoke to me of my home, of my mother, of how it felt when he held me close in my frail girl form, of the hungers I felt then. "I need you."

The Bengal tiger's honey-colored eyes found mine. He saw Lazar, and he saw me, and then he jerked his head, chuffed, and lashed his tail. I read his meaning clear as a book. In tiger form we spoke the same language. *Go, and thank you. We will make sure they do not follow.*

With one last look back at the skirmish, I sprang over the few tigers between me and Lazar and padded after him down the hallway. I was all at sea, leaving behind the tiger-shifters. And I didn't like the way Lazar had stared at me, as if I wasn't myself. As if he didn't know me.

"Wow," I heard Amaris say. "Dez?"

"Wow, indeed," Caleb's face as he gazed at me had an appreciative little smile that made me think maybe I was myself. "Let's go. We'll need to hurry."

They all ran ahead of me, back the way we'd come, but as we came to the terrace and the open air, a strange rumble shook the ground and a small avalanche of dark rocks tumbled down the face of the cliff above us.

"Keep going!" Caleb shouted.

The dire wolves led the way back into the narrower passage, with London, Amaris, Caleb, and Lazar close behind.

But I stopped. A horrible, unnatural thought flashed through my mind, and I pushed my gaze up the rattling cliff, up to the peak that was shaped like an enormous sleeping cat.

The mountain shuddered. The giant stone cat's tail twitched.

That's a mountain. It can't be alive.

I stood frozen, not wanting to believe it even as horror beyond horror overtook me.

The cat was no longer asleep. It stirred, and boulders crumbled away at its sides. The falling debris cascaded down in a landslide as the creature stretched, arching its back.

The moonlight ran along its flanks, illuminating ruddy fur and dark black stripes, touched with white around the paws and throat.

I knew who it was then. Stone and tiger. This world and our world. A nightmare brought to life.

Orgoli. In a tiger form larger than an aircraft carrier. His great head cocked to one side with fluid grace that should have been absurd in a thing so huge. The tail, thick as a redwood, lashed like a whip. The great eyes, glowing like silvered lakes in the moonlight, searched the peaks around it, ears the size of satellite dishes ready to receive any sound.

He hadn't seen me yet. I forced my legs to function and slunk back into the shadows on the terrace, literally shrinking in size as I tried to take in how huge he was, how I couldn't let him see me, how I had to get my friends to safety.

Now.

I vanished back into the mountain tunnels, sprinting after the group. I caught them easily, and unable to speak to them in my tiger form, and nipped at their heels to make them run.

We made our way without stopping through the stalagmite caves and the narrow passages, emerging into the full night of the forest. If we were lucky, Orgoli would waste time searching inside the mountain for us, or perhaps even be stalled by the battle going on between his former prisoners and his guards.

If he found us, we wouldn't stand a chance.

The tiger-shifters deserved a chance to escape, too. I'd released them only to send them into pitched battle and then abandon them. Would any of them survive? My heart ached as we jogged downhill, ignoring the strange songs and flickering light filtering through the trees.

I remembered the fierce joy on the face of the Indian man just before he shifted into his tiger form, and the respect with which he'd addressed me before I left. He, at least, would rather go down fighting. But I couldn't help feeling that I'd found the last tiger-shifters only to lead them into final extinction.

The trees lay behind us as we raced down the grassy slope toward the swamp. London barked at the dire wolves, and they pulled ahead, scouting for dry land much more quickly and accurately than we could. As we skirted a drowsy group of giant ground sloths, the same ones we'd seen earlier, and headed into the mire, I looked back.

The bog lay quiet under the pulsing moon. The faint thump of drums and flutes floated faintly toward the sky. Tiny purple and green lights rose from the waters around us and danced like fireflies. One buzzed past me, looking more like a diminutive person with dragonfly wings and a feral grin than a fly. Or maybe it was a trick of the markings.

"Beautiful creatures," Amaris said as one flew past her face. "I wonder if sightings of them are what lead to stories of faeries in our world."

She kept jogging along, staring at the turquoise light flitting just ahead of her, hypnotized. It circled in closer.

"Ow!" She slapped at her face as a turquoise light landed there. Her hand came away smeared with glowing blue light and blood. The creature, one wing damaged, hissed at her and fluttered away. "It tried to scoop out my eye!" There was a jagged cut near her eyebrow.

A yellow glow and a pink one glided right up to the black dire wolf. He snapped at them, allowing a red one to come at him from another angle. He jerked his head away, but the red light had latched on to his eye. He whined, slapping at it with a paw, until the white wolf bit down, crushing the red light in its teeth. There was a tiny, terrifying screech. Then the white wolf was licking glowing red liquid from its lips with satisfaction.

We avoided the floating lights after that, swatting and swearing if they came anywhere near. Amaris wanted to take a breather and use her healing ability to tend to the dire wolf's eye, Lazar's punctured arm, and all the scratches on Caleb, but none of them would stop.

I had deep gashes in my shoulders and neck from my fight with the Amba, but the brief taste of their blood had been more than enough to refresh and strengthen me. I had to slow my pace to keep behind the others to make sure we weren't being followed. I felt as if I could run forever. If there hadn't been too many of us, I would have thrown everyone on my back and galloped them to Morfael in half the time.

In a small dark corner of my tiger brain, I wanted to taste more of the Amba blood. If I had more, I might be able to grow even larger, run faster. Kill Orgoli. I wanted him dead, but I also understood him.

That's why he ate his children. Their blood, the blood of any Amba, made him stronger, made him able to become far bigger than anyone else. That's why he now ruled over the Amba, and over Othersphere.

What if I killed Orgoli somehow? It didn't seem possible, given his enormous size and strength. But if I managed it, if I ate the one who'd eaten so many himself... how powerful would I become? How much better would this world be without him? How much safer would the world back home be?

You're no better than Orgoli.

But thinking it wasn't the same as doing it.

Right?

We crossed the swamp with only a few scares—toothy creatures snapping at our heels from the water, and one dark swoopy thing brushing our heads with its wings before it disappeared—and entered the Red Wood. The leaves nearest us rustled, as if stirred by our presence. The rustle spread outward from there like ripples in a pond, spreading the word that we were back. Was it a warning to the other trees, or was it like ringing the dinner bell? As we walked, the red leaves tilted and turned, keeping their never-blinking eyes upon us.

To make sure she kept her distance from the thorny grass and white-trunked trees, Lazar gave Amaris a brief recital of the attack we'd faced.

She was touched that we'd all bonded over her. "I know it was just a trick of the mist or whatever," she said. "But when we get home, I'm making you all the biggest Bundt cake our world has ever seen."

"As long as you don't make it in Othersphere," Caleb said. "Where it might turn into a cake with a genius IQ and pointy teeth."

The air did start to smell like a wood fire on a beach at night once we fully entered the wood. Amaris started joking with Lazar about the time they'd tried to get Ximon to roast marshmallows with them over a bonfire at their compound in the desert. When Lazar slowed down and began to fondly reminiscence, Caleb snapped: "Ximon was probably burning books in that fire, too. Now speed up."

Lazar's face shut down, and he accelerated his pace, batting at the mist that wanted to gather around the bandages on his punctured arm. They were seeping blood, and he was looking a bit pale. We needed to get him, and everyone, home fast.

London saw me looking over my shoulder a couple of times and made an inquiring yelp. I was still in tiger form, unable to explain, so I just shook my head. But she started looking back, too.

A distant crack of thunder split through the deadened silence of the wood, and we all lifted our heads. We couldn't
see the eternal storm yet, but I couldn't help feeling that it
was calling out, reassuring us that there wasn't far to go.

"Good thing," Caleb said, looking up from his watch.
"Just five minutes till Morfael has to close the window."

"We'd better run," Lazar said. "Come on!"

The humans broke into a jog, with the wolves and me
keeping up easily. Even though I'd gotten smaller after seeing
Orgoli on the mountain top, my tiger form remained bigger
than ever before. The dire wolves' heads barely reached my
abdomen. I could take one stride for every four of theirs.

The white-trunked trees thinned out and the wind swept
the scent of ozone and rain over us. The blue mist retreated,
and the curtain of dark gray cloud that heralded the storm
was visible above the treetops ahead.

The dire wolves were in front, with London close behind,
staying close to Amaris. Lazar came next, then Caleb, and
me, so it was only Caleb and I who first saw the pale, elongated figure step out from behind a tree and beckon to me.
She wore a cloak woven from golden scales that glittered in
the moonlight over a dress of dark green. Her hair was red
striped with black, the long locks writhing in the wind like
snakes around her narrow white face.

"Sarangarel, my daughter." Her voice was dark and husky,
like a tiger's growl made almost human. "Don't go."

CHAPTER 11

Caleb stopped dead, staring. I was frozen in place.

My biological mother, Khutulun, strode up to me with long, graceful steps. Her feet were shod in sandals made from bark. She came close, looking up and raising one long-nailed hand to stroke the fur on my cheek. Her touch sent a strange shudder through me.

"You have seen him," she said. "Now you know why we need you here."

"Orgoli?" Caleb asked me tightly. "Did you see him here?"

I met his black gaze, and then looked over my shoulder, ears perked for the sound of heavy paws, listening. Caleb frowned, snapping a look backwards as well.

Khutulun eyed Caleb, a small smile on her red lips. "If you wish, your lover may stay here with you."

Caleb let out a sharp laugh. "Dez, we don't have a lot of time."

Khutulun's smile widened. "Or he may go." She turned her tip-tilted green eyes to me. "Whatever you wish, my dear."

I shifted to my human form in a single heartbeat and stood before my biological mother now clad in the soft white thistle-down dress that appeared effortlessly when I needed it. I was taller than she, but otherwise I knew we looked much alike in this world. Here at last I was facing her, the one who gave birth to me. Maybe in her face, her words, I would find a clue as to who I was.

Her face broke into a wide, genuine smile. She leaned in to me. Cold lips touched my wet cheek. "My beauty," she said, then ran a hand over the thistledown clothing that automatically appeared around me. "I see your connection to this world is fully intact again, for the flowers come when you have need of their warmth, just as they always have for the Amba."

I pulled away. Her breath smelled like blood and carrion. It should have disturbed me more than it did. In the corner of my eye I saw Amaris, London, and Lazar turning around to stare.

"Orgoli is here," I said to Caleb. "He's in tiger form and big as a building. You have to get the others away, now."

He was standing very still, his eyes flicking between Khutulun and me. "What about you?"

"She will stay here." Khutulun took my face in her hands and turned my head to look at her. "With those who know her best."

"Do you?" I asked. My whole heart was in the question. "How?"

"I see myself when I look at you," she said. "I hear my own voice, for I created you. You belong here with those who are like you, where the song of making runs through us all. And the song of death. It's all one. And I know—you long to be a part of it."

She was right. The hymn of Othersphere resonated through me. The connection to it, to everything, was intoxicating, yet calming, as if every atom inside me vibrated in harmony with every other atom in the world.

"Dez!" Lazar was running back toward me. "Don't listen to her!"

Khutulun raised her thin eyebrows at Lazar, unafraid. "Or is that the one you wish to keep with you? I don't like him."

"This won't take long," I called to him. "Go! Take the others back home."

"No!" Lazar slowed down but kept coming. "You can't trust her!"

Caleb glanced at his watch. "We've got four minutes, Dez. That's it."

"I just need two," I said.

"Are you insane?" Lazar kept coming. "She's a creature from another world, an alien!" He was headed right for me, reaching to take my hand. I backed up.

Caleb got between us, grabbing Lazar by the lapels. "Dez is from another world too, *brother*. If she wants to talk to her biological mother, that's her decision."

Lazar shoved Caleb away and backed up a step himself, his face flushing with anger. "You can't stop me from helping her."

Khutulun viewed them, amused. She leaned into me, her voice low. "Look how they fight over you, Sarangarel. Many more will fight for your love before you are done."

"I don't like it when they fight," I said.

Khutulun smiled. "Oh, I think you do. I know I did in my day."

I ignored her, yelling at Caleb and Lazar, "Stop it! You need to get out of here!"

"But you like to fight yourself," Khutulun said. "You've tasted the power that victory brings." She raised delicate eyebrows, a knowing smile on her lips. "No longer can anyone keep you away from me, from yourself."

"Morfael told me that you wanted me back sooner," I said. "But it would not have been safe for me to come back then."

Her smile faded. "So your uncle would have you believe. I would never have endangered you."

"Morfael's a good man," Lazar said loudly past Caleb. "Don't let her turn you against him."

"Let her talk to the woman," Caleb said. He was still blocking Lazar from coming any closer.

Lazar looked at him like he was the idiot. "She's vulnerable here! Do you want her to stay?"

"It doesn't matter what I want," Caleb said. "And it doesn't matter what you want."

Khutulun sighed, as if they were boring her. "Neither one is worthy of you," she said. "After you've defeated your father, you will find one who is."

I looked down at her. She smiled. Her incisors were longer than a human's would be, like fangs. I put my tongue against my own teeth. They were the same. She was right. I'd felt it the moment I came through the window. This was the home a part of me had been longing for.

"The power you have here is far greater than anything to be had across the veil," she said. "We are at war. We need you."

"We need you, too, Dez!" Lazar said, trying to move closer again, and coming up against Caleb like a wall. Lazar's fury finally turned on his brother. "Let me talk to her!" And he swung his fist.

Caleb ducked. "Not exactly the time or place for that shit."

London barked. Behind her, the storm clouds swirled forward around her, Amaris, and the dire wolves. Drops of rain hit my face, and lightning stabbed up from the ground right between the brothers, sending them both reeling back. It was as if the storm had read my mind, keeping them from fighting. Then I remembered how the storm had spoken inside my mind. Maybe I could do the same.

"Dez!" Lazar called. "You know that...thing doesn't want you for yourself. She needs you to help her get what she wants."

Khutulun dismissed him with a gesture. "Don't let petty squabbles waste your time. Your true family, your true purpose is here. *You* are here."

I could feel the blood singing in my veins when I was here, and that song connected to everything around me. Here I spoke to storm and water and fellow Amba. There was nothing like that connection back home.

I looked over at Caleb and Lazar, circling each other warily as the rain beat down, brothers who could never truly be brothers. There was nothing like them in Othersphere.

I should stay.

But the tiger-shifters. They didn't belong here. "Did Orgoli bring the tiger-shifters here through the veil?" I asked Khutulun.

"Yes, shortly before you were born." Khutulun gestured with one hand and the wind changed. Somehow the rain started bending around her, leaving us both dry. "The Amba have always tried to save the creatures about to die off in your world. Many shifters, as well as animals and plants have been brought through the veil. This is how we learned to speak like you, and how we know you are not like those genocidal humans."

"That's why all these extinct species live on here," I said. "You were trying to save them."

She shrugged her narrow, elegant shoulders. "It started off as an amusement, I think, millennia ago, but eventually it became a duty. Even as the bright, worked metal of your world encroached on ours wherever the veil was thin, destroying our own species, it allowed us to bring through a few who were about to die out there. Lately, there have been too many to save—humans are ruthless. But at least with our control over the weather, the water, the plants—well, most of the plants." Here she threw a rueful glance at the Red Wood.

"We can find for each species a place where it will not be extinguished."

So that explained the giant sloths, the flying dinosaurs, the bat-shifters. There were probably many others. For hundreds of millions of years, the Amba of Othersphere had been preserving creatures our world thought long gone. Even Orgoli had continued the tradition. "Then why did he put the tiger-shifters in prison?"

Khutulun's thin eyebrows drew together in a delicate frown. "Orgoli has been recruiting shifters to his cause. He thought they would be loyal and mighty because they are much like Amba. But a few moons ago, the tiger soldiers from your world rebelled against his tyranny. He killed many, and then threw the rest in his dungeons, hoping they would rethink their stance. But they are stubborn." She brightened. "They would follow you! As will the Amba who currently follow Orgoli. They will switch allegiance to you easily, for Orgoli is cruel and much hated."

"So that mountain is the home of the Amba," I said. "Where he kept the tiger-shifters imprisoned."

She nodded. The green irises of her eyes were like fractured stained glass of a hundred different shades from emerald to olive. They took on a faraway look. "Our home was beautiful once. He has made of it a charnel house." She focused on me. "With your help, that will change. Everything will change."

London barked. I glanced over, barely able to see her through the encroaching storm. She barked again, clear and short. A warning.

"*Kept* the tiger shifters imprisoned?" Khutulun asked with sudden attention to my earlier words. "Why did you say 'kept' as if they are no longer?"

I paid her no mind. I heard it now. I felt it in the ground. Huge feet were galloping this way.

"Orgoli's coming!" I shouted.

London sent me one laser-blue look, then turned and ran into the storm, herding Amaris and the dire wolves in front of her. With her nose and ears, they would probably find the window, even in the fog.

"Go!" I shouted at Caleb and Lazar. "Get them through the window! I'll watch your backs."

"No!" Lazar shouted, pushing past Caleb finally to grab my hands. The rain had turned his golden hair dark. "You're coming with me."

That's how he was. Always catching me when I fell, always looking out for me. But he was wrong this time. "Lazar," I said, sliding my hands away from his. "You need to let me do this."

Caleb, his dark eyelashes spiked from the wet, raindrops falling from his lips and black sleeves, leaned in and took his brother cautiously by the elbow. "Come on, man," he said. "Dez can look after herself."

Lazar jerked his arm free, turning on Caleb. "You don't want her to stay here any more than I do!"

Caleb's black eyes flicked over to me, their corners edged with something both sad and slightly amused. "Yeah. But what does Dez want?"

I couldn't help smiling back.

Lazar saw the smile. He caught our shared look, innocent though it was. His fists clenched, he roared out in frustration and punched his brother right in the face.

Caleb, caught off guard, reeled back.

"Oh, my God!" I shouted, as Caleb regained his footing and put his fists up. "Will you ever stop?"

The ground shook. Nearby, trees thudded and crashed, wood cracking, leaves rustling as loud as the thunder. Their lidless eyes were staring not at us, but toward the center of the forest. Something immense was running through the Red Wood as if it were a grassy meadow.

I saw Orgoli as a ripple of movement. Black striped orange

fur a blur over the red and green leaves. He neared. The wind from the storm battered the forest more fiercely, hammering down rain and hail upon him.

I am with you.

The storm. I felt its thoughts like a melody in my head.

"You must decide," Khutulun said.

For a moment I thought she meant I had to decide between the brothers. But then, with one blink of her huge green eyes, she was gone. In her place towered a tiger as tall as a mammoth, but longer, leaner, crueler.

She lashed her tail, knocking a tree sideways, and growled at Orgoli's approach.

"You're coming home with me!" shouted Lazar, a desperate look in his eye. He bent low and grabbed my knees, his shoulder at my hips, beginning to lift me over his shoulder like a sack of laundry.

"No!" Caleb reached to stop him, even as I shoved at Lazar's shoulders with all my strength, twisting away.

The nearest white-trunked tree creaked like an old door and then toppled over as a tiger over ten stories tall swatted it aside. His whiskers were the size of logs, his ears big enough for three to walk inside abreast. With an ear-shaking blast he roared at Khutulun.

Lazar teetered backwards at the sight, releasing me. I regained my feet and gave him a shove toward the center of the storm. He staggered and half fell into Caleb, who caught him.

Orgoli's eyes were seas of molten gold. They followed Caleb and Lazar's movements almost lazily, barely acknowledging Khutulun. It was they who had stopped him before, back on Cherry Drive.

Then, almost too fast to follow, one of his giant paws lashed out at them.

In that moment I shifted, jumping to land between Orgoli and the boys. His paw hit me instead of them, like a truck going full speed. Pain knifed through me; ribs cracked. I slammed into Khutulun, knocking her prone.

I'd been expecting that. I shifted back to human. Health, power, complete oneness with my body suffused every corner of me and seemed to pass beyond the boundaries of my skin, rippling out through the world. I bounded to my feet, exhilarated.

"Hey!"

Orgoli's head swiveled toward me, the ears, now dripping with rain, cupped in my direction. Caleb had gotten Lazar to his feet. They were running deeper into the storm. Lazar cast one last look back at me before the clouds swallowed him up.

They might make it out. That thought would once have comforted me, but now everything had narrowed down to this world, this moment: to Orgoli, to battle, and the strength of the storm all around.

The great cat Khutulun stood up behind me. I felt no change in her even, rapid breaths, so she was uninjured. But she was shrinking away from Orgoli. She was afraid.

So was I. My mouth was dry. The rain washed down my face, wetting my lips. But the fear was only one small part of this moment, and it fed my anger, my desire to dominate and overcome this giant before me.

"Sorry to distract you from taking over another world by invading this one," I shouted. The storm all around us beat itself against Orgoli's thickly furred, impervious hide. "Would you like me to stay?"

The monstrous tiger curled one lip in a snarl, revealing fangs as long as I was, and rumbled out a growl that shook the earth. My heart rumbled, too. I flexed my fingers, knowing soon they would bear great claws, claws that would sink deep into Orgoli's skin.

"Thinking about swallowing me whole?" I asked, throwing my arms out wide, internally sending out a plea to the air, the rain, and the very molecules around me for help. I knew without a doubt that the storm would hear me, for we were one. "Go ahead!"

The great head lowered; the vast muzzle opened. I looked

up into the immense maw as it descended on me, hot breath like a slaughterhouse bearing down.

You will not touch her.

With a pulse like the beating of a great heart, an immense shaft of lightning clouted Orgoli across his black nose. His yowl nearly split my ears. He reared back, shaking his head, paws batting at his face.

I shifted to tiger form in that moment. The electricity in the air set my fur on end and jolted me with its vitality. I leaped for Orgoli's throat. It didn't matter that I was one-quarter his size. My teeth were sharp, and I hungered. My claws sank through his fur and into the skin with gratifying ease. I could smell the power inside him. I wanted it, and it would be mine. My fangs sank into his flesh, whiskers guiding me to find a vein.

Hot blood like no other touched my tongue. The richness of it, the liquid force within it smacked of omnipotence. The world teetered around me as I savaged his throat, shaking my head, fighting for more.

Orgoli thrashed, whacking Khutulun again. She flew a hundred feet back. She would have slammed into a tree, but she shifted in mid-air into something with wings and flew raggedly away.

Wings?

Yes, yes. It all made sense now. One day I would have wings, too. If I drank deeply here I could do that—and more. I nearly laughed at Khutulun's retreat. She was a fool not to be here with me, feasting. But I didn't need her. The potency of Orgoli's blood was all I needed. I bit him again.

He howled horrifically and swiped at me. The blow slammed into me like a falling building, knocking the air from my lungs and tearing me off of him. I soared through the mist, into the heart of the storm.

I landed hard. My back snapped, and everything below my waist went numb.

It didn't matter. I licked my muzzle, wanting every drop. I

could still flex my front claws, and they could still rend and find me more blood. I would immerse myself in that power and lose myself there.

"Dez!"

I looked up from licking my bloody paws, ears flicking back with irritation.

"Dez! You've got to shift!"

Through the swirling mist and rain I saw a peaceful night scene as big as life, like a painting someone had propped up in the middle of the storm for my amusement. It depicted a quiet suburban park at night, still wet after a rain.

Quiet, except for the tall, angular figure singing out a vibrant chord of notes. Ranged next to him were four large doglike figures, a girl, and two boys. At their feet was a brown rope, lying as if it had just fallen from their hands.

"Shift, Dez!" The blond boy shouted at me. He started forward, as if about to walk through the painting. Through my drugged haze, I vaguely recognized him, and the dark boy beside him who stopped him.

Lazar called out a note, telling me to shift, to remember my human body, to reject the tiger, to heal, to come back. I knew his intention, but its potential was undercut by its journey through the veil. The song of Othersphere was much stronger. It was pumping through my heart.

I went back to licking my paws, my muzzle, my whiskers. Every drop was another beat of the heart of the world ringing out inside me.

"That won't work," Caleb was saying. He sounded far away, unimportant. "It won't translate across the veil."

Lazar whirled on him "At least I'm trying to help. At least I haven't given up on her, the way you've given up on everything!"

"I am trying to help, you stupid shit!"

To hell with them. Let them argue till the end of the world. I would stay here. I would shift, heal, and drink Orgoli's blood until I was so powerful no one would ever dare cross me. I would grow so large, be so fearsome, that everything and everyone would fear and love me forever.

I licked my paws as the earth trembled beneath me. Orgoli was coming through the storm. With its help and with this new strength I could grow even bigger than he, big as the moon itself. . . .

The air around me sparked. My whiskers fanned out, and a huge fork of lightning thrust down like a spear and struck the ground between my front paws. Heat scorched my face. I shut my eyes and smelled burning fur. Thunder shouted at me; it roared.

Don't be a fool.

The storm.

A deluge of feeling shook me back to pain, to fear, to the realization I was dying. Love and anger flooded through me too. Me, Desdemona Grey. Not Sarangarel. I wasn't only a tiger feasting on her enemy. I was the girl who had climbed the Lightning Tree as a child, who grew tomatoes, hated Las Vegas, who loved animals and my mother and the snow.

The fog parted and a paw bigger than a boulder touched the earth beside me.

I looked up at the tiger towering over me. I could shift to human to heal, then in a blink shift back to tiger, leap on him, and begin the fight again.

I could be Amba. Or I could be a girl.

I shifted back to human, for that was also what I was. My back healed with the change. I could feel my legs, my two almost-human legs. To be completely human again, all I had to do was step through the veil.

Caleb and Lazar had stopped arguing. London barked a command at me. Morfael's eyes were glistening with effort to keep the window open. He beckoned.

The tiger's paw lifted, claws extended.

I jumped through the window, tumbling into the bodies of my friends and my teacher like a bowling ball hitting a strike. Morfael lurched backwards. The note he was singing was cut

off, and the window snapped closed. The rain and wind were
gone, as if they'd never been.

The cold Burbank winter night air was still. All around us,
crickets were quietly chirping.

Gulping in air, I put my hands to the wet familiar grass
and lifted my very sore, very unclothed human body up. I
was tall but no longer filled with otherworldly grace. I
pushed my long red hair, no longer striped with black, away
from my face. Naked after a shift again except for the ever-
present Shadow Blade. No fabulous thistledown gown to
shield me here, but with the Shadow Blade once more on its
belt around my waist.

A long black coat settled down over my shoulders.
Caleb's.

"Thanks," I said, shoving my arms through the sleeves.
Around us, the others were getting to their feet. Morfael
dusted blades of grass off his long sleeves.

"Any time," Caleb said. His dark eyes caught mine with
an intensity that belied his casual words; then he turned
away.

CHAPTER 12

During the drive back from Burbank I said very little. The sudden loss of the music of Othersphere was like going deaf. The metal of the car felt so wrong, so hard. The fake leather of the seats had no inner life, no music to connect it to the rest of the world.

London and Amaris filled Morfael in on everything that had happened while smiling mindlessly at each other, with Caleb and Lazar chiming in with their own funny commentary. The two of them went on to dissect the biology of Othersphere and to speculate how it accommodated the once-extinct species that lived on there. Some of their ability to work together there seemed to have endured the crossing of the veil. The only thing that got through my shock was the pleasure of hearing them finish each other's jokes about the eye-gouging faeries, or speculations about what would happen if a giant sloth had wandered through the window into the park at Burbank.

I woke up the next morning alone in the dorm room. As

usual, I had slept later than everyone else. I forced myself to shuffle up the stairs to the empty dining room and drink a cup of coffee, even though I hated the biting taste. I ate automatically, feeling empty, thinking.

I kept thinking about the tiger-shifters, the looks on their faces when their cages opened.

Then there was that look Caleb had given me after covering me with his coat. It wasn't unlike the look in his eye months ago, a look that was burned into my brain—the look of utter desire and love that had brought him back to this world, the feelings that had kept him from being overtaken by a creature from Othersphere, who, it turned out, was Orgoli.

And there was Lazar, who also loved me, although he'd bitten back the words. A boy who was always there when I needed him, a boy who desired me, too, and who made me feel safe like no one ever had before.

I cleaned my cereal bowl, dried it, and put it away, and saw a half-full bag of chips with the top folded over, neatly clipped closed.

November will polish that off.

I caught myself. November wouldn't be snacking here any time soon. November was gone. I really could've used an infusion of her sarcastic perspective right now. But she hated me.

She and Siku's family were attending the big shifter council meeting to discuss the tribes' uniting against the Tribunal. Something I'd been trying to get them to do for months. But they hadn't invited me. It was hard to blame them now that I'd seen where I came from.

If I'm not a shifter, or a human girl, what am I?

The ground seemed to teeter under my feet, even though all was still. I grabbed the edge of the dining room table to steady myself. Was I Desdemona Grey? Or was I Sarangarel, the Amba who could depose Orgoli's tyrannical rule and set his prisoners free and make things right?

Was I really even a person? It was like I didn't exist.

A door clicked shut nearby and multiple sets of footsteps clattered on the wood floors. I heard Arnaldo saying, "Okay, but just one more bowl of cereal till lunch or there won't be any left for breakfast tomorrow."

He walked in, lean and brown, fresh from outside, leading his younger brothers, Luis and Cordero. He saw me, and his eyes lit up. "Dez!"

I shoved away from the dining table and threw my arms around him, squeezing tight, not caring what his brothers thought. My throat was tight, and I kept my eyes squeezed shut until I could get hold of my emotions.

He hugged me back, laughing a little at my enthusiasm. "It's good to see you, too." He pulled away a little. "I heard you had an interesting time...." And stopped when he saw my face, my lips tight as I fought to hold back tears. "You okay?"

I shook my head, unable to speak.

He gestured to Luis and Cordero, pointing at the kitchen cupboards. "Go ahead and get it yourselves. But just one bowl each, okay?"

" 'Kay!" The boys ran to open the cabinets, and Arnaldo led me into the living room.

We sank onto the sofa and I started to weep. Huge, heaving, ugly sobs wrenched themselves out of me in convulsive waves. Arnaldo just put his arms around me again and let me cry. Eventually, the convulsions ebbed, and he got up to find a box of tissues. As I blew my nose, I started talking, about freeing the tiger-shifters and how it felt to leave them behind, about Lazar and Caleb quarreling, fighting, hating each other, and about how my biological father was a tyrant, a monster.

"She asked me to help her overthrow him," I said, grabbing another tissue to wipe at my eyes. "Khutulun, my biological mother. God, I look so much like her, Arnaldo. It scares me. I kept staring at her thinking—is that me? Is that who I have to become? And she said I had to stay, that I could make things better there. She was relying on me. But then, when Orgoli attacked, she barely stood up to him. She ran away at the first sign of trouble and left me. I knew I didn't stand a chance against him, but I bit him, and his blood..."

I paused, glancing up at his patient brown eyes, staring at me with intense attention. "I'm going to sound like a vampire or something, but his blood was like the other Amba blood times a hundred. Just a taste of it and I felt like I could rule the world. I wanted more. I almost didn't make it back because I was too busy having these crazy dreams of taking over Othersphere and making everyone there stop fighting and behave themselves." I took a breath. "Do I sound like a crazy person?"

Arnaldo shook his head, smiling a little. "No more than usual."

I laughed a little with relief.

"When it comes to Caleb and Lazar, I wish I could be more help," he said. "That's not something anyone else can tell you—how you feel. Caleb pretends he's over you, but that's so obviously not true."

"Really?" My voice was very small.

Arnaldo rolled his eyes. "Oh, please. He protests way too much. And Lazar's pretty obvious, so you don't need me to tell you about that. You're probably going to have to make a choice," he said. "Which sucks, because someone's going to get hurt."

"I hate hurting people," I said.

"Well," Arnaldo appeared to ponder something. "I don't think Lazar could handle a polygamous thing. You know, you having two boyfriends. Or three." As I broke out laughing, he smiled and kept talking. "Caleb—maybe. He's been around, seen the world. But Lazar's got that whole conservative upbringing to overcome."

I leaned back on the couch cushions, giggling at the ridiculousness of it. "Oh, God, it feels good to laugh."

Arnaldo's grin subsided as he thought further. "Here's the

thing I've learned," he said. "People need a leader when they
go into battle or conflict. You've done that for our group for
a while now, and you're good at it. That kind of thing needs
someone in charge, someone making the decisions. If we all
sat around discussing every little move we made during a
raid on the Tribunal, we'd never get out the door."

"But?" I asked. I knew there was more coming.

"But there's a different kind of leadership. I mean, what
you really want is for everyone to be safe, and happy, and
loved, right?" He smiled. "That's why you were tempted to
fight Orgoli. You said you want to use his power to force
everyone to behave the way they should. For the tiger-shifters
to be free, for your biological parents to love you, for Caleb
and Lazar to shut up and get along. You want all of us to
treat each other kindly, to be a family.

"I totally get it, because that's what I want for Luis and
Cordero. Sometimes I order them to stop hitting each other,
or I send them to their rooms. And sure, that's okay when it's
called for. But really I mostly just need to show them I love
them, that I respect them. Tyrants and dictators can't order
people to love and respect each other. You could be a tiger as
big as the world and eat up everyone who opposes you, but
that won't make people act like a family. It'll just leave you
all alone at the end." He shrugged. "Where's the fun in
that?"

A fragile understanding was creeping over me. I sat very
still, trying not to disturb it.

"The good news is that no matter what your mom said
when she tried to make you come home, you know she loves
you. That's not going to change."

"No," I said. "That won't change." I looked at Arnaldo
again, leaning back against the brown couch cushions in his
jeans and worn sweater, all long angular arms and legs, a boy
who had stepped in to take care of his brothers when his father couldn't be a parent. That was real strength, the kind
that mattered.

"Thanks," I said. "I think that helped."

"Oh, good!" He leaned forward, grinning. "Because half the time I have no idea what I'm doing or saying, you know? We're all just fumbling along, trying to make the best of things."

"You fumble along better than most of us," I said.

"I'm not so sure." His face took on a worried cast, his thin lips pressed tightly together in thought. "My dad's lawyer, that hawk-shifter who sits on the North American Shifter Council? I talked to him this morning about a few things, and he told me where the big council meeting is taking place tonight."

"Oh." I didn't say more. I didn't want to push him to tell me where it was. But suddenly, more than anything, I thought that we all needed to be there. The future of the otherkin depended on what happened in that meeting, and my friends all deserved to be a part of it.

"It's happening in the Sierra Nevada mountains, about four hours' drive from here," Arnaldo said.

"Oh, sorry." Lazar had walked in, with Amaris and London close behind. They were unzipping their jackets, cheeks flushed from being out in the cold.

"Did I miss a morning class?" I asked.

"Just tracking in the snow," Amaris said, taking off her gloves. "Morfael said not to disturb you. It was mostly catch-up for me and Lazar, since we don't have extra sensitive noses or hearing like you and London."

"But I went along anyway," London said, and took Amaris by the hand.

Amaris smiled and pulled London's hand to her heart. Their eyes met. "I don't want her to be too far away just yet," Amaris said. To London, she added, "I feel safer with you there."

A huge grin was taking over my face. Lazar looked down, as if to give them some privacy, but he also looked a little uncomfortable. The warmth between the girls was palpable.

They were just holding hands, but the way they looked at each other spoke of something much deeper and more intimate.

London's electric blue eyes shot over toward me shyly. She wasn't used to being openly affectionate with anyone in public. But I was happy to see she didn't let go of Amaris's hand. "Want some cocoa? I'm making some."

I shook my head. "No, thanks. You guys go ahead."

Amaris tugged on her, and they vanished down the hallway toward the kitchen. November wasn't here to do it, so I waggled my eyebrows at Arnaldo the way she would have.

He exhaled a laugh and said, "Finally, right?"

"How are you, Dez?" Lazar asked, taking a tentative step toward me. "Did you sleep well?"

"I'm okay." Feeling a little weird around him, I gestured at his arm, which no longer had a bulky, blood-soaked bandage wrapped around it. "Did Amaris heal you?"

"Yeah, all better." Lazar hesitated, his eyes darting over to Arnaldo.

There was an awkward pause.

Arnaldo's eyes zoomed back and forth between us, until, with a smothered smile, he got off the couch. "I'd better make sure Luis and Cordero aren't eating everything in the fridge."

As soon as he walked out of the room, Lazar crossed the open space between us. "I'm sorry," he said. "I overreacted yesterday. I see that now."

"Thanks," I said. It was a relief to talk about it. "There was a lot going on, for all of us."

He nodded and sat next to me, looking down so that his dark blond eyelashes brushed his slightly tan cheeks. "I could see that you were different there. You were . . . magnificent."

My heart jolted in my chest. I couldn't speak.

"Not that you aren't amazing here, too." His lips, plusher than Caleb's, lifted in a self-deprecating half-smile. "But it was scary to see that you might belong somewhere that I didn't. I was afraid I'd lose you. That's why I acted the way I did." He lifted his eyes to mine, not smiling. "But Caleb was right. It's not up to me to decide where you belong, or who you belong with."

I put a hand on his arm. "You did it because you care. And you're probably right about my biological mother. She sure turned tail and fled fast when things got tough."

He put his warm hand over mine. "I just don't want to make your life any more difficult or get in your way."

"Are you crazy? You've helped me these last few weeks more than I ever thought possible." I scooched closer to him, so that our heads were inches apart. "Please keep getting in my way. I like it."

He leaned his forehead against mine, his shoulders relaxing. "Will do."

"Are you a little uncomfortable with what's going on between Amaris and London?" I asked, keeping my voice very low.

He leaned back, eyeing me with appreciation and chagrin. "Do you think Amaris noticed?"

"I think she's too happy and grateful to notice anything other than London's big blue eyes," I said. "You want your sister to be happy, don't you?"

"Of course." He looked down at our intertwined hands. "Some of it is the strangeness of seeing my sister be in a relationship with anyone. This is her first."

"Sure," I said. "And?"

He took a deep breath, exhaling in a sigh. "I was raised by a terrible man, who taught me to judge and kill and hate. He said such relationships were an abomination, sinful. And I know he's wrong. I see how happy Amaris is and I feel in my heart how wrong he was. But . . ." He couldn't finish.

"It's hard to escape an upbringing like yours," I said. "You should be proud of how far you've come."

"I have far to go." The muscles in his jaw clenched. "Amaris and London are another reminder of that."

I kissed him on his cheek, feeling the recently shaved smooth skin under my lips. He smelled like warm, freshly dried laundry. I remembered another time, when the two of us had stood facing each other in the laundry room of a Vegas casino, and he had told me his darkest secret. "You give me hope," I said. "For all of us."

He was staring at me with wide, almost childlike eyes, and the longing in them nearly made my breath stop. "How did I live before you?" he asked, his voice as soft as down. Then he leaned close and pressed his lips gently, almost reverently, to mine.

"It's okay," I said against his mouth. "We'll be okay."

He shook his head, tracing my lower lip with his fingers. "Whatever happens, you must know I will always love you."

I slid my arms around his neck, and he kissed me again, deeper now, more urgent. He wrapped both strong arms around my waist and crushed me against his chest, kissing me with an edge of desperation I'd never felt in him before.

A door opened nearby, and a buzzer sounded, startling us out of the kiss.

I looked up to find Caleb standing there with fresh snow on his black hair and the shoulders of his coat, looking right at us with a face that seemed to be carved from marble.

Next to me, Lazar's shoulder muscles tensed as he saw his brother. I flushed, my cheeks ablaze. I wanted to pull away from Lazar, to deny what Caleb had just seen, but I forced my body to stay still. This was the reality, and withdrawing wouldn't change that. It would only hurt Lazar, and he deserved better.

For a long, horrible moment, nobody moved.

The buzzer went off again. Someone was calling via Skype. Caleb's dark eyes moved from me curled up against Lazar to the computer. His expression hadn't changed, but I could tell he was being careful not to give anything away.

Arnaldo clomped down the hall from the kitchen and tapped the keyboard to see who was calling. "Holy crap," he said, sharp eyes looking over his formidable nose at the three of us. "It's Ximon. Again."

"He's alive," I said, trying to reason through the emotional tumult going on inside me at several different levels. I disentangled myself from Lazar. "Unless . . ."

"Unless it's Orgoli," Caleb said at the same moment, taking off his gloves and crossing the floor to the computer.

"I'm putting him on the big monitor," Arnaldo said, typing. "Amaris, London!" he yelled down the hallway. "It's Ximon calling if you want to come see. Or not."

"Again?" That was London.

"Coming," Amaris called down the hall, and then lower, to London: "I have to see his face."

Amaris and London clattered into the living room as Ximon's face appeared big as life on the huge monitor on the wall.

Amaris gasped. Her father's cheeks were hollow, his skin a yellowy-gray. His once large, glittering eyes had sunk deep into their sockets, and his lips were cracked and peeling. For the first time since I'd known him, he wasn't wearing a white turtleneck, but a dark blue T-shirt and a gray jacket, which hung loosely on his thin shoulders. He looked like he was dying.

But his dull eyes lit up as they caught sight of Amaris on his own monitor. He leaned in, squinting.

"Is that you, Amaris?" His once sonorous voice cracked with effort and emotion. "Are you safe?"

Amaris grabbed London's hand as if for strength, looking up at her father resolutely. "Yes, Father. I'm fine. My friends brought me home."

"Thanks be to God," Ximon breathed, shutting his eyes with seeming heartfelt prayer.

"And to the rope we found in your basement," London said.

"I was wrong about you," I said to Ximon. "Where are you now?"

Ximon opened his eyes. Behind him were the wood grained cabinets and mock-marble counters of a generic suburban kitchen. "In one of the Tribunal safe houses in Pleasanton, not far from where you saw me last," he said. "I came to myself here sometime last night and found these clothes, but I'm afraid to leave, in case the creature possesses me again while I'm walking or driving."

"That would correspond to about the time Orgoli showed up in Othersphere," I said in a low tone to the others.

"Did you say you saw him in the other world?" Ximon asked. "Did you defeat him?"

Lazar and I exchanged a look. "No, Father," Lazar said. "We helped Amaris escape, but the creature, Orgoli, was too powerful to fight."

Ximon groaned. "Which means he'll be back in here soon." He tapped his own chest and swallowed, his jaw trembling. I saw for a moment a deep, terrible courage in his lusterless eyes, a look I'd seen on Caleb and Lazar's faces at times. "I must tell you what I've learned."

"Do you know what his plans are?" Caleb asked.

Ximon nodded. I moved to the edge of the couch, stifling my instinct to scoff. Given what he'd been through, it made total sense that Ximon was helping us. It was like we now had a spy inside Orgoli's camp, albeit one who could only report in during the brief intervals when Orgoli was back in his own world.

Ximon's hands moved underneath the monitor, as if gathering something, and then he lifted up a stack of papers and tapped them on the table before him to get them straight. His every movement seemed to take concentration. "The creature continues to inhabit my body because the objurers still loyal to the Tribunal think he is me, and will do all that he asks. He has received a report back from our connections inside the National Ignition Facility, which is . . ."

". . . where the world's most powerful laser is kept." Arnaldo said, finishing the sentence.

Ximon nodded. "Exactly. He had hoped to steal the laser somehow, or to duplicate it, but the latest report indicates that would be nearly impossible to do by stealth, given the extreme level of security at the facility."

"What does he want with the laser?" Caleb asked.

"Always so impatient, so reckless." Ximon's cracked lips twisted in a strangely fond smile. "I'm getting to that. Since he cannot steal it or duplicate the machine quickly, Orgoli plans to storm the facility with his remaining Tribunal troops and use the laser to open a permanent window between our world and Othersphere. This will allow him to bring through demon troops, which he plans to use to subjugate this world and destroy its technology."

"Dear God," Amaris whispered.

I stood up. "When?"

"Tomorrow," Ximon said. "Tomorrow night, after midnight."

"That gives us time to . . ." I stopped myself, looking at Arnaldo. We could go to the shifter council meeting tonight, but I couldn't tell Ximon anything I didn't want Orgoli to know.

"Why tomorrow?" Caleb asked.

Lazar shot him a look of understanding. "Yes, why is he waiting till then?"

"I . . . I can't be sure." Ximon's brow wrinkled as he shuffled through the papers in front of him. "I have only seen his e-mails, sent out to the remaining objurers in the Western half of the United States and Canada, calling them to arrive here tomorrow morning for a . . ." He focused on a paper in front of him, reading out loud, " 'the definitive infiltration and appropriation of the NIF's laser technology by midnight of the date in question.' " He looked up at us. "The date is tomorrow, midnight."

"Maybe he needs time for his troops to get there?" Caleb asked, looking at his brother for his thoughts.

"Possible," Lazar said. "Did he send out e-mails or make

calls to his associate Bishops in Asia, Europe, or South America?"

"I didn't see any e-mails going out to them. He might've made calls. . . . I don't remember. But then I don't remember a lot." Ximon brought a glass of water from off camera and took a noisy sip. "He did get an e-mail from the Bishop of Northeast Asia, which he hasn't answered, telling him his recent actions haven't been authorized by the Assembly of Bishops, and that he could be subject to demotion if he disobeys. But, of course, this creature cares nothing for the Assembly, and so far it's a first warning and sent only to him. By the time the Assembly sends a second warning out wider, the deed will be done." He uttered a frantic little laugh. "Normally, I'd be worried about his actions leading to my demotion. But that's the least of my problems now."

"Do we have time to go get him?" Amaris asked, her voice almost too soft to hear.

"To get Father?" Lazar asked, voice incredulous. "Why?"

"He needs help," Amaris said, shrinking back from him a little. "Look at him."

"Help?" Lazar's face had drained of all color, his brown eyes dark as he stared at his sister. "Where was he when Mother needed help? Where was he when she was screaming in pain, dying before our eyes?"

"I know, I know!" Amaris put up her hands, as if to ward Lazar off, even though he hadn't moved toward her. "But shouldn't we try to be better than he? Shouldn't we do for him what he would never do for her?"

"You don't know, sister," Lazar said, half choking. "You don't know the half of what he did. Or you would never ask me that question."

Amaris frowned and took a tentative half step toward Lazar. "Lazar—what . . . ?"

"We can't risk going to get him," Caleb said. "I'm sorry, Amaris."

"But..." she started to say.

"He's right," I said.

London squeezed Amaris's hand, and Arnaldo was nodding, his face very serious. "We can't risk your father turning into that creature anywhere near us right now," Arnaldo said. "He'd kill us all."

"They're right," Ximon said. His broken voice was unexpectedly tender. "You must stay far away from me. All of you. But thank you, Amaris, my daughter. For allowing me to see your compassionate heart remains, in spite of all I've done." He carefully, meticulously arranged the papers in front of him with shaking hands, blinking back what might have been tears in his suddenly too bright eyes. "I wish I knew more about their exact plans for the attack on the NIF, but at least now you know the basics. Lazar will tell you the capacity and breadth of our weaponry. There are fewer than fifteen objurers working with him as I speak." He looked over his shoulder. "The e-mails indicate perhaps twenty more will arrive for the infiltration tomorrow."

"Those numbers are low," Lazar said. "Have there been a lot of defections?"

"Ever since the debacle at the particle accelerator, the number of recruits and objurers has diminished considerably," Ximon said. "I am scheduled to go before the Assembly next month to explain the low numbers, the recent failures." He smiled, tired lines creasing around his eyes, but with a flash of his old ultra-white-toothed arrogance. "I don't need to worry about that any longer."

"Father..." Amaris started to say.

Ximon coughed, a deep-chested, body-wracking cough. It was the sound of weakness, of exhaustion, of the human body near the end of its strength.

He controlled the cough and jerked his eyes up to the camera. Sparks of gold and green shot through the brown irises. His nails looked like they had grown thicker, longer.

"He's coming. Must go," he said, his voice thick. "I'll try not to let him find out that I've told you anything for as long as I can. He mostly ignores my thoughts now anyway." He put a hand out and touched the monitor, as if reaching for the faces of his children. "Good-bye. Pray for me."

The screen went black.

CHAPTER 13

There was a long moment of quiet after Ximon ended the Skype call. I looked over at Amaris. Tears were running down her face. London had both arms around her shoulders, holding her tight. "Why am I crying?" Amaris asked. "I hate him."

"Because he's your father," London said.

"He loves us," Caleb said. "Or as close to love as a man like that can get."

"Why is he so awful?" Amaris asked, but not as if she expected an answer.

Lazar was looking off into the distance, brows drawn together. "I wonder," he said, "what his father did to him."

Caleb's dark eyes flashed over to his brother's face, startled. Amaris put a hand over her mouth, pushing down her distress. The three siblings, for a moment at least, exchanged long questioning glances.

"Did you see anything like troops while you were in Othersphere?" Arnaldo asked, pulling everyone's attention back to the present. "Ximon said Orgoli was planning to bring troops over from Othersphere once he used the laser to open the permanent window. But who could he be talking about?"

"He has the tiger-shifters locked up for a few months now because they didn't want to be his troops," I said. "But other than that . . ."

"There were the dire wolves," London said.

"But you took care of that," Amaris said, wiping at her wet face and trying to smile.

"There could be more of them," London replied.

"There are still Amba loyal to him, according to my . . . to Khutulun, anyway," I said.

"I'm guessing troops that Orgoli would have aren't the traditional type to be housed in barracks or on army bases," Caleb said. "Othersphere is too different. They would be other animals, or . . ."

"The bat-shifters?" I asked, remembering the human figures in the trees that had shifted before our eyes. "If they were brought over by the Amba hundreds of years ago, they might still be loyal."

"Exactly." Caleb shot me a look that said I'd just completed his thought. "And they might not be the only ones."

"If the Amba have been bringing shifters over before they went extinct in our world for that long, he could have hundreds of different types loyal to him now," Arnaldo said. "What if there were dinosaur shifters?"

London blinked. "Wow. T-Rexes storming down the suburban streets of Livermore, California," she said.

"Pterodactyls over the Golden Gate Bridge," Caleb said, nodding. "People in San Francisco only think they've seen it all."

I said nothing, thinking about the tiger-shifters. It was almost too bad they'd rebelled against Orgoli. If they'd remained loyal, they'd have a chance to come home.

I looked up to find Caleb's thoughtful eyes on me. The look there made me blush unexpectedly. I dipped my head down so no one would see. He said, "You want to go back, don't you?"

Lazar turned to me, taken aback. "To Othersphere?"

I didn't say anything. I didn't want Lazar to feel bad, but Caleb hadn't even had to ask. He knew me so well. His black boots took a few steps toward me. "We could send you through again," he said.

That brought my head up, eyes blazing up at him. "Do you think . . . ?"

He was nodding, a little smile on his lips. "There's time before the attack."

"What?" Arnaldo was also puzzled. "Why? We have that shifter meeting tonight."

"Oh, right." I slumped a little, my stomach sinking with disappointment. "I need to go to that meeting tonight and warn them. Maybe they'll help us against Orgoli."

"That's right!" Arnaldo said. "I know where the meeting's being held."

"It's going to be tough to convince them there's a threat out there bigger than the Tribunal," I said. "But we have to try."

My skin prickled. I looked up to find Caleb staring at me again with an intensity I didn't understand.

I tilted my head at him inquiringly. He frowned, his dark eyes darting over to Lazar, still standing next to him. Was that a guilty look? Or an angry one? He turned away, saying nothing, and I didn't know what to think.

"November will be there," London said. "She's seen Orgoli in action. She'll back us up."

"So at least maybe the rat-shifters and bears will help," Amaris said.

"We'll need to get going in the next hour or so," Arnaldo said. "It's a four-hour drive."

"Okay." London tugged on Amaris's hand. "Let's go get ready."

"There's got to be more we can do," Arnaldo said, as the three of them headed down the hall. "What if I called in an anonymous bomb threat to the NIF? That'd get them to beef up security at least. Luis! Cordero! I need you downstairs right now please."

The boys' feet pounded down the stairs after them. Caleb and Lazar were still standing in front of me, side by side.

"I'll talk to Morfael," I said, standing up and trying to sound as if my heart was in it, as if my very bones weren't dragging with weariness and a desire to be elsewhere.

Caleb made a tiny move toward me, beginning to lift his hand, before he stopped himself and stuffed that hand in his coat pocket. "Maybe you can go after all this is done," he said.

I nodded, staring at the floor between his feet. "Maybe."

"Why would you want to go back there?" Lazar came closer to hunker down in front of me, his eyebrows drawn together in concern. "I know it's where you're from originally, but Orgoli and his people tried to kill you."

I was too tired to explain. How could he not understand, after seeing all those tigers trying to free themselves, seeing them fight alongside me?

"It's the tiger-shifters," Caleb said, his voice flat, as if he too were suppressing some kind of emotion. "She wants to bring them home."

I gave him a brief, grateful smile.

Understanding dawned over Lazar's face, quickly overtaken by something closer to dismay. "Of course." His voice sounded odd, distant. His glance went from me to Caleb, and then back to me. "I should have realized."

"It's okay," I said, and suddenly wished to be anywhere else. The tension between the brothers, the strange glances between me and Caleb just moments after he'd seen me kissing his brother—it was all too much. I needed to go outside to clear my head.

"Was Morfael outside?" I got up, pretending not to notice Lazar as he reached a hand toward me, and moved toward the front door, grabbing my coat from the rack.

"Yeah." Caleb watched me go, not moving. "Over by the stream last I saw him."

I reached the door before Lazar caught up and touched my shoulder. "Hey. Are you okay? I'm sorry if..."

"Don't be sorry." I turned back to him as he automatically reached for my coat, helping me into it. Back in the living room Caleb cast a glance at us and then walked away.

Lazar saw my eyes looking past him and turned in time to see Caleb's black coat disappearing down the hall. He shook his head.

"What?" I asked.

Lazar gave me a melancholy smile. "I still don't know you as well as he does."

"What?" I didn't quite know what to say to that. So I shook my head dismissively. "Don't be silly."

But it's true.

"You should go back to Othersphere, if you want," Lazar said.

"I do want," I said. "But right now we have to get the shifter council to listen to us. They may hate me, but I think I need to be there because I..." I swallowed. "I know the most about Othersphere."

"And about Orgoli." He nodded. "Do you want me to come with you to talk to Morfael?"

"I need a minute," I said. "I'm sorry. It's just...a lot right now."

"Yeah." He nodded and tried to smile. For a moment he looked as he must have as a little boy, putting on a brave face. "I'll go pack."

I leaned in and kissed him. I meant it to be a quick kiss, but he took my shoulders in his hands, pulled me close, and kissed me hard and hot. One of his hands slipped down to my lower back, pressing my whole body against his.

For the first time, I was a little hesitant to kiss him back. I needed space, not touching right now. But I allowed myself to melt into him. Supporting my upper back with his other hand, he bent me over backwards, like a sailor giving his sweetheart one last kiss before he boards his ship.

"Good-bye," he said, and released me slowly as I came back to my senses.

"I'll be right back," I said, not sure what I was reassuring him of. I needed to be alone, to have time to think, to understand.

"Sure." He backed away, not smiling, his brown eyes big and bright on my face.

I opened the door and the cold winter air rushed over me like a sigh of relief. I stepped out and pulled the door shut, pausing as the flurry of flakes whispering down from the sky skittered over my cheeks and stuck to my eyelashes.

It must snow in Othersphere, I thought as I made my way toward the creek. Caleb had called forth a snowy scene once for me when we were in Vegas. It had looked a lot like the woods here in the Spring Mountains, only with taller, older trees and white hares as big as poodles.

It felt so good to be outside, to breathe fresh air and hear my boots crunching through the snow. I tilted my head back and stuck out my tongue. Darts of cold hit it as snowflakes melted. Then I stopped moving and listened.

It wasn't Othersphere, but for a moment I thought I could hear the snowflakes tumbling gently through the air, hear their waltzing dance as a breeze swirled them around. The tree branches creaked softly, the pine needles murmuring from branch to branch.

Maybe this world had a music to it, too. It was just buried deeper, tougher to find.

As I walked, a stocky little bird with a bright blue back and rusty vest landed on a branch near my head, a round, reddish-black berry in its beak. I recognized it from my lessons with Morfael as a male Western Bluebird, native to this part of the world.

"Hello," I said softly.

It fixed its bright black eye on me, and then took off toward the creek. I followed, and kept spotting its deep-blue wings fluttering ahead of me. It turned right before hitting the water, and I went with it. Sure enough, thirty yards later, I saw a lean, black-clad figure crouching by a tree. It was Morfael, his bony white hands gently moving aside some snow. He stood up as the bird flew right toward him and landed on top of his carved wooden staff.

The bird chortled quietly, not moving as I walked up to my teacher. *My uncle.* At his feet I saw some green stems tipped with yellow.

"The primroses are about to bloom," he said. "I know I shouldn't help them, but I couldn't resist clearing away some of the snow."

"Do you miss Othersphere?" I asked. "Since you can never go back?"

"At times," he said. "Each world has its own beauty."

"I wish I was there right now." I looked up at the bluebird, still perched on his staff. "But it scares me, too."

Morfael considered me, still as a statue except for his eyes. "You can go back. You are part shadow walker."

"I could go back?" I asked, my heartbeat picking up speed. "Now?"

He shrugged. "It was the others who needed me to open a window for them, and the rope, to ease their transition. You may part the veil and walk through whenever you wish, but with a cost."

I didn't respond at first, thinking. "It'll be more difficult each time, won't it?"

His lips crooked upward. "Yes. Because most of you is genetically tied to Othersphere, leaving there will require more effort each time."

"And it wasn't easy the first time," I said.

"Precisely."

"Is that where I belong?" I asked. "Am I meant to go back there and just . . . stay?"

Morfael reached up and gently stroked the bluebird's back

with one long finger. "I have never been one to believe that anything is meant to be.' " he said. "But I have no evidence of this, only a feeling. So I tell you not as a teacher, but as your uncle, that I was born between the worlds, that my heritage speaks of constant travel and exploration, of never staying in one world for very long. I did this for most of my life until I came here, with you. I have remained in this world for nearly fifteen years, longer than I've ever stayed anywhere, and I have never been so happy."

I found that I was smiling. Morfael had never spoken before about his own feelings. It warmed me through and through. "How does someone know where they'll be happiest?" I asked.

"I'm not sure you do," he said, "until you try it."

Trust Morfael, and life, not to have any easy answers. "I do know I want the tiger-shifters to be free, to come back here, if that's what they want. At least they should have the choice."

"But?" He arched one colorless eyebrow upward.

"But we have to warn the shifter council meeting tonight because Ximon called." And I told him everything we'd learned. "Will you come with us to the meeting? I think you carry a lot of weight with them, even if they are kind of afraid of you."

He nodded. "And after that, I will go with you to this facility Orgoli is planning to take over. Opening a permanent door in the veil is a drastic violation of the fabric of both worlds."

Relief washed over me knowing he would be there, even as his words filled me with new anxiety. "If he succeeds in making this door, is there any way to close it again?"

"I won't know," he said with a ghost of a smile, "until he tries it."

The council meeting was taking place in a lodge off of Pine Creek Road in the Eastern Sierra Mountains, not far from

the town of Bishop, where Morfael had briefly been hospital-
ized a couple of months ago after the Tribunal attacked his
first school.

We were piled into the SUV, jammed in tight together along
with our gear as we turned down Pine Creek Road, passing
brown desert scrub and the tiny mining community of Rovana.
Ahead, the Eastern Sierra escarpment rose abruptly, brownish
red near the bottom, transitioning quickly to thick white on the
peaks, still thoroughly coated in February snow.

We wound higher; the road got narrower, and trees green
with pine needles sprang up around us. At the narrow turn-
off we spotted a large man with his long black hair tied into
a ponytail keeping watch from the shadows. He was barrel-
chested and wearing only a flannel shirt and jeans in the
below freezing weather. Probably a bear-shifter.

Arnaldo spoke to him, dropping the name of the hawk-
shifter Alejandro, member of the local council, and the man
waved us past. The dirt road led to a snowy meadow turning
pink in the last rays of the setting sun. It bordered a thick
pine forest and a large building made out of rough-hewn
logs. A battered sign in front read: BEAR CREEK SPIRE LODGE.
CLOSED FOR WINTER.

The parking lot was already full of trucks and SUVs, and
the shuttered windows on the lower floor leaked a lot of
light. Two people at the entrance, a man and a woman, eyed
us suspiciously as we piled out. Arnaldo ran up to speak to
them. As I stepped out into the crisp air, my crazy hearing
caught the sound of applause coming from the lodge and
then a familiar voice speaking.

London's wolf-shifter ears were almost as sharp as mine.
"Is that November talking?" she asked. "This I've got to see."

We clattered up the wooden steps to the lodge, and the
guards waved us through, giving Morfael wary glances, but
saying nothing to stop us.

The reception area just inside was deserted, including the

check-in desk and the long tables set with plastic cups, water pitchers, and large plates of half-eaten meat and cheese.

Brighter light filtered through the closed double doors to the left, along with November's voice.

"If a rat-shifter like me can hang out with Siku's family of bears, if Siku and I could fight alongside a wolf, an eagle, and a fricking tiger-shifter . . ." she was saying as we headed for the doors.

Arnaldo pushed the doors open as we entered a large room filled with people on folding chairs, all circled around a worn podium, where November was standing without a microphone, still speaking. ". . . then why can't all shifters of all tribes come together just once to destroy the enemy that wants to destroy us?"

Applause broke out, but not everyone was clapping.

At our entrance, heads turned. Next to Arnaldo, London was striding with her three dire wolves trotting around her, then me and Caleb, Amaris, Morfael, and Lazar shepherding Luis and Cordero. We'd agreed in the car to let Arnaldo get the council's attention, and then for London to tell everyone about our trip to Othersphere and the threat Orgoli presented. As the "purest" shifter who had actually been to Othersphere, London would be considered the most trustworthy and legitimate among those of us who had been there. She'd protested a little at first at taking on such an important role, but with encouragement from us all, particularly Amaris and the unspoken pack support of her dire wolves, she'd finally said yes.

As callers and Tribunal-connected people, Morfael, Caleb, Lazar, and Amaris would be considered less trustworthy by a crowd of shifters, and so agreed to remain more in the background unless they were needed. I, as a pseudo-shifter, would hover somewhere in between.

There had to be over a hundred people in the rough-hewn ballroom, some standing along the walls or sitting in the aisles, and most of them seemed to be holding out phones, tablets, or laptops so that friends and family back home could watch and listen in as well.

"It's the tiger-shifter!" a woman exclaimed nearby.

"Those aren't wolf-shifters," someone else whispered as the dire wolves passed.

People on the far side of the room started to stand up to see what the fuss was about, and November frowned, looking around for the disturbance, until her shining brown eyes landed on us.

"Holy shit!" she said, which caused a ripple of laughter and more heads to turn.

"Sorry to interrupt," London said, projecting her voice almost too loudly in her nervousness. "But we've got news all of you should hear."

"Not all of these people were invited here," November said. "And not all of them are shifters."

"We're all otherkin," Arnaldo said. "One way or another."

A woman with short gray tufted hair in a big blue flannel shirt and jeans stood up from her chair next to the podium, and I recognized her as Jonata, the lynx-shifter who represented the big cat tribe in the local council meetings. "Desdemona? It's good to see you. We were just about to hold a vote."

"Before that, we need to tell you about an impending attack," I said.

"Attack?" a man asked from the crowd.

"From the Tribunal?" someone else said.

Arnaldo and London had reached the podium. "Kind of from the Tribunal," Arnaldo said.

"But kind of not," said London.

"Let us explain," I said, moving up near the dire wolves, who stood around London like a furry phalanx.

"You don't have any right to speak here," November said. "You're not even really a shifter."

"That's funny," I said. "You were just talking about working alongside a tiger-shifter. Did you meet another one somewhere I haven't heard about?"

"Let them talk," said a man with a piercing voice, seated next to Jonata. I recognized his hooded eyes and long face. It was Alejandro, the hawk-shifter from the local council who'd helped Arnaldo gain custody of his brothers while their father was in rehab.

"Agreed," said the small woman next to him, pinning up her slippery black hair. She smiled at me, and I smiled back in recognition. It was the rat-shifter from the local council, who along with Jonata and Alejandro and a few other bear and raptor-shifters, had fought beside us in the desert outside Ximon's particle accelerator, where Siku had died. "These are the young people who engineered the Tribunal's great defeat near Mercury, Nevada," the rat-shifter continued. "And who burned down their compound in the Mojave desert before that. I think they've earned the right to speak."

Next to the rat-shifter I saw the wolf and bear council members look at each other, frowning, but they didn't object. They were probably curious to hear what we had to say before they shot it down. The rest of the audience, roughly equally male and female, murmured and moved restlessly in their chairs.

"The majority of the council agrees to let these people speak," said Jonata, moving a few feet away from the podium. "Ms. Anderson?" She leaned in toward November, who hadn't budged from where she stood. "Please allow your friends the podium."

"Friends!" muttered November, but she shuffled to the side.

"Yep," London said in a low voice only those of us near the podium could hear. "We're your friends whether you like it or not."

Arnaldo moved up to the podium, pointing to a spot on the floor to indicate where his younger brothers should take a seat. Lazar ushered them over there and sat down next to them. Amaris followed suit. Caleb stood off to the side, leaning against a wall along with a bunch of very tall, broad-shouldered people who were probably bear-shifters.

"Fellow shifters and guests," Arnaldo said. "We've uncovered a new kind of threat, one that comes not just from the Tribunal, but from Othersphere itself."

The murmuring in the room ascended to a rumble. London moved to take Arnaldo's place. Her knuckles gripping the sides of the podium were white, but her voice was strong and more assured with every word. "We were just there, in Othersphere. We've seen the threat. We know it's real."

"What are those?" asked a man seated nearest the head wolf-shifter. "They're not like any wolves any of us have seen, and we know wolves!"

Sharp laughter and shouts of "Yeah!" came from the group around him. They must be the wolf-shifters, one of the most distrustful tribes because they'd always been specially targeted and visible, often mistakenly labeled werewolves. They were another good reason to make London our main advocate. If we could win over the wolf tribe, we'd win everyone.

"These are dire wolves," London said, placing her hand on top of the head of the black dire wolf seated on his haunches next to her. "A species that lived here in America about ten thousand years ago. They followed me back from Othersphere."

Growls of disbelief reverberated off the walls.

"Bullshit!" shouted the wolf-shifter leader. His thick reddish hair stood nearly on end, his sideburns bristling. "They're some new kind of dog the humdrums have bred so they can pretend to be ordering wolves around."

"They look a lot like the drawings of dire wolves in the Tar Pits Museum," a woman's voice said from the wolf crowd.

Arguments broke out all over the room, loud enough to

pull Jonata back to her feet and slam down the wooden gavel sitting on the podium. "Quiet!" she shouted.

The noise lowered to a buzz. "We have voted to let them speak." She turned to London. "Tell your story, Laurentia."

I'd almost forgotten that London's given name was a long Latin mouthful that translated into "wolf." London nodded to Jonata gratefully, caught Amaris's encouraging eye, and then said, "It began when a girl from our school was kidnapped. This is Amaris, and she's the daughter of Ximon, the notorious Tribunal Bishop you all know and hate."

"You brought a Tribunal member here?" The wolf-shifter council leader stood up, incredulous. "Traitor!"

Someone else called out "traitor!" too and others started to argue with them. The group of wolf-shifters was a roiling sea of confusion and anger. I wondered if any of them were London's estranged family.

London watched them, breathing hard, and then her ice-blue eyes narrowed in a look I'd seen in her wolf form just before she attacked.

"Let me speak!" she barked.

As if on cue, all three of her dire wolves threw their heads back and howled.

The wolf-shifter crowd went silent as a windless night, every eye wide and staring as the three great wolves sang a keening, haunting cry of wild nights hunting under the moon, of pack and cub, of loss and birth. My skin pricked with gooseflesh at the melancholy, sacred sound.

London placed her hand on the head of the black dire wolf, and all three let their yowls trail off. Every person in the room sat still and quiet.

"As I was saying," London continued. Her voice was still strong, but there was a tiny smile at the corners of her mouth. "Amaris left the Tribunal, along with her brother Lazar, because they wished to escape their father's abuse, and to learn the ways of the otherkin. Then Amaris was kidnapped by Ximon, or so we thought..."

And so London told the story of how we'd figured out that Ximon really was possessed by a creature from Othersphere, how Morfael had opened up a window to that world, how I'd commanded the storm, and how the calling abilities of Lazar and Caleb had allowed us to track Amaris to her prison, and to defeat the deadly creatures who tried to kill us.

"You would've loved it there," I muttered to November, who was listening with an expression that managed to combine severe irritation and wonder. "London's wolf form was as big as pony, which means your rat form would be . . ."

". . . huge." November's irritation increased, but her eyes were full of longing. "Oh, man, that would've been cool."

"We missed you," I whispered. "And we could've used your unique brand of encouragement, let me tell you."

"Oh, shut up," she snapped, but quietly, as London continued to talk. "You can't win me back with your feeble attempts at flattery."

"And I can't believe you weren't there to witness London and Amaris holding hands," I said.

She gaped up at me, the irritation wiped off her face. "You telling me Wolfie's finally getting laid?"

I waggled my eyebrows at her, and she snorted. "That explains why she's all alpha and in charge tonight."

"Maybe," I said, still keeping my voice down. "I think her friendship with you taught her a lot, too."

She snorted again, but with less conviction. I nodded toward a tall, handsome bear-shifter couple along the wall behind Caleb. The man had familiar deep-set eyes, sharp cheekbones, and long straight black hair.

"Are those Siku's parents?" I asked November quietly.

"Yeah," she answered. "His brother and sister are seated in the row beside them. Great people."

"We'd love to meet them," I said. "If that's okay."

"Actually," November hesitated, and for a moment I worried she was going to refuse. But her cheeks colored pink, and she said, "Actually, they asked to meet all of you, too. I think it might be nice for them, to talk with you guys. About him."

"It'd be nice for us, too," I said.

She didn't respond, listening to London talk about finding the tiger-shifters in their cells. But warmth was spreading through my chest, and I felt happier than I had in a very long time.

London was doing a great job. November even stepped up when London asked her to confirm that she'd seen Orgoli in the house on Cherry Drive. That seemed to convince a lot of people that Orgoli actually existed, and that he was indeed using the Tribunal and Ximon.

But when London got to our most recent conversation with Ximon, when he'd told us about Orgoli's plan to attack the National Ignition Facility in order to use their laser to open up a window to Othersphere, the crowd muttered restlessly.

Jonata shushed them, which allowed London to finish. "So we need to make a plan to stop him before he brings an army from Othersphere through the veil that could destroy us all."

She stepped back from the podium to an uneasy quiet. Jonata moved up. "I believe a proposal has been put forward that we table the plans to attack the Tribunal and focus instead on this invasion from Othersphere."

A bear-shifter stood up in the crowd. "Why should we bother? This NIF laser is a humdrum project, guarded by humdrums. They're the ones whose property will be destroyed; assuming it's not another trick of Ximon's. Let the humdrums deal with it."

"Yeah," a wolf-shifter shouted in agreement. "They've never helped us. Why should we help them?"

"They don't even know about us," Arnaldo said.

"They don't want to know about us," countered the wolf-shifter. "Let them deal with the consequences."

"We can't leave it to them. They're unprepared. And Orgoli has a history of subjugating shifters," London said. "He
kidnapped and imprisoned all the remaining tiger-shifters.
We'll be the first people he comes after."

"It's probably another one of Ximon's tricks!" shouted a
rat-shifter. "Maybe he's in league with this thing from Othersphere."

"In that case, we have even more reason to go there," said
London. "You want to put a stop to the Tribunal? Well, it's
locally been taken over by Orgoli. Two birds with one
stone."

"Odious expression," said Alejandro the hawk-shifter
under his breath.

"It sounds like we'll need each tribe to vote internally and
then have their representatives convene tomorrow morning
with their decision," Jonata said, half turning to us, but speaking loudly enough to make it an official announcement. "This
is a lot of information."

"Yeah, never going to happen," said the wolf-shifter council member, standing. "I can tell you that right now."

"What a crock," said a rat-shifter to his group. Everyone
was standing up, ending their phone calls, stretching.

Laughter. "Tigers as big as mountains," said another.
"Come on!"

"Wait!" I shouted. "We can't take that long to decide. Orgoli's attacking the NIF tomorrow night. We need to make a
plan now!"

There were more sarcastic mutterings and dismissive ges-
tures. The wolf-shifter leader shook his bristly head, grinning
to show sharp canine teeth. "You overplayed your hand,
tiger-girl. Nobody's going to risk their life because your crazy
daddy's coming to town."

More laughter.

A distant, terrible scream tore through the hubbub. The
sharp-eared crowd of shifters cocked their heads or jerked
their gazes toward the parking lot, alarmed.

A dull, constant thud above us got louder. I recognized it instantly.

"Helicopter!" I said, raising my voice over the sound of its approach.

"The Tribunal?" November said.

With a terrible rattle of gunfire, the wide shuttered windows behind the podium burst inward. Burning pain shot through my thigh and shoulder as I threw myself to the ground. All one hundred people in the room did the same, shouting in alarm.

"It's Orgoli," Caleb said. "He's found us."

CHAPTER 14

Bullets clattered through the windows again, sending shards of glass and wood knifing through the room. I'd crawled behind the podium somehow, even though my shoulder and thigh felt as if they'd been punched and my sneakers were shredded.

My friends and most of the folks on the ground had gotten down behind chairs for cover, but I heard a few cries of pain. The wolf-shifter from the council had a deep bleeding cut down his back, and Arnaldo's arm was sliced open near the shoulder. Amaris elbowed her way over the debris-strewn floor and laid her hand on his arm, but he shook her off, pressing against the wound. "I'll be shifting any second," he said.

Caleb's gaze traveled over the blossoming blood spreading over my shirt and my pants leg. "Dez, you've got to shift."

I looked down and saw that I'd been shot. No wonder crawling had been so difficult. I tore my eyes away from my own blood. That could wait a moment. "Now we know why Orgoli was waiting till tomorrow to attack the NIF. He knew about this meeting, and he wanted to wipe out as many shifters as he could here, all at once."

Caleb looked up as the helicopter thumped closer. "He's got something big planned."

My leg was numb and slippery with red. Pain surged so acutely I had to focus so as not to vomit. Close by, London was crouched over the black dire wolf where it lay still in a spreading pool of blood. Arnaldo crawled across the floor to his brothers, yelling in his piercing tones, "The plan we talked about—now!"

Luis and Cordero, lying on their stomachs on the floor, tore their eyes from their older brother's wound and shifted in a blink into brown eagles, too young to have white feathers on their heads. Leaving their clothes in a puddle behind them, they heavily took wing and flew out through the double doors.

The helicopter's blades slashed closer to the roof. Something above whistled through the air, falling.

Morfael's pale gaze lifted, and with a sudden gesture, he raised his staff. Caleb saw him, and as Morfael sang out, hard and fierce, Caleb's voice joined in, blasting out the same edgy note.

The roof exploded. Fire erupted like a Las Vegas fountain. Burning chunks of wooden logs and metal shrapnel burst toward us. The crowd, with no time to move, screamed.

But the flare of flame curled and recoiled as it hit something else. The splinters of wood and flashing metal slammed into an invisible wall created by the note that Caleb and Morfael were singing, and were repelled.

A bomb. The helicopter had dropped some kind of bomb on us, expecting to kill everyone in the room. Only Morfael's presence and quick thinking, with Caleb's help, had saved us all.

The room surged with fur and feathers as people broke for the double doors, shifting as they went. Near Caleb, Siku's family and those around them warped into their bear forms and began smashing at the side windows with their paws, peering through the broken glass, and then ducking down as bullets answered back.

A few shifters roared, cheered, and cawed their delight and anger up at the black body of the helicopter, now completely visible as the debris from the explosion slid down the clear shield in an arc to land harmlessly on the floor.

Lazar was focused on it, his brown eyes glinting gold. "It has a shadow!" he shouted toward Caleb. "But it's hard to see."

Caleb frowned up at the whirling bladed thing, humming, his eyes sparking the same bright yellow. "We can call it forth," he said to Lazar. "If we all do it together."

"Like in Othersphere." Lazar nodded.

"Morfael?" Caleb eyed his mentor.

Morfael narrowed his gaze up at the flying machine. "Rare for such technology to have a shadow. All the metal will make for a good challenge. Let us begin."

He sang out a low, strangely amorphous note. Caleb, listening hard, added his own voice at an even deeper register, drifting up and down a semi-tone. Lazar concentrated, staring up at the hovering copter, and then called out a third note to complete the chord. Together, they formed a complex foghorn effect, both soft and penetrating, deep and simple. It enveloped the roof like a gauzy blanket.

One of the objurers on the helicopter had surveyed the lack of casualties below and yelled something to his compatriots, reaching for an automatic rifle.

"Get out, everyone!" I shouted.

"Hurry!" Arnaldo echoed, moving forward to shove people through the double doors.

The room was emptying fast, bodies, human and otherwise, pressing against the doors. Two of the smaller black bears had made it out of the side windows without getting shot.

The foghorn note grew in volume. The three men intoning

it had moved closer together, gazes directed upward. The objurer above shouldered his rifle and took aim right at them. I could hear the story behind the song now, fainter than it had been in Othersphere, but still there. It spoke of a clumsy metal bird that couldn't fly who longed to become one with the sky. Then he sacrificed his life for his family and he was reborn. As a cloud.

The sound altered by one note, reaching a crescendo. Morfael pointed his staff at the helicopter, and a black, cloudy ray shot out of the staff, pushed by the voices of the callers, and struck the nose of the machine.

With a hiss of air, the helicopter vanished, replaced with a small, puffy white cloud such as you might see sailing through the blue sky on a summer's day. It looked out of place hovering so close to the ruined roof of the lodge.

The objurers didn't have time to register the shift. Their helicopter had been transformed into a cluster of white vapor. All four plummeted fifty feet down, screaming. They crashed through the broken, bombed roof of the conference room to hit the floor with a hideous wet smack in the center of the room and lie still.

Nearby, Amaris and the other two dire wolves barely noticed, gathered around London and the black dire wolf. Amaris buried her hands in the dark fur and closed her eyes, a peaceful look coming over her face. For a moment hope surged in me. Amaris was a healer, and if the dire wolf was still alive, she could save it.

But Amaris's mouth turned down, and her eyes when she opened them were filled with tears.

She didn't have to say anything. London bowed over the dire wolf, hands clutching his fur, and the other two dire wolves did, too. Then London threw her head back, teeth bared, and shifted into her shining, silver wolf form. She wasn't as big as back in Othersphere, but she was still a head taller than the dire wolves. Growling, she leapt through the shattered shutters, breaking away the remaining glass. The other two wolves arced after her. A second later, a man outside cried out, and was quickly silenced.

"Dez, you're hit!" Lazar had run over to me, grabbing Amaris to bring him with her as he did so. She followed him, wiping her bloody hands on her jeans, her pretty face drawn and worried as her eyes kept darting toward the windows, hoping for a glimpse of London.

"I'll shift in a second," I said. "Have you got any silver ammunition in the car?"

He looked confused. "Yes, but against objurers...oh!"

Amaris grinned, getting it the same moment her brother did. "Orgoli. He may look like Ximon, but he still hates silver." She got to her feet, and Lazar did the same, both crouching to keep their heads low.

"Good idea," Lazar said, and then he leaned in and kissed me, hard and fast. Something almost sad flickered behind his eyes, which then was banished in favor of his game face. "Now, do us a favor and shift, okay?"

"You got it," I said. As they turned to head out the doors, I shouted, "Lazar! Amaris!" They paused, looking over their shoulders at me. "Stay safe."

Amaris nodded, smiling. But Lazar's face was deadly serious, the look of a man who might have to kill the thing that consumed his father, and thus kill his father as well. He set his jaw. "See you outside."

Electric agony lanced up my leg, and I reeled, dizzy. It was time. I sought the black heart inside me, the window to Othersphere that always chafed and churned there. Now that I'd been to the other world, I could practically smell that stormy air, hear the faint strains of the concert of creation there.

It was done. I was as I should be, sleek, strong, and striped. I stretched, arching my long back, digging my nails deep into the wooden floor, feeling the pain-free power in my legs, the grinding might of my jaws, the sharp tips of my fangs ready to bite. I shook out my whiskers and turned my ears to catch Morfael's voice speaking urgently to the council leaders with Caleb standing by.

I paced up to hear him tell the council leaders they needed to gather their people to counter the remaining attackers. Even the wolf-shifter had his red-gray head bent, listening.

"Cats into the wood to the west of the parking lot!" Jonata shouted at the retreating backs of people, mountain lions, bobcats, and lynx. I caught sight of a jaguar, too, up from South America. The cat faces with their triangular noses, their gold and green eyes, turned to her, listening, and then like liquid, they wound their way through the legs and bodies around them.

"Rats to their vehicles!" announced the young lady rat-shifter. "Through the windows, my friends!" She grinned, and then she was gone, replaced by a huge black rat with a pink nose. Like a furry tide, the rats in the crowd poured out of the cracked windows.

Bullets clattered against the walls, but were stopped by something invisible before they reached the rats, vanishing as if into an invisible shield. Morfael was holding his staff out in that direction, humming lightly. I'd seen him do it before, only now I understood—the bullets were shooting through the veil, into Othersphere. So the rats, staying low to the sill, moving too fast to tell one from the other, swarmed outside. A woman's voice called out in bewilderment. A high, horrible screaming cut across the night, and the guns went silent.

The hawk-shifter council member had no bird-shifters to command nearby. His people had been the quickest out the doors. He nodded to Morfael, shifted, and flashed out the window after the rats.

The bear-shifter leader morphed into her grizzly form, nearly as big as Siku, and tore off the last bit of her blouse with her teeth. Most of her people were heading out already. I spotted a large brown rat on the back of a grizzly, probably

November catching a ride on one of Siku's family, as it loped out the double doors.

The wolf-shifter was frowning, watching his fellow council leaders go. The wolves were by far the largest group still in the room, howling and whining to each other, waiting for their leader's decision.

A loud bark sounded from the window. London's head appeared above the sill, her blue eyes gleaming. Every wolf in the room turned to stare, tails high as question marks. London gave them a low, commanding howl, and then bared her fangs at the council leader.

He lowered his head, eyes slitted, and growled back, still in human form, and transformed into a ruddy wolf as big as a Great Dane. In one bound, London sprang over the sill and was on him. Her teeth fell upon the ruff of fur at his neck. He was stocky and muscular, but London used her long legs for leverage, as Morfael had taught her in class. She forced him onto his side, growling, and held him there.

The other wolves circled them, yapping, and a second later the council leader whimpered, his tail curling between his legs. London shook him hard one more time and released him. As he got slowly to his feet, the wolves around her wagged their tails, coming up to lick her legs and yip their approval. It all happened so fast. One second she was fighting the council leader, the next she was leading him and the others back out the window, where her dire wolves were waiting.

If I could have smiled as a tiger, I would have. I purred instead.

"She has done well," Morfael said to me, Caleb, and the empty room. "I believe the shifters will be more than a match for the few remaining Tribunal members. Their organization is no longer the force it once was. With Ximon not quite himself, it's in disarray."

"They haven't recovered since Dez tore them apart back at

the particle accelerator," Caleb said, his eyes coming to rest on me.

I chuffed at him, purring louder. It was an admission from him, that my idea to raid the particle accelerator wasn't a failure after all.

"Let's hope this is the beginning of the end," Caleb said. "But also, Orgoli didn't count on you being here." He turned to Morfael.

Morfael didn't acknowledge the compliment. His glittering eyes were narrowed at the broken windows, assessing. "There is still cleaning up to do. Finish this quickly," he said. "Once Orgoli realizes that Ximon's Tribunal troops have been neutralized here, he will bring his Othersphere troops through the veil ahead of schedule."

Caleb took a deep breath, a line appearing between his dark brows. "You think he'll go right for the laser tonight?"

Again, Morfael did not bother to reply. He expected us to keep up with him now. "Be careful. Orgoli won't take this kindly," he said.

"Careful's my middle name," Caleb said with a grin, taking a book and a small pack of cards out of his pocket. He looked at me, hefting them like weapons, the smile hardening into the fierce, joyful determination I remembered from our times in battle together. I whipped my tail, a purr rumbling through my body as I sprang into action once more with Caleb, something I hadn't ever hoped to do again.

Morfael was already gliding out the double doors. I ran to the broken front windows and put my front paws on the sill to survey the scene, Caleb striding up beside me.

The rats had swarmed over one of the white Land Rovers the Tribunal had positioned in front of the windows. I could barely see the automatic rifle they'd mounted in front of the moon roof under the teeming fur and whiskers. Not far from there, a white pickup truck with the windshield smashed in was surrounded by London and her wolves, who were finishing off the three objurers there.

Thirty feet back and to the side was another white Land Rover with a man standing up through the moon roof, firing an assault rifle at the mountain lions, grizzlies, and lynx pouring out of the lodge's front door. The bullets hit three that I saw, but their friends dragged them behind other parked cars where they could shift and heal.

Farther out in the parking lot, I could see Lazar and Amaris over by our SUV, putting together a long, shiny gun.

Because they'd survived the bomb, the shifters had been able to effectively neutralize the Tribunal with very few casualties. I saw Lazar aim his gun at the man with the assault rifle and fire once. The man's body shuddered as the bullet hit him in the center of his chest. He crumpled without a sound. The cats and bears slinked closer as the driver of the car fumbled to get the car in gear, hauling on the wheel.

"Where is he?" Caleb asked under his breath.

I was wondering the same thing. Orgoli was nowhere to be seen.

"Either he's in that car"—Caleb pointed to the Land Rover with the man and the assault rifle—"or he's hiding nearby, watching."

My ears turned, scanning to catch the slightest giveaway sound amidst all the scuffles, rendings, and gunshots. As soon as Caleb said "hiding," I felt that's what Orgoli would be doing, allowing his Tribunal men to do the dirty work. He wouldn't want to draw upon his otherworldly powers around them, lest they realize he wasn't Ximon after all.

My eyes settled on the dark woods to our right, which began a few feet from the slushy parking lot.

"If I were Orgoli, I'd be close to nature," Caleb said. His dark eyes were resting on the same patch of forest. "Hiding in the trees."

I meowed, and jumped lightly over the windowsill to land in the parking lot. The snow on the ground was covered in paw prints. If anyone came by here tomorrow, they'd have to wonder at the comingling of wolf and lynx, of bear and rat.

Caleb followed. As we ran past the churning mass of wolves, the remaining Land Rover pulled out of its parking space. Its back wheels spun on the slippery ground; then it took off with a squeak.

But not fast enough. A brown streak of mountain lion and a grizzly the size of a small shed, moving faster than its size would seem to allow, reached the back end of it. The lion used the rear bumper to launch itself onto the car's roof, clawing through the open moon roof. After the cat was up, the bear leaned onto that bumper and bounced the rear end of the car on its tires like a basketball.

The lion hung on as the car bounded up and down, rocking the two objurers inside. That gave a smaller black bear time to run up and slam its right paw into the driver's side window.

The glass smashed inward. The driver tried to duck, but I saw his terrified, bloody face gaping back at the toothy muzzle at his window. The black bear opened its jaws and lunged for his throat.

"Guess we don't need to worry about that car anymore," Caleb said as we got to the edge of the parking lot. Overhead, several raptors were circling, wings wide.

We turned to the thicket of trees, bordered by a meadow to our left, but stretching out as far as my excellent night eyes could see before us.

I tuned out the sounds of final struggle going on behind us and concentrated on the woods as I scanned, looking for anything too regular in shape, anything that might be a vehicle, or a person. I could hear Caleb's even breathing and how his battered dark coat slid against the crisper cloth of his cotton shirt.

Other things were breathing, too, over fifty feet away, deep in the woods. Three hearts were beating somewhere behind a clump of fallen logs and bracken. I ruffed gently at Caleb, stepping forward on silent paws. I didn't have to look at him to know that he was letting me go first because I was the one with the superior hearing and sight, because I was the one able to move as silent as the moonlight.

He let me get about fifteen feet ahead of him, then he, too, stepped as quietly as he could onto the snow-covered pine needles that carpeted the forest floor. He had the paperback book in his right hand, and the playing cards in his left. To someone who didn't know how callers could pull the shadows of ordinary objects from Othersphere, it would have looked completely incongruous, even comical, as if he and the huge tiger were headed into the woods for a game of bridge or a book club. I didn't know what the book and cards could become, but if Caleb brought them, they must be useful.

I didn't approach the screen of logs and bracken directly, but circled around to the side, avoiding stepping on any noisy sticks, my tail snaking through the low bushes. Caleb moved very quietly for a human, and his black coat helped him blend into the dark places between the gray trees, but to my tiger ears his movements were as clear as gunshots. At least I knew exactly where he was, in case he got into trouble, and Orgoli was probably using Ximon's inferior human ears at the moment.

The three heartbeats remained in place as we approached, with no change of rhythm. Wood creaked as someone leaned on it. Something flashed like a glass reflecting moonlight, and I paused. Caleb straightened behind me. His breathing sped up.

I focused, and edged closer, and human shapes came into view. The three figures were in the dark, using binoculars to peer through the spaces between the fallen logs that lay piled haphazardly between them and the parking lot.

We stood twenty yards to their left. If they turned, they would see us, but their gazes were fixed ahead on the rout of the Tribunal forces. It was the lens of one of their binoculars that had caught the light through the branches above. About thirty yards back, a dark-hued truck sat parked, empty, on a dirt track.

I smelled gunpowder and traced the outline of shoulder harnesses and guns on two of them. Long rifles were laid on the logs beside them. The third man stood a little apart from them, both feet on a log so that his white-haired head was higher.

It was Orgoli, still wearing Ximon's body like a Halloween disguise. Perhaps he didn't wear a gun because he was from Othersphere and, like me, he had a tendency to destroy worked metal.

Was there anything left of Ximon in there, as he witnessed the death of so many of his followers at the hands of the otherkin? Whether Orgoli succeeded or not, we were witnessing the end of the Tribunal's power on this continent. Did Ximon know that as Orgoli stared out at the slaughter through his eyes?

One of the men grunted in disgust at what he was seeing and grabbed the rifle at his side. He shouldered the butt and slid the tip through a hole between the logs, squinting through the sight.

"Don't be a fool." It was mostly Ximon's deep voice, speaking quietly, but now that I'd heard Orgoli speak, I felt the difference in the vibration in my gut. "One gunshot will bring them all down upon us."

"How can you just stand there and allow this?" the objurer hissed. "Your plan has destroyed us!"

Orgoli took the binoculars away from his face. It was very dark, but my tiger eyes saw clearly that although he was not happy with the outcome, he wasn't horribly distressed either. "There was no way for me to know Morfael would be here," he said. "My spies told me that shifters don't trust his kind, and he wasn't invited. I knew the girl and her friends were strong in battle, but I underestimated their ability to bring the otherkin together. In all the Tribunal's research, they never anticipated this." He turned to the two men. "It's more your failure than mine."

"The research is yours," the other objurer said, and by

her voice I could tell she was female. "All of it was directed by you."

Caleb placed the hand holding the playing cards on the top of my head, hefting the paperback book in the other. Our gazes met, and he mouthed, "Close your eyes," slowly shutting his own eyes as he did so. I looked back quickly at Orgoli.

He was smiling with Ximon's teeth, a hungry smile. "No, it was not my research."

"But . . ."

"Come!" He began to turn toward us. "We need to get to Livermore. Now."

I closed my eyes.

Beside me, Caleb's body coiled and threw the book. Simultaneously, he called out a single bright note. I wished I could see the expression on Orgoli's face as he heard it, as he turned toward the sound he knew had to be the voice of Ximon's son.

The back of my eyelids flashed brilliant white, and instinctively I scrunched them closed more tightly. The book Caleb had thrown must have been a dazzling light source in Othersphere.

Orgoli cried out a sound like a combination of Ximon's scream and a tiger's painful roar. The male and female objurers also yelled in surprise and pain.

"Open them slowly, but go!" Caleb said to me.

With my whiskers fanned out and my ears cocked, I was nearly as functional blind as I was with sight. If I could get Orgoli before he shifted into that glassy black rock form, I just might be able to take him. He cut off his yell quickly and took quick, fumbling steps toward his car.

I could see it in my head, exactly where he stood. In a split second, I mapped out the route I would take, moving around the tree directly ahead of me, leaping over that bush, and then . . .

I took off running. The light still beat against my eyelids, so I kept them tightly shut. I dodged around the pine tree, feeling its branch brush over my back, exactly as I'd anticipated. As I jumped over the bush, I heard Ximon calling out, "Shoot! Shoot them, over to the left!"

I heard the objurers fumbling with their guns. One already had a rifle in hand, but both would be shooting blind. I had only one more leap. Ximon's footsteps moved faster, tripping over logs.

But the air in front of me was warping, changing. A breeze brushed my whiskers that shouldn't have been there. It smelled of a forest older than this, of a river. . . .

I slowed and cracked my eyes open. Light flooded my senses, but I was ready, focusing only on the area where I knew Orgoli to be. A man-shaped form stumbled across my vision, blurry still, but it was he. I gathered my muscles to leap, pulling my lips back in a ferocious snarl, so ready to sink my fangs into the man who had killed Siku, who had kidnapped me and Amaris, who had tortured his children and forced Lazar to murder his own mother. In my tiger form I had no doubt—Ximon would die as I killed Orgoli. That was as it should be.

My eyesight sharpened, and I saw where the breeze was coming from. Orgoli had opened a window to Othersphere. It was small, three feet high, three feet wide, but he stooped and was halfway through it. If I leaped upon him, my momentum would carry us both through. Since we both had shadow walker blood, we didn't need a rope or anyone's help to step into Othersphere.

In a split second I had to decide—go through the window and possibly kill Orgoli and Ximon with the blow, or if I failed in that, be stuck there with an Orgoli fortified by Othersphere, an Orgoli I couldn't kill if he became a tiger the size of a mountain.

"Dez!" Caleb called. There were other sounds, behind

him. The two objurers had gotten their guns. They fired once each, but I heard the bullets whistling past Caleb.

The bright light went out. Nothing but moonlight. My pupils opened wide. I knew I had to do everything I could to kill Orgoli, no matter what the risk.

Everything seemed to slow down, each moment fraught with meaning and decision. I turned to get one last look at Caleb, to say good-bye with a glance before I pushed the monster through the window and went with him.

Let's be done with this.

Caleb was looking right at me, his face falling into lines of horror as he saw what I was doing. I saw love, acceptance, and terrible, terrible loss.

He was probably going to lose me if I went to Othersphere now and faced Orgoli. I was going to die. He knew it, and he would never get over it.

But he accepted it.

I knew in that instant that I loved him more than I'd ever loved anyone or anything. This was the boy who knew me best, who loved me no matter what my shape, who would fight by my side without me asking, yet knew when I had to travel my own path. He wasn't perfect, but he was the one for me.

The one I would probably never see again.

At the same time, in my peripheral vision, I saw the objurers raise their rifles. The woman aimed at me. The man pointed his rifle at Caleb.

One bullet would not kill me. I had only to shift.

But at that distance, so very close, the shot would kill Caleb.

The window to Othersphere was five feet away. Orgoli had only one foot left in this world. If I was going to kill him, I had to do it now, while he was still in his most vulnerable, human form.

But if I did that, Caleb would die.

He's going to die anyway.

There wasn't time to save Caleb, but I couldn't vanish and just let it happen.

My momentum kept me charging forward, but instead of going through the window, I leaped right over it, swinging my hindquarters around so that I faced the way I'd come, flying backwards.

As I landed, the window snapped shut. Orgoli was gone.

Caleb looked taken aback. He didn't understand why I hadn't gone. Then his dark eyes swiveled to see the muzzle of the gun pointed at his face.

I wasn't going to make it. Even as I gathered every fiber of my being to leap upon the objurer firing at Caleb, I knew I couldn't stop it.

Something else was going on, farther away. Footsteps were running toward us. I couldn't tell exactly, and it didn't matter. Caleb was about to die, and I loved him, and he would never know.

He turned his eyes away from the gun and looked right at me. Something in his eyes, still sparking with gold, told me that he knew. He saw my love for him in my own eyes. He felt it.

The female objurer moved to keep me in her sights. The male objurer's finger tightened on the trigger as he stared down his barrel at Caleb. I jumped for him.

A gunshot rang out. Caleb's face took on a startled look.

But he was still standing. No bullet wound appeared on his body; no blood blossomed on his clothes.

The male objurer collapsed. The rifle fell from his hands as I dropped to the ground beside him. He was dead. A bullet had buried itself into his temple.

Somehow Lazar was on top of the pile of logs holding a long silver rifle. The barrel was still smoking as he swiveled and fired once at the female objurer. She fell over, a red hole in the side of her head, her eyes still open.

All I heard for a moment was my own breathing, my own heartbeat.

Then there was Caleb's heartbeat, his blood pumping safely through his veins. He stared up at his brother, who hoisted his rifle onto his back and climbed down off the logs.

"You guys okay?" Lazar asked. Behind him, Amaris's concerned face appeared as she climbed up and over the log pile. "We saw you walk into the woods and figured we'd follow in case you needed help."

"Glad you did." Caleb strode forward and held out his hand. "Thanks."

Lazar looked a little startled at the gesture. As he shook Caleb's hand, an incredulous smile crept over his face. "You're welcome."

I bounded over and butted my head into Lazar's side. He laughed, grabbing the fur at my neck. "You, too."

"Where's Orgoli?" Amaris asked, coming to stand with us.

"Stepped into Othersphere," Caleb said. "Pesky shadow-walker abilities. But he'll be back soon. He said something about attacking Livermore now, tonight. Didn't he, Dez?"

He turned to me. His cheekbones were slightly flushed from the excitement, his black and gold eyes bright. They seemed to speak without a word, reminding me of all that had passed, also unspoken, between us just now.

I couldn't contain myself. I purred and pushed my head against his waist. I wanted to shift, to be a girl again and throw my arms around his neck, to whisper that I loved him in his ear. But the lack of clothing I would have in my human form, along with the presence of Lazar and Amaris, would have made that more than a little awkward.

Especially because Lazar was my boyfriend, and he'd just saved Caleb's life.

Caleb laughed, scratching the ruff of fur at my neck as he knelt down and kissed my forehead. "I know. It's kind of hard to think about strategy and our next move after all that."

"All what?" Amaris asked.

"Oh, man, you should have seen it!" Caleb stood up. "Just as Orgoli was about to step through and vanish into Othersphere, Dez was jumping for him. It was fifty-fifty whether she'd get to him while he was human and take him out, or if they'd go through the window together and he'd shift into mega-tiger first. I thought . . ." He paused for a second, and it sounded like his voice nearly choked up before he got control. "I thought she was gone, and then she saw that guy with the gun aimed at me and let Ximon go. But she couldn't have reached him." He turned to Lazar. "You saved my life."

Lazar's direct brown eyes were moving back and forth between me and Caleb, looking very serious. He reached out and shook Caleb's hand again and said, equally seriously, "That's the least I could do."

Caleb shook his hand back, and I could see him regaining control, recalling that Lazar was my boyfriend, that he and I, until so very recently, had been estranged. "What's the situation in the parking lot?"

"So far, everyone's okay. Let's get back there," Amaris said, leading the way back around the pile of logs. "But London and the shifters seemed to have everything under control."

"She'll be pack leader next," Caleb said.

"You know it." Amaris smiled proudly.

"I think the council leaders are trying to reconvene in the parking lot, once we're sure there's no further threat," Lazar said. He looked down at me. "You're sure there's no one else in the woods back there?"

I nodded in my awkward tiger way. I'd detected nothing but the very empty car back there.

The front porch lights were still glowing on the lodge and they showed the giant empty hole where the roof of the conference room had been. The windows and their shutters were gone. The parking lot was a tangle of fur, the sky still teeming with raptors. Those experienced with Tribunal attacks had already dealt with the bodies, for they were nowhere to be seen.

I spotted Morfael, tall and skeletal among the sinuous animal bodies, saying something to a grizzly bear. The lynx-shifter of the council, now back in human form and sporting another flannel shirt, was walking up to them as the hawk-shifter spiraled down. Clumps of people were shifting near their cars or hunting for keys and clothing in the wreckage of the conference room.

"I'll tell Morfael what happened with Orgoli," Caleb said, breaking off from us. "Dez, you're going to shift before you go, right?"

He knew what I intended to do, of course. Caleb always seemed to know without my telling him. Lazar looked down, his jaw clenched, as if he also understood.

"Go?" Amaris asked. "Go where?"

Caleb hesitated, as if realizing he might've said too much. "I'll let Dez explain," he said and jogged off toward Morfael.

"Amaris, would you mind finding London or . . . something, for a minute?" Lazar asked, his voice taut. "I need to talk to Dez."

"Sure." Amaris kept her voice neutral, but her eyes were wide and a bit worried.

I was worried, too. A knot in my chest was tightening. Amaris trotted off toward the wolf pack circling around London, and Lazar and I walked over to our SUV, not talking. Did Lazar want to wait to yell at me when I was in human form? It had to be something bad, given the way his eyes wouldn't quite meet mine. He'd just saved Caleb's life. I couldn't tell him now that I still loved his brother. I owed Lazar too much to hurt him.

I shifted and got into my clothes in the back of the SUV while Lazar cleaned his rifle and reloaded. If Orgoli's plan was to get to Livermore and the laser as soon as possible, and to bring through his troops tonight, there was no point in packing up the weapons.

I climbed from the back of the SUV up to the front. He was seated in the passenger seat, staring out the windshield at all the parking lot activity. I thumped down into the driver's seat.

"I know you're going back to Othersphere," Lazar said calmly, "to get the tiger-shifters."

I nodded, relieved that he understood that at least. "If they're still alive, they deserve a chance to come back home."

"And we could probably use them at Livermore." The faint moonlight coming through the windshield outlined his strong nose and square jaw in profile. The tawny brown of his irises glittered faintly. "If Orgoli brings troops through, it's going to be a hell of a fight."

"If they're willing to fight with us, it could help a lot," I said, wishing I could read his expression or his voice better. This didn't sound like he was mad at me, or as if he'd noticed something between me and Caleb.

"I'm sorry to have to tell you this before you go." He finally turned to look at me. All I saw there was determination, an iron will clamped down to get him through whatever he was about to say. "But I don't think it can wait."

"You can tell me anything," I said. "Any time you want."

His gaze faltered, eyelids veiling his eyes for a moment, as if what I'd said meant something to him, meant a lot.

"We can't see each other anymore," he said. His voice was nothing but resolute. "I need to end it."

Someone had scooped out my insides and left nothing but a collapsing space. "But . . ." I started to say. The word "why" was coming next, but I didn't seem to be able to say it.

"It's been coming ever since we went to Othersphere," he said. "I'm too conventional."

"Conventional?" That didn't make sense. What was he trying to say? Growing up in a cult run by your own crazy father wasn't exactly normal.

He shook his head a little, as if angry with himself. "That's not the right word. It's like when I told you that I want

Amaris and London to be happy, but still there's a part of me that struggles with their relationship. That part of me has trouble with you because . . . you're not exactly what I thought you were at first. In Othersphere, you looked so different. And I learned you're part shadow walker, which is something up until a day or so ago I thought was a creature out of old wives' tales."

"I'm too . . . weird for you?" I asked. What he was saying didn't hurt because I couldn't believe it. "You had no problem with me being a tiger, but getting taller and thinner when I'm in Othersphere is a problem?"

"It's not how you look," he said, then immediately regretted it. "And it's not how you are, either. It's my problem. My narrowness."

"You're not narrow," I said. "You're the most willing to grow person I've ever met. You're the most considerate guy ever. You're willing to think about other people's feelings all the time because of everything you've gone through."

"But it's a constant struggle!" It came out vehement, almost angry. He shook his head at himself again. "Don't you see? I know some of my feelings are wrong, and I don't act on them. I never would. I try to be better, always, because I couldn't live with myself if I ended up like my father. But it's not natural or easy for me, the way it is for you and for—" He hesitated. "For a lot of people."

"Oh." I still didn't quite understand. "So us being together. It's hard work for you."

"It's been the best time of my life," he said quietly. He cleared his throat and said more firmly, "When I saw you in Othersphere, looking like that creature, your biological mother, I knew in here"—he pointed to his head—"that it was still you. Still Dez, no matter what name she called you. But in here"—he pointed to his heart—"it felt like you had become a demon, an alien thing I've been taught my whole life to hate, to objure, to kill."

"Some part of me is that creature," I said. "So your heart wasn't completely wrong. I'm Dez, but I'm something else, too."

"And I can't live with it," he said. "The constant battle inside my head where you're concerned. You deserve better."

"There isn't anyone better," I said. I meant it. I didn't want him thinking he was a bad man for having this struggle. "It's the fact that you win that battle every single time—that makes you the best man I know."

He took a deep breath. "There's more." His eyes flicked back and forth between mine as he girded himself for what he was about to say. "I've realized that I was drawn to you because you were, you are, the person who inspired me to change. I wanted to be better, to be worthy of you. But . . ." He looked away, out the windshield. The silence told me what he could not.

"But that's not the same thing as love," I said flatly.

He exhaled a breath as if he'd been holding it for hours. "Exactly." He stared at the snow, which had begun to gently fall on the hood of the car. "I'm sorry."

I'd been afraid that Lazar loved me more than I loved him, that I would hurt him too much if I broke up with him because I loved his brother. Turned out he could still hurt me.

I stared at his handsome profile, so like his brother's but creased now with those premature lines around his eyes and between his brows. His life had been so hard. He'd endured abuse and become what he hated most. But he'd fought his way back and become so good. The conflict was there, written on his striking face. And it only made him more beautiful.

It would be a lifelong struggle, and he deserved to have all the help he needed to win it.

But he didn't want or need my help, not anymore. Or at least that's what he was saying. Through my hurt, I saw that he was masking his own pain. This was incredibly hard for him. Why was he doing it then?

Why wasn't he meeting my eyes?

"There's something else," I said, surprising myself by saying it. "What is it?"

"God help me, isn't that enough?" The anger in his voice was savage. He reached for the door handle blindly and was out of the car, moving across the new snow of the parking lot, his silver rifle still in his hand.

CHAPTER 15

I don't know how long I sat in the car. It couldn't have been very long, but it felt like hours. The outside cold was numbing my toes, ears, and the skin across my cheekbones as I sat there and stared out at the shifters conferring with Morfael and Caleb.

I saw Amaris and London, now back in her human form wearing borrowed clothes, kiss as the snow fell on their heads. I saw Arnaldo grab new clothes for his brothers out of the back of the SUV and wave at me, smiling. I saw him hug them and wrap their scarves just a bit more snugly around their necks.

I saw November, still in rat form, run up to Lazar, who stood alone on the edge of the parking lot, and shift into her petite human form. There, naked right in front of him, she cocked her head to one side, and asked what was probably an impertinent question.

And because he was "conventional," as he called it, and

kind, Lazar took off his heavy jacket and wrapped it around her as she danced from one freezing cold foot to another. He shook his head at her as she said something, but she threw her arms around his neck and practically forced him to pick her up in his arms, so that she wouldn't be barefoot in the snow.

He walked her back to a truck nearby, probably the one she'd come in with her family or Siku's parents, and politely turned his back as she threw off his coat to get dressed. She playfully walked around in front of him wearing only a T-shirt and jeans and, still talking, she jerked the bottom edge of her T-shirt up and flashed him. She wasn't wearing a bra.

He laughed. I saw his teeth flash. His head bowed as he shook it in mock disapproval at her. I couldn't help laughing a little, too. It was so like November, and so over the top.

Maybe he would be okay.

Maybe I would, too. Lazar had saved me from having to make a difficult decision. When I'd thought Caleb was going to die, I'd realized that he was the one for me. But I couldn't have stomached the thought of abandoning Lazar for his own brother. Now I didn't have to worry about that.

I leaned over to my backpack and got out the Shadow Blade, strapping its sheath around my waist. I got out of the SUV, slamming the door, and froze, staring at Lazar as he talked to November. He was refusing to pick her up in his arms again and pointed at her now boot-clad feet in protest.

Was that why he'd broken up with me? Had Lazar seen that it was inevitable and deliberately saved me the trouble?

I walked hastily over to the group of shifters near Caleb and Morfael, feeling as if I was going to jump out of my skin. I needed to do something, to act instead of being acted upon. I needed to get out of my own head and over to Othersphere so I could free the tiger-shifters. They'd been there too long already.

First, I needed to know how to get myself there, and second, I should find out what everyone had planned while I was gone.

"What's wrong?" Caleb said in his non-whisper quiet tone as I moved to his side.

"Later," I said. "What's going on here?"

As the council leaders continued to consult with Morfael and their constituents, Caleb quickly explained that they were coming to a consensus to send their best fighters now to Livermore. Arnaldo had called in a bomb threat anonymously in the hopes that the humdrums would beef up their security. But Morfael had told them that Orgoli was capable of walking through the veil to arrive deep inside the facility. If he could gain control of the laser for long enough, he'd open a permanent window through the veil within the NIF itself and bring his troops in there, a window so permanent you didn't need a special bit of rope to get through it.

"The rats think they can infiltrate the NIF," Caleb continued. "And probably then sneak more shifters inside. If they can track down Orgoli and stop him before he gets control of the laser that would be best for all. Worse comes to worst, they can throw a fire alarm switch or alert the humdrums of an intruder."

"Worse comes to worst," I said, "Orgoli's there right this minute, and we're too late."

He nodded. "We've got to hope it will take him some time to convert the laser to his purpose."

The shifters were breaking off, heading for their cars. Jonata, the lynx-shifter, winked at me, smiling, and headed toward a truck with a pride of cat-shifters around her.

Morfael was leaning heavily on his staff, lips pursed as he stared out over the parking lot.

"So," I said, hating to interrupt what appeared to be deep thought. Although knowing Morfael, it could just as easily be an open-eyed nap. "Can you tell me how to get through the veil?"

Morfael lifted his head abruptly, as if coming awake. He slung his moonstone eyes at me like an accusation. "You know how."

"What?!" I threw up my hands. He could be so frustrating. "I've never done it before."

"What have you done many times that involves bringing something through the veil?" Morfael said, his voice cutting, his demeanor screaming out "must I do everything?"

It couldn't be that simple. "Shift?" I said. "But that's not the same thing as walking through the veil in my human form."

"Not exactly the same, no." Morfael tapped the tip of his carved staff against my collarbone. "But you've got everything you need right here. Now, go!" He pointed off into the woods, where Orgoli had disappeared. "I've got enough to worry about here."

I watched, astounded, as he clomped off toward our SUV, where I could see Amaris and London had gathered with Arnaldo and his brothers. November was tugging Lazar there now.

"Holy crap," I said. "You'd think I asked him to cut up my food."

"I think he's worried," Caleb said, taking a few steps toward the woods, looking back at me to make sure I'd follow. "In my coat, I've got the twine to help you get the tiger-shifters through. Come on. You should probably cross over right where Orgoli did, I guess."

"I guess," I said, reluctantly keeping up with him. I cast another glance at Morfael. My other friends near the SUV all waved at us, all except Morfael and Lazar.

Caleb waved back, calling out, "I'll be right back." To me, he said, "Just want to be sure you get through okay."

"Thanks." Unexpectedly, I felt shy now that we were alone. I tried to focus on what Morfael had said. My connection to Othersphere was deep inside of me. Somehow that was what I needed to get there physically across the veil. Could I somehow pull that window out of my body and manifest it in the air?

"What's wrong with Lazar?" Caleb asked.

I looked up at him, startled. "Wrong?"

"He didn't wave. And something's been off with him since we got back from Othersphere."

I debated for a long second about what to say. Caleb would learn it one way or another. "He broke up with me," I said. "Just now."

Caleb stopped walking, his face blank with astonishment. "*He* broke up with *you*?"

He cast a look back at Lazar, and then started walking again automatically, frowning and staring down at the ground.

"Yeah." I kept pace with him, not wanting to say anything more.

"I'm sorry," he said. "I just thought he—" He broke off abruptly. "Sorry. It's none of my business."

"I was surprised, too," I said.

We'd reached the edge of the parking lot and entered the woods, crunching without fear this time over the fresh snow.

"Are you okay?" he asked.

"It's for the best." I looked down at my worn sneakers, one of my last whole pairs. I'd need to head to the thrift shop to get more clothes for shifting soon.

"Maybe you shouldn't go to Othersphere alone at a time like this," he said, his black eyes sliding over to me cautiously. I opened my mouth to contradict him, but he shook his head. "I take it back. This is the perfect time for you to go to Othersphere alone."

"Exactly!" I said. How well he knew me. How perfectly our strides matched as we walked side by side. I wanted to take his arm, to press up against his side as we walked. But how weird would that be, minutes after breaking up with his brother? "I can't wait to get over there and do something useful."

"Action girl." A smile touched his eyes. "Not a passive-aggressive bone in your body."

I knew then what I had to do. It was breaking a confidence, but I was about to head into Othersphere and perhaps never come back. Lazar would never tell Caleb on his own, and if I didn't do it now, Caleb might never know.

"I need to tell you one thing before I go," I said.

"Oh?" His voice was deceptively casual.

We were approaching the pile of logs and bracken where Orgoli and the objurers had been. I braced myself to see the bodies of the two Lazar had killed, but they were gone. The shifters had been thorough in their cleanup. They had thousands of years of experience in dealing with the aftermath of battles with the Tribunal.

Caleb stuffed his hands in his pockets. "You don't have to tell me anything about the two of you, you know."

"It's nothing to do with me," I said. "You need to know why I started trusting him. It's about how his mother died."

Caleb stood there as I told him everything Lazar had told me back in the Neptune Casino in Vegas—how when he was twelve years old, Lazar had tried to drive his dying mother to the hospital against his father's orders. How Ximon had dragged Lazar from the car and beaten him, breaking several bones. Ximon had then dragged Lazar's mother, weak from advanced, untreated breast cancer, over to lie before Lazar, put his own gun in Lazar's unbroken left hand, aimed the gun at Lazar's mother, and forced his son to pull the trigger.

I tried to keep it short and nondramatic. It wasn't a story that needed any embellishment. As I got near the end, Caleb's shoulders hunched, as if he was in pain, and he pulled his coat close around his body. When I was done, he looked as if he might be sick. I knew exactly how he felt.

"Okay," he said. His face, handsome as a carving by

Michelangelo in the moonlight, was pale and quietly murderous. His flexible voice spoke of anger, of sorrow, of understanding.

"Please don't tell him I told you," I said. "He hasn't even told Amaris because he's afraid she'll hate him and blame him for their mother's death."

"I won't tell her. But she'd know whom to blame," he said with venom that took my breath away. "I knew Ximon was a monster, but this . . ."

"If I didn't know better, I'd think Orgoli was Ximon's own evil come to life," I said.

"To think I almost felt sorry for him the last time we saw him." He looked back toward the parking lot. "It explains a lot."

"I would have told you sooner, but I promised Lazar I wouldn't tell anyone, ever," I said. "That promise meant a lot to him, and I wouldn't have told you now except, well, I might not come back."

Caleb turned to look down at me. It was very dark under the trees here, but a spot of moonlight glittered in the depths of his black eyes. "You'll come back," he said. There was no doubt in his voice.

The intensity in his face gave me goose bumps. We'd stopped on the spot where Orgoli had crossed through the veil, standing closer together than we had in a long time.

"I have an idea about how to cross over," I said. "I hope it works."

"It will," Caleb said. "Can I help?"

"I don't know," I said. "I'm going to try to manifest the window to Othersphere that I feel inside me."

He nodded, lifting his brows. "Go for it."

I closed my eyes, feeling around for that connection and there it was, inside and behind my heart as always, seething. I tried to picture it as a black window, roiling with energy; then I mentally asked it to step out of my heart and into the world.

It seemed to move, and then recoiled back to its home, as if reluctant to go anywhere else.

Caleb was humming, so low it was almost imperceptible. He broke off as I opened my eyes, sighing in exasperation. "It's your own uncertainty that won't let it go. But remember how you felt when you were in Othersphere? It was as natural as breathing."

"Yeah, but I didn't get myself there," I said.

"You will," he said. "Try it again."

I closed my eyes again and leaned into the note coming from Caleb. It reminded me of Othersphere, a tune that wasn't a tune really, just a part of the bigger musical production going on around us all the time. That was how Othersphere felt, like a dance, a song so complex that it became simple again. This was also simple. Just connect myself to that song.

I didn't ask this time. I simply did it, taking hold of that part of me and throwing it out and open. Whatever Caleb was doing made it seem inevitable and natural, just another part of the pattern.

I opened my eyes as a familiar-smelling breeze brushed my face. There in the air was a door a little over six feet high and about two feet wide which opened into a very different wood than the one we stood in. The trees there weren't pine, but larger, taller, more worn, with trunks that looked like many trees braided together and nearly square leaves that were almost blue. The temperature was warmer, perhaps sixty degrees. But it was also a moonlit night there. The timing of day and night in Othersphere seemed to correspond to our world, if not the seasons.

Caleb, smiling, grabbed my hand and raised it into the air. "Desdemona Grey, ladies and gentlemen!"

I laughed, my pulse racing at his touch and at the prospect of venturing, on my own this time, back to the place where I was born.

I squeezed his hand. "Thanks," I said. "You really helped."

He shook his head, remembering something, and grabbed

it from a long pocket inside his coat—a length of the rope from between the worlds.

I reached for it, but he pulled it away. "Better if you don't touch it till you have to, I think. Here." He stepped in close and wrapped it around my waist several times. I breathed in his familiar stormy scent, stared at his lips and dark eyelashes from a few inches away.

He tied the rope off and stood there, very close. We were breathing each other's breath now, heart to heart. Our gazes met. Then his eyes fell to my lips, and I stopped breathing. He took my upper arms in both his hands and pulled me close.

"Just in case," he said, one arm sliding around my back, the other encircling my waist. He kissed me with a fierceness that made my knees buckle. My lips opened under his as I pressed against the whole lean line of his body, curving into him, sliding my fingers at last up the back of his neck and into his thick, unruly hair.

It would have gone on, except that he wrenched his mouth from mine and said, "Go." He took my shoulders with his hands and pushed me away. "Now. Or I'll never let you leave again."

I took a step back. I was smiling. "I'll see you soon," I said, and walked through the window I'd made in the veil.

CHAPTER 16

The air breathed happily around me, sighing as it ran over the singing leaves. Small creatures ran flashing under the darkling branches, and stars peeped down from their spheres. My skin exchanged melodies with the breeze; my lungs breathed deep the ballad of moss and wood, of sweet dirt and fresh brook. All were there with me in this time, this place, and I with them.

I looked back and saw Caleb still standing on the other side of the veil, snow waltzing down on his dark head, wind trilling over his long black coat. The music was there, too, if I just stopped to listen.

He raised his hand: not a wave, but a hail. I raised my own hand, now with its otherworldly long, tapered fingers, in return. The same connection I felt to the earth and water, to the air and wood here harmonized now softly between the two of us.

It took only a thought to pull the window back to where it belonged. It vanished from view and lodged once more against my heart. That heart was now housed in a different body. As before, the trip through the veil had transformed me into something taller, more fluid, leaner, and perfectly in tune with all around me. With the window gone, the bond with Caleb had disappeared, too. But I wasn't alone. Nothing in Othersphere was ever alone.

I stood in the wood I didn't recognize. The branches rose thick with their blue-green leaves, leaving open triangular chunks to the night sky. The ground was covered not in grass, but in a yellow-green moss that climbed a foot or two up the twisted tree trunks and over the rocks and roots.

The scent here was off. Something had walked this way recently. I knelt and ran my hand over the moss, and its indentations crooned a story of a man with white hair who had been here. Orgoli's feet, in Ximon's boots, had stood here and then he had shifted into a great striped beast, a tiger spirit Amba, only as big now as a horse. He could become larger if he wished. I was learning that the size of our Amba body was determined by our emotions and, in some cases, how much blood we had recently drunk. The more powerful the creature we ate, the greater our own power, for a little while at least.

The great tracks led me over to the braided trunk of a nearby tree, where my pointed fingernails traced four deep scratches running parallel deep into its knotted bark. The tree's chant told of Orgoli, sharpening his claws there, of him leaping up the trunk, climbing high into its branches to where the breeze ruffled his ears so that he could see the great cliff of the Amba's mountain palace off in the distance.

The cliff. I followed Orgoli's trail, climbing up the tree, thanking it silently as I did so, to poke my head above the top of the forest. The moonlight resounded here without the leaves to obscure it. It shimmered through the light wind and filled the trees with life. It wasn't just the sun that fed the plants here, I realized, but also the moon. They'd learned to turn its silvered light into food and strength.

From here the treetops ran into the distance like the rooftops of a great city. To my left I could see a distant mountain range, capped with snow as white as cake icing under the moon. To my right, a few miles away, rose a great cliff, gleaming like ivory marble veined with black and purple. I was too far away to see the balcony where we'd stood during our rescue of Amaris. But that had to be the place, for a peak shaped like a slumbering cat presided over it, the ears still pointed up alertly, even in sleep.

I gripped the branches between my hands and asked.

What did he do after he climbed up here?

The tree reverberated with a remembered great roar, one that could be heard for miles. Orgoli had sent out a call to all within the sound of his voice. He would do it several more times on his way home. He was calling in his army.

I climbed down and shifted with an ease that felt like breathing deep. A great tiger creature once more, I sprinted toward the marble cliff. I had no idea if there would be a way for me to enter the home of the Amba at its base, or even if the tiger-shifters were still there, but that was the last place I'd seen them, so it was where I had to start.

My great leaping strides ate up the miles, and if I ever doubted which way to go, I bounded up a tree to check my direction. Soon the cliff was visible through the leaves, looming ahead. I came to the river I'd seen winding through the valley when I'd looked down from above, and plunged into the rough–flowing water without hesitation, paddling easily through the rapids to climb up the other bank and shake my coat dry.

I paused as I got close, taking in great, even lungfuls of fresh night air, and drank from a creek that wound off the river. With every lap of my tongue, I tasted the clean rocks under the water, the algae that lived on those rocks, and the fish that swam between them. Something that glowed blood red swam lazily past me, circling up to another finned fish thing that shimmered indigo. They circled each other in a slow, elegant dance, then merged, their colors shifting with the union to a gleaming royal purple. The resulting creature swam upstream, out of sight.

I walked over to a tree and rubbed my face against it, marking it instinctively, and then paused as a similar scent reached my nose. Another Amba had been here within the past few hours, one like me, from this world.

I sniffed around the wide base of the tree, ears cocked for any approaching sound, and found more smells. This was when London's superior nose would have been useful, but my tiger senses were sharp enough to distinguish three different Amba scents, apart from my own, and six sharper, muskier scents which I recognized as the tiger-shifters. Those scents were slightly older, while the Amba's were more recent, which meant that six of the tiger-shifters had run through this way, chased by three of the Amba.

I followed the tiger-shifter tracks, nose to ground, as quickly as I could. The Amba stalked them the whole way. I wasn't ex-perienced enough to know how old the scents were, but they seemed relatively fresh. As I moved along, the trees were fewer, and the grass grew as high as my head, rustling like taffeta in the breeze as the moonlight brushed fingerlike shadows along the ground.

I heard a deliberate crackle in the grass and swiveled to face it, fangs bared. Another swish from behind me and I re-alized—I was surrounded by twelve tiger-shifters. They slunk toward me, stripes like grassy shadows on their backs, snarling. Off in the distance, I now smelled blood and the dead flesh of the Amba that had followed them.

Ambush.

I had walked right into it, as the Amba had. The tiger-shifters were smart, and against twelve of them, I probably didn't stand a chance. I got quiet and stilled my tail. I didn't quite know how tigers communicated, but somehow I'd understood what the In-

dian tiger-shifter had "said" to me back in the cells before I left
him. So, with a combination of body language and chirps, I
did my best to indicate:

I'm a friend. I'm the one who freed you earlier.

They seemed to understand, because they hesitated. One
snarled an order:

Go get our leader.

And a second tiger-shifter turned and ran off into the
brush.

I sat down, trying to look as harmless as possible. The
tiger-shifters exchanged glances and questioning rumbles. In
the distance, I heard a roar, and a familiar tiger bounded
through the grass. By his stripe pattern I recognized him as
the Bengal tiger-shifter I'd sort of befriended back in the
prison cells.

His honey-colored eyes got wide at the sight of me. I
bowed my head, flipping the tip of my tail nonchalantly in
greeting.

He relaxed, and around him the others did, too. He
chuffed, whiskers fanning forward, and I understood him to
be greeting me as a friend, as someone welcome to the group.

I stood up slowly and made a similar greeting, looking
around and also trying to ask him:

Where are the others?

Maybe it was the connection I felt to all things in Othersphere, or maybe it was that tigers really did talk to each
other with roars and tail twitches. Or maybe it was a little of
both, but he answered me very clearly.

*Thirty of us are free, thanks to you. The rest of those left
alive were locked back up in the cells. We do not have the
power to open them up.*

I roared joyfully.

I do.

He roared back, just as jubilant. The other tigers did the
same, and the night trembled under the barrage of our cries.

I chuffed and turned my ears to the cliff that still loomed nearby.

If you take me there, I will free them now. I can also take you home, back through the veil, if you wish.

The Bengal tiger's whiskers retracted, hugging his striped muzzle, his ears flattening in surprise.

But you are from this place. How can that be?

I chirped and tilted my head.

A long story. But your world is now my home. And Orgoli is planning to take his battle there, to dominate that world as he dominates this. So I cannot promise you life there will be any better.

The Bengal shook his ears.

Free us all, and we will make sure he flees our world in terror, or dies.

He looked around at the others, and they were stamping, chuffing, growling their approval.

I bowed my head once again, but my tail lashed.

Lead the way.

The Bengal bowed in return, and then chirped to one of the others.

Bring everyone to the Climbing Tree. Now.

That tiger-shifter sprinted off into the grass, and the Bengal came up alongside me, smaller than I was, but sinewy and strong.

Come.

He took off running toward the cliff. The others poured after him. I followed, keeping up easily, one stride of mine matching every two of theirs, galloping at a steady pace as the dark-veined cliff towered closer. As we reached the bottom of it, I saw what he must have meant by the Climbing Tree. A wiry tree hugged close to the wall of the cliff, mounting higher and higher until it became more of a thick vine, spiraling upward as far as my neck could crane back to see.

The Bengal glanced at me.

It is far. They may be waiting at the top to attack.

I nodded. I didn't want any more of them to die, if possible. And as both an Amba and Orgoli's daughter, I might be able to put a stop to the fighting.

If you will allow, I will go first.

Tigers don't smirk, but he waved his tail appreciatively, and gestured upward.

After you.

At first the climb was easy. I thought of all the lessons in climbing up and down Morfael had forced me into, and I was grateful. The tree's branches were thin, but they were solid and spread out both horizontally as well as vertically. I could feel the tree's ancient song coming up through the pads in my paws, and I thanked it for allowing me to dig my claws into its tough bark, for bearing my weight and all those coming after me.

After about a hundred feet, the branches turned into one thick creeping stem, which warbled a peculiar refrain as it wound ever higher. My body adjusted to the harsher tune, but after climbing for another thousand yards straight up, with no end in sight, my shoulders were aching.

The wind teased the creeper, buffeting my fur and causing the vine to sway. I tightened my grip and while I waited for it to move a little less, I dared to look down.

My stomach dropped, and my fear shouted out at top volume. The vine's song seemed to catch that refrain and echoed it back. My fear increased. The vine was feeding it. I dug in tighter, hunching closer to the sheer wall, and forced myself to growl a soft, contrasting deep note. The plant I clung to resumed its wandering jingle and my heartbeat slowed.

The forested valley lay over a hundred stories below me, spread out like a black and silver map under the luminous moon. Directly under me, the tiger-shifters were strung down the vine like striped flowers. Some were panting with effort, straining as they climbed, muscles trembling.

The Bengal was right behind me, teeth bared in a grimace of effort. He ruffed at me, as if to say: *We will make it. Don't stop.*

So I continued the ascent. A sharp cramp ran through first my right, then my left front paw. A deep tremor quivered in the powerful muscles in my front legs and traveled down my back, joining in a painful tune with my aching joints and raw paw pads. I took more weight onto my back paws, trying to use the front ones mostly for balance, but soon my back legs and toes began to cramp.

The agony song inside me was reaching a miserable crescendo. I grasped upward with my front right paw, dug in, pulled up. But the cramp there didn't allow me to dig in deep. I slipped. I skidded jarringly down the vine three feet until my left paw caught hold, my back legs dangling. Scrabbling to get them back on track, I clamped my jaw around the thick stem until all four paws once more grasped the plant.

I looked down. The Bengal was just a foot beneath me, shaking with effort. If I'd hit him, we both would have fallen to our deaths, and probably hit a few more shifters going down. There were clouds beneath us now, obscuring the trees.

I continued on, unashamedly using my jaw for extra hold when I needed it. Every foot we gained was agony. I began wobbling with both weakness and with fear that we wouldn't make it back home in time to be of help.

Just as I felt I couldn't haul my body one more inch up that cursed vine, the greenery spread out above me, crowned with bushes twisted into familiar strange shapes. We had reached the lip of the Amba balcony. I crawled, shaking, up and peered over its edge.

A huge paw with claws the size of steak knives extended, swiped at me. I ducked. The razor-sharp talon slit open one of my ears, but missed my eye. I forced my back legs to push off the vine and leapt up and over the head of an Amba in tiger form lurking at the top of the Climbing Tree. He must have heard us coming.

In mid-air, I saw there were four of them on the balcony, all in tiger form and ready to pounce, rake, and kill.

I shifted before I hit the ground, curling and rolling from the impact in my elongated semi-human form. Three of the Amba swiveled to follow me as I uncurled and put one hand on the hard marblelike rock, and that gave me an idea. I was Orgoli's daughter, and they needed to know that, fast. If Khutulun was to be believed, there was a chance the Amba were looking for a reason to abandon Orgoli. I needed to give it to them.

I imagined my skin was like that pale, black-veined marble, inflexible, shiny. I thought of my joints and decided they would be like Morfael's, angular and skeletal. I listened deep to the song of the mountain beneath my feet and felt that vibration invade all the tiny atoms that made up my body. I asked them to sing in time with the mountain.

I stood up, and up, taller than ever before, my limbs hard as milky glass, my joints clicking, my tongue and my blood the only flexible, warm things about me.

The Amba's gold-green eyes widened; their lashing tails curled with questions. They hesitated.

I extended a shiny, long-jointed hand out to the Amba as they prepared to leap. I recalled Orgoli's deep, DNA-rattling vocal vibration, and intoned, "Stop! I am one of you."

Not exactly Shakespeare, but all three Amba about to attack me backed up a step, ears flattening. The fourth split his attention between me and the vine, where I knew the tiger-shifters were still clinging, exhausted and about to drop. I had to do this quickly.

"I know you serve Orgoli," I said, and as I spoke, I pointed to the mountain peak shaped like a cat and did my best to send out all my intentions into the air around me. I'd communicated with a storm, and the trees, the tiger-shifters, and the vine. Something about Othersphere and the connections between all things made such communications possible. I could only hope that even if I spoke English, the Amba here would get the gist.

"I am his daughter, and I ask you to help me oppose him," I said, gesturing with hands out as if in opposition. I pointed to the vine, and bared my shiny teeth. "Tiger-shifters there. Allow them up, and together we will free this place from a tyrant."

The four Amba growled to each other in a way that seemed to question my words, to wonder, to be tempted by them. The one by the vine roared at me, flicking his whiskers with disdain. I knew then that they understood me, for I comprehended him completely.

You would then hold blood-rule in his place. How is that any better?

An excellent question. The Amba were not fools, to exchange one dictator for another. The term I heard as "blood-rule" spoke of death and imprisonment, of terror and a deeply unnatural craving for power. It indicated that Orgoli had upset the balance here. If the Amba were like tigers, they were loners, living only in family units, able to care for themselves as long as they had enough land to hunt on. I thought I knew the answer to his question, but had no way to be sure if it would actually appeal to them. But it was better to be honest, and hope they understood that I meant well, at least.

"It's time for blood-rule to end," I said. "It's time for the prison to be opened, for each Amba to rule himself only, to live in harmony with all."

Another Amba bared his teeth and shook his muzzle.

Orgoli cannot be killed. He has drunk too much of our blood.

Not exactly a resounding vote in my favor, but not quite a

"no" either. I reached deep inside, pulling out every convincing vibration my voice could manage.

"Right now the tyrant seeks to open a door in the veil, so that he may conquer another world. He calls upon his army to join him. On the other side of the veil he is weaker. If you will allow me to take these prisoners back to that world, we will destroy him."

No.

The Amba by the vine paced forward. I saw the Bengal tiger peek up over the edge behind him, but I couldn't take my eyes off the Amba. If he and the other three refused me, the tiger-shifters and I were dead.

The Amba lifted the right side of his upper lip in a snarl.

No, do not destroy him. Send him back to us weakened. We will deal with him.

The other three roared approval.

I tried not to collapse in relief and gestured to the Bengal that it was safe to come over the edge. He crept up cautiously, but the Amba were already ignoring him and putting their heads together. They were agreed. The biggest, the one by the vine, spoke.

Spread the word. Allow this one to pass unharmed.

This one had to mean me. Two of them sped off, each through a different door, into the mountain. As the rest of the tiger-shifters wearily made it off the vine and safely to the stone balcony, I asked the Amba, "Where is Orgoli now?"

He was last seen by the wolf door. We were to stay here and guard the mountain. But he headed toward the great sea, calling all others to follow him.

"The great sea," I said. I had no idea how directions worked here, but I figured the wolf door was probably the one where we'd first encountered London's dire wolves. "If I exit through the wolf door, how do I find the great sea?"

Down the hill, toward the moonrise. Skirt the swamp. If you follow its edge, you will come to the great sea.

I looked up at the moon. It was over to my left, and it looked like it was still rising. I pointed. "That is the direction of the moonrise?"

The Amba didn't roll his eyes, but he wasn't impressed. *Yes.*

He didn't say *duh*, but for the briefest moment he reminded me a little of November. I stifled a giggle. The Amba wouldn't take kindly to being compared to a rat-shifter, I was sure, but the longing to be with my friends pierced my heart. This being in Othersphere was exhilarating, and the prospect that I just might succeed in bringing the tiger-shifters home even more of a thrill. But how much sweeter would it all be if my friends, my team, my family, were there to share it with me.

"Come!" I gestured to the tiger-shifters. With a breath, I shifted to my tiger form and dashed through the broken doorway that led to the prison cells.

It didn't take long to free the remaining tiger-shifters. The roots covering the entrance to their cells moved away at my touch, and over fifty of them surged out. The Bengal shifted to his human form and explained what was going on to the others in his own language.

I asked a tall redheaded woman who spoke both Russian and English to see if our plan was okay with her group of Siberian tigers. She grinned toothily and shouted some phrases at them in Russian. They answered back with an affirmative roar that made the walls shake.

There were nearly a hundred of them all told, and after they all shifted into tiger form, the narrow passageways of the mountain rang with their chuffs and meows of excitement. *We're going home,* they all seemed to be saying.

And we get to fight Orgoli.

Once outside the wolf door, we stopped briefly at a stream so everyone could drink their fill. More than a few snapped at creatures in the water with their jaws, or snagged wiggling, scaled things from the shallows with their paws and wolfed them down, licking their whiskers in satisfaction. They were scrawnier than they should have been, but the water, food, and freedom made them bat playfully at each other and tussle like kittens as we moved along.

We galloped through the wood where my friends and I had spotted the bat-shifters. There were none in the sky that night, and no drums or lights in the distance. It wasn't hard to follow Orgoli's path with nearly a hundred tiger noses looking for the trail. We also identified other catlike smells, some reptiles with very large clawed footprints, elephants or mammoths, and a few creatures that smelled like humans, but were muskier, hairier, and prone to using their knuckles when they ran. I tried not to think what an army of gorillas and dinosaurs would do to downtown Livermore, California, not to mention Orgoli's ability to make the earth quake, and I prayed we could stop him before he got far.

At the edge of the swamp, I turned the thundering herd of tiger-shifters toward the moonrise to our right, following the watery boundary. The scents of Orgoli and his army grew stronger. I thought I could identify tracks of hoofed creatures and hopping ones, crawling ones and many-legged ones. Their scents shimmered through the wet air, blending with the odors of dank plants, and those pesky eye-gouging faeries, who smelled like charcoal. They left us alone after the tigers swallowed a few whole.

After a few quick miles, the horizon up ahead shone like silk under a lamp. I smelled salt. The soil beneath my paws fell away like sand, and the waters of the swamp swirled and ran with melodic current, expanding into the chorus of a delta as they reached the sea. The closer we got, the farther out it seemed to spread before us, flat as a lake under the moon. Soon we were slogging through sand, up and over huge dunes, which alternately obscured and revealed the great ocean now a few hundred yards ahead.

From a distance away, a harsh sound cut across the accord

of the sea and river, sand and spray. It wasn't music at all, but a noxious, unnatural racket, like a buzz saw mixed with a downed power line.

My stomach constricted with dread. A noise like that here in a world where everything sang together in harmony could mean only one thing.

As if in answer to my apprehension, something like a crab scuttled across my paw away from the sound. As I descended the dune, the entire downward slope came alive with tiny crawling things, scurrying en masse in the direction we had come from, away from the horrible din.

A throng of shapes crossed the moon, throwing winged shadows on the drifts. They, too, were flitting away from the sound. Off in the distant waves I thought I saw leaping arcs of water creatures fleeing off to sea.

Which meant that Orgoli might have trouble getting his army to go closer. It was the only hopeful thought I could conjure, because I knew what this meant. He had opened his permanent door in the veil between this world and the other.

We topped a large bluff and saw it, a large, irregular hole in the air, perhaps forty feet wide and fifteen feet high. Unlike the other windows through the veil I'd seen recently, this one's perimeter was blurry with spiky movement, like the maw of a giant, invisible creature with electrified teeth. The sickening sound seemed to come from this boundary, where the cut had been made.

It was as if a puzzle piece had been cut out of the veil. Where, I wondered, was the missing piece? Maybe the laser in Orgoli's hands had destroyed it. Could it ever be replaced?

I slowed down, chuffing at the tiger-shifters around me. They braked, too, and I came to a halt at the top of a high summit about three hundred feet away from the doorway. The tiger-shifters paused there, too, ears up as we surveyed the scene.

Hundreds of animals were moving toward the doorway, coming at it from a slightly different angle than we were, circling the base of a lower dune ahead. I saw a bright-green crocodile as long as an RV snaking along next to a woolly mammoth. Ahead of them, a rhino covered with long white hair charged along, followed by several skittering gray spiders as big as German shepherds. To one side, a pride of mane-less lions nearly as big as I was prowled, while above their heads a swarm of shining red and black beetles massed, wings sparkling in the moonlight.

But there was something wrong with the sand. About fifty feet from the door it was no longer white, but gray and dusty, more like soil than sand. And to the left, where the ocean had sparkled under the moon, the water was gone, dried up for hundreds of yards out to sea. Perhaps a mile or so away I could see the sparkle of moonlight on the ocean again. Past the doorway, the gray sand stretched as far as my gaze could reach, flattening the dunes, blowing around aimlessly in the ocean breeze.

It reminded me of the blighted area we'd come across in the swamp, where Lazar had found the skull. We'd thought it might be a kind of graveyard, but the barren area around me was too big, too utterly devoid of any life to be that. This was something very unnatural, very wrong. I could feel in my bones that it was spreading. Maybe the doorway had brought this ugliness to Othersphere, but how then to explain the plagued area of the swamp?

The only visible life was the teeming mass of beasts, and I couldn't find Orgoli among them anywhere. But there were hundreds of bright purple frogs, several ostriches taller than giraffes, nearly a dozen small horses with three toes per foot, and warthogs as big as cows. Nearest the door, hesitantly stepping over its buzzing bottom edge were over a dozen bipedal creatures that looked like skinny gorillas. I squinted. It was hard to tell from this distance, but they looked like drawings I'd seen of early hominid species, which had gone extinct before *Homo sapiens* roamed the earth.

One of them stepped over the threshold and was not

pushed back as Caleb had been when he'd tried to go after Amaris without wearing the special rope from between the worlds.

So that was the power of this doorway. Anything or anyone could cross it. No shadow-walker blood or help was needed now, no twine or songs or Lightning Tree necessary. Once they overcame their reluctance, all of those animals and shifters would pass through, to fight. Many of them would probably die.

Then I saw something that made my heart stop. Not far away, just down the dune from where I stood, were several tigers that looked very much like the Bengal by my side. But they were just different enough that I recognized them from my homework at Morfael's school. They were two of the sub-species of *Panthera tigris* that had gone extinct in the last hundred years—the Caspian and the Bali tiger.

We can't kill them.

These innocent animals had been saved from extinction in our world and now were being drawn into battle with us, where we would probably send them into extinction again. Even the thought of slaughtering one of them made me feel sick.

The Bengal growled low.

We don't wish to kill them either. Where is Orgoli?

I turned to him, tail lashing.

He must be through that doorway.

I looked again. A few of the animals, including the early hominids, had made it through the doorway, but most of those closest to it were shying away from its aberrant energy.

Farther on, limbs flailed. Was it some kind of fighting, a tussle or struggle? I craned my neck but couldn't see more. Was it my friends, fighting Orgoli? I needed to know. I needed to go. We had to get these animals out of here and put a stop to the real villain. Now.

I could speak to those most like us at least, the Bengal suggested, indicating the Caspian and Bali tigers below, which were already staring up at us, lips curling in uncertain snarls.

Please do.

The Bengal beckoned to the nearest tiger-shifters and they began a careful descent toward the tigers below, making every effort to chuff and show by tail and posture that their intentions were friendly.

I needed a way to speak to all the creatures down there at once. To tell them to go home, that Orgoli was not their friend, that this world they were invading was no longer a place where they could live, for it had already wiped out every other creature like them.

I felt deep sadness for the world then. That it could no longer be home to the Caspian and Bali tigers, to the giant crocodiles and flashing red beetles. Mastodons, purple frogs, and three-toed horses, none would be welcome in our polluted, industrialized world. Our world was the poorer for their loss.

I vowed to myself with the holiest words I could find—by the Moon, by my Mother's love, by my friends and my soul and my stripes—that when I was home and safe, I would go to college, I would study ways to reclaim species on the brink of extinction, and I would do everything in my power to save them.

But first we had to save these below us, and defeat Orgoli. And survive.

A flutter of wings neared me, and a strange red bird with black stripes on its wings circled over my head.

Sarangarel.

That voice. It was in my head, but I knew it. It was my birth mother, Khutulun. I squinted up at the bird as it glided down and, with a flick of its feathers, landed on my back. I curved my spine around in a C to see her better. She looked like a tiger-striped cat that had sprouted feathery wings, with

a tigerish fuzzy muzzle and ears and a sleek furry bird body
that sprouted orange-red feathered wings. Her feet, embedded in my own fur, were taloned like an eagle's.

You're a bird.

That was all I could think to say. I thought how she had
flown away when Orgoli had attacked me in his biggest
form, how quickly she had abandoned me. So much for the
blood tie she always seemed to invoke. My friends had stood
by me more solidly than she was capable of. Once I had
thought she might be the key to finding myself, but now the
only thing I felt for Khutulun was indifference.

I fly, but am not a bird.

She preened a little.

Then fly away, I thought back at her. *Go. You're no use
to me.*

*You could fly, too. You can be anything you like in this
world, for the Amba are one with everything here. With Orgoli gone, this world is yours.*

Even if what she said was true, I didn't want to own a
world. The idea was ridiculous to me now. I wanted . . . her
help.

How can I speak to all those animals below? I asked. *Can
you communicate with all of them at once?*

She peered down her striped nose at the river of creatures
ebbing around the buzzing by the doorway. Several indistin-
guishable shapes scuffled near its edges, and I caught my
breath, wanting to somehow rush past the crowds and get
there.

Why would you wish to speak to those who are beneath you?

My anger and dislike for her rose precipitously.

That's no concern of yours! I lashed my tail and bared my
teeth. *Tell me how!*

Khutulun's eyes in this form were still tip-tilted and green.
They examined me with cold calculation. I felt the deep cunning behind them working its will.

I will tell them anything you wish. If you promise to stay in this world forever, to take it back from Orgoli, and to protect me.

I shivered. There it was. The thing I could do to save all those animals. And if I sent them safely home, I would no doubt save many of the shifters fighting against Orgoli on the other side and probably my friends as well. Orgoli alone would still be tough to defeat, but it was better than facing an army.

The ground on the other side of the doorway heaved upward with a brain-rattling *harrumphing* sound, as if a great beast under the floor had wakened.

Your father wreaks havoc on that world, Khutulun said inside my head. *While you stand here and refuse me.*

Oh, she was good. All that guilt to get me to stay with her. I tried to picture a life without Mom, my real mom, and Richard, without Arnaldo and his brothers, London, Amaris, Morfael, and Lazar.

Without Caleb. A pain deep as the great sea struck my soul as I thought of him. I would never see Caleb again.

But saving all those animals, maybe saving the world from Orgoli—that was worth a sacrifice.

You will be living where you were born, as was meant to be, Khutulun said, her husky voice crooning. *You can help heal this world from all the damage Orgoli and your world have done. And every night the moon will sing you to sleep.*

The moon could sing to me back home, if only I stopped to listen. And back home there was a lot of healing and helping to do, too.

But maybe that home wouldn't exist if I didn't do this to stop Orgoli.

You promise to tell them exactly what I say? I asked. *And you promise that all of them will hear you?*

Khutulun leapt from my back to take brief flight, then shifted in mid-air with such precision that her suddenly humanoid feet gracefully touched ground. Her tall, elegant form was clad, as mine had been, in soft white thistledown woven into a long, warm, clinging dress. Nature in Othersphere cooperated with the Amba, acting in perfect concert to keep us warm whenever we needed clothing, to help us move through and around the world, and to part the clouds of the eternal storm. It spoke to us and helped us. Orgoli had violated that covenant. Perhaps I could restore it.

Khutulun's head in her humanoid form was as high as mine in my tiger form. She stretched out a graceful, long-fingered hand and stroked the fur on my cheek.

"I will do as you say," she said, now speaking aloud. "If you will make me that promise."

I looked back at the horrible doorway. An exotically spotted ibex with huge horns and a giant buffalo had crossed the threshold, and charged off to one side, out of sight. Whatever fighting had been going on before was no longer visible. I had to help. Somehow. If I promised to come stay with her when all this was over, maybe I could pull the creatures back and fight Orgoli with my friends before I came back forever.

I . . .

A terrible roar split my ears, and a striped blur flew up the dune to leap, paws outstretched, right for Khutulun.

She reacted too fast to follow, jumping to one side as the Bengal tiger twisted in mid-air, trying not to miss.

He landed on the sand at my side, twisting and snarling, ready to leap again.

I put a paw bigger than his head on his back and shoved him down, digging my claws in enough to hold him, but not deep enough to draw blood.

Hold, please.

He struggled, but not with his full strength, snarling at her.

Let me kill her! Why do you protect this vile thing?

I glanced up at Khutulun. She was backing away, her already pale skin now so paper white I could see the tiny blue veins running beneath it. She was afraid of the tiger-shifter. But that made no sense. He and his kind hated Orgoli, too.

I know of no reason to kill her.

The Bengal slowed his struggling, still growling at Khutulun.

It was she who helped Orgoli imprison us. She is his ally and mate!

A chill ran down my spine, even as I told myself that the Bengal had to be making a mistake.

But then why was Khutulun shaking her head, stepping back from us both, moving carefully on the shifting sand beneath her feet?

"No," she said. "I was Orgoli's mate twenty years ago, when he brought your kind through. That's where you remember me from. But you were just a child then, and not long after that I broke with the tyrant, for he wished to consume my child, my daughter. . . ."

The Bengal shot me a look of dawning comprehension.

You are her daughter.

I nodded.

She lies. In her tiger shape she helped Orgoli and his friends to round us up, to put us in prison. That was only months ago.

Another tiger-shifter paced up, the Caspian and Bali tigers not far behind her. She growled at Khutulun, crouching and ready to pounce. This tiger shot an angry glare at me when she saw I had the Bengal pinned.

He speaks the truth. She is the tyrant's ally!

"Not anymore." Khutulun's voice shook as she backed farther away. "I broke with him again. Don't you see? We're on the same side now."

I lifted my paw from the Bengal, and he slowly got up.

You broke with him recently, not years ago. That's why you tried to contact me a short time ago, I said to her. *By possessing my mother at the Lightning Tree.*

"I contacted you then because at last I was free to do so!"

Khutulun looked behind her as a few tiger-shifters circled there to surround her. "Your father kept me prisoner, forced me to do as he asked, and as soon as I could, I ran away and tried to find you."

The Bengal paced closer to her.

You laughed well enough as you stood by the tyrant's side when he locked us away.

The female tiger-shifter, who looked like the Russian female I'd spoken to earlier, lashed her tail and bared her fangs.

She joined him in killing and eating those of us they could not imprison. Such a crime cannot be forgiven.

I stared at Khutulun. Had I ever really hoped she might help me learn who I was? The mysterious figure who had seemed to want me back these last few months looked ashen. She evoked nothing in me but disgust.

You didn't want me back in your life because you loved me, I said. *You wanted me back because you quarreled with Orgoli, because you needed my help to kill him and save your own hide.*

"You need my help!" Her voice rose, shrill and commanding. "You need me to speak to all the creatures down there. You made me a promise."

But I hadn't promised anything. The Bengal had interrupted in time.

And if Khutulun could communicate with all the animals in Orgoli's army—why couldn't I? I was her daughter, after all. . . . Like the moon rising, rays of light crept through the dark corners of my mind, and I saw how it could be done.

I don't need you, after all. You knew all along I could speak to them myself. You're a liar.

All the pleading fled her face, replaced by disappointment and shrewd calculation.

Very well then. Go, and die under your father's claws.

I nodded, and inwardly said good-bye to my dream of a birth mother who might define me. The death of that dream was surprisingly easy, for it had been replaced by the reality—that, as Caleb had said, I was who I chose to be. That would not be Khutulun.

Be careful, I said to the tiger-shifters. *She is dangerous.*

I turned my back and began descending the dune.

"Fool!" Khutulun shrieked as the tiger-shifters closed in. "You walk away from the ultimate power! You could have everything! No, you shall not have me!"

I heard the warping of air as she shifted and the whoosh of tiger-shifters as they pounced.

A terrible squeal accompanied by a desperate flapping of wings, and Khutulun flew raggedly over my head, whimpering, one leg dripping red. She curved her black-striped wings away from the doorway and disappeared against the dark sky, heading back toward Othersphere's greener slopes. I didn't try to watch her go.

I climbed the next, lower dune, and looked down at the great bears and snakes, the frogs and the herons and the mastodons clustered near the doorway, cawing or trumpeting or baying unhappily. I reached out with every atom in my body—pushed outward in all directions, into the sand, the air, out to sea, and I asked them all, animal and rock, plant and ocean, to hear me. I'd been able to communicate with a storm, after all, and with a tree, and with tiger-shifters. Why not with all of them?

Friends, I said. *Please do not go.*

Hundreds of animal heads turned to me. If they had ears, they were at attention, even though I had not spoken out loud. Except for the unnatural drone from the doorway and the sweet lapping of the waves on the sand nearby, this part of Othersphere was silent.

Whatever Orgoli promised you, it was a lie. I am his daughter, and I know, for he tried to kill me. He slaughtered his way into ruling this world, and now he's using you to conquer another. But you will die there and gain nothing. Don't go.

The silence was broken by a hundred different sounds, animals of every shape and size braying and honking and rumbling in confusion. Among it all I caught a thread of one main emotion—fear. Fear of the doorway, of death beyond it, but mostly fear of Orgoli. They had followed him because they were afraid.

The tiger-shifters moved up behind me, quiet, watchful. The other animals flinched at the sight of them, probably reminded of the Amba.

We won't hurt you, I said. *Go back to your homes. We will put ourselves now between you and Orgoli. We'll make sure he never hurts any of you again.*

I only hoped I could make good on that promise.

At the fringes of the group of beasts, a few rhinos snorted and ran off. A cloud of red and blue parrots rose up and swooped back to their forest. The rest moved uneasily, edging away, but not yet certain if it was really safe to leave.

Come.

I walked down the side of the dune, the tiger-shifters following. As we approached, I came face to face with a giant horned reptile, a dinosaur I remembered from books in early science classes as a triceratops.

Which meant that the Amba had been collecting animals from our world for tens of millions of years. This gentle-eyed creature, with its fearsome pointed horns and herbivore's teeth, waggled its huge head at me and stepped carefully aside to let me pass.

I nodded, thinking *Thank you,* and began to move past it. An eight-foot-tall bipedal kangaroolike creature with mighty legs meant for jumping and a pouch on its belly hopped to get out of my way.

Beyond her, a creature seven feet high at the shoulder with great antlers spreading more than twelve feet across waited, with six or seven others like him grouped nearby. I recognized them as relatives of the elk that sometimes gathered near Morfael's school. A baby of that group had once walked right up and stuck his nose in the small of my back while I was kissing Caleb.

I couldn't smile in my tiger form, but I paused and extended my nose delicately toward the great elk.

He eyed me with a cautious liquid gaze, then ever so slightly stuck his own bulbous nose out toward me and sniffed. I exhaled softly at him, purring. He lifted his head high, as if no longer worried and bellowed out a cry that I understood in some way. It was a call to go home, to leave this place, never to bow to tyrants again.

The crowd of animals stirred, then parted before me, and the small herd of elk dug their hooves in and took off, running down the beach along the water's edge under the bulging moon.

I kept walking toward the doorway, and they all made way. Some were nervous, some curious. Some bolted away. The crowd was thinning. The purple frogs had hopped off; the beetle swarm flittered into the distance. Mastodon and antique ostrich, warthogs and families of giant shrews. They all waited as I passed, then turned and walked or scurried away.

Thank you, I thought.

Nearest the doorway stood a great tawny cat-creature with two long curved fangs like tusks curling down from its upper jaw. A *smilodon*, a prehistoric relative of the modern tiger, all sinew and deep-chested power, coiled violence waiting to spring. Behind it slunk a slightly smaller female and two youthful cubs, all watching me with vigilant green eyes.

I paused and bowed my head to the great cats. Then, with the tiger-shifters doing the same behind me, I strode past them and up to where the doorway stood, buzzing and droning like a huge fly eternally flinging itself against a windowpane.

The doorway looked out though a hallway made of shining tubes and metal struts, supporting a heavy structure of some kind above. Fifteen feet down that hall, the room opened up. It was semicircular, filled with the blue gleam of steel and mirrors; a metal walkway led up to a steel door. As I stood there a red light began to flash, and a claxon rang out an alarm. The humdrums knew something was going on.

A clatter of hooves gave us a moment's warning before the giant ibex I'd seen go through the doorway came leaping around the corner up ahead and down the hall. I barely made it out of the way as it galloped past me, burrowing through the mass of tiger-shifters, who hastened to let it through.

What had frightened it? I lifted my paw to cross the threshold.

Heavy pounding sounded from near the hallway entrance, and hissing as a buffalo, followed by two very hairy naked hominids with tiny foreheads and alarmed expressions, and three forty-foot-long boa constrictor type snakes thicker than my tiger body bolted and slithered toward us.

We were readier to give way to them, and they didn't pause as they fled. The snakes fanned out to dart between the legs of the tiger-shifters as they headed back to their swamps.

"Did you see that?"

I swung my head back around at the familiar voice, coming at us down the hallway. A petite girl I knew all too well sauntered toward us. Her short-cropped hair was standing on end and she was naked as the day she was born. What a sight for sore eyes, showing all her pointed little teeth in a wide grin as she put her hands on her hips and surveyed the bevy of tigers before her.

"Did you see?" November asked. Behind her, a dozen more small human figures scurried, including one who looked like the rat-shifter on the local council. "Snakes—running from rats! Well, rat-shifters anyway. I ought to try it with all of you!"

She bared her teeth in a mock grimace and laughed. I crossed the threshold without a second thought to run my rough tongue up her face, purring.

"Ew!" She scrubbed at her cheek. "Good to see you, too, Stripes, but we need to get busy. We got in the rat way, but now we need to open that door"—here she pointed to the metal door at the top of the stairs near the flashing red light—"and let our friends in. Because Orgoli's busy destroying the machinery right around the corner. And Arnaldo told me we'd better stop him or we'll never be able to close up this ugly old hole. Orgoli's bigger than my brother's RV, and he's mad." Her shining eyes flicked to the tiger-shifters amassed behind me. "Wanna bring your friends to a fight?"

CHAPTER 17

The answering roar rattled the metal tunnel around me.

November narrowed her eyes against the blast of sound. "Guess they understood me. Oh, hey, what's this?"

She stooped over to pick up something she'd stepped on, a broken black shard of glass about three feet long. The Bengal beside me nosed it curiously.

Carved figures writhed along it up to the sheared-off end. I knew it as well as I knew November. I'd seen it when it was whole in Orgoli's hands as he took on his shadow-walker form. It was his staff, or part of it, broken.

"What the hell's Orgoli's thingie doing here?" November said. "Here's another bit of it." She hunched down and came back up with a smaller splinter of shiny dark glass, sharp as a knife, with one carved anguished eye still visible.

I looked around. Above and behind the door, thousands of tiny metal tubes wound around each other, coming around to lock. Above me, the red light was still blazing, the alarm loud and obnoxious to my ears. I focused my thoughts on it, feeling the "wrongness" of worked metal, and told it, "Shut up!"

The alarm went silent, and the light went out. There was blessed quiet and minimal light, which suited my tiger-shifter eyes just fine.

"Whoa!" said Toby.

I sliced the Blade through the metal door. The amorphous edge firmed up and bit down happily, as if eating the metal. It cut through the steel as if it were paper, right through a large metal bolt and another locking mechanism.

I pulled the blade out and tugged on the door. It swung open without a sound.

"Awesome," said Toby.

"Let's go!" Jules scampered through the open door, which led to a cement hallway. Toby followed and I peered after them. The lighting was low here, too, every third fluorescent panel in the ceiling faintly aglow for the night.

A familiar pair of figures came running around the corner toward us, one blond as a sunny day, and the other dark as the Shadow Blade: Lazar and Caleb. It lifted my heart to see them side by side. Behind them strode Arnaldo, Amaris, London, and her two dire wolves. There were others, too, but not many. Where were the rest of the shifters?

November's brothers skidded to a stop and waved at them. "This way! This way!"

I waved, too. My friends caught sight of me and smiled. But the two brothers' faces were the most revealing. Each bore the same expression of extreme, almost exhausted relief at seeing me. Caleb waved back, and began shrugging out of his coat immediately. Lazar started to run alongside Caleb. Then, as if remembering things had changed between us, he made himself slow down and let Caleb get ahead of him. There was pain on his face, but something more. My throat tightened as I realized he was looking at his brother with love, and acceptance, and the tiniest bit of pride. As if he'd done something to help Caleb smile at the sight of me.

Maybe he had.

That was why Lazar had broken up with me. To atone for killing Caleb's mother, he'd given Caleb his heart's desire. Me.

Unshed tears pooled in my eyes. Caleb ran up, holding his coat to throw it around my shoulders with a flourish like a cloak. He wrapped it around me, and then enfolded me tightly in his arms. I could hear his quick, steady heartbeat, and I buried my face in the curve of his neck, inhaling his thunderstorm scent. No wonder I loved him. He smelled like the air around the Lightning Tree and the eternal storm in its shadow.

He pulled back, hands warm and strong on my shoulders, and caught my eyes with his dark gaze. His smile checked and faded. "What is it? What's wrong?"

I shook my head, smiling and wiping my eyes as I put first one arm, then the other through the sleeves of his coat. "I'll tell you later."

The ground heaved upwards beneath our feet, causing the metal staircase to creak alarmingly, and all the machinery in the room to sway and bounce. I caught hold of the wall with one hand and Caleb with the other to stay upright. Thirty feet over our heads, the blank white ceiling cracked from one corner to the other.

"Hope he can't keep that up too long," Caleb said. "Or he'll bring the roof down on all of us."

The rest of my friends had caught up, panting a little from running. I smiled at Lazar, and then quickly looked away, happy to see everyone else looking well. "So good to see you all."

"Welcome back, Dezzy!" Amaris shouted. She and London were holding hands, looking adorable.

"Glad to see you," Lazar said quietly. His eyes on me were warm but cautious.

Caleb was looking past me at the tiger-shifters. "I see you brought back some friends." His hand surreptitiously rubbed my back in tiny circles. "Well done."

"Where's your army?" I asked. I was trying not to lean into him too obviously here in front of Lazar, before anything could or would be explained to the others. But being here, next to Caleb, I felt a huge wave of relief breaking over me. I wanted to do nothing more than rest in his arms, tell him everything. But that would have to wait, assuming we survived the rest of the night.

"The other shifters are busy incapacitating the humdrum guards and all that," London said. "The place is on a pretty strong lockdown, so it hasn't been easy. Once it was clear, we ran ahead to see if Orgoli had opened the door yet."

"He has," I said. "But November and her friends shooed back the animals that crossed over. And I told the rest to go home. That seems to be what they're doing, so he should be alone."

"Still won't be easy," Caleb said. "Where is he?"

"He's around the back of the laser machinery there, destroying it."

"Why doesn't he just, you know"—London wiggled her fingers toward the bank of lasers—"call forth some shadow and send it all back to Othersphere."

Lazar hummed as she spoke, squinting down at the laser bank. "It doesn't have a shadow in Othersphere," he said. "We got lucky with the helicopter tonight. The higher tech something is, the less likely it'll be attached to anything in Othersphere. And this laser's about as high tech as this world gets."

"If we can't get the lasers going again, we'll never be able to close the doorway," said Arnaldo. "We figured out that Orgoli would need something powerful from Othersphere to use as a focus for the lasers. Morfael thinks he has a focus we can use to shut the door again, but the lasers need to be working. If you can stop him, maybe we can reprogram it."

"A focus for the lasers . . ." I was thinking hard. A lot of what Arnaldo said usually went right over my head, but something about his statement clicked now. "November found what looked like shards of Orgoli's staff right in front of the doorway. Could that have been his focus?"

"That must be it!" Arnaldo's eyes lit up, but then his face fell. "What the hell do we have as powerful as *that* to reverse it?"

Light footsteps padded down the hallway, accompanied by a well-known tapping sound. Morfael's gaunt figure, wrapped in black, glided down the hallway toward us. He was holding his own wooden staff out, hitting the floor lightly in front of him as he came. I waved. He lifted a bony white hand in greeting.

Arnaldo was staring at Morfael's staff. "No way. We can't ask him to give that up."

"I don't think you'll have to ask," I said.

An explosion of horrible snarls and snappings erupted behind us.

Three tiger-shifters flew over the top of the half-sphere of machinery in the center of the room, bloody, legs flailing, and squalling in pain. They landed with painful thumps on the hard floor below us. All three stirred, still alive, and I knew they could shift soon to heal.

"Let's go!" Caleb shouted.

I put one hand on the stair's railing and vaulted over it, dropping twenty feet to land easily on the floor below. *Thank you, cat-shifter strength and dexterity.*

Caleb, Lazar, and Arnaldo ran full speed down the stairs, followed by London and her dire wolves, with Amaris nearest the back, waiting to see if her healing abilities would be needed.

I didn't wait, but tore off Caleb's coat, tossing it to him even as I shifted. I was tiger once more, and I chirped a request to the tiger-shifters in this part of the room to go up the stairs and help the other shifters deal with guards and humdrums—in a nonlethal fashion. The room was getting crowded, and if Orgoli's earthquake brought the building down, I didn't want every tiger-shifter now on earth to be killed. Something good had to come of this.

The tiger-shifters swarmed up the stairs we'd just come down, snarling promises to do as I'd asked, and I sprinted around the corner of the laser machinery, ears cocked to hear anything useful.

As I ran through the curving hallway behind the lasers, I heard painful meows and felt a low rumble in my chest. Orgoli's growl. There was also a faint, human whimpering, a more erratic heartbeat than the tiger-shifters'. Who could be in there with them? Maybe it was one of the rat-shifters somehow unable to shift into rat form.

The hallway opened up to a large room a hundred feet square lined with computers and equipment. Some of them were sparking and gouged, smoking. But it was Orgoli who filled the room. He wasn't mountain peak–sized here, but still he was five times as big as I was. He looked a veritable dragon of a tiger, over twenty feet high and sixty feet long. His coat was bloody orange-red, slashed with stripes so black they reflected no light. His fierce head was spattered with blood, and strips of flesh hung from his teeth.

At his feet lay the Bengal tiger, my friend, his abdomen torn open, eyes eternally open. Sadness and rage overtook me as his body shifted for the last time, back to human. As Siku's had done.

A weak, very human whimpering came from a huddled form wedged tightly in a corner under a shelf of hard drives. It was Ximon, arms wrapped around his knees, rocking ever so slightly back and forth. His gray shirt and pants were ragged and dirty, his body wasted away. His white hair was patchy, and his once glittering, intelligent eyes were dull with fear and confusion. He stared right at me, that mindless whimper issuing from the back of his throat.

After using Ximon's body to step through the veil and escape back at the lodge, Orgoli must have stepped back through the veil here at the NIF, still inside it. He'd used Ximon's fingers to set up the lasers, to fire them, and open the doorway. But in stepping back through the door to his home world, he'd shed Ximon like a skin, and left him here while he gathered his army, romping back to the NIF in tiger form while Ximon cowered in the smallest cubbyhole he could find.

How dare you? I snarled at Orgoli. Tiger to tiger, communication was easy. *This is our world, not yours.*

It will be mine soon, little cub, he replied, his huge tongue scraping some of the red from his whiskers. *For too long your world has drawn power from mine while we sheltered your outcasts.*

Are you saying our world draws power from yours? I was incredulous. *But you created that unnatural hole in the veil. You are the violator.*

You began it hundreds of years ago, he answered. *It wasn't enough to draw your healing and your animal forms from us, but you had to invent technology that bled through the veil. Your bombs have wilted forests all over my world. This ugly place has begun to choke the life out of the great ocean. If it were just your own oceans, your own creatures, your own moon which you destroyed, I would not waste my time with you. But your world is too connected to ours. I must destroy your technology, and the brains behind it, or my world will continue to slowly die.*

I remembered the dead seashore I'd seen as we approached the doorway and the blighted section of the swamp we'd spotted as we crossed it. Orgoli was telling the truth. Othersphere had taken our threatened species and given them homes safe from human slaughter and incursion. In return, our human technology was slowly eating its way through the veil, killing off their pristine ecosystems.

There's got to be some way both worlds can survive, I told Orgoli.

This world will survive, he said. *But your precious humans will not.*

It's too late, Orgoli, I told him. *Your army has fled. You cannot defeat this whole world without them. You're alone.*

So. He lashed his tail, molten eyes slits of heat on me. *Then it is time for me to eat you at last, little cub. Your blood will make me strong enough to destroy all your friends, the shifters, and my brother, too. One way or another, my world and I will have revenge.*

I didn't wait for him to finish. My friends were coming down the hallway, and I was the distraction. I slinked to one side, as if about to run away. As Orgoli dodged to one side to stop my retreat, the fake-out gave a clear view of his throat, and I sprang. He lifted a paw to bat me away, a millisecond too late.

I dug my claws into his fur and skin. The heady smell of power streamed up through his skin as I sank my teeth into his throat.

He roared, choking, and shook his head, trying to dislodge me. I knew I wouldn't have long, so I bit deeper, feeling the sinews and muscles taut beneath my jaws, seeking his jugular. A gush of hot blood spurted into my mouth and down my throat. I gulped and guzzled. As I did, my body grew, my muscles flexed with new strength, enabling me to chomp down even more ferociously on Orgoli's throat.

Life sang through me with the blood, and ecstasy took me. My body lengthened until my back feet touched the ground. In seconds I'd grown to twice my original size, big enough to torque my spine and use my paws for leverage. I shoved at Orgoli, wrestling, trying to get him onto his side. If he was down, then perhaps I could finish him. Finish him and drink him all.

Somewhere out there in the periphery of my vision, Lazar and Arnaldo were running up to the smoking computers and setting up a laptop. The dire wolves leapt fearlessly onto Orgoli's back, biting at the thick fur near his spine, unable to get a hold. London shifted to her wolf form.

November nearly stumbled over Ximon huddled in his corner, and she recoiled in horror. "Lazar!" she called out. "It's your horrible father!"

I needed to get Orgoli out of the area so that Lazar and Arnaldo could set up the laser and close the doorway. He swatted at me, but I pushed myself away and raced down the hallway, back to the main room.

Giant paws padded after me. I glanced back as I rounded the corner in front of the laser array, and saw that not only was I larger, but Orgoli had shrunk a little during our fight. But he still towered over me, reaching one paw out like a cat batting at a mouse. I sidestepped the blow and scampered down the short hallway toward the open door to Othersphere.

The gathered animal army which had clustered there was gone. Instead, hunkered down behind low gray dunes, thirty feet back from the door lurked ten or twelve Amba. They had come as they'd promised, and were all in tiger form, tails low to stay hidden, but with the ends twitching in anticipation, their eyes narrowed with the focus of the hunt.

They'd asked me to give them Orgoli in a weakened state. If I ran through the doorway I could only hope he'd follow. I was nearly there, five feet from the threshold, when Orgoli hurtled forward and grabbed me by the shoulders with front paws bigger than mattresses.

He latched on, claws knifing through my skin, and pulled me into him, his great head lowering, fangs stabbing for my throat.

I would not survive the bite. His teeth were like swords, his muzzle big as an oncoming train. I struggled with my last ounces of strength, bringing my back legs up to kick and rake, seeking purchase on his arms, his belly, anything, to draw blood, to disable or maim.

But Orgoli calmly used one back paw to step down on my two back legs and laid his great belly and chest right down on top of me, driving all the air from my lungs. I was pinned, suffocating, unable even to cry out. With one paw he daggered his claws deep into the bone of my shoulder blade, and with the other he deliberately severed a tendon in my left front leg. Red streaks of agony blurred my vision. I was going to die, and with my blood inside him, Orgoli would grow strong again.

The great teeth neared as I pushed, shoved, wiggled, trying to fend them off. Events lurched forward in distorted chunks as time slowed.

A beloved voice was calling my name.

Caleb.

I wished that I had told him I loved him today. I wouldn't get another chance.

The voice called again, ordering me to do something. But the point of Orgoli's incisor began to impale my skin, cutting through the thick muscles around my spine and throat.

"Dez!" Caleb's voice cut deeper than Orgoli's claws. "Not a tiger! A house cat! I call upon you—get smaller!"

I would have laughed if I had any breath. The answer was so simple. And it wasn't to become stronger, larger, or more powerful.

I closed my eyes and obeyed the call.

Instantly, my wounds healed. The teeth pressing into my throat slid up and away. The great paws flexed, empty. The giant, smothering body no longer pressed down. I was small, compact, and lithe.

Far above me now, Orgoli's eyes were wide in bewilderment. He focused down on me as if not quite taking in what he saw. He dabbed a paw at me, testing to see if I was really there.

I darted between his paws just as I had slithered between the writhing stems of the bloodthirsty thorn bushes of Othersphere. While Orgoli blinked down at where I'd been, I zipped along the hallway toward a tall figure in a long black coat. Like climbing a tree, I scrambled up Caleb's leg and into his arms.

His warm lips brushed the top of my head. "Well done."

Nearby, Lazar led a more focused-seeming Ximon with November right beside them, a strange glint in her eye.

London and her wolves were there, too. Behind them, Arnaldo was gesturing up at Morfael, who descended the metal stairs, holding his great wooden staff in his hand. The lasers must be ready to fire again.

Orgoli was pawing at the floor, looking around, confused. His huge head turned, to look over his shoulder, about to catch sight of us.

A blur of movement surged out of Othersphere, and he tensed, roaring. The Amba were coming.

I climbed onto Caleb's shoulder, craning my head to look over Orgoli's huge body. Six Amba, not much smaller than Orgoli, leapt right through the doorway. He disappeared under a maelstrom of slashing claws and bared teeth.

The earth heaved upwards, a vast beast awakening beneath us. The tunnel of tubing around us shuddered and screeched. Dust and small pieces of the ceiling hurtled down around Morfael. Arnaldo, hand over his head, dashed into the mouth of the tunnel, but Morfael ignored the tremor, moving in a stately manner toward us.

The shaking had not dislodged the Amba. They were caterwauling, biting and shoving Orgoli toward the doorway. Blood splattered the sides of the tunnel and coated the metal walkway with sticky redness. Orgoli fought, fiercely, desperately, but I had drained him. Every time he threw off one of the Amba, another jumped in to take its place, to harry him some more. The scene in the shiny tunnel of tubes was like a pile of angry striped snakes, twisting and thrashing and slipping in their own blood.

London launched herself at the wriggling pile of Amba, her dire wolves following. But they didn't bite or attack; they shoved, pushing Orgoli toward the doorway. Once he was there, Arnaldo and Lazar could use Morfael's staff as a focal point for the lasers and shut it forever.

"To hell with it!" November shouted, and ran up, arms out, to also shove at Orgoli's back end. His hind legs were braced against the floor, scrabbling desperately.

"Yes." It was Ximon's voice, a quavering shadow of what it had once been. His eyes were bright and feverish. "Yes, be gone foul demon!" He slipped away from Lazar, and walked up behind November and the Amba as they propelled Orgoli forward.

November whirled on him, her face a mask of hatred and disgust. "You're the demon, you sick old man," she said. "You're worse than he is. You killed Siku."

Ximon's face fell, his watery eyes staring at her. "You're not wrong, little fiend. You're not wrong at all."

Morfael entered the tunnel and extended his staff to Arnaldo.

But Arnaldo was shaking his head. "I've been trying to tell you. I don't think it'll work. Given my calculations based on the material November gave me, your staff is less dense than Orgoli's because it's wood, not stone. We need more material from Othersphere for it to work."

The brawling ball of Amba was squirming over the threshold of the doorway. A few Amba had been hanging back, with no room to enter the fray, and now they surged forward. The wolves backed off and November grabbed Ximon by the back of his shirt to shuffle him back. The Amba leaned into Orgoli from behind and pulled at him from the front with one last, all-out effort.

Then, like a tooth being pulled, he slid out of our world into Othersphere.

Arnaldo ran forward, gingerly holding Morfael's staff in one hand, shaking his head. "I'm telling you, guys, it won't be enough. We need something else from Othersphere."

"Well, let me just pull out my handy slab of Othersphere and give it to you," November said, running her hands nervously through her hair, making it stand up even straighter. "Come on! Just try it."

On the other side of the doorway, Orgoli had one of the Amba by the throat. I could see he was growing bigger as the blood ran down his gullet. A small winged creature flitted above them and shifted.

Khutulun, bigger than all of them in her tiger form, stared through the doorway at me. As the other Amba piled on top of Orgoli to hold him down, she dipped her great tiger head and sank her teeth into the back of Orgoli's neck. He jerked in surprise and pain.

I felt vaguely sick. Was that what I had wanted to do? Was that who I was becoming? More than anything, I wanted the doorway closed now.

Lazar was at Caleb's side. "We need to shut that door."

Caleb was patting his pockets. "I know. If Orgoli doesn't threaten us, then she might. But I don't have anything from Othersphere."

Orgoli let go of the Amba and flailed in Khutulun's grip. I dug my needlelike claws into the worn cloth of Caleb's coat. It was like witnessing a slow execution. Khutulun closed her jaws around Orgoli's throat for one more time. He kicked weakly, paws trembling. Then the great golden eyes rolled over, and he lay still.

Khutulun raised her bloody snout and licked her whiskers with relish. *Come, little cub. Join us.*

I knew what I had to do. I jumped down from Caleb's shoulder and shifted into human form, wearing nothing but the Shadow Blade.

"Dez?" Caleb was automatically pulling his coat off and wrapping it around me from behind.

I unbuckled the shell clasp on the leather belt around my waist and held the Shadow Blade and its scabbard out to Arnaldo. "This is from Othersphere," I said. "Take it."

"Are you sure?" Arnaldo reached out hesitantly.

Caleb grabbed my shoulders, turning me partway around to face him. "Dez, that's the part of you that's connected to Othersphere. If you give it to Arnaldo, it'll be destroyed."

"And I'll lose my bond with Othersphere," I said.

I looked back at Morfael. His moonstone eyes were shining, his narrow lips pulled back in his strange version of a smile. "I won't be able to walk through the veil whenever I want. I'll be just another tiger-shifter." I couldn't help smiling. Joy sang in my heart as I looked at the faces of my friends. "Here in this world, with all of you."

"Fine." November snatched the Blade from my hand and shoved it at Arnaldo. "Hurry up."

"Let's do it!" Lazar pivoted and ran down the tunnel, over to where his laptop was set up, hooked into a computer bank.

Arnaldo took the Blade from November warily, and laid it carefully on the floor right on top of the buzzing border of the doorway, jerking his hands away from it as if shocked. "Back up!" he shouted, waving us away from the doorway. "Back up to the end of the tunnel. Lazar, get ready to fire."

London and her dire wolves herded Ximon back down the tunnel, away from the door, with November and Arnaldo following.

On the other side, Khutulun stepped over Orgoli's body, coming toward us, blood dripping from her lips. *This is your last chance. Come be what you really are.*

I slipped my hand into Caleb's. He lifted it up and kissed my palm, and we backed up the tunnel together slowly. "I am already myself," I said. "I am what I chose to be. Good-bye."

Khutulun neared the doorway, her gaze circling it, calculating.

We reached the end of the tunnel. Ximon, wobbly and be-
wildered, hesitated there, staring down the metal hallway at
the doorway, at Khutulun, at Othersphere.

"Here," said November to London. "I'll get him."

The wolves backed out completely. November took Ximon
by the shoulders, standing at the mouth of the tunnel. "All
clear, Arnaldo!" she called.

"Ready!" Arnaldo shouted.

Lazar pressed a key on the laptop, and the entire half-
sphere of tubes and metal piping lit up. A hum of electricity
hit my skin.

"Aim!" Arnaldo said, lifting his right hand.

Lazar pressed several more keys. "Target acquired." He
poised his index finger over the last key, eyes on Arnaldo,
waiting.

Khutulun paced along the perimeter of the doorway,

Good-bye, and good riddance.

Silhouetted in front of the giant bank of glowing machinery, November's hands on Ximon's thin shoulders tightened.

I had a strange, sick premonition. "November!" I shouted.
"Wait!"

"Fire!" Arnaldo ordered at the same moment.

Lazar tapped the key.

"So long, asshole." November shoved Ximon into the tunnel.
He stumbled forward, clattering down the metal hallway.

Caleb, Amaris, and Lazar staggered forward a step at the
same astonished moment. Caleb would have kept going, but
I tightened my grip on his hand instinctively, pulling him
back.

Amaris cried out wordlessly. Ximon tottered into the doorway to Othersphere and turned back, just a thin, lost silhouette, teetering on the brink. I couldn't tell if he was through
the doorway or not.

The high hum of the machinery hit a peak. Hundreds of

thousands of red laser beams struck Morfael's staff and the Shadow Blade at once. Everyone winced back at the brightness, throwing hands in front of their eyes, squeezing lids shut, turning heads away.

There came a soft *whumph* of air. Like a window swinging shut.

The light assaulting my eyelids dimmed. I opened them cautiously.

The doorway, the staff, the Shadow Blade, and Ximon were all gone.

CHAPTER 18

Everyone was staring at November, aghast. She dusted off her hands, as if her work was done, and gazed right back, unashamed. "He thought Othersphere was hell," she said. "So that's where he deserves to go."

Tears were pouring down Amaris's face. Caleb and Lazar exchanged wordless glances, and then walked over to their sister and put their arms around her. The three of them stood like that for a long moment. In spite of the horror of all that had just happened, my heart lifted a little to see the siblings so bonded at last.

An alarm clanged, startling me. The red light by the open metal door flashed. My tech-fu had only shut it down for a short period of time. With my connection to Othersphere severed, I'd probably never be able to do such a thing again.

I was smiling. That was fine by me.

"Better get out fast," Arnaldo hollered over the claxon.

"The shifters outside can't knock humdrums unconscious indefinitely."

November was the first up the stairs.

Detaching himself from Lazar and Amaris, Caleb came to me, hands outstretched.

"I'm sorry," I said. "About your father."

His expression was more pensive than upset. "And I'm sorry," he said, "about your biological father."

We started up the stairs after Lazar. Amaris came right after, with London and her wolves clustered around her in silent support.

"Thanks," I said to Caleb. "Part of me is horrified—at the Amba and Khutulun, and at November."

"The other part of you thinks Orgoli and Ximon got what was coming to them. I know," he said, as we walked side by side through the metal door. As always, he'd read my thoughts exactly.

We quickly wound our way through the NIF hallways, passing unconscious guards at various checkpoints, and burst outside to the parking lot. Surrounding it was a chain-link fence topped by razor wire with a large, grizzly bear–sized hole in it.

I'd expected to find the tiger-shifters milling about, and a lot of other kinds of shifters, too, but there were only three large SUVs waiting outside the fence.

Jonata, the lynx-shifter on the council, climbed out of one of the trucks and waved. We streamed toward her over the parking lot, Morfael elegantly bringing up the rear.

"So good to see you," she said as we climbed through the hole in the fence, shaking everyone's hands as they passed her. "Everything all right?"

"Orgoli's dead," I said. "The doorway's closed for good. And Ximon . . ."

I looked up at Caleb. "We don't need to worry about him anymore," he said.

"Where is everyone?" I asked.

"Oh, we shuttled the tiger-shifters and everyone else out of here lickety-split when the alarm went off again," she said. "Various cat-shifters volunteered to house the tigers till we can get them back to their own countries." She leaned into me, smiling. "They told us how you saved them. Nice job."

"There was a Bengal, a kind of leader," I said. "Can you let them know he died fighting Orgoli?"

She pressed her lips together in regret and nodded. "Of course. Some of them expressed a wish to come visit you at the school."

"Great," I said. Arnaldo was motioning us toward the school SUV. Sirens were approaching in the distance.

I heard incredulous shouts down the dark street, which was unusually deserted even for such a late hour.

Jonata grinned. "Better get going. Bears and mountain lions on the road can only keep the cops busy for so long."

She climbed into her truck, and the woman beside her hit the accelerator. "Whose car is that?" I asked, pointing at the third car.

"Mine," Caleb said. "Confiscated from the Tribunal at the lodge." He bent in close to me, hand reaching into his own coat, which I still wore. His face got within inches of mine, and he smiled, drawing out a set of keys. "Hey, pretty girl. Want a ride?"

I nodded, laughing low. "One second."

I turned and ran over to throw my arms around first London, then Amaris, Arnaldo, and November. "Yes, even you," I said, squeezing her tiny form against me.

Her voice, muffled against my chest, said something very rude about what I should do with myself.

"Even me," Lazar said as I let November go. He put both arms around me and kissed me on the cheek.

"I know why you did it," I whispered. "You broke up with me for Caleb's sake."

He pulled back, his face relaxed and resigned. "You're what he wants most in this world, what he needs," he said. "We talked a little on the ride over," he said. "Not about that, exactly. But we might end up brothers after all."

"Oh, Lazar," I said, my face flushed with a thousand emotions. "That's wonderful."

Caleb appeared next to me. Lazar drew away self-consciously, but Caleb reached his hand out to Lazar to shake. "Well done today, brother," he said. "We'll see you back at the school."

"Class begins tomorrow morning at six a.m.," Morfael said, opening the passenger side door. It was weird to see him without his staff.

Everyone groaned, until Morfael's face lit with a wide, teeth-baring grin. He climbed into the shotgun seat, as we all looked at each other.

Lazar shut the door, looking vaguely astonished. "I think he just made a joke."

"It better be," November said from the depths of the SUV. "Get inside, handsome. If you sit next to me and keep me warm, I promise not to shove any more of your relatives through the veil tonight."

"Shut up, 'Ember," London said.

"Yeah," said Amaris, who was snuggled with London in the back. "For once, shut the hell up."

November's eyebrows shot up toward her hairline. She opened her mouth to make a smart-ass remark.

"You heard her," Lazar said warningly.

November shut her mouth, smirk wiped away. Lazar climbed in. He did sit next to her, but not close enough to keep her warm. Her eyes slid up and down his long lean body, and the smirk returned.

"See you all in a few hours," I said.

Amaris and London waved. In the driver's seat, Arnaldo tapped the horn softly and grinned. November stuck her tongue out and Morfael lifted one hand in blessing or farewell. Or both.

Lazar leaned out to grab the door handle to pull it shut. His brown eyes were rueful, but smiling ever so slightly. He leaned into me, his voice low. "This is going to be an interesting ride home."

The door slammed shut, and I ran back to Caleb's SUV. He was already revving the engine. I climbed into the passenger's seat and saw he was holding his phone up, talking to someone via Skype.

"Hold on, she's right here," he said, and handed me the phone. "Someone wants to talk to you."

"Desdemona!" My mother's sweet face, slightly distorted by the wide-angle lens of her laptop camera, peered at me, grinning so big I could see her back fillings.

"Hi, Mom! Everything okay?" I beamed back at her, warmth spilling out of my heart into every corner of my being. It was so good to hear her voice say my name, the name she'd given me after fighting so hard to adopt me from that Russian orphanage all those years ago.

She flapped her hand at the camera. "I'm fine. Caleb called just now and told me you had a bit of an adventure but that everything's fine. You're a sight for sore eyes, my girl."

I shot an amused glance at Caleb. He was cranking the wheel and stepping on the gas, grinning. "Oh, Caleb called you, did he?"

"He's a considerate boy," Mom said.

"He's the best boy I know," I said.

Caleb, smile widening, reached out and put his hand on my knee, sliding his fingers over it and down the inside of my thigh. Heat burned its way up my thighs where he touched me. I tried not to gasp in front of my mother and smacked his hand.

"So you went there," Mom said. "To that other world."

I nodded.

"What was it like?"

"Beautiful, magical, dangerous," I said. "But I can't ever go back."

Her face was very serious. "I'm sorry, honey," she said. "I know it was important to you."

"It's okay," I said. "Because this world is all those things, too. And it also has everyone I love."

Mom sniffed, blinking. Her eyes were sparkling a little too brightly. "I love you, honey."

"Love you, too, Mom."

She wiped her eyes quickly and raised her voice. "Caleb, you drive her safely back or you'll be hearing from me!"

"Yes, ma'am!"

"Talk to you soon, Mom," I said, and ended the call.

I looked out the windshield. Caleb had turned onto a smaller service road and kept the headlights off. We bumped along, guided by the light from the stars. Over on a parallel road, a horde of flashing police cars, sirens blaring, zoomed back the way we'd come. The sight stirred a few memories.

"Coming back from battle under the evening sky with Desdemona Grey," Caleb said. "It doesn't get any better than this."

"I can think of something even better," I said, and ran my hand over his knee and down the inside of his thigh.

Caleb shot me a look and lifted his foot off the accelerator. The car rolled to a stop, and he turned the engine off. His dark eyes had a reckless, determined look that turned all my muscles to jelly.

"Come on," he said, grabbing my hand. He opened his car door and pulled me out his side of the SUV. I stumbled onto the dirt road, wearing nothing but his long dark coat, and into his arms.

Caleb's lips met mine with wild certainty as his hands slid under the coat to circle my bare waist. "Was that what you were thinking of?" he murmured against my mouth.

"Yes," I said softly. "That's even better."

Around us crickets were chirping their concert to the night. The moon peeped from behind a bank of clouds rimmed with silver, and the nondescript side road on the half-deserted edge of town was transformed into a glowing wonderland.

BEYOND
THE
STORY

EXTINCTION AND BEYOND

While I was writing *Othermoon* in 2011, the Western black rhinoceros, a subspecies of rhino that dwelled mostly in Cameroon, was declared officially extinct due to poaching. The news was painful to hear. I love animals. The world is a magnificent place thanks to its incredible biodiversity. Every time another species is destroyed by humans, everyone loses.

The problem goes far beyond the rhinos and elephants being slaughtered in record numbers for their horns and tusks, beyond the fact that tigers are vanishing from India, Russia, Thailand, and Indonesia due to trade in their parts and destruction of their habitat. The horrible truth is that dozens of species, plants, and animals are going extinct every single day, at a rate that far exceeds any since the mass die-off of the dinosaurs sixty-five million years ago. Scientists believe we're in the middle of the sixth mass extinction to happen in the last half billion years, with species being lost at 1,000 to 10,000 times the normal "background" rate. (For more information on the extinction crisis, try this site: www.extinctioncrisis.org)

No one knows the diversity in the world, not even to the nearest order of magnitude. . . . We don't know for sure how many species there are, where they can be found or how fast

> *they're disappearing. It's like having astronomy without*
> *knowing where the stars are.*
> —EDMUND O. WILSON, biologist and environmentalist

The difference between the time of the dinosaurs and now is that currently 99 percent of all extinctions occur because of humanity. We're the ones bumbling into pristine environments and polluting or destroying them. We're the ones hunting down elephants for ivory or smuggling rare turtles off their beaches. Illegal trade in wildlife is the third largest in the world, after drugs and arms, and the money fuels terrorist and insurgent organizations all over the world.

> *It's the next annihilation of vast numbers of species. It is*
> *happening now, and we, the human race, are its cause.*
> —RICHARD LEAKEY, paleontologist and conservationist

Now that I've thoroughly depressed you, time for an injection of hope. We're the problem, so we can be the solution. A lot of organizations are working to make things better. Check out the links at the end of this piece for places you can go online to help. And don't despair—bald eagles were down to 412 breeding pairs by 1950, but then the US protected them by law. Now their numbers are estimated to be over 200,000! And in the 1940s there were only around 40 Amur tigers left in the wild. Today those numbers are closer to 400. Change for the better is possible.

> *Few problems are less recognized, but more important than,*
> *the accelerating disappearance of the earth's biological re-*
> *sources. In pushing other species to extinction, humanity is*
> *busy sawing off the limb on which it is perched.*
> —PAUL EHRLICH, Nobel Prize–winning scientist

So now you know why I included so many extinct species in *Othersphere*. I wanted readers to feel the magnificence of nature and appreciate how much we still have to lose. In my books, the Tribunal has wiped out most of the different kinds of shifters. No one has heard from the tiger-shifters in nearly twenty years, and other shifters fear that means they, too, have been made extinct.

Then Dez and her friends go to Othersphere and find— well, I'm not going to spoil it here in case you haven't read the book, but I featured a number of species that have gone extinct over the millennia to showcase the issue of extinction, and because the animals are supercool.

> The extermination of the passenger pigeon meant that mankind was just so much poorer; exactly as in the case of the destruction of the cathedral at Rheims. And to lose the chance to see frigate-birds soaring in circles above the storm, or a file of pelicans winging their way homeward across the crimson afterglow of the sunset, or a myriad terns flashing in the bright light of midday as they hover in a shifting maze above the beach—why, the loss is like the loss of a gallery of the masterpieces of the artists of old time.
> —THEODORE ROOSEVELT, 26th President of the United States

Here are some fun facts about the extinct animals I featured in *Othersphere*.

Quetzalcoatlus
The largest creature ever to have flown in our world, named after an Aztec god, this pterosaur was as large as a private jet airplane. The exact dimensions are debated, but the coldblooded creature's wingspan was at least thirty feet wide. Compare that to the largest flying creature currently on our earth, the condor, with a wingspan of "only" ten feet! You can see footage of an animated *Quetzalcoatlus* flying here:

video.nationalgeographic.com/video/education-videos/
edu-fly-mon-10-quetzelsize

Megatherium
This ancient ancestor of the tree sloth was one of the largest land animals on earth until about 8,000 years ago.

They were over twenty feet long and weighed up to five tons. Like elephants, they lived in large family groups. We have fossil evidence of their footsteps, which show they often stood up on their hind feet, probably to reach foliage to eat. But scientists believe they might have also opportunistically dined on carrion killed by carnivores, using their huge claws and massive strength to drive off the likes of sabre-tooth tigers and dire wolves. Here's a fantastic video animation of a *Megatherium* taking food from predators:

www.youtube.com/watch?v=OY-OWgVgvtc

Dire Wolves

Canis dirus ("fearsome dog") was 25 percent larger than the modern gray wolf, with a bite 130 percent more powerful. But this North and South American creature was very similar to modern wolves in that they hunted in packs and lived in large family units. There's a long, fascinating video documentary online about dire wolves here:

www.youtube.com/watch?v=0V7hDJvkzjw

I have a particular fondness for the dire wolf, not only because they remind me of London, but because I vividly remember my first visit to the Page Museum at the La Brea Tar Pits as a child, where I stood aghast at the sight of an entire wall covered in dire wolf skulls. Also on display there: ground sloth skeletons, camels, extinct horses, mammoths, and of course, *Smilodon*, aka the saber-toothed cat. If you're ever in Los Angeles, it's a great place to visit. Or check it out online:

www.tarpits.org

For if one link in nature's chain might be lost, another might be lost, until the whole of things will vanish by piecemeal.
—THOMAS JEFFERSON

Last, but certainly not least, my personal favorite, for obvious reasons. . . .

Caspian, Java, and Bali Tiger Subspecies

The Bali tiger (en.wikipedia.org/wiki/Bali_tiger) was around the size of a leopard, the smallest of the tigers, with males reaching only around 220 pounds. The Javan tiger (en.wikipedia.org/wiki/Javan_tiger) was a bit larger, with males reaching up to 310 pounds. Because both were isolated on islands, they each evolved to have distinctive fur colors, stripe patterns, and head shapes.

The Caspian tiger (en.wikipedia.org/wiki/Caspian_tiger) was around the size of the current Bengal tiger (animals.nationalgeographic.com/animals/mammals/bengal-tiger) with a wide range around the southern end of the Caspian Sea, from Turkey through Iran, all the way to the western deserts of China. One fascinating tidbit about the Caspian tiger is that the Kazakh people referred to it as the "road" or "traveling leopard" because it would follow migrating herds of preferred prey over large distances, which is markedly different behavior from its more territorial cousins in Siberia and India.

The Caspian tiger was most closely related genetically to the Amur or Siberian tigers (my favorite, of course; animals.nationalgeographic.com/animals/mammals/siberian-tiger), and some scientists have proposed introducing Amur tigers to the areas where the Caspian tiger once ranged. But without large tracts of undeveloped land containing a large prey population, the proposed region is currently unsuitable for re-introduction. Alas.

What is man without the beasts? If all the beasts were gone, men would die from a great loneliness of spirit. For whatever happens to the beasts, soon happens to man. All things are connected.
—CHIEF SEATTLE

If you're wondering about species currently at risk or recently extinct around the world, here are two links with lists,
information, and photos (there are a lot more if you go looking):

wwf.panda.org/about_our_earth/aboutcc/problems/
impacts/species extinct-animalz.blogspot.com

> *To hunt a species to extinction is not logical.*
> —Spock, in *Star Trek IV*

Should we bring back species that have gone extinct?
That's the fascinating question raised by recent advances in
cloning. It's similar to the thought that crosses Dez's mind in
Othersphere when she comes across tiger subspecies in the
other world that are extinct in ours. It would be fascinating
in some ways, but problematic in others.

You can read about both sides of the issue on the National
Geographic site here:

www.nationalgeographic.com/deextinction

The full cover story National Geographic did on "de-
extinction" is here:

ngm.nationalgeographic.com/2013/04/125-species-
revival/zimmer-text

> *Nobody made a greater mistake than he who did nothing
> because he could only do a little.*
> —Edmund Burke, Irish statesman and philosopher

If you're wondering "What can I do to make a difference?" below are some of the things I do. It doesn't seem like
much, but the more of us who try to make things change, the
more likely it is to happen.

But do your own research and make up your own mind.
I've included links with more information, but it's easy to
find your own as well.

1. Sign up to get updates from organizations like www.WWF.org and wildlifeconservationnetwork.org. They'll keep you informed and give you easy ways to contact your legislators and leaders all over the world who can make a difference for wildlife.
2. Try to live as sustainably as you can. This means different things for different people. You can try recycling, composting, eating mindfully, conserving energy, gardening, and so on.
3. Avoid supporting the trade in illegal wildlife or abuse of wild animals, particularly when you travel. For example, when I went to Thailand, I decided not to go to one of the controversial tiger temples or parks there, where visitors handle the tigers. It's very tempting to go because the animals are so intriguing, but if you see an animal behaving in a manner contradictory to its wild nature, odds are that animal is being grossly mistreated. For that reason, I also avoid giving money to any venue where wild animals are forced to perform.
4. Raise awareness via social networks (without being too obnoxious). I try not to deluge people with requests to sign petitions and so on when I tweet or post on Facebook, but I've seen the power of social media. Education is the key to making any lasting change.
5. When you support charities, consider organizations that protect wildlife and preserve natural habitats. Along with the World Wildlife Fund (www.wwf.org) and the Wildlife Conservation Network (wildlifeconservation network.org). I recommend (no surprise here if you've read my books) the Snow Leopard Trust (www.snowleopard. org), Tiger Time (tigertime.info), and Panthera (www. Panthera.org), which focus on conservation of big cats.

Here are some lists by reputable sites of other things you can do:

wwf.panda.org/about_our_earth/biodiversity/what_you
    _can_do
www.wikihow.com/Help-Endangered-Animals
www.thedailygreen.com/environmental-
    news/latest/extinction-tips-47051605

In wilderness is the preservation of the world.
    —HENRY DAVID THOREAU